TALL, *Royal* AND GRUMPY

NYLAH MONROE

Paperback ISBN: 978-1-7394953-0-5
E-book ISBN: 978-1-7394953-1-2

Book cover art: Sonia Gx (@artbysoniagx)
Book cover design: Books and Moods
Internal formatting: Books and Moods
Editing: Amy Briggs
Proofreading: Jesse Briggs

*Dedicated to those who would much rather have Prince
Grumpy than Prince Charming…
With a soft Dom personality*

CONTENT WARNINGS

This book is an adult romance *with explicit sexual content,* suitable only for those aged 18 and over.

It contains mentions of *an abusive past relationship, vague mentions of suicidal thoughts, mentions of family death, a light Dom/sub relationship, light Dom drop, and some degradation.*

Your mental health matters, so please tread with care if any of these subjects are likely to trigger you or speak to someone in the event that they do.

Nylah xx

P.S. I'd like to point out this book is written in British English with a few twists to make things work in the world of Neves. So, if certain words don't seem right to you, it doesn't mean they're wrong.

PLAYLIST

Princesses Don't Cry - CARYS

Enchanted (Taylor's Version) - Taylor Swift

Sparks Fly (Taylor's Version) - Taylor Swift

Humraah [Companion] - Asim Azhar

There's Nothing Holding Me Back - Shawn Mendes

Middle of the Night - Elley Duhé

Train Wreck - James Arthur

Heartbroken - Diplo, Jessie Murph & Polo G

Dirty Thoughts - Chloe Adams

Until I Found You - Stephen Sanchez & Em Beihold

What was I Made For - Billie Eilish

Skyscraper - Demi Lovato

Ranjha [Beloved/Romeo] - Jasleen Royal, B Praak, Romy & Anvita Dutt

Everything Has Changed (Taylor's Version) - Taylor Swift ft. Ed Sheeran

THE WORLD OF NEVES

THE STATE OF JAHANDAR

Climate
Hot summers, monsoon showers, and cool nights

Terrain
Hot summers, monsoon showers, and cool nights

City/town structures
Old shipping routes via rivers influenced the building of its towns and cities around them, creating clusters of hubs

Known for
White marble and dolphins, which are under the protection of the crown

Currency
Raal and Rupees

No. of Regions
43

Monarchy lineage
Hereditary

THE STATE OF TOUMA

Climate
Cold, wet winters and warm summers

Terrain
Mainly flat with lots of forest areas and an eastern mountain range

City/town structures
A mixture of big cities and towns within countryside all of which have some preserved old structures and protected areas

Known for
Advancing tech industry, red brick structures, and traditional marketplaces

Currency
Sterling and Pence

No. of Regions
45

Monarchy lineage
Semi-elective (by monarch)

THE STATE OF KHAAS

Climate
Long periods of warm weather perfect for efficient and profitable farming

Terrain
Generally flat with stretches of fertile, green land, but hilly towards south

City/town structures
A smaller population means there are more towns than big cities situated between land used for agriculture and pastoral farming

Known for
Big houses and strong horses, which are much sought after for racing

Currency
Dinar and Koor

No. of Regions
27

Monarchy lineage
Hereditary

THE STATE OF RAVEN

Climate
Wet and mild, though summer weather is unreliable/ unpredictable

Terrain
Generally flat but areas of low mountain terrains dotted around and several big islands off its eastern coast

City/town structures
Big, bustling, planned cities with lots of skyscrapers and modern architecture with smaller towns surrounding them

Known for
Being the economic, financial, and business hub of the world, and a competitive higher education system

Currency
Quan and Cents

No. of Regions
40

Monarchy lineage
Semi-elective (by monarch)

THE STATE OF DALE

Climate
Distinct seasonal climate of winter, spring, summer, and autumn

Terrain
Grassy hills and mountainous terrain all over the land mass

City/town structures
Citizens long learnt to adapt to the terrain, building cities on mountain sides and using shared technology with Touma and Raven to create strong infrastructure between

Known for
'Flying' trains built on raised platforms, successful pastoral farming, and Crimson Cast folk (people with ruby red eyes and silver hair)

Currency
Lira and Pence

No. of Regions
38

Monarchy lineage
Hereditary

THE STATE OF PRIO

Climate
Warm and steady climate, and equally cold in winter

Terrain
Flat terrain but very rocky around its coasts with lots of small islands, clustered mainly around southern border

City/town structures
Some cities and towns were abandoned after a period of poverty and famine in the recent **100** years when two siblings in the royal family went to war with each other before their cousin intervened and took control

Known for
Caves of hidden minerals and precious stones, and the sustainable mining and production system of them

Currency
Jolda and Won

No. of Regions
33

Monarchy lineage
Elective (by board and monarchs)

THE STATE OF SHAH

Climate
Cold weather—snows heavily during their long winters—that is very predictable as it follows the pattern of the northern winds

Terrain
Big snowy mountain ranges with valleys between

City/town structures
Cities and towns have been built between valleys and around mountains, connected by curling roads and railways

Known for
Sustainable manufacturing industry, and domesticated wolves, which are common pets in the mountainous regions

Currency
Tala and Fren

No. of Regions
35

Monarchy lineage
Hereditary

THE LOST ISLANDS

A cluster of islands to the east of Shah and north of Khaas. The islands don't belong to any specific state but are under the collective care of all seven. They are all sites of preservation and natural wildlife, maintained to sustain the ecosystem of the world.

Each state is run by a **monarchy** as a whole, but states are split into **regions**.
Regions are governed by a local body known as the **Regional Council**, with **council ministers, civil servants,** and **a head councillor**. Within regions, cities have **Local Councils** too.

Local Councils are the middlemen between the citizens and the Regional Councils. The head councillor is the middleman between the Regional Council and the **Imperial Cabinet**—a group of ministers and the leading royals.

The whole structure is known as a **government**.

The states have established knowledge on tech, science, and the world they live in, but there are **no religions** in the world. Some states are more specialised in certain areas than others.

PR (Post Rebellion) refers to the years after the rebellion that formed the modern states.

AR (Ante Rebellion) refers to anything before.

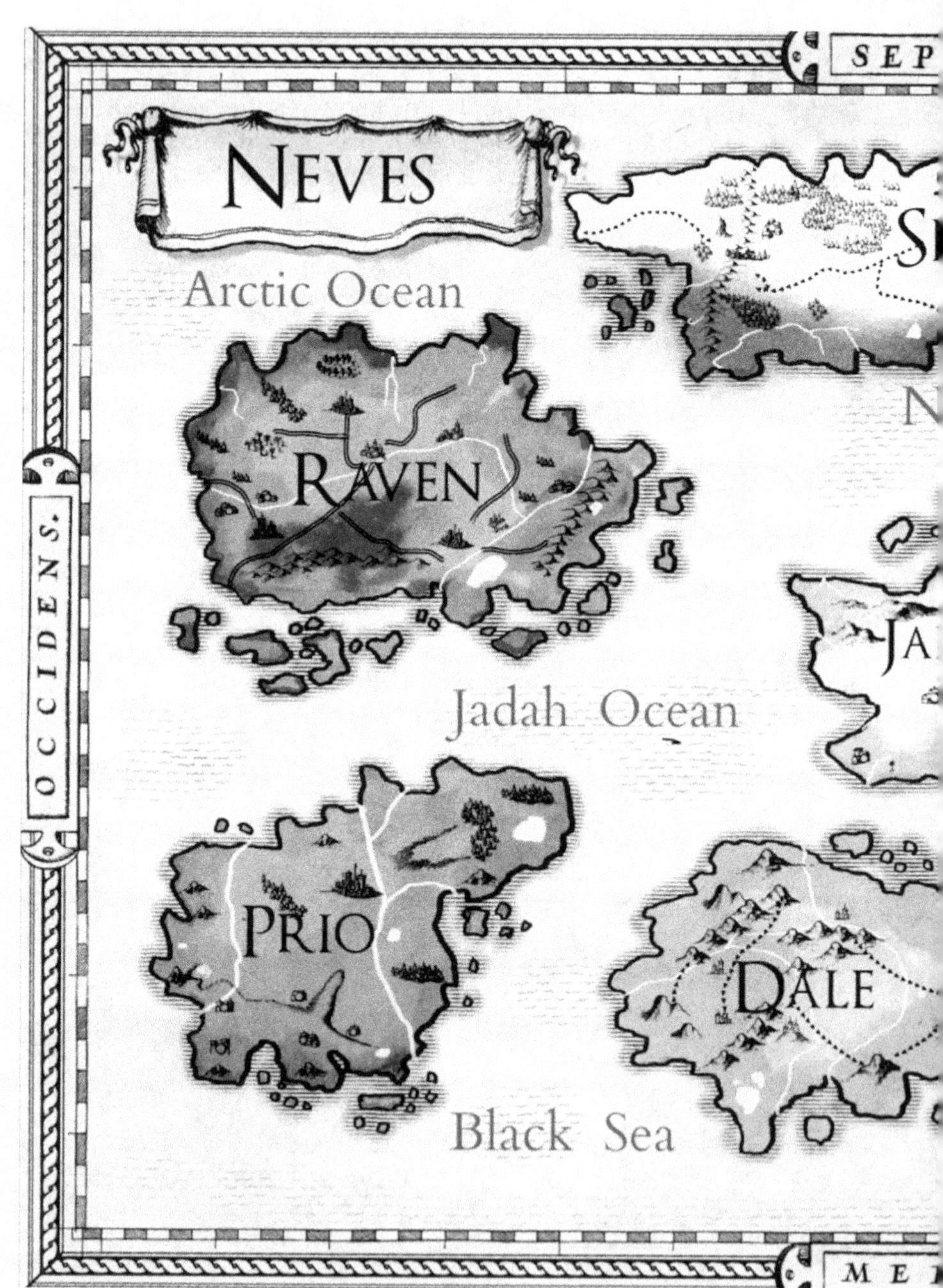

SEP
NEVES
Arctic Ocean
S
RAVEN
Jadah Ocean
JA
PRIO
DALE
Black Sea
OCCIDENS.
MEP

R I O.
THE LOST ISLANDS
ORIENS
Sea
Red Passage
Ocean
KHAAS
AR
Lehanto
Pursian
Sea
TOUMA
N
W
E
S

PROLOGUE

Long ago, several hundreds of years in fact, the world of Neves was ruled by three powerful clans and their head families.

The Kalb Clan. The Russo Clan. And the Ghanim Clan.

Despite day-to-day animosities, the three clans lived in relative peace on a land called, Azaad Bay, with six other lands shared equally between them.

Unfortunately, a vicious plague spread across Azaad Bay and the other territories. Many people fell victim to the illness, including the male heads of the Kalb and Ghanim clans, leaving their women to rule. After several years of slow recovery, both women of the Kalb and Ghanim clans decided to hand down their power to their grown children.

Youngest daughter, Raven, and only son, Shah, both left Azaad Bay to watch over the two lands of clan Kalb, while eldest daughter, Toumila—who went by the name Touma—remained to support her mother and their clan people there.

From the Ghanim family, youngest daughter, Prio, and second son, Khaas, were sent to watch over their people, while eldest son, Jahandar, strengthened the clan in Azaad Bay.

What neither clan knew, was that for Touma and Jahandar, staying behind was about far more than clan politics.

It was about the broken stones in the wall that divided the Kalb territory from Ghanim land, creating a gap just big enough for two opposing worlds to collide. A place where a rebellious little girl had curiously climbed over only to find an upset little boy sitting under a tree with a broken wooden doll in his hand.

They didn't know each other's names at first, but that didn't matter to them. The little girl returned the day after and brought one of her own dolls for the boy to play with.

That gap in the wall became their place. Their secret hideout where they played dragons and knights—the boy was always the dragon much to his dissatisfaction—and shared the food they'd stolen from their respective kitchens.

It was where the boy's heart first skipped a beat as the little girl he once knew suddenly looked rather like a pretty young lady to him. And it was where their noses bumped when they shared their first kiss before the young lady burst out laughing and fell over.

But their hearts broke when they were old enough to understand the reason for the wall.

Their love was never meant to be. *It couldn't be.* And yet even knowing what was meant to keep them apart, they both returned day after day to see each other. That was, until the little boy and girl had become two grown leaders.

"We ought to stop meeting here," Touma would say, laying on the grass, wrapped in her lover's arms.

"We ought to meet more often," he would reply, teasing his fingers through her hair.

"Jahandar. I very much mean what I am saying. I shall not return here again."

"One more day, my love," he would say. "Please. Return on the 'morrow and I promise it shall be our last."

They both knew their words rang untrue. They would return again and again for as long as they could.

But something changed.

"I must marry," Touma said to Jahandar one day. "Mother has—"

"What? No." Jahandar sat up from their spot under the tree. "You cannot. I will not allow it."

She sat up with him. "Jahandar—"

"We made a vow to each other."

"As children," Touma bit out angrily. "And we are no longer children. Mother is sick. The clan elders are fretting, and I can no longer be selfish. I must find a strong partner to lead with."

"And that is me!" Jahandar thumped a hand against his chest. "We vowed to lead together. We vowed to unite the clans and search for a new path. We shall do so."

She laughed a hollow sound. "Why must you act thus? Has it not occurred to you that our world is changing yet naught has come of it? The clans are still enemies. *We* are still enemies."

He cupped her face in his palms, tilting her fiery eyes up to his. "My love. When my heart beats as fast as the wings of a ruby-throated mockingbird for you, how could you be my enemy? I take flight whenever you are near, and I wish never to leave the skies."

"The skies are turning grey."

"Then we shall find a way for the sun to shine through."

"With what plan?"

He smiled. "You were always the knight as a little slip of a girl. Now let me be your knight, Touma."

They planned the union of their clans and their future together for days, weeks even.

All for nothing.

Unfortunately, the youngest son, Zorro of Clan Russo, had plans of his own.

With both parents well and alive and without a land of his own to rule, Zorro grew jealous of the other clan's children, and after insistently requesting to rule, he was soon granted his wish. On one condition.

He was to oversee the Russo land to the southwest of Azaad Bay, but only if he led together with his older brother, Dale. But this left Zorro furious, and he vowed to find a way to rule on his own. And

over the next few years that was exactly what he began to do.

He started by diminishing Dale's power and influence over their clan leaders and people, rallying more folk day by day in his own support. Enough that he managed to spread his power and influence all the way to clan Russo's southeastern land too.

But it wasn't enough.

Zorro succumbed to the age-old tale where his greed for power became an unquenchable thirst. He took one sip and wanted more. He drank a glass full and craved another. He found a river of it and searched for its source.

What if I could rule all the lands of Neves?

Once the second land was almost entirely under Zorro's control, he started building a mighty army, preparing to declare war against the Kalb and Ghanim clans, which would for all intents and purposes end any notion of balance and peace.

He claimed himself to be the sole ruler of all the lands. *"Zorro Jahan,"* he would call himself—*Zorro of the world*—the King of Neves.

Dale saw what his younger brother was doing and fearing the clans would be thrown into an everlasting war, he sent letter after letter to warn his parents. But upon finding out about his older brother's betrayal, Zorro had Dale imprisoned and convinced their parents to join his effort.

After much trying, Dale managed to escape and hid on a supply ship heading for Azaad Bay, where he eventually found his way to Touma Kalb and informed her of Zorro's plans for war.

Realising the scale of the threat coming from Zorro, Touma knew immediately she had to inform Jahandar and sent an urgent telegram. She knew without a doubt he would come.

Together, the star-crossed lovers left behind the plans for their future and gathered their siblings to start preparing for a possible war with Dale's help. But Zorro's attack came quicker than they had anticipated, targeting the most northern land—under the rule of Shah Kalb who was ill-prepared for any impeding battle.

One month of fighting turned into four, four months into a year, and a year became five.

But hope finally came in the sixth year when fighting side by side, Touma and Jahandar were able to infiltrate Zorro's territory, cornering him in his own camp.

When the news spread that Touma Kalb—the fierce warrior Queen who led an army of 30,000—had killed Zorro in battle, his once vicious army surrendered in the face of defeat. And quickly, the end of what had once seemed like an endless war came into sight for all people of Neves.

But with no hope of ever rebuilding the three-way clan rule that had once been integral, Touma, Jahandar, and Dale—with their other four siblings—decided a new era of rule was needed.

It wasn't the united future Touma and Jahandar had always hoped for. It was a divide that tore them even further apart.

Splitting the lands between the seven of them, they declared each land to be an independent state ruled by their own individual monarchies so that no monarch of one state could interfere with another State's affairs unless it threatened the peace of their lands.

21st February 1 Post The Great Rebellion of Zorro, or Post Rebellion (PR) as it was quickly shortened to. That was the date and year the peace treaty was signed, and the seven states were declared.

The states were named Jahandar, Touma, Dale, Raven, Prio, Shah, and Khaas, each after their first ruler.

And that is the tale of how the modern states of Neves were founded. But while the story of war may have come to a favourable conclusion, Jahandar and Touma's tale did not.

They sacrificed their love for their world, and the world?

Well, maybe it was its cruel working or its mercy, but not once in the eight-hundred years that followed did a descendant of Touma and a descendant of Jahandar fall in love and complete the incomplete union.

Until now.

CHAPTER 1
Esmeralda

Kai shoved me hard against the wall with a harsh grunt, pressing my cheek to the cold stone as he trapped my forearms against my back with one large hand of his.

I struggled in frustration, but it was fruitless as he pressed his front against my back, pinning me between the stone wall and his muscular frame. His hand in my hair. His breath heavy in my ear.

"Baby girl," he snarled. "Just because I'm being kind and giving you time to get used to me, doesn't mean you can forget I always get what I want. Whenever I want it. However I want it." He pushed a thigh between my trembling legs, and I arched against him with as much hatred as there was lust in my glare. "And there is nothing stopping me from taking you right now."

My eyes widened, but I didn't struggle. I just spread my thighs to accommodate him.

He smirked down at me. "You want me too, baby girl. I know you do." He dipped his face into the crook of my neck, letting out a deep, arrogant chuckle as I shook my head. "Yeah, you do, love. I can smell your arousal dripping down your thighs. Now all you've got to do is keep those pretty legs spread for me so I can taste it."

"Sorry, but how can this guy smell her arousal if he's not actually between her legs?"

My fantasy vanished before my eyes—again—as my best friend's voice yanked away the hazy state blanketing my mind. Exasperation threw a tantrum inside me, and my head snapped around to the girl curled up in the other corner of the velvet settee.

"Mariyah," I half snapped, half whined.

Mariyah stopped fiddling with the loose bun of dirty blond hair atop her head, her sky-blue eyes appearing grey in the dim lighting of the living room as they flicked to me. "What?" she said with a shrug. "It's true though. Unless this girl's smelling fishy, why can he smell it from so far away?"

A growled chuckle rumbled from my mouth. "I don't know. It's a movie, anything is possible. Now would you please just let me…let me *concentrate?*"

The whole north-south magnet, opposites attract thing? That was mine and Mariyah's friendship. Literally and metaphorically.

She was tall, I was short. She had straight blonde hair; mine was waves of chocolate-brown. She had a big arse, I had the big boobs. I liked to watch movies in silence, and she liked to do a full-on commentary as if it was a football game or something.

I just wanted to imagine my own version of the movie-adaption of the mafia romance book we both liked and were watching on the last night I was staying with Mariyah at her parent's house. But I should've known that was going to be an impossibility with her inability to keep all her intrusive comments to herself.

"You're trying to concentrate?" Mariyah asked in confusion before her brows shot up to her hairline. A blush crept onto my cheeks as she threw her head back and laughed loudly. "Oh, you're doing it again, aren't you?"

"If you know, then shut up."

I got two minutes of silence before Mariyah snorted. "I'm just trying to imagine it but I really can't." She snickered. "Orange would never. He could never!"

She chuckled harder as she unfurled her legs, all long limbs and a curvaceous figure clad in a skin-tight T-shirt and leggings despite it being a cold early February night outside. Then she lifted her hands and curled her fingers into circles, holding them apart in front of my face.

"Look, this is your Orange." She shook one hand. "And this is a mean, dirty-talking Dom like our mafia don, Javier over here, okay?" She shook her other hand towards the TV screen opposite us. "Can you see the two circles do not touch or overlap? That is because the two are mutually exclusive and could never align into one person." She chuckled, dropping herself back against the armrest. "There is no point trying to imagine your sweet, charming Prince Orange as Javier."

I knew she was right, but I still twisted my mouth to the side. "You don't know that," I said, not exactly sounding convinced myself. "He might be a secret Dom."

Mariyah scoffed with eyes full of disbelief. "Oh, come on, Ez. He's a prince—"

I lurched forward, scrambling to clamp my hand over her mouth. "Shh! Shehryar's upstairs!"

Mariyah's parents had been away on government business for the whole week I'd come to celebrate my twenty-third birthday with her in the State of Raven. It was the first time I'd been back to see her since we graduated from university more than a year ago. She was the only friend I'd made in my three years studying economics in Raven, and I loved her to bits.

Obviously, with me being the Crown Princess of the State of Jahandar, I hadn't been allowed to come and stay with her alone. My private secretary-slash-bodyguard, Shehryar, who was also the closest thing I had to a *real* brother, was upstairs in the second guest room.

He was unlikely to hear anything, but I never knew with him. Shehryar had the hearing of a bat, the sixth sense of a shark, and the sight of an eagle, and I didn't need him asking me questions about my prince crush who Mariyah had nicknamed, Orange.

She softly pulled my hand off and carried on in a quieter voice as if she'd never been interrupted in the first place. "And not just any prince, Ez. He's the one the world calls, *The Perfect Prince*. And a man who outshines even a fairy tale prince *cannot* be a Dom."

"I know." I huffed and slumped back against the sofa. "But Dom or not, it doesn't even matter."

"Yeah, for it to matter, you would actually have to talk your way into his bed, instead of just pining over him silently from across the room."

I gaped at Mariyah as she giggled like a triumphant little bitch, and without thinking, I grabbed the cushion between us and whacked her with it. *So much for proper princess behaviour.*

"That wasn't funny," I said, but annoyed laughter laced my words. "I'm trying, okay."

"Trying?" Mariyah nearly bellowed in incredulity before she lowered her voice. "Esmeralda, you have been crushing on this man for what, six, seven years, and you have yet to have one proper conversation with him. And you've been to so many of the same royal events as him too!"

I wanted to argue that she was wrong. The problem was she wasn't wrong.

The prince, nicknamed Orange—my crush of nearly seven years—was Kai Touma.

Twenty-nine-years-old, he was the first-born son of King Rami and Queen Leila of Touma. Not to mention, he was tall, dark, and handsome, and charming in a quiet, understated way. Plus, his smile… he had a dimple.

I had grown up in the same royal circle as him. We attended the same events and birthdays and New Year's parties. And yet other than the basic pleasantries, she was right, I had *never* had a proper conversation with him.

Ever.

How that was even possible, I didn't know. I had no idea what I was doing wrong.

"Rub it my face why don't you." I threw the cushion at her lap.

She wrapped her arms around it with a smirk sitting on her full lips. "I will. Maybe it will finally spur you into action."

She threw the cushion back at me and it smacked me right in the face. "Mariyah!"

"You have to talk to him this Peace Celebration, or I swear, Esmeralda, I will find Orange and tell him myself that you like him. Actually, no." She waved her hand around. "Forget talking to him. Just straight up fucking seduce him. Befriend him and seduce him."

I threw my head back and laughed. I hadn't even managed to speak to the bloody man, and she thought I could seduce him? *As if.*

"I'm serious." Mariyah crossed her legs and shuffled towards me. "Two weeks is enough time to seduce a man and look at you—you're gorgeous."

"It's not about my looks—"

"Shut up and look at me." I sighed but met her gaze head-on. "Now repeat after me. *Befriend him, seduce him, bed him, and then shower him with roses.*"

My mouth tugged in amusement. "Mariyah—"

"Say it. Manifest it."

I bit down on my bottom lip, hesitant to do so, but I quietly forced myself to. "Befriend him. Seduce him…bed him. And shower him with roses."

"There you go!" She pointed a finger at me. "And you better try. Like I mean try, Ez."

I knew Mariyah was right. I had to try to get Kai's attention this year.

And if I didn't manage to, then maybe it was a sign I needed to give up on my crush.

Especially considering he'd been engaged once before already.

"That's everything," Shehryar, my secretary, bodyguard, confidant, and everything in between, said, ducking his head to get his six-foot-five, hulking frame through the doorway into the living room.

I stood opposite Mariyah, ready to head to the airport to fly back to Jahandar late the next morning, but reluctant to leave. Mine and Shehryar's suitcases sat in the corridor where he'd left them.

"Did you double-check your room?" he asked, adjusting the sleeve of his crisp black suit jacket.

"That's the fourth time you've asked me, Sher," I said, grinning up at him.

He angled towards me, looking down at me through stern pale green eyes set under even more stern thick, arched eyebrows. To an outsider his expression might have been scary, especially with his tall, muscular build and shoulders as wide as a bull's. His short, soft brown hair didn't really soften the harshness of his face nor the shadow on his jaw. But I knew he was a big, loving, softie underneath that mask, so nothing about his glares and warning gazes bothered me.

That didn't mean I was stupid enough to mistake his softness for weakness or incompetence. When it came to his guard over me, what he said was what I did. No whining or questions asked.

"But yes, I didn't forget anything," I assured him.

"What does it matter if she forgets anything, anyway?" Mariyah said, waving him off with her hand as she put herself right in front of me. "I can post it to Jahmal Palace." She smirked at him over her shoulder. *Up at him.* Because she was five-nine, but he still stood a whole head taller than her. "And then you can tear it apart like a chew toy until you're satisfied it's safe for our dear Crown Princess."

Her condescending tone brought darkness down across Shehryar's expression. Frustration and daggers as he glared at the back of her head, and something…*else.* Mariyah's fair skin was faintly flushed too.

Neither of them seemed to realise it was so damned obvious what their anger at each other really hid, but I thoroughly enjoyed watching them try to act as if there was nothing there.

Mariyah pulled me into a tight hug. "Call me as soon as you land, okay?"

"I will," I said, squeezing her back.

"And do remember what I said? Or do you need me to repeat myself here?"

"No," I said quickly, ignoring the way I could feel Shehryar's piercing stare narrow on my suddenly hot face. "I remember."

"Good. I expect regular updates too."

If there's anything to update. I didn't say that though; I just nodded. "Tell your parents I said thank you for letting me stay. Next time, I'll come when they're here too."

"I will." Her arms tightened around me. "Take care of yourself, okay, Ez. I love you so much."

"I love you too."

We clung onto each other for a minute longer before Shehryar said we had to leave if we wanted to stick to the security schedule. So, I untangled myself from Mariyah and followed Shehryar to the black, bullet-proof Jeep waiting in the driveway.

As he drove us away, Mariyah's figure waving in the doorway getting smaller, a heavy stone sunk through me, pushing away all the happiness I'd felt for the last week.

CHAPTER 2
Esmeralda

"**H**ow was your trip?"

My hand froze, hovering in front of my mouth, but I recovered just as quickly and lowered the forkful of chicken in garlic sauce back to my plate.

My brother, Kareem, might initiate a conversation with me once in a red moon on the rare occasion he actually ate dinner with me, but that didn't mean it was a good thing. It never was with him.

I straightened in the long-backed wooden chair that had graced the private dining hall of Jahmal Palace for over two hundred years. My eyes drifted ahead to where the young King of Jahandar sat at the other end of the matching table. There might only have been a five-chair difference between us on the long ends of the table, but to me, it felt like I was sitting miles apart from him.

"It was very pleasant. Thank you for asking, Your Majesty," I said in the perfectly polite tone of a princess like I wasn't talking to my own brother but to a complete stranger. I watched him carry on eating without batting an eye up in my direction. "Thank you again for allowing me to spend my birthday in Raven with Mariyah on such short notice."

Kareem hummed a bland sound then took a sip from his glass of water. "I made an exception this once because Shehryar vowed you would be ready for your presentation."

Ah. My stiff shoulders sunk.

So that was why Kareem had agreed. Shehryar had convinced him behind my back. *Again.* As much as I loved Shehryar for doing me the favour, I hated that my asking hadn't been enough for Kareem to agree.

Kareem's lashes finally lifted, subjecting me to his pointed, empty stare.

There was no doubt that he was my brother. Everyone always made the same remark wherever I went with or without him. *We were our father's children.*

Same warm golden skin tone. Same chocolate brown hair, although Kareem's was less wavy than mine, sitting in a short, combed-back style on his head. We had our father's slim noses, neither thin nor full lips, and high cheekbones. But while the features looked pretty and feminine on my face, they looked elegant with a masculine edge on Kareem.

The only difference between us—other than height—was that Kareem had the late Queen, our mother's eyes. A rich brown that shone shades of gold in the sun but turned sharp and cool whenever he looked at me. Never holding the same warmth that mother's eyes always had.

"You asked to lead on this year's environmental strategy presentation," he said, "so even with this disturbance of going to Raven, I expect your full focus on making it perfect."

I gulped hard. "Yes, Your Majesty. I will do my best."

"I didn't ask for your best." I nearly flinched at how quickly the words flew off Kareem's tongue. "I expect nothing less than perfection. I don't have to remind you that your work doesn't only reflect on Jahandar's government. It also reflects on me. And what you present at the Peace Celebration cannot in any way undermine me in front of the entire world."

I understood. I did. I understood why he emphasised perfection so much.

However, just because I knew he had a job to do didn't mean

his harsh words and doubt didn't sting. They always did, digging another hole in my heart before I had even had the chance to fill in the previous one. I would never tell him—I couldn't—but I just wished for the occasional word of support instead. Acknowledgement I was doing well. Some sort of praise. Just a smile. Something. Anything.

I would take measly scraps from him at this point. But even hoping for that was hoping for too much.

"Yes, Your Majesty," I said stiffly, swallowing the wobble in my voice as I dropped my gaze.

I wouldn't cry. *A princess doesn't cry in front of others.* I kept up a brave front, showing nothing, feeling nothing. I straightened my spine and continued eating in a perfectly mastered manner despite having lost my appetite entirely. Chew. Swallow. Repeat.

Unable to taste anything but the sticky heat of never-ending sadness in my mouth.

Kareem excused himself from our late dinner and took his dessert in his office, allowing me to abandon the rest of my main and refuse dessert from a distressed butler who insisted I take it before accepting I wasn't going to give in.

I made my way up to my bedroom on the second of four floors, the wide corridors of the marble palace lined with gold-trimmed red rugs and centuries worth of history. All this beauty presented in the form of carvings in the walls, paintings, old furniture, tapestries, swords, and armour.

"Princess," a woman called out just as I wrapped my fingers around the handle on the engraved door of my bedroom.

I looked over and flashed a genuine smile at the woman sauntering over to me with Shehryar following closely behind. I almost laughed when I realised they were wearing identical troubled frowns. *Like mother, like son.*

"Mama Katiya," I said, eyeing the plate covered by a silver serving lid she held in one hand.

Dammit, how did she find out so quickly?

If Shehryar was the closest thing I had to an actual brother, then his mother, Katiya, was the closest thing I had to a mother. At least since the late Queen had passed away.

Mama Katiya was the head maid in the palace, though she mainly worked with me as she'd been my nanny since my birth. She'd had Shehryar when she was nineteen, so she was only in her mid-forties. A tall, lithe woman with a figure that had filled out gorgeously with age. Besides having matching frowns with her son, their pale green eyes were the same too.

"You did not finish your main, nor did you take your dessert," Mama Katiya said worriedly, her eyes roaming all over me.

"I left the dining hall five minutes ago," I muttered with a grin. "How do you know already?"

"I always know, my dear." She placed the back of her free hand to my forehead but took it off when she seemed satisfied that I didn't have a temperature. "Do you feel nauseous?"

I shook my head. "I'm fine, Mama. Just not that hungry. I think it's the jetlag."

She cocked one lush hip as she sighed. "I understand, but please try to eat a bit more. I had Nina plate your dessert so you could eat it in your room."

Mama Katiya settled the plate in my hands. "But—" I started.

"You have to try, my dear. Please."

A buzzing sound pulsed through the corridor, and as Mama Katiya pulled off the beeper attached to the belt loop of her black dress, I glanced to Shehryar looking for help with the dessert in my hands. But he smirked back at me silently.

"My gosh, I just left him there a minute ago. What has he done now?" The older woman huffed and clipped the beeper back on her dress. "My dear, I have to go, but promise me you'll eat some more."

What Mama Katiya wanted, she got, so I pursed my lips together and nodded. "Okay."

"Good night, Esmeralda," she said and kissed my forehead.

"Good night, Mama," I replied as she scurried off.

The moment she turned the corner, I shoved the covered plate in Shehryar's direction. "Sher, can you please eat—"

"No." He shook his head once sternly, his hands locked behind his back. "You know what my mum's like. If she finds out I ate it instead of you again, she'll kill us both." I narrowed my eyes at him, but he flashed me a grin. "I'm sorry, Princess, but I value my ears."

"Fine," I said with an understanding smile because I valued mine too. They were still ringing from the last time Mama Katiya found out Shehryar ate something I claimed to have to eaten.

I poked him in the chest. "I know you convinced Kareem to let me go to Raven."

His smile vanished and he defensively pulled his already bull-sized shoulders wider. But it didn't make him look scary. It turned him into a gentle giant, soft and guilty but fiercely loving too. "I won't apologise for doing that."

"I know. But I wish you didn't have to."

His face contorted in that adorable way men's faces softened with sympathy yet hardened protectively, with awkwardness bridging the two emotions.

"Do we have a busy day tomorrow?" I asked to put him out of his misery.

He shook his head, immediately straightening into his professional stance. "We'll spend the morning working through your environmental strategy presentation with the advisory team. Then in the afternoon we will attend a tour of the new community centre in Baytown City."

"Okay, that sounds all right."

"It should be. But you should still get an early night and rest."

I hummed my agreement. "I'll try."

Resting his hand against the back of my head, he pressed a kiss to my hair. "Good night, Esmeralda."

"Good night, Sher."

He rubbed my head with the affection of an older brother. "Call me if you can't sleep."

"Okay."

As Shehryar headed back down the corridor the same way his mother had left, I headed into my room and started preparing for the night ahead.

A comfortable hoodie. Snacks. A romance novel. A hard maths exam paper. And a games console.

Everything an insomniac needed to get through ten hours of lonely darkness.

CHAPTER 3
Esmeralda

Six busy days of attending Imperial Cabinet meetings with ministers to finalise Jahandar's actions for this year's international agendas and showing face at other events, all while practising my presentation passed by in a single breath. And the day Kareem and I were to leave for the State of Touma caught me like a lioness sneaking up on its prey, her claws swiping out way too quickly.

Just like that, I found myself sitting in the public dining hall of Touma's main palace, Chaukham Palace, dressed in an evening gown of Jahandar's national colour—dark red.

There was a pulse beating so heavily in my chest that I could feel it in my throat.

He was there. Orange—no, Kai was right there. *So freaking close to me.*

He wasn't in the seat next to me, no, but he was only eleven seats away on the opposite side of the table. *Eleven seats away!*

He hadn't been there when Kareem and I arrived at the palace earlier that afternoon. Only Kai's mother, Queen Leila, his uncle and younger brother to the King, Prince Arsh, and Kai's youngest brother, the third prince of Touma, Adam, had been there to greet us.

Apparently, Kai, King Rami, and the second prince of Touma, Fay, had gone to Vray Manor and Westcombe Palace to await Raven and Prio's arrival, hence his absence.

I'd almost been convinced Kai wasn't going to turn up at the welcome dinner with all sixty plus members of royalty from all seven states in attendance, excluding all the children under fifteen. Spread across two dark oak tables dressed in flowers, crystal glasses, silver cutlery and empty plates of food, with gold chandeliers spreading a bright yellow hue all across the historic room. But when he entered the hall with his family, my excitement and nerves hit a new degree of measurement.

My hands were shaking in my lap as the penultimate course of nine was served, and I was doing my best to focus solely on what Princess Dabira of Shah was saying to me from opposite the table. But my eyes kept searching out the man who made my heart pound erratically.

Gosh, I was so jealous of the Dowager Queen of Khaas who was sitting next to Kai, laughing at whatever he'd said to her. I would have traded my every organ for the older woman's seat.

"There is only a month left now for my Shadow to have her four pups," Princess Dabira said, her hand falling over her heart as her mahogany cheeks glowed with delight. "But I can say with my whole heart that I am already attached to every one of them. Unfortunately," —she let out a theatrical sigh— "my mean brother, *the dear King*, has already made me promise to give all but one of them away."

The blue eyes of the seventeen-year-old Prince of Raven, sitting next to Princess Dabira, lit up. "You're going to give them away? Do you possibly think I could have one?"

The woman chuckled, nudging the boy with her arm playfully. "Well, we'll have to speak to your parents first, won't we? Having a pet wolf is a big responsibility."

"I've already spoken to them about getting a wolf before, and Father said..."

I was listening. Honestly, I was. *But,* while the young prince distracted Princess Dabira with talk of getting a pet wolf, I took the small window of time to glance at Kai again.

A soft sigh fell from my mouth as my heart flapped harder in its cage again.

My Orange, Prince Kai, was beautiful. *Fact.*

Not in a feminine or pretty way, no. Not at all.

His features were masculine and maybe even a little stern. His face was permanently shadowed even though he was always cleanly-shaven, his nose was straight and strong, mouth thin and wide, jaw sharp and square, with ink black eyes set under dark, straight brows.

But maybe it was the way he held himself, his expression always warm and open, or the starry twinkle in his eyes—just like his mother's in colour. Or maybe the way his raven black locks of hair softened his features, but he just had natural charm and elegance that made him beautiful.

Dressed in his official uniform of a black suit trousers and a tunic decorated with embellished gold buttons, braided ropes that wrapped under the sleeve of his right arm, and a red belt tied high up around his waist, he looked every bit of the handsome prince he was and so much more too.

"Is the conversation boring you, Princess Esmeralda?"

I nearly jumped out of my seat like a frightened cat when the quiet, playful voice came from my left. My blush stung hot across my face when I found Prince Arsh of Touma, Kai's uncle, grinning at me.

Objectively speaking, Kai's uncle and King Rami's younger brother, Prince Arsh, was what I considered a silver fox. Though, actually, his short brown hair was only grey around the sides. In his mid-forties with a cheeky smile and a tall, athletic frame, he was known for being easy-going and very sociable. I didn't think I'd ever seen him not smiling.

Except, looking at me, his grin was cheeky and amused, and his hazel eyes danced with mischief.

Like. He. Knew.

But he couldn't know, right? I hadn't been staring that blatantly, had I? Had I? *Oh, shit...*

"No, not at all," I managed to get out relatively evenly with a smile.

"Then I suppose…" His eyes moved past me, but I didn't dare follow to see who or what he was gazing at. "You're simply more interested in being seated over there?"

The lift of his brow only added fuel to the embarrassment that tore through me, scorching my skin from head to toe, no doubt in blotchy, red patches.

I cleared my throat, shifting in my chair. "No, I'm happy where I'm seated."

"Are you certain? You wouldn't, you know—rather sit next to my nephew?"

Oh fuck…

I wanted to deny it, but my tongue was swollen and glued to the roof of my mouth in panic. So, I tried to shake my head, though I couldn't tell if it was actually moving or not. "I don't know…"

Prince Arsh chuckled. He was enjoying my fluster far too much. "Ah, you don't know what I mean?"

A weight dropped through me and launched back up to my throat as I flicked my attention around us. Because if he'd noticed then—

"Relax, Esmeralda," he whispered, and it was the oddest thing, but I actually found myself loosening under the softness of his tone. "You play a very subtle game, so I doubt anyone else noticed." His tilted his head giving me a slight nod like he was impressed. "It took me a while to realise who you were looking at."

I stared at him, muted and unblinking for a small eternity, trying to figure out how I was supposed to play this off. Apparently, I didn't want to. "Are you…are you going to tell him?"

He shook his head immediately. "I wouldn't dare." He leaned into me. "But I could swap you into every seat next to him for the next two weeks if you'd like?"

My mouth twitched. The idea was tempting, but… "I think that would be too obvious."

"A few seats it is then."

"Wait, that isn't what I—"

A harmony of clinking sounds from the heads of both tables cut through my sentence and ended all the conversation in the hall. With a light scrape of chairs on the solid wood floor, Queen Leila and King Rami of Touma stood up from their seats at their respective tables.

King Rami's gaze moved around the hall as he shifted his weight, bracing a large hand on the gentleman's cane he used to support an old injury to his leg. Yet even with the cane, he still looked fit and handsome. With a big, charming smile, a kingly beard streaked with grey, a lean, tall build just like his younger brother, and beautiful light brown eyes, bordering on hazel.

"Now, I know," he said, "that everyone of us is rather excited for dessert, so I thank you for your silence, and I promise, Leila and I shall keep this welcome short and sweet."

The King of Touma nodded to his wife, and Queen Leila smiled elegantly and tipped her heart-shaped face up, making the diamond crown on her head shimmer in the light. "Thank you all for attending the 875th Peace Anniversary this year, and we are delighted to be hosting this special anniversary celebration…"

I watched, smiled, clapped, and laughed with everyone else as the King and Queen made their welcome speech, bantering like a sweet couple rather than two powerful rulers of a state.

Somewhere during their speech, when a cheer echoed around at the mention of Prince Arsh planning the annual royal scavenger hunt, my attention naturally trailed around the table.

Accidently finding Kai. Or unconsciously searching for him.

Just as his blacker than black eyes found mine.

It was as if everything stopped. My brain. My heart. My breath. The sound in the room. The world.

I sat as still as a statue, expecting him to look away like it was nothing.

But from across the table, eleven seats away, his mouth stretched. Curled up into a perfect grin with just enough teeth and warmth and…

My world tipped, fluttered, shook. Just cartoon-style *kaboomed.*

Pressed deep into his right cheek was the very dimple that had stolen my heart all those years ago.

CHAPTER 4
Esmeralda

It was two in the morning, and I laid awake on the king-sized, wooden-framed bed, staring at the crystals on the chandelier as the moonlight coming in from the window twinkled through them.

My insomnia might have been keeping me awake, but it was Kai's smile replaying in my mind that had me perma-grinning to the point my cheeks were aching.

Was there such a condition that caused someone to literally be unable to stop smiling?

Because I was entirely sure that was what I had developed. Or caught—maybe it was contagious.

I could have aced an audition for the role of a horror-movie clown.

I kept telling myself it was just a smile. Just a smile that probably hadn't even been for me but for his uncle. Even if it had been meant for me, Kai had just been polite, nothing more.

But my stupid heart that stupidly craved anything from him was dancing like a stupid fool in my chest, filling me with giddy bubbles and butterflies and all things stupidly fluttery.

But it was the best feeling ever to be noticed by him.

A giggle fell from my mouth before I slapped my palm to my lips like someone might have heard me. I groaned immediately after, squeezing my eyes shut as I rubbed a hand over my face.

I'm being silly.

How was I ever going to get him to see me as a woman if I grew excited over every little thing he did like some teenage girl? Not only that, but I was the Crown Princess of Jahandar before I was a woman attracted to a man. I had a duty to do. These two weeks weren't just for fun and games.

I needed to stop thinking about his smile immediately. Or at least stop squealing about it.

Deciding a late-night stroll was the right call, I threw myself upright and climbed off the bed, heading into the walk-in wardrobe next to the ensuite bathroom.

The room I'd been given was spacious and decorated like the rest of the palace—history frozen in time in every nook and cranny. High, painted ceilings, intricately carved cornices, and a hanging golden, crystal chandelier. The floor was covered in a worn red carpet, dark oak furniture that included two bedside cabinets, a dressing table, and a velvet-cushioned chaise that sat against the wall between the large window seat and balcony doors.

I pulled on an oversized black hoodie over my stripped blue, matching pyjama shorts and cropped shirt, then headed back out and shimmied into a pair of blue, bunny-eared slippers.

The sensor lights turned on in the corridor as I stepped out from the room. I pulled my hood up over my hair and walked down with no particular destination in mind.

I ended up on the balcony level of the palace's three-floor library first and spent an hour whizzing between the shelves on each floor. I gasped when I found four sets of bookcases tucked at the back of the second floor with romance books and vowed to come back and explore it when I had time.

My hunt for the palace kitchen next ended in success. I peeked inside, but I didn't grab anything to eat. I wanted to get permission from the head chef first before sneaking any food.

At some point, the giddy feeling consuming my belly settled, leaving space for tiredness that turned my yawns frequent and long.

I took a confused, almost-got-lost route back up to my assigned bedroom, only recognising the correct corridor by the painting of a forest hanging on the wall.

Except the moment my fingers brushed the round, metal handle, a viciously tight latch wrapped around my upper arm, stuttering the beat of my heart. My shock hadn't quite reached its peak when another hand gripped the back of my hood and tore it off my head.

By that point, I was already being yanked around and slammed back against the door.

The impact knocked a gasp out of me, but my body reacted instantly, recalibrating and planning, working on muscle memory to use everything I'd practised with Shehryar on self-defence.

My hands shot out and pressed against the huge, grey torso of the man—I might not have seen his face, but I knew it was a man—gripping onto hot, shifting muscle as I readied myself to force my knee up into his groin with as much strength as I could manage.

Then my gaze flew up. And I froze solid.

My mind in survival mode might not have recognised the obsidian black eyes looking down at me through square-rimmed glasses, but my heart could have recognised them anytime, anywhere.

That—he—Orange… *It was fucking Kai.*

The shock ringing through me reflected back in Kai's glaring eyes as they widened. He suddenly let go of me and flew a step back, leaving me to slump against the door, shaky and baffled.

Why—he—what—what? What was freaking happening?

"Princess Esmeralda," he rasped, his voice deep and rich but quick and breathless. "What are you…what are you doing here?"

I'd heard his question, but my mind was reeling so hard from the sight before me, struggling to figure out whether it was a figment of my desperate imagination or not.

Because my crush—Orange, the prince—who had been present at dinner was *nowhere* to be seen.

Kai was wearing a hoodie. With navy-blue pyjama bottoms—*and a hoodie!*

Grey and fitted around his huge shoulders and biceps in a way that threatened drool to spill out the corners of my gaping mouth, before trimming down and sitting loose around his waist.

Maybe it was the fit of the fabric, or maybe it was because he'd never been up in my personal space before, but he was so much bigger than he'd ever looked from a distance. *Taller and bulkier.*

He towered over me. My eyes were pretty much level with his sternum, which had to put him nearly a whole foot taller than me. And his size. Fuck. He wasn't built like an ancient warrior in the same way Shehryar was, but Kai was still *built*. His shoulders, chest, and arms hard, wide, and strong.

He was definitely not the lean, athletic prince he looked in his uniform or a three-piece suit.

He was a cross between those college rugby players they called *jocks* in the State of Raven and a…a hot nerd—glasses, tight-jaw, his raven-black hair poking out from underneath the pulled-up hood.

Glasses. *He wore fucking glasses.*

And a frown too, I belatedly noticed, so intense as he studied me to the point his thick, straight brows practically merged into the rim of his glasses.

"Princess Esmeralda. I asked you a question." His voice was lower, darker, and damn if it didn't shake through my chest in the most perfect, delicious way.

Yet the stern edge in his tone had me straightening, snapping out of my trance and really seeing the man before me. And shit. He didn't look like my quietly charming Orange one bit.

"I, uh…I was just heading back to my room." I tried to smile but my face muscles refused to comply as I awkwardly pointed my thumb behind me.

His eyes and frown only hardened more, piercing into me in a way that made me want to squirm uncomfortably—*who was this man glaring at me and where was my Orange?*

"This is not your room. It is *mine*."

My blood ran cold.

Actually, it turned to ice like a frozen lake in the northern parts of Shah. Before a volcano suddenly erupted beneath it, shattering the ice, and sending a torrent of molten lava sizzling through me.

Oh. Fuck.

I had the wrong room. I had the flipping wrong room! And worse. It was Kai's room.

I jolted away from the door. "I—I am so sorry," I said, wishing the floor would swallow me whole or that I would just drop dead. "I thought this was my room, so I…"

His frown barely let up as he shifted on his feet. "Your room is down the next corridor on the right."

Oh fuck. Oh fuck. I messed up, I messed up, I messed up.

I sidestepped out from between him and the door, fumbling with my hands. "Of course." I took another step back. "Thank you, and I apologise. Good night." Grimacing and cursing at myself, I quickly spun away and began striding back down the corridor.

You stupid, stupid, stupid—

"Why are you awake?"

I didn't want to, but my feet immediately stopped, and as much as I wanted to hide forever in embarrassment, I had no choice but to turn and face him. I couldn't exactly make a run for it either—I would have to face that humiliation for the rest of my life if I did.

He was still eyeing me through his glasses with caution, a deep crevice between his brows.

"I, uh…I couldn't sleep," I said automatically and smiled and shrugged. "You know…new place, new bed. So, I thought I'd tire myself out with a quick walk. I just…ended up getting a bit lost on my way back."

Some stupid part of me hoped he'd smile it off, but what I got was just more silent glares from the man who wore Prince Kai's skin. If anything, his frown intensified with a fraction of a shift of his right brow, and I felt myself shrinking into my hoodie.

"Good night," I said again, and quickly spun away without daring to look back.

What on Neves just happened? What did I just do? Who the fuck was that glaring man?

Because that sure as fuck wasn't Orange.

And he sure as fuck didn't like catching me mistakenly trying to enter his room.

Great. Perfect. What a brilliant start to *Operation befriend him and bed him.*

CHAPTER 5
Esmeralda

"How was your night, my dear?" Mama Katiya asked as she drew the curtains back from the balcony doors that morning—the human hours of the morning.

I rubbed a hand over my nest of hair as I glanced from her to my personal stylist, Rose, picking out my outfit through the open door of the walk-in wardrobe.

Shehryar would be here within the hour, and then the trio I never travelled without would be complete. But instead of getting up, I threw myself backwards into the sea of pillows with a groan.

"Oh, are you okay, Princess?" Mama Katiya said.

Okay? After that disastrous encounter? Fuck no. I was definitely not okay.

I was forever going to remember the painting hanging in the corridor of my bedroom wasn't of a forest, but of a meadow of flowers. Though, I wished I could have forgotten what happened after.

But as the day passed on, and I ended up close or next to Kai multiple times through the first public conference of the Peace Celebrations, it became increasingly obvious that the world just wasn't going to let me do so.

Honestly, I couldn't tell what bothered me more. That he hardly interacted with me the whole time, or that his demeanour was exactly that of Orange's despite the way he'd frowned at me last night.

They could have been two different people—charming twin and… grumpy twin.

I was almost convinced I'd dreamt up the frowny Kai of the night, which I knew I hadn't, but I couldn't comprehend how they blended together into one person.

By the end of the conference, I realised it didn't really matter, because I was never going to get anywhere with him when he thought I was a creep who tried to steal into random men's rooms in the middle of the night.

How did I fuck up so badly on the first night?

"Would you like to run through your presentation for tomorrow now or later after a rest?" Shehryar asked as he walked me up to my room—*the correct one*—when we returned to the palace.

"After dinner, Sher. But only very quickly," I said. "So, go rest until then, and enjoy yourself for a few hours. And no thinking about work or messaging me work-related questions."

His defiant posture made it seem like he was going to argue the resting thing, but his shoulders relented, and he nodded. "All right. But if you need me, Princess, you call me. *Immediately.*"

Ten minutes later, I came out of the room dressed in a burgundy, knitted jumper dress and leggings, and made my way down to the palace kitchen. If things with Kai hadn't exactly gone to plan, I could at least make sure the kitchen staff were okay with me snacking my sorrows away.

Delicious smells of spices, sweetness, and fresh bread snuck into my nose as I pushed the swinging metals doors of the kitchen open, a single circular window in each one. The kitchen was a maze of industrial cookers, sinks, and silver countertops and islands dotted around, with staff everywhere creating a harmony of sizzling and clattering sounds. They were all so focused on their pre-dinner prep that no one noticed I'd entered. Until one young man came bouncing in his step towards me.

The young man's brown eyes popped before he doubled over in a dramatic bow. "Your Highness," he said, his grin bright and friendly.

The freckles across his nose added to his boyish charm.

I returned his smile. "Hello…"

"Ah." He practically jumped forward. "I am Michael, His Highness Prince Kai's equerry."

Of course. Of course, the one person I ran into for help had to be linked to the man whose attention I couldn't grab in the right way. The world was taunting me.

"Oh, well hello, Michael. It's a pleasure to meet you," I said. "You couldn't happen to direct me to the head chef, could you?"

A sweet frown took over his brows, crinkling his freckled nose. "Was there something wrong with any of your meals?"

"Oh, no." I shook my head. "I simply had a question about some snacks."

"Oh. Oh, of course then, allow me to lead the way." He didn't even wait a second. He spun around with a flourish and marched ahead. I followed by his side. "The head chef is Nur, and his nephew, Pierre, is the sous chef. There are two head pastry chefs. Lola is on holiday, but my husband, Roger, is here today." He glowed as he said that. "They're in the pantry, planning orders and meals and whatnot, so I'll introduce you, Ma'am, to them all."

"Nur, Pierre, Roger," Michael called out as we reached the far right corner of the kitchen where there was a big silver door half open.

"Michael," a man's voice came from inside. "You only just left Roger and I cannot and will not—oh."

In the open door of the pantry stood an older man I assumed was the head chef, Nur. He was of a sturdy build, neither short nor tall, and had the typical silver hair and ruby red eyes of someone from the Crimson Cast, with soft wrinkles around his eyes and strands of white in his hair.

His striking gaze went wide, and he stepped forward and bowed. "Your Highness."

Two other men suddenly appeared behind him. It was quite obvious which one was Nur's nephew.

Michael's husband, Roger, bent his head immediately as he spotted me, but Nur's nephew, Pierre, admired me from head to toe with his ruby red eyes. He seemed older than me, maybe close to Kai's age, and must've only been half Crimson Cast, because his short, wavy hair was a silvery brown, with the faintest of freckles splashed across his light, olive-coloured skin. Pierre was tall like Kai, but leaner, more athletic, but honestly, he was objectively really handsome too.

His eyes met mine and they glinted in a mischievous, arrogant way that was insightful and funny.

The man was a flirt. He knew it. I knew it. The world knew it. And he clearly loved it.

His wide mouth stretched into a cocky, lop-sided grin as he stepped out from behind Nur and leaned over in a flourish of a bow. I couldn't help but smile at his show as he took my hand gently in his larger, roughened fingers and brought it to his mouth, pressing the softest kiss to my knuckles.

"Crown Princess Esmeralda, what a wonderful and beautiful surprise to see you down in our kitchen; I couldn't have wished for better company to join us," he said and let me slip my hand from his. "I'm Pierre Farhan, the sous chef of the kitchen, so if you ever need anything, Your Highness," —his voice dipped a tone— "you can call upon me whenever you want. I'd be more than happy to help."

His uncle, Nur, made a choked sound. "Really now?" the older man said, sarcasm lifting the depth of his voice. "Wasn't it just a moment ago that you said to me it was completely unfair I hadn't given you any leave over the Peace Celebrations, and that you wanted to take a break?"

Pierre didn't even glance across to see Nur's incredulous expression. "I have no idea what you mean, Uncle Chef. It seems the exhaustion of age is playing with your memory. Maybe it's time to consider retirement."

Roger and Michael covered their amusement with coughs from where they were huddled together, and I pursed my lips together trying not to laugh as Nur's pale skin flushed pink. "Why, you—"

A chortle burst from Pierre as he flinched away from his uncle. "I'm kidding, old man. Relax."

"Do you know what? Go. Go now. Go check on everyone's prep

while I talk to Her Highness," Nur instructed, waving the clipboard in his hand at Pierre like he was swatting a fly away.

"But Her Highness likes my company, don't you?" he said and nodded himself. "It would be rude to leave when she has asked for me to stay."

I chuckled. Oh, I liked him. He was cheeky and cool, yet he still genuinely seemed like a good person.

"Her Highness did not ask you to stay."

Pierre edged closer to me, but still kept a respectful distance. "Would you like me to stay, Your Highness?"

"I think," I said, grinning through my words, "you should probably listen to your uncle."

"Dammit," Pierre mumbled, but next to him Nur looked rather smug. "All right, fine, as you wish. But please do not leave before I get a chance to speak to you."

I agreed to Pierre's condition before he, Roger, and Michael disappeared, leaving me to ask Nur about digging through the kitchen for snacks. To no surprise, he was more than happy to let me and even forced me, *respectfully,* to add my favourite snacks to their daily orders from their suppliers. By which point, Pierre returned and stole me away from his uncle to show me around the kitchen.

I was with Pierre and Nur around a silver island in the middle of the kitchen when Prince Adam of Touma—the youngest son of Queen Leila and King Rami—walked over, running a hand through his hair. He startled a bit when he noticed me, while Nur and Pierre bowed their heads to him.

"Princess Esmeralda," Adam mumbled and stooped his head.

I smiled widely and nodded back at the awkward teenager. "Hello, Prince Adam."

I had always liked Kai's polite and shy youngest brother. He was a tall, lanky eighteen-year-old who had yet to fill out his frame, but it was obvious he was a just a younger version of his father with the same light brown eyes, dark hair, and warm skin tone.

"Oof, is the revision taking its toll, little prince? You look…" Pierre pulled a mock wincing face.

"Thanks," Adam grumbled but his lips curved up tiredly. "I needed something to eat."

"Of course," Nur said. "What would you like, Your Highness? Would a sandwich suffice?"

"Thank you, Nur, a sandwich would be great."

As Nur headed off, I turned to Adam with my brows furrowed. "Revision for what?"

"A maths mock exam the week we go back to school."

My eyes widened. "What happened to no schoolwork over the Peace holidays?"

Pierre chuckled, but Adam's face scrunched in distaste. "Our teacher doesn't think the celebration is a reason not to have an exam."

"Shoulda pulled the prince card like I told you to," Pierre said, shaking his head.

"I could help you revise if you want," I offered without a thought.

Adam blinked at me but then slunk his gaze away shyly. "No, it's okay. Thank you for offering."

"Are you sure?" I didn't have anything else to do until after dinner when I'd meet with Shehryar to practise my presentation, and unfortunately, Operation Kai was currently on hold, so...

"I'm free right now." I playfully flicked my hair. "And I don't usually brag, but maths was my strongest subject. Full marks nearly all the time."

Consideration darted across his face then he nodded awkwardly. "There are a few past paper questions I'm struggling with..."

Kai

I rubbed the back of my neck with a firm hand as I pushed open the ground-floor doors to the palace library.

Bloody Neves, I was tired. And hungry.

The morning conference had been draining, and sitting in my office, staring at a computer screen for two hours after hadn't exactly helped. One and a half hours longer than I had intended to. I had only wanted to triple check my presentation for tomorrow, but I was... distracted.

First, it was her laugh, and now this. That. Her. Outside my bedroom.

I shook the thought away as a frown fell heavily on my brows. I'd come to the library to return the books piling up in my office and take a five-minute break, not be distracted further.

In the library, my steps were silenced by the thick red carpet rolled out through the middle, and dark wooden shelves and bookcases lined either side, not a single one empty. I didn't notice it at first, but the further I walked down, the clearer the murmur of voices coming from the back became.

I recognised the timbre of my younger brother's voice immediately. But the softer, familiar feminine voice... *Who was that with Adam?*

Suddenly, the woman's voice shot through the library. "Adam!"

"Esmeralda!"

Esmeralda? As in Princess Esmeralda?

The piercing clatter and bang that followed rang through me so loudly that I lost all hearing before fear and concern for Adam slammed me into action.

I dropped the books in my hands, scattering them across the floor, and rushed to the other end. I nearly stumbled into one set of table and chairs as I came to a stop. And the sight...

Princess Esmeralda stood over my little brother where he was sprawled on the floor by a fallen chair. A teacup in her hands tipped in his direction. Its content gone.

A lion's roar of protective rage tore through me

She'd spilt tea on Adam. She'd burned him. She'd hurt Adam like Meg had.

"What on Neves is going on?" I didn't recognise the booming voice that left me.

Their heads flew up, but I directed all my anger at the wide-eyed princess.

Fuck, I should have known. After catching her trying to go into my room the night before, I should have known she was going to cause more trouble. But I made the mistake of giving her the benefit of the doubt. Hadn't I learnt my lesson already?

I charged over to Adam, taking his arm and pulling him up to his feet. It completely slipped my mind that I was a prince, bred in the way of politeness when I saw the spillage stain over Adam's left thigh. I flew around to stare down the princess. "What did you do to him?"

She flinched, shrinking into herself, and I should've felt guilty for speaking that way to a woman, but I didn't. Couldn't and wouldn't— not if it meant my family got hurt again.

"It's not…" She shook her head and scrambled to put the teacup down on the table. "I didn't—"

Adam tugged at my arm, futilely trying to pull me away from her. "Kai, relax. It was an accident."

"An accident? How was spilling tea on you an accident?"

"That isn't what happened, Prince Kai," Princess Esmeralda stuttered. "I didn't—I wasn't—"

"Then how was Adam burnt?"

She flinched again, her warm golden skin turning red and blotchy over her cheeks and neck.

"Would you just listen first before yelling," Adam said.

"I'm sorry." She shook her head, her greyish-brown eyes growing damp. "I didn't mean—"

I'd heard more than enough. I needed her to leave before I caused an international scandal by raging at another state's princess. But I couldn't just let her get away with hurting Adam without consequences either.

"Leave the library now," I snarled, "before I inform King Kareem of the antics you've been pulling."

I had never in my life seen anyone visibly blanch the way she did. Turning so pale she almost looked bloodless, her eyes so dark and stricken she looked near lifeless. It was as if I hadn't threatened to tell on her but threatened to torture her with ancient instruments.

I felt a pang of guilt fire through my chest.

Silently, she straightened her spine, yet she looked so small and fragile like an injured bird. Hardly able to look me in the eyes as she clasped her hands in front of herself. "I apologise. It was my fault," she muttered, her voice steady but barely above a whisper.

And then she walked away. Shoulders back, chin high. Strong and regal.

"What was that?" Adam snapped just as the door closed behind her. "You're such an idiot, Kai."

"She hurt—"

"No, she didn't. She saved me." He shook his head. "The tea didn't spill on me. It spilt on her hands."

A cold wave rose through me with painful slowness. "What?"

"I was swinging on my chair with the cup in my hand. I tipped the legs too far and the tea would have fallen all over my face if she hadn't grabbed the cup, *burning her own hands*. Not me." Adam shoved me in the chest. "And you just yelled at her like a bloody idiot."

I swallowed slowly as I looked from the fallen chair to Adam to the wooden doors of the library, processing what he'd just told me.

The small ounce of guilt I felt just moments ago?

That turned into a heavy paw clawing at my chest, shredding my anger and insides to pieces as Princess Esmeralda's pale expression filled my mind.

Shit.

CHAPTER 6

Kai

It was raining outside. *"Chucking it down"* as the saying went in Touma.

The sound was irritatingly loud in the silent darkness of my room, battering the window and balcony doors like fingers drumming constantly on a table. Quick, harsh, and annoying.

I scrunched my face into a tighter frown and sunk deeper into my silk bedsheets. But I kept watching shadows of droplets—at least the blurs of them I could see—splatter on the far wall where it was painted in the dim light of the bedside lamp.

I hated winter and its ridiculously cold weather. But I despised rain most of all. Ironic considering I was from a state with a cooler, wetter climate. From the way it turned the sky grey to the way it made everything look miserable, to the sound of it caging me in and how it crawled on my skin.

My hate for rain was worse at night.

Being an insomniac meant I rarely ever slept anyway—two or three hours of sleep was a good night for me. But on nights when it rained, the impossibility of sleep reached new heights, forcing me to lie awake and listen to the chatter of rain outside until it convinced me to find sanctuary elsewhere.

But…on nights when I had been an absolute prick to a princess for mistakenly thinking she'd hurt my little brother when she'd done quite the opposite, not being able to sleep and therefore being forced to listen to the rain seemed like the punishment I deserved.

"Shit." I scrubbed a hand over my face before throwing myself over, turning my back to the window.

I fucked up with Princess Esmeralda. I'd been wrong for letting my own distrust pin her as a pretty villain when I had no real evidence of her being one. And what was worse, I had yet to apologise.

Cursing again in frustration, I shoved the duvet off and sat up. I grabbed my glasses off the bedside cabinet and climbed off the bed. Then I picked up the grey hoodie lying at the end of my mattress and pulled it on over the long-sleeved top I already wore. No number of layers could ever be enough to protect me from the rain and cold. Even if I was still inside.

Slippers on, hood pulled up to cover my bed hair, I left my room, stopping when I reached the next corridor around the corner. I scowled down the hallway at the door to Princess Esmeralda's room.

Shit. I had to apologise quickly. And soon.

I scrubbed a hand over my mouth and continued on the usual route of my nightly walks. But less than a few minutes into the stroll, I found a palace guard pacing restlessly in front of the arched garden doors. He peeked out where one door was partially open before he quickly swung around.

He stuttered to a stop. "Prince Kai," he said with a bow.

As much as I wanted to avoid getting too close to the pelting of rain echoing from outside, I approached the guard. "What's wrong, Raj?"

Raj wrung his black-gloved hands and tugged at the coat of his red livery as his eyes flicked to the gap in the doors. "Her Highness, Crown Princess Esmeralda is outside," he blurted.

I blinked. "What?" Surely my ears had deceived me because Raj hadn't just said—

"Crown Princess Esmeralda is sitting outside in the rain. In nothing but a thin nightshirt and shorts. With no jacket and no umbrella. I tried to stop her, I really did, but she refused to listen to me."

Again, I blinked, my numb mind failing to comprehend his explanation. Because there was no way she was crazy enough to do that. *She couldn't be.* Surely, she knew that the rain in Touma was freezing cold in comparison to Jahandar's monsoon showers.

Before I could recall my abhorrence for rain, I charged for the open door and yanked it fully open, exposing myself to the cold downpour.

My jaw collapsed to the floor.

There she was. Princess Esmeralda. Sitting on a nearby bench under a black metal lamp with her back to the door. No umbrella and no jacket either just as Raj said.

"How long has she been out there?" I asked.

"I—I don't know." He looked at his watch. "Maybe ten minutes."

My blood ran cold as if I'd been the one outside. "Ten minutes? And you didn't think to go get her out of there? You know how cold it is when it rains."

Raj's face paled. "I tried, Sir, but Her Highness—"

Without another thought, I stormed away from the guard to the tall wooden wardrobe nearby. There was no time to put a coat on, so I grabbed the longest umbrella hanging on the door and picked up my old pair of trainers off the cupboard floor, charging back over to the door. As I quickly shoved my feet into the trainers, I couldn't help but feel like this was my fault.

Why else would she be sitting outside in the rain in the middle of a freezing cold night? Unless she just enjoyed playing Raven Roulette with her health and wanted to get hypothermia. In which case, it might not have been my place, but I was going to set her straight when I got her inside. And then finally, I was going to apologise too.

With that plan in mind, I opened the umbrella and braced myself before voluntarily charging out into the pouring rain for the first time in my entire existence. When I rounded the bench, whether she saw me or felt me, her gaze drifted sideways. Then up and up until her wide eyes met mine.

Princess Esmeralda shot up from the bench, stumbling back a step. "Prince Kai."

I just about heard her breathless voice over the consuming noise of the rain. I was too focused on trying to control the irrational frustration filtering through me at the sight of her.

Her shorts, of some light colour, were plastered to the very top of her thighs, her shirt had become a second layer of skin, and her hair was beyond dripping wet and combed back off her face.

She was fucking *barefoot* too.

My brows bunched together fiercely. "What are you doing out here?" I demanded loud enough to ensure she could hear me.

Her gaze flicked to the side, but she stayed silent, so I stepped closer, covering her with the umbrella. Her big eyes grew wider as I reached for her hand. "You need to get inside."

"No." She pulled back, stumbling out from under the protection of the umbrella. "I'm staying out here."

I gaped at her.

She was mad. *This girl was insane.* There was no other explanation as to why she wanted to stay outside where the wet wind was biting away at her skin.

I gritted my teeth. "With all due respect, Princess Esmeralda, you cannot stay out here in the freezing cold rain."

She tipped her chin up. "I'm perfectly fine, Prince Kai. I want to be out here. I *need* to be out here."

Need to be? Oh, she needed to be sick, did she? And get me wet in the process? *Yeah, right.*

I stepped closer to her. "You're going to risk getting hypothermia if you stay out here."

She shrugged one shoulder. "Then I will take the risk."

"No, you will not." The frustrated words left me before I even realised they had. "You are coming inside. *Now.*"

For a long moment, her expression remained blank in shock. Honestly, I was a little shocked myself too. This was *not* the polite prince I had always strived to be. But I meant it, with everything in me.

She recovered quickly, giving me her own little scowl—if that's what it could even be called. "*With all due respect,* Prince Kai, you cannot tell me what to do."

I moved closer again. "If you weren't being so stubborn then I wouldn't have to, would I?"

Her mouth pulled apart before snapping back together. "I'm being the stubborn one? What about your insistence on taking me back inside against my will?"

This is what I got for coming out into the rain for her. A mouthful from this tiny—

She's a princess. Remember that, Kai? A crown princess. Currently higher in position than you.

But I was pissed off for reasons I couldn't even properly explain. "You will thank me tomorrow morning when you wake up dry and well."

I latched onto her hand—which was wrong of me on so many levels, and had I had a single rational thought left, I would never have done it—before she pulled away again.

I couldn't imagine it was anything other than indignation that flashed in her eyes as she twisted her small, soft hand in my larger, rougher one. "Prince Kai."

"We are going inside," I said, trying to tug her back under the umbrella.

She leaned her weight away. "Prince Kai, you cannot—"

"Esmeralda!"

I made two mistakes.

One, I had dropped her title without her permission and yelled at her. *Again.*

Two, I pulled at her too hard. *Way too hard.*

Instead of dragging her under the umbrella, I dragged her straight into me. *Flush against me.*

I could feel. Every. Wet. Inch. Of. Her. Body. Through every piece of clothing I was wearing.

Every curve. Every dip. Like she was naked. And once that realisation, was in my head, I couldn't unthink it. And I definitely couldn't unfeel it.

The surprising swell of her breasts, soft, soaked, and squished to my chest. The full curve of her thighs. The size of her, slim yet curvaceous. Small. The top of her head wasn't quite level with my shoulders, but she fit perfectly against my taller, wider frame.

And then there was her ridiculously pretty face. Nobody should have had the audacity to be that pretty. Droplets trailed down her skin, her eyes grey under the lighting, big, beautiful and entrapping. Her cheekbones were delicate but high, the arch of her brows was strong, and her supple lips were just parted.

Whatever frustration I had been feeling was forced to move over as a new emotion entered the mix.

The kind that made my breaths feel hot and heavy in my lungs and made me lose focus on everything but her. It slipped low inside me, tracing the path of her body down until it reached my stomach. *Lower.*

If I hadn't registered the disgusting prickle of dampness settling across my shoulders, I might have fallen into the clutches of the tempting feeling. But I snapped out of the trance, not releasing her hand, just remembering that she was soaked to the bone, that I hated rain, and we needed to get back inside quickly.

Without offering Princess… *Forget it, I already dropped her title anyway*—Esmeralda the chance to argue otherwise, I dipped my head and charged for the door, pulling her behind me.

"Prince Kai," she called.

"Would you please place this somewhere to dry and then lock the doors?" I said to Raj as I stepped into the warmth of the palace and handed him the dripping umbrella. I hardly stopped in my stride through the hallway.

"Prince Kai," Esmeralda snapped, tugging for her hand, demanding my attention.

I gave it to her. I stopped and swerved around, meeting what she clearly intended to be a fierce stare, if she were an angry kitten that is. She was so close that I noticed the green speckles that coloured her greyish-brown eyes before her long, wet lashes fluttered and she shifted back meekly.

She must've seen the silent warning in my heavy stare because she didn't utter a sound after that, and soon enough I reached her room.

I opened the door with my free hand, turned on the lights, and pulled her inside, closing the door behind us. It wasn't polite to say the least. Not to mention the back of my neck was crawling from the way my hoodie was soaked and growing uncomfortable. But I didn't care in that moment. All that mattered was getting Esmeralda warm and dry.

"You need to get those wet clothes off and take a hot shower," I instructed and headed into the walk-in wardrobe just like the one in my room. I grabbed two fresh white towels from one cubby along the back wall and headed back out. "Or—"

All the syllables disappeared from the tip of my tongue when I looked at Esmeralda. For the first time, I saw her properly in full lighting, standing with her arms softly wrapped around her belly.

I saw far more than what I probably should have been seeing of her. All the golden warmth of her bare skin layered under the wet baby-pink nightshirt and shorts clinging to her slim, curvy body.

As well as the fucking white lace of her bra and knickers underneath.

This time, the hot, heavy feeling punched me right in the groin, gripping my bloody balls with surprising strength. It was so tempting to just stand there and stare and take my fill of her.

Kai, you bastard, she's cold!

The warning whipped through my head and had me quickly glancing away. *Up.* I found her face and kept my eyes there. No matter how much the surprising shot of heat begged me to look lower.

I walked forward and held the towels out for her. "Or at the very least dry yourself well," I said, hearing the slight breathless croak in my voice and cursing myself.

She took the towels. "I'll shower."

My jaw locked.

Don't imagine her in the shower. Don't imagine her in the shower. Don't imagine her in—too late.

How was I supposed to stop myself when I'd already seen her soaked to the skin?

"Okay." I wanted to smack myself in the face for how raw my voice sounded as I turned away, charging into her ensuite to run the shower for her. I didn't know why I did it. I really should have left her room a century ago for propriety's sake and my own fucking sanity.

In the newly decorated, black and white bathroom, the walk-in shower was situated in the middle of the opposite wall behind a floor-to-ceiling panel of glass that was open on either side. I headed straight for it and turned it on.

Only when I circled around, Esmeralda was standing a few steps behind me. And in the brighter light of the bathroom…fuck. At least she'd moved one arm to cover her chest.

"Thank you," she whispered, her voice shaking with her trembling.

I kept my eyes above her shoulders and nodded, then headed past her to escape this situation. But for some damned reason I stopped in the threshold of the bathroom. "Go to sleep, Princess Esmeralda. Please don't go wandering outside again."

She was quiet for a moment then said, "I can't. Sleep, I mean. I can't sleep… I have insomnia."

I stilled in surprise that she knew the same struggle as me, and my shoulders softened instantly. I spoke next without hesitation; it wouldn't have been right to offer anything less.

"Then." I glanced across my shoulder without looking back at her. "Once you've showered, would you like to come down to the kitchen for tea?"

Her answer came delayed again. "Aren't you going back to sleep?"

I shifted my weight around. "No. I have insomnia too."

Several more beats of silence passed. "Okay. I'll come down to the kitchen."

CHAPTER 7
Esmeralda

I had absolutely no idea what had just happened in the last hour of my life.

One minute I'd been sitting in the ice-cold rain absolutely convinced Kai hated me, that my failure had been inevitable, and how I had no choice but to give up on him.

The next, I was arguing with him, slamming into him, feeling the hot, hard muscle of his body against me, and being dragged up to my room by him.

It felt so surreal that the cogs in my brain froze, halting all my emotions. Even as I'd showered and changed, except for the constant bucking of my heart, I'd felt nothing.

But as I walked down the silent corridors of Chaukham Palace towards the kitchen in an oversized grey T-shirt, black leggings, and slippers, my emotions came back to life with a sudden jumpstart of my heart. And with vengeance.

Oh gosh, oh shit, oh fuck…

Forget that my nerves were buzzing enough for a fusion reaction, I was so fucking embarrassed over taking so long to realise my soaked pyjamas were completely see-through.

But with what little dignity I had left after flashing Kai, I tipped my chin up and headed through the swinging kitchen doors. "Prince Kai?" I called out once I found my voice.

"Over here, at the back."

My heart skipped a beat, sending a wave of blood to my skin. I felt like a skittish cat, my hairs standing on end, but I craved this man's attention too much to run away, so I headed towards his voice. When I found him in front of a stove near the back of the kitchen, my stupid heart missed a beat again. Then raced off into the sunset like it was the end of a show, leaving me struggling for air.

He was so breathtakingly beautiful.

Kai had swapped his grey hoodie and pyjama bottoms for a black top that hugged his built torso in a way that was perfectly fitted and not two sizes too small. The best part though, was that he'd paired the top with a dark blue, knitted cardigan.

A cardigan. A fucking—

"You didn't dry your hair."

I clapped my lips together as my lashes snapped up to find Kai's ink black eyes on me through his glasses, his mouth pressed firm, and his brows pinched in a scowl.

I hoped with my entire existence he couldn't see the blush spreading over my face and neck as I shuffled towards the side of the counter. He had two mugs and a small tea strainer waiting next to the stove with loose tea leaves simmering away in a saucepan.

I tucked my towel-dried hair behind one ear. "My hair dries quickly naturally, and I didn't want to wake anyone up with the noise of a hair dryer, so I didn't bother."

His frown only hardened, and it should have made me shift uncomfortably like last night.

It didn't.

Because there was no malice in his scowl as it travelled over my hair. He was just...scowling. Maybe like he was thinking, but more like it was just natural for him. And it was kind of cute actually.

He nodded to his right. "Take a seat. It's almost done."

I did as he said, taking a seat in one of the navy-blue stools along the kitchen island where I'd been chattering away with Nur and Pierre in the morning. From there, I watched Kai with my chin resting on my right palm, biting down on my bottom lip to stop myself from moaning in absolute bliss.

He was just making tea, but the concentration on his face, the way his arms flexed as he poured the liquid into the two mugs. His flipping outfit! I might as well have been watching a hot porn video.

I snapped straight, not wanting to be caught swooning, when he picked up both mugs and came around to put one in front of me. I thanked him and wrapped my hands around it.

"What tea is this?" I peered into the clear golden liquid in the white ceramic and took a deep breath of the flowery, almost sweet scent.

"Jasmine tea. Honey or sugar?"

"Uh...none, I think."

He stared at me like I'd grown a second head. My choice personally offended him apparently, and I felt the strongest urge to giggle, half in shock and the rest in pure amusement. Instead, I ogled as he carefully measured a level teaspoon of honey and stirred it into his tea. Then he meticulously tidied up after himself, even washing the saucepan, spoon, and strainer he'd used.

When he was finally satisfied, Kai stood on the opposite side of the kitchen island with his hands resting on the surface on either side of his mug, staring at me. Not exactly frowning, but he had a stern resting face—jaw set, brows faintly dipped, eyes dark and piercing. Dark. *Gorgeous.*

It wasn't exactly an awkward silence, but it was weird, nonetheless.

I smiled at him. He shifted on his feet, his brows dipping lower as he tugged on his left earlobe.

I couldn't help it, the chuckle erupted from my mouth before I could cage it in.

Who was this man? This stern, grumpy prince. Was this really my Orange—the man the world called *The Perfect Prince*? But he seemed so damn adorably awkward.

Kai's brows shot up before they settled back into a furious pucker. "What's so funny?" he grumbled.

"I just…" My laughter settled into a wide smile. "I've never seen you like…*this* before, so it's a little weird. Funny—not in a bad way, of course. It's just…*different.*"

His glare softened as he looked down at himself but then tightened again. "I cannot wear my uniform day and night, Princess Esmeralda."

I rolled my bottom lip into my mouth sheepishly. "It's not just the clothes." I trailed my gaze over the regal yet harsh lines of his face.

"I could say the same thing about you," he muttered in reply.

Heat crept through my cheeks, and I sat straight—*yes, because he'd never seen me in my underwear before tonight.* "I guess so," I swallowed, struggling to meet his fierce stare. "I, uh, apologise if I offended you, Prince Kai."

For a second, he was still. Then his thick lashes dropped. A lock of his raven black hair flopped over his forehead as he tugged at his left earlobe again, twice.

"Kai."

I blinked. "Sorry?"

He looked up. "Call me Kai. And you didn't offend me."

My stupid heart did an excited flutter in my chest like he'd just told me he loved me. "Then please call me Esmeralda." He gave me a single, awkward nod.

I glanced to the stool next to me. "Do you want to sit down?"

He slowly came around with his mug in his hand and set it down on the counter. The kitchen seemed to shrink as he folded his big frame into the seat. I suddenly felt so small and surrounded by him. And so damn aware of his scent.

I'd noticed it before but not like this, not from this close, but he smelt…enchanting. Like a magical forest—woody, fresh, but kind of sweet too with a vanilla undertone. It was delicious.

As he tried to get comfortable, his right thigh ended up pressed against my leg. Hard, warm, and muscly. And gone way too quickly as he tore it away like my touch burned him. But I could still feel the tingling, heavy imprint he'd left on me.

"Sorry," he muttered, tugging on his earlobe.

I swallowed and tried to disguise my fluster behind a smile. "It's okay. You're big, so you need more space to fit."

Kai's gaze snapped around and like a slap across the face, I clocked the not-so-innocent way my comment could be interpreted. *Fuck...*

"Tall—tall, is what I meant," I quickly corrected, embarrassment exploding through my face. I picked up my mug and burned my tongue on a gulp of tea in an attempt to cover up the blunder. "So." I cleared my scorched throat. "You have insomnia?"

"Hmm, I do," he said, thankfully sounding unbothered by what I'd said seconds ago.

"Can I ask how long you've had it?"

"For as long as I can remember. Even as a child. Yourself?"

I shrugged softly, the sensitive topic dampening my excitement over talking to him. "For about eight years now. Since the late Queen—I mean our—*my* mother passed away." I avoided Kai's gaze, but I felt and heard him shift in his stool. "One night I could sleep, the next I couldn't." Trying to lighten the heavy mood, I smiled. "So, yeah. That's it really."

He was absolutely still for a breath, then, "So now you spend your nights sitting in the rain determined to get hypothermia?"

I blinked once. Twice.

He had just...he just cracked a joke. With the straightest face ever. *Why was that so sexy?*

I grinned, big, fat, and pouty. "No." I scowled playfully; his eyes travelled my face. "I wasn't trying to get hypothermia. It's called rain therapy, to help you relax. Have you never heard of it?"

He grunted, his *not-exactly-a-frown* turning frownier. "There is nothing therapeutic about rain."

"You don't like rain?"

"No. I hate it."

I gaped a little. "My, that's extreme. What did rain ever do to you?"

His jaw locked and he glared at me without an answer.

I chuckled softly, teasingly. "Gosh, I didn't know the future Crown Prince of Touma was such a grouch. What would your fans think?" *Forget that I was one of them.*

His frown melted away completely. "How...how do you know that?"

Unlike Jahandar's hereditary line of succession where the eldest child was automatically heir, Touma's wasn't. The heir to the throne could be chosen from any of the monarchs' children—on a few occasions, nieces and nephews too—and Kai's parents had yet to officially pick.

"Adam told me in the library," I said. "Although, honestly, it's not hard to guess it would be you. Prince Fay is more interested in focusing on his career as an artist, and Adam said he wasn't particularly interested in the crown, so that only leaves you."

"You're right." He eased into his chair. "Although Adam shouldn't have told you. It was supposed to be a secret until the end of the Peace Celebration."

"Relax." I poked his arm, nearly choking when I met nothing but rock-hard muscle. Kai's gaze flew down to the place I'd touched him, and I blushed. *Bloody woods, why had I done that?* "Don't go telling him off. He didn't mean to tell me, and he already asked me to keep it a secret, so don't worry. Your secret is safe with me."

Why I expected him to return my smile, I didn't know. *He didn't.* He just looked at me with such intensity, completely unreadable, until I found myself struggling to breathe and think properly.

"I'm sorry."

Air flooded back into my lungs. "What?"

Shame oozed from Kai as he lowered his head to look down at his mug. "I'm sorry. For the night you were lost, and for earlier today—yesterday. In the library. I shouldn't have accused you of trying to hurt Adam. I was an idiot, and you didn't deserve to be shouted at. And I'm...sorry."

He visibly swallowed, waiting for my reply with a twisted expression I'd never in my wildest dreams thought he could make. And it was like an arrow right to the heart—my ultimate weakness.

Yes, it had really hurt when he'd shouted at me, when he'd threatened to tell Kareem, but I could easily forgive him. It had been a mistake that I could see how guilty he felt for.

I smiled at him. "It's okay, Kai. Adam is your little brother. I would've been surprised if you *hadn't* reacted like that when it did look like I had spilt the tea on him." I shrugged a little. "I suppose, I should have stuck around longer to better explain what had happened. I just…when you brought up Kareem—I mean, the King—I kind of panicked."

I shouldn't have told him that. It didn't matter that he was my crush, he could expose my secret to the world. But maybe it was my hopeful heart wanting to trust him, or the way he patiently sat, not pushing, not asking, just waiting, but I knew I could tell him in full confidence.

With an awkward smile, I tipped my head to the side. "A secret for a secret? I don't…it's complicated but…Kareem and I don't really get on."

He frowned, but there was something different about this one. He looked surprised behind his glasses. I couldn't pinpoint why, he just did. Though he didn't probe further.

I wiggled my brows, needing the suffocating feeling in my chest to go away. "I know, shocking, right? Almost as shocking as your hate for rain."

He grunted and the sound could have passed for a laugh. My heart definitely took it as one, triumph ringing through it. "Hating rain is rational, not shocking."

"Hating rain is completely irrational! It's like…hating a child for no reason."

He scowled with such ferocity as he tugged at his ear, but my heart? It danced with abandon like he was giving me the biggest of grins.

"Drink your tea, Esmeralda."

I was convinced I was about to float off the chair in absolute bliss of hearing my name on his lips. My skin buzzed as I watched him while he focused his attention on his tea. Then filling my lungs with his enchanting scent, I took a sip from my own cup.

"Are your hands okay?" he mumbled. "From the tea, I mean."

I nodded as I wiggled one set of fingers. "Yes, they are. Thank you." I leaned into him a little. "Congratulations by the way, for being chosen as heir."

He nodded once, no smile in sight. "Thank you." But his voice was soft.

I couldn't stop taking sneaky glance at the new version of Kai next to me as we finished off our tea.

This handsome grouch.

And truth be told...my heart was still pounding for him.

CHAPTER 8
Esmeralda

I had woken up this morning feeling ecstatic after my blissful two hours of sleep post spending three hours talking to Kai in the palace kitchen.

Now all that happiness was dead. Gone. Finished. Annihilated. Ruined.

It was lost in the anxiety, panic, and worry as I watched the other crown princes, princesses, and royals present their environmental strategy plans on the stage in the big auditorium, filled with thousands of people for the morning session of the conference.

Touma, Shah, Prio, Khaas had had brilliant plans, taking a human-animal-welfare central approach for their one, five, and ten-year strategies.

I hadn't taken the same approach.

I had worked on a more economic strategy and suddenly, all those months, days, and hours I'd spent working with Kareem, top economic advisers, the Imperial Cabinet ministers, and Regional Councils all felt pointless.

Pathetic. Not good enough. Rather than perfect, my presentation felt heartless, and that mean voice in my head just kept getting louder and louder and meaner. And sounding evermore like Kareem.

I had no doubt my brother was seething in his chair after seeing the other, *better* strategies. He would never let me take on such a big task again. He would isolate me even more. I would never be perfect in his eyes. Never good enough. Never to be praised by him. Never loved by him.

He would expose me. He'd get rid of me. A fake. A fraud. I would have nothing left.

I flicked nervously at my nails in the seat behind Kareem in one of the seven groups of chairs at the front of the auditorium. In each group, the other active royals of all the states were sitting among their families and imperial ministers.

I glanced anxiously between Raven's middle-aged Crown Princess, wrapping up her presentation, and the back of Kareem's head. It was my turn next.

A heavy hand pressed down on my rapidly bouncing knee under the full-length skirt of my dark blue dress. I nearly jumped out of my seat as it frightened me out of my head.

On my left, Shehryar's pale green eyes were filled with concern, a folder with my presentation slides and script in it resting on his lap. He squeezed my entire knee in his bear-sized palm. "Breathe," he whispered.

The breath I was holding in gushed out and then flooded right back in.

He smiled and nodded softly. "Once more."

I did. In then out. Once more. Replacing the tension in my muscles with feigned composure. Because I was a princess. I couldn't and wouldn't have a meltdown in front of everyone, especially with all the media reporters lining the walls and front of the stage.

"We've practised so many times. We've triple checked all the statistics too. You are prepared."

I lifted my mouth in a wobbly smile. "Everyone else's presentations are better."

Shehryar dipped his head, looking right at me. "Yours is just as good."

I couldn't stop shaking my head. "But it's all just economic policy."

"Which the advisers supported and recommended, and the ministers all approved of too."

The urge to argue otherwise was still there but I kept my lips pressed together, holding in the flood of words that wanted to convince Shehryar I wasn't good enough.

"You're going to do great," he said softly, and I willed the assurance in his piercing stare to soothe my anxiety.

It did. A bit. Enough for me to ease into my chair. "Thank you, Sher."

He smiled and gave my knee one final squeeze before a loud applause danced around us. The Crown Princess of Raven was taking a bow upon the stage.

When the older princess began her descent from the stairs, the conference emcee called out, "To present Jahandar's environmental strategy, please welcome onto the stage, Her Highness, Crown Princess Esmeralda."

More applause rang out and I pushed my shoulders back and stood tall, taking the folder from Shehryar. I didn't look at Kareem as I passed by him and made my way to the wooden podium on the left side of the stage.

"Thank you, Vikram," I said into the small microphone, looking at the speaker tucked in the corner of the stage as I took my script out of the folder. "They have hidden you behind a curtain, but we all know you're the true Wizard of Roz, keeping this conference running smoothly."

Vikram bowed his head with a massive grin plastered across his face and light cheers echoed through the hall of thousands of seats. I took the opportunity to look around quickly.

First to Shehryar, who gave me a nod and a toothy grin. Before I dared to look at Kareem, whose smile appeared pleasant to others, but I knew his eyes only held contempt for me.

My heart kicked hard when my gaze then collided with Kai's.

Intense. Unmoving. Confident. *Beautiful.*

There was no nod, no charming smile, nor a grumpy frown, no emotion overtly there that I could pick up on. And yet the warmth of happiness I had been feeling this morning bubbled up again.

With a newfound confidence, I tipped my chin up and began my presentation, silently vowing I was going to use the previous night's success to talk to Kai again today.

Or tonight.

Kai

I covered my yawning mouth with the side of my hand as I closed the door behind me and made my way down the corridor past my bedroom.

It was after midnight, so the halls were pin-drop quiet. Exhaustion from the first full-day conference of the Peace Celebrations had sent everyone to bed as soon we returned to Chaukham Palace. I was tired too, but my growling stomach was demanding to be fed so sleep evaded me.

On my way to the kitchen, I passed by the night guard, Raj, humming to himself in front of garden doors that were completely shut tonight. *Thankfully.*

"Your Highness," he said and bowed.

"Raj," I greeted in reply.

"Crown Princess Esmeralda—"

The mention of her name caused me to stop as my heart plummeted.

Bloody woods, she hadn't gone outside again, had she? It wasn't raining tonight, but it was still freezing cold. *Dammit, was she genuinely trying to fall ill?*

"Is she outside again?" I asked, stomping back towards Raj.

"Oh, no, no, Your Highness." He shook his head swiftly. "I was just going to tell you she passed by a while ago." My shoulders eased, but the guard shifted on his feet. "It's just…this is the third night she's been awake, so I was just wondering if Her Highness doesn't—can't—sleep. Like you."

"Hmm, she doesn't. But you keep that to yourself, Raj."

"Of course."

It felt a bit wrong disclosing something she'd told me in confidence, but if it meant there was someone to keep an eye on the pint-sized, babbling troublemaker, then it was fine. Good even.

"And if she ever needs anything—"

Raj smiled widely. "I will not hesitate to help her."

"Thank you, Raj," I said and looked down the corridor. "Did she say where she was going?"

"I believe she was on her way to the kitchen."

Same as me then. And for some reason that knowledge sent the faintest little buzz through the left region of my chest. But not exactly the left. Somewhere in the middle. More on the left though. Not low enough to be a gurgle of hunger from my belly—*never mind. Just forget it.*

The little buzz grew in strength by the time I reached the kitchen to find the lights on inside. It was probably just because I had a surprisingly good and long conversation with her last night. I was looking forward to talking to her again seeing as I hadn't interacted with her much during the conference. We'd ended up on different sides of the room nearly the whole time, though I'd caught her gaze a few times. And her smile. *She had a nice smile.*

As I entered the kitchen, a quiet giggle fluttered over from the right just ahead, and I went towards the pretty sound like a moth drawn to a flame.

I found her sitting on the kitchen island we'd sat at last night. Not *on* a stool. She was actually sitting on top of the counter, having pushed one stool to the side.

Esmeralda held a book in one hand, and a half-eaten, orange ice-lolly in the other. Her soft brown, wavy hair fell around her shoulders, tucked behind her ear on one side, as she grinned at whatever she was reading.

The sight of her eating an ice-lolly in winter should have sent shivers of disgust through me. There were no shivers. Just a flare coming to life behind the steady thudding inside my ribcage as I couldn't seem to swallow through my tightening throat.

She was wearing shorts again. Grey cotton ones that barely covered the top few inches of her warm golden, supple thighs. Paired with a grey T-shirt that was cropped enough that if she leaned back even a centimetre, I'd get a glimpse of the soft curve of her belly underneath.

It was so tight across her chest.

For such a small woman, she had a rather ample chest that she'd somehow managed to shove into the T-shirt. But the strain on the fabric was obvious. *So damn obvious.*

Kai, eyes!

With a screech of braking tires and a jolt, I tore my gaze away from her, embarrassment and frustration burning through my face. I tugged at my left earlobe, scowling furiously somewhere past Esmeralda. Not trusting myself to look at her.

For fuck's sake, what was wrong with me? I didn't normally behave as if I had never seen a pretty woman before.

Yes, but this is the pretty woman you've been thinking about a lot.

My eyes, with a mind of their own, caught on her again, and I scrubbed my fingers over my mouth.

She was lost in her own world, her gaze tracing the words on the pages of the book. As if she heard my thoughts, her head snapped up and her eyes darted left. Once. Twice on a glistening, wide-eyed doubletake.

"Kai!"

There was so much familiarity and excitement in her voice that a bolt of electricity zapped through my chest. Blood poured through my ears again, making them itch, making me want to—I tugged at my earlobe, swallowing around the feeling as my brows slipped down.

No one had ever said my name like that before. It was…weird. Pleasantly so.

Trying not to appear flustered, I ran a hand through my hair and moved towards her. "What are you doing?"

Do the fucking book and ice-lolly not give it away? Idiot.

"Just reading." She lifted the book in her hand then the ice-lolly. "And eating an ice pop."

I glared at the bitten cylinder of ice on a stick. "In the middle of winter?"

She grinned. "Yes, because there is no season for ice pops." I grunted my disapproval. Her smile widened as she put the book down. "What about you? Having jasmine tea again?"

"Not tea. Food." I flicked a judgemental glance to her ice-lolly. "Real food."

She gaped at me, pretending to be outraged though she clearly wasn't. "*Excuse me.* But where I come from, ice pops are an *essential* food."

As if to prove her point, she bit down on one side of the orange-coloured lolly, only for the other side to fall off the wooden stick. She squealed with her mouth closed, catching the falling ice in her left palm. Then quickly rolling it onto her fingers, she pushed it between her red, swollen lips.

"What?" she muttered around the ice with a defiant tilt to her chin and blushing cheeks.

Her fumble and obvious embarrassment were cute. Seriously. I had to turn away as the weight on my brows lifted and the tightness of my lips melted.

Esmeralda awkwardly held her palm flat, the juice from the ice-lolly glistening on her skin. Without a thought to it, I ripped off a tissue from the kitchen roll sitting at one end of the island.

But instead of giving it to her to wipe her hand like I bloody should have, I wrapped my fingers loosely around her wrist and held her palm up so I could clean the sticky liquid.

She stilled. It was obvious, but I didn't feel it instantly. I was too busy glaring at the task at hand—*no pun intended*. All until I lifted my lashes and found her eyes, huge and round and completely unmoving, her cheeks even more pink than before. I didn't need my glasses to see the shock in those captivating kaleidoscope irises of hers.

It was my turn to freeze.

Shit. What the fuck was I doing?

I was wiping a grown woman's hand for her like she was a child. And one I hardly actually knew too. At least not enough to do something so…so…intimate.

My ex-fiancée would have hated something like this. She had always said my attempts to care for her or help her were overbearing and annoying. That I was being condescending.

My therapist had told me otherwise. It had taken some time to believe her, but that didn't mean I was dumb enough to think what I was doing to Esmeralda was okay. It was bloody weird.

I tore my hands back, almost knocking myself in the chest. "Sorry," I muttered, struggling to meet her gaze. "You didn't need me to do that."

It might have just been my ears, but she seemed to let out a shuddering breath as she cupped her hand in the other. I braced myself, waiting for the onslaught of her disgust to hit me.

"No, no, it's okay," she said quietly. I blinked—*wait, what?* She smiled a little shy curl. "Don't apologise. I didn't mind." Her shoulders lifted. "I mean, we're friends, right? So it's fine."

"We're friends?" I blurted out on a croak.

Her face fell. "Oh…I thought…" She shifted uncomfortably. "We're *not?*"

Shit. That wasn't what I meant.

"No," I said a little more aggressively than I needed to. Esmeralda flinched and her face turned paler. *Fuck, I made it worse.* "No, I meant yes. Yes, we are friends…we're friends."

Esmeralda's mouth cautiously tipped, but it wasn't exactly a smile. "You don't sound sure."

I moved my weight from foot to foot, rubbing at my ear. "No, I'm sure. I am."

"Really?"

"Yes."

She cocked her chin, eyeing me with a glimmer of amusement. "Can you shake on it?"

My brows bunched together, but I stuck my hand out. After a second, Esmeralda's smile stretched, and she fit her palm against mine. She had a surprisingly firm grasp.

"Friends," she said.

I was way too aware of how soft her hand felt against mine. "Friends."

Our hands stayed intertwined between us before our fingers slowly slipped apart. My skin prickled as I dropped my hand to my side. I could still feel the cold imprint of her slim fingers.

"I'm—" My voice sounded ridiculously gruff, so I cleared my throat and tried again. "I'm going to get something to eat. Would you like anything?"

"No, thank you. I've already had what I wanted."

Before I moved away, my gaze fell to the lolly stick still in her hand. Resisting the urge to simply pluck it from her, I pointed at it. "I can bin that for you. If you would like me to."

"Thank you."

I pinched the stick from her using the tissue, binning it on my way to the larder room at the back. Returning with three tangerines and two protein bars, I sat on the stool next to where she sat on the counter, making sure I didn't bump her leg this time.

It was too late to move without seeming rude by the time I realised her lap was right in my eyeline. And when she crossed her bare thighs over… It was completely out of my control that my gaze was drawn to the movement.

"I thought you said you were getting real food. That's not real food," she said, wriggling her bottom on the counter.

My jaw locked and I stabbed my thumb so hard into one tangerine that juice was pooling around it, and I was entirely sure I had orange peel under my blunt nail, deep enough that my thumb was going to hurt in the morning. That was my deserved punishment for ogling at her inappropriately.

I viciously tore off the skin, taking my frustration at myself out on the innocent piece of fruit. "How so?" I grumbled.

It was easier to keep my stare away from her legs once she started talking. She spoke so much and at times so fast, as much with her mouth as she did with her hands and eyes.

And shit. Because it was cute.

CHAPTER 9
Esmeralda

"You have a beautiful voice, Princess," Pierre purred.

I faltered mid-sentence as a furious blush struck my face but tried to carry on reading from the book in my hands like he hadn't said anything.

"Paired with your accent…damn. I could listen to you all day."

My cheeks ached with how hard I was smiling. "Then stop talking and listen."

"But I like talking to you too."

"Pierre," I warned playfully, looking up from the page.

"Okay, all right, I'll shut my mouth," he said with a chuckle and slumped his shoulder against the shelves with his arms crossed over his chest, stretching the fabric of his thin, black V-neck jumper.

After a morning conference celebrating the special achievements of some of Neves citizens from all seven states, and a private tea and cakes session after lunch in Chaukham Palace with all the royals, the reigning monarchs had left in a number of cars to head into the city for their annual walkabout.

The other princes and princesses had dispersed back to their temporary residence quickly after that, though Prince Arsh and Prince Fay had suggested an outing for some of the younger ones, taking Adam and Princess Dabira of Shah too.

Kai had headed to his office, and I had ended up in Chaukham Palace's library, reading a *Tregency* romance that I had picked up from the shelves when Pierre found me. Hence, we were both tucked against the shelves while I stood upon a small stepladder and read aloud to him.

It was the first time I had seen Pierre without his chef's coat on. He'd been hiding chiselled yet lean muscle under it the whole time. Paired with the way his stance showed-off his torso so well, objectively speaking, Pierre was pure eye candy. But I felt nothing. *Because he wasn't Kai.*

I glanced back at the page. "*He stumbled to a stop in the threshold of the room. Time slowed as his heart dropped out of his chest, the shatter as it hit the floor piercingly loud. His Juliet was laughing with another man. His best friend."*

"That's what you deserve Marquess for shutting her out, idiot."

I grinned. *"Was he too late? Had she chosen Rauf instead?"*

"Of course, she has. Juliet has a brain."

"Pierre!" I laughed, lowering the book to glare at him.

But instead of Pierre's voice, I heard Kai's. "Esmeralda."

My heart imploded in on itself, and I jerked my head up so fast I nearly gave myself whiplash.

Kai stood at the end of the aisle behind Pierre, looking as perfect and as gorgeous as he always did. He still wore the dark grey, three-piece suit from this morning, only rumpled where he'd loosened his tie and undone his waistcoat buttons. And fuck, those two casual touches were so bloody sexy paired with the natural frown on his brows and the five o'clock shadow on his jaw.

"Kai. Hi." The air in the library had disappeared or my lungs were malfunctioning.

"Why if it isn't my favourite prince," Pierre said, pulling off the shelves.

Kai pressed his lips together and nodded at the sous chef. He stretched his shoulders wide as he pushed one hand into his suit trouser pocket. "Pierre."

"Wow," Pierre said, shaking his head. "So you're gonna act like we haven't been best friends since birth just because there's a pretty princess here? I see how it is."

I grinned between them, and Kai's jaw shifted—locked or rolled, I couldn't quite tell. "That's not how it is," he uttered gruffly, then angled his gaze to me. "Are you ready to go?"

I snapped the book shut. "Yes, I am."

So, I had somehow ended up making plans with Kai to go to the palace stables before he'd disappeared into his office. Mariyah was going to be so proud of me.

"Dammit." Pierre sighed. "I need to know if Juliet forgives Thornwell or not. Will you read to me again, Princess, after dinner before I head home? Please?"

"Deal, but only because I need to know too."

"See you at eight then, Your Highness." Pierre took my hand and pressed a light kiss to my knuckles.

The moment he disappeared around the bookshelves, my attention zoned in on Kai like only he existed. As if I wasn't surrounded by my favourite thing in the world, books. His beautiful frown etched itself deeper on his face as he watched Pierre walk away. From his side-profile, I saw his cheek suck in until his jaw looked like the sharp edge of a knife.

I climbed down the two steps off the stepladder, catching Kai's attention. "Shall we?"

It took a second or two, but he hummed his reply and stepped back, letting me head past him.

Chaukham Palace's stables were like something out of a storybook. A huge, weathered oak building with several stalls curving out in a semi-circle on one side, situated in a huge, fenced paddock that was split in two. There were a few horses poking their heads out of the stalls on the side, and Kai patted the nose of a white horse we passed as we headed to the open doors of the structure.

I had changed out of my dress into more comfortable slim-fit jeans and a white long-sleeve under a zip-up dark green jumper. Kai said there was a pair of riding boots for me to use at the stables.

He, on the other hand, had only taken his suit jacket and tie off, and had donned the thickest, longest parka coat I had ever seen in my life. Like it was meant to be worn in the Tundra strip in northern Shah, rather than during a warmer winter day in Touma.

But the older, tanned man with a trimmed salt-and-pepper beard didn't seem to question Kai's odd choice of riding gear as he turned away from a young boy checking the stirrup dangling from the side of a gorgeous chocolate brown horse. No doubt a Thoroughbred reared from the strongest of horses from the State of Khaas.

"Prince Kai," the man chirped happily over a bow. "I see you've brought a guest with you."

Kai returned the man's smile softly and gestured to him. "Princess Esmeralda, this is Jorge, the stablemaster."

"Good afternoon, Jorge," I said, offering the older man my hand. "I know you were only expecting Prince Kai, so I hope you don't mind me turning up like this."

Jorge quickly yanked one leather glove off and shook my hand. "Not at all, Your Highness. I'm very happy you made a trip to my stables. Will you be accompanying His Highness on his ride?"

I tilted my head hopefully. "If that's not too much of an ask."

"Of course not," he said with a chuckle. "We can have a horse saddled up within a few minutes. And seeing as you are here, we can ready a horse of your own choosing too."

I beamed at the older man. "I'd love that." I immediately started scanning the stables.

"Jorge, Princess Esmeralda will need to borrow a pair of boots in a size five," Kai said behind me.

"Of course. Aladdin."

"On it," the young boy said, handing the reins of the brown horse to Jorge.

"And don't forget Prince Kai's jacket and boots!" Jorge called after him just as I stopped in front of the third stall on my right.

Inside stood a black giant, showing off its side-profile as it munched on a hanging bale of hay. At least seventeen hands tall, powerful yet lean, and from what I could see of the magnificent creature, every inch of it was obsidian black. It's bottomless eyes, it's neat mane, it's coat shining so brightly like it was dressed in silk.

"Who's this?" I asked.

"Who? Ah—wait, you mean, Bucky?" Jorge said with surprise. "Ah, wait, wait, Your Highness, I wouldn't go too close!"

The panic in the stablemaster's voice halted my steps. "Is he untrained?"

"No, no, he's not untrained, it's just… Bucky can be a little aggressive is all. We'd have to see how he takes to you, Ma'am."

Jorge's eyes moved past me, and I followed their direction to see him looking at Kai. Kai replied to their silent conversation with a nod. "It's okay, Jorge. Bring her an apple."

"Of course." Once Aladdin returned with two pairs of boots and a worn black jacket, the older man scurried off in the same direction as the young boy had gone in.

"An apple?" I repeated to Kai.

He made his way over to my side. "Hmm. If he takes it from you, you can ride him."

At the sound of Kai's voice, Bucky flicked his head over to us and stared. The horse stepped forward and threw his head over the stall door, kicking it like he was beckoning Kai over. Kai went to him.

"Is he yours?" I asked, sounding and feeling like the air in my lungs was being replaced with heavy, giddy gooeyness as I watched Kai stroke the horse's nose with a soft smile on his mouth.

"Hmm."

How it was possible for one soft sound to convey so much affection I had no idea, but Kai managed it. I felt it right in my chest as an overflow of bubbles. Seeing him care so much for an animal was dangerous. It was pushing my crush to the edge of a cliff that led to a bottomless pit called love.

"I found him as a foal, injured and abandoned in a ditch while I was on a trip with Fay and a few friends to the south a few years back."

Well…hello, cliff edge of love. We finally meet.

I tried to resist you, I did, but then he told me he'd rescued a baby horse like it was some normal thing to do, so it really was out of my control.

Shit, why? Why had he told me he'd rescued Bucky? How was I not supposed to turn to a puddle of love and lust at the thought of him trying to calm a frightened little foal, covered in dirt as he got the poor creature out of the ditch?

Thankfully, Jorge returned at that moment, so I didn't have to try to come up with a coherent response that wasn't, *"I think I'm in love with you."* But once the apple was in my hand and both Jorge and Kai stepped back, the weight of what I had to achieve dawned on me.

There was truth in the idea that animals were the best judges of character. So, if the horse didn't think I was trustworthy, then that was bound to doom the progress I was trying to make with Kai. In other words, I had possibly just shot myself in the foot. *Shit.*

Please take the apple. Please take the apple. Please take the apple.

I repeated the chant in my head as I approached Bucky. The horse went completely still as he glared me before shifting backwards, rustling the hay under his hooves. *Well, that was a great start.*

Trying not to feel deterred, I lifted the apple up and out to him. "Hey, Bucky," I cooed. "I have a little something for you." He huffed through his nose roughly.

Damn. Being judged by a horse was tough.

I waved the apple at him in case he'd missed it. "You won't take it?"

Nothing. Bucky didn't move, he just ruffled his head.

Too scared to look at Kai, I glanced over at Jorge. "Has he ever taken an apple from anyone before?"

Jorge tilted his head awkwardly. "Other than Prince Kai himself, uh…*no.* But that doesn't mean—" The man let out a choked breath instead of the rest of his sentence, his eyes bulging wide.

That's when I felt it. The puff of warm air that prickled over my palm and fingers. The sound of a sniff and a snort. And finally, a brush of wet, wide lips as the weight of the apple vanished from my hand.

I came face to face with Bucky, his night sky eyes consuming my soul, as he made quite the statement with his loud crushing and crunching and munching.

He took it…

"Hi," I whispered in awe, delight slowly tugging the corners of my mouth up.

"He took it," Jorge's voice came out as a whisper, then loudened. "My oh my, he actually took it."

A chuckle of relief shook my shoulders as I glanced at the man. "Does this mean I can ride him?"

"Yes, yes, of course," Jorge said, grinning widely. "I'll grab a saddle. Aladdin, give Prince Kai and Her Highness their boots."

"It's okay, Aladdin, you can leave them there."

My heart hiccupped when Kai spoke, like for a moment I'd

forgotten he was there. The thought was instantly inconceivable as he approached me.

His steps were near silent, but they thudded loudly through me. Anticipation entwined around hope to create a tightrope strung up high in my chest. Because he was looking at me.

Not looking at me but *looking at me*. Right into me. Pawing at my body, searching me, demanding I lay myself bare to him. I was breathless and high on the feeling of being a captive in his gaze.

He stopped right in front of me, and I tipped my head back to stare right up at him, waiting.

He bent into me. "What did you do to my horse, Esmeralda?"

For the life of me, I couldn't breathe. The flame that combusted into a wildfire in my chest cut off the path of air from my mouth to my lungs. Molten heat rippled over my skin in every flipping direction, so fast and so hard my body shook, but my thighs clenched too.

Why had he sounded like that?

There was no grumpy grumble in that question.

It was gruff. Rough. A little breathless and maybe a tiny bit hoarse as he said my name.

Like there was an undercurrent in his question. In the way he stood so close to me. And it didn't make sense, because why? What? How? When? *Excuse me, why?*

Despite the heady buzz whirling through me, I smiled. At least I hoped it was a smile on my mouth and not a *fuck-me-Daddy* wobble, because my face was burning so hot it felt numb.

I wanted to say something cool and mysterious or funny that would leave a lasting effect on him, but all I could pathetically muster was a quiet, breathy, "Nothing."

My hands were still shaking as I swapped my trainers for a pair of brown riding boots. But with Bucky saddled and Kai in a shorter but equally thick coat, Jorge brought me a stepladder to climb onto Bucky. Then Kai took the reins of both horses and led them out of the paddock.

But before he climbed onto the brown horse's saddle, he turned to Bucky and patted him on the neck with a heavy hand.

"Be good to her," he whispered to the horse.

Maybe I wasn't meant to hear it. But I did.

And I nearly melted off the horse into an unconscious puddle of delight on the floor.

CHAPTER 10
Esmeralda

"**S**o, if Bucky is your horse, who's horse are you riding?" I asked Kai after several quiet minutes.

Our horses walked side by side with lazy gaits as we headed through the forest surrounding the back of Chaukham Palace.

It was beautiful. So peaceful and enchanting. The sky above was bright even though it was blanketed in a layer of pale grey clouds. A few robins danced between the short evergreens and tall, leafless trees. Fallen branches were scattered among bushes and sprinkles of winter wildflowers. And it wasn't muddy thankfully, but it was damp from the rainfall a few nights ago.

"He's mine too," Kai said. "I have three horses. Bucky." He rubbed the long silky neck of the horse he was riding. "Big Guns here, and a mare, called Dahlia."

"You named your horse *Big Guns*?"

His brows puckered in a wince. "No. Fay did. I lost a bet."

"Ah." I chuckled.

We fell quiet again, and no matter how hard I tried, I couldn't focus on anything but him.

I loved that we weren't talking but it wasn't awkward in any way. But most of all, I loved how even with the light frown on his face, somehow, he looked so peaceful as he enjoyed our surroundings.

It was beautiful. *He was so beautiful.*

I was completely content just watching him, but a part of me couldn't help wanting his attention, wanting to talk to him, wanting…

A lightbulb lit up above my head.

"Want to race?" I said.

"Hmm?"

I lifted Bucky's reins. "Do you want to have a race?"

"Here?"

I nodded. "Here until the clearing you mentioned."

He frowned. "You don't know your way through."

"You said it was just straight, didn't you? That's fine. I've ridden through a forest before."

That didn't seem to ease his scowl. In fact, it deepened, which made me grin.

I arched a teasing brow. "Are you just pretending to be worried because you're scared of losing?"

"No," he grumbled instantly.

I laughed up at the sky. "Ah, the *Perfect Prince* is afraid of losing."

His jaw locked, and it wasn't threatening, but the depth of his eyes appeared to deepen by a mile. "I don't lose, Esmeralda."

A warm shudder tingled down my spine at the deep, dark way he said my name and settled low in my belly. I pressed my thighs close to the saddle as if clenching up would give me any control over the faint tingling. It didn't.

I was a good crown princess. Well-behaved and polite, and I did my best not to cause any trouble. Call it an adrenaline rush or something else, but with Kai, I didn't want to be good or well-behaved or perfect. I wanted to goad him and challenge him and tease him.

"Prove it," I said, tipping my chin up. "Race me."

He didn't say anything, but his hands tightened around Big Guns' reins. I felt a grin spread across my mouth. "Three," I counted, shuffling on my saddle. "Two." Kai did the same. "One…go!"

Kai and I flicked the reins in our hands in near-perfect sync and both horses were off, flying through the forest neck and neck, and the rush was exhilarating. The cold breeze lashed my skin, whipping through my hair. Hooves thumped rapidly against the forest floor, beating through my chest.

I veered left around a huge tree trunk and Kai went right, and when we met around the tree again, our gazes clashed for a second. Despite his scowl of concentration, his golden skin flushed from the cold, there was a bright twinkle in his eyes that electrified my insides.

A loud chuckle blossomed from deep within my throat as I leaned down over Bucky with a new flood of adrenaline pumping through my blood. I pushed him harder and faster with whispers of encouragement, nudges, and near-free rein, all while I threw giddy grins in Kai's direction.

Just as Bucky passed Big Guns, the clearing on the other side of the forest came in sight. I cheered the beautiful black horse on, squealing with the excitement of a child, and Kai too began urging Big Guns faster, loud enough for me to hear.

I shrieked a sound of triumph as Bucky launched into the clearing ahead of Big Guns. He raced further onto the open stretch of grass before I pulled softly on his reins to slow him down. My hands just about cooperated, both numb from the cold and trembling from the adrenaline rush.

When I trotted Bucky around to find where Kai and Big Guns had stopped, the moment my eyes landed on him, a heady laugh brewed in my chest.

Maybe because the whole situation felt so surreal or maybe I hadn't felt so alive in such a long time, but I laughed hard and long until tears prickled the corners of my eyes.

And it felt so fucking good.

More so because I was sharing the moment with the guy I was falling violently fast for.

Kai

She laughed. Esmeralda was laughing…

And she'd laughed in front of me before, at my expense too. Teasing chuckles and husky giggles that had captured my attention for longer than they should have. But not like this. Not like…

Exactly like that night on the balcony.

During Shah's New Year's party less than two months ago, when I'd escaped the loud music and constant chattering of over a thousand guests to the veranda at the back of the hall.

I had willingly gone out into the freezing cold of that night just to find some quiet. Standing in the shadow on the balcony, I'd instead found Esmeralda taking solace there too.

She'd been by a tall lamp that lit her up as if she were under a spotlight. A lone star on the big stage. Her back had been to me, her hair and long, black silk dress fluttering in the icy breeze. But when she'd turned her head, instead of making myself known, I'd slipped further back into the shadows.

Because she'd been on the phone, I'd told myself since, so I hadn't wanted to disturb her. She'd been speaking too quietly for me to have caught any of her conversation, but I'd stayed stuck there, rooted to the floor just watching her.

It was like I was seeing her for the first time. The elegant, beautiful young woman she was. Which of course had felt ridiculous because I'd seen her so many times before. More than I could count. And she'd always just been another princess. A *young* princess.

I had been about to leave when I realised what I was doing was creepy and fucked up.

But then she'd laughed.

Head thrown back. Breathless and loud. Graceful yet absolutely carefree. So damn intoxicating.

I hadn't been able to forget the sound or the image of her standing under the lamp. For the first time since, I felt like I was seeing that side of her again.

Like that night, the hairs on my body stood on end as her laugh rushed over my skin like a warm, fuzzy wind. It entrapped me. Left me tumbling as it spun me this way and that. Made me breathe it in and hold in it even when I was already breathless from the race.

It lured every ounce of my attention to her. To the pretty laugh lines outlining her mouth, and the softest crinkle around her big, greyish-brown eyes. Every inch of her radiated pure, sweet joy.

She was stunning. So much more mesmerising than that night. And I...

My heart was pounding.

Exactly in the rhythm of the horses' hooves as they raced. Hard and dangerously fast. It shouldn't have been sustainable, and yet it didn't slow down from exhaustion.

Fuck, fuck, fuck. What was wrong with it? *What was wrong with me?* My chest felt hot and itchy, or maybe achy, like my ears. I wanted to scratch and pull at my ribcage to soothe the feeling. But I couldn't move. I didn't want to move, but I couldn't relax either. And for the life of me I couldn't take my eyes off Esmeralda. I just...

I wanted to go to her. See her from closer. Hear her laugh from closer. *Feel her closer.*

I didn't recall urging Big Guns towards her, but he started moving under me, taking me where I was being pulled by some invisible string. Esmeralda flashed me a big, beautiful grin, and a new wave of hot blood attacked my face.

Fuck. Did I—towards Esmeralda—this feeling—I, uh... attraction...

She steered Bucky to meet me halfway, and I started panicking.

Was it showing on my face? Could she tell how much she affected me? Had she noticed I couldn't—*hadn't* taken my eyes off her? That she had messed with my head?

Would she think it was weird? That *I* was weird for finding myself attracted to her in such a short amount of time? Especially when I'd been horrible to her for one of those days and nights.

What if she thought I was a creepy old man for being attracted to her? I was going on thirty this year, and she was twenty-two—no, twenty-three. *Shit.*

My brows sunk and scrunched as my thoughts spiralled. I tugged at my earlobe, trying to get rid of any lingering evidence of what she'd

done to me.

Esmeralda pulled Bucky to a stop next to Big Guns. "What was that about never losing, huh? *I don't lose.*" She mimicked a deep male voice. "That was it, wasn't it?"

I relaxed a little under her teasing. Maybe she hadn't noticed the tsunami that was threatening to drown me because of her. "I don't sound like that," I muttered.

She giggled, swaying with the back-and-forth steps of an eager Bucky. I stared down into his eyes sternly, warning him not to get overexcited now that he'd had a good, hard run. As if he could read human expressions to know what I meant.

"Ooph, just look at that glare." She gave a mocking pout. "Are we sulking now, Mr Perfect Prince?"

I thought I hated that nickname. But why didn't it sound so bad when she used it? *Why was she so cute?* And yet that mischievous swirl of light in her eyes caused my teeth to clench.

"What?" she sassed. "If you have something to say, say it."

Something sharp jabbed through me, riling me in a warm, prickly way. The feeling was newly awoken. One I'd suppressed, but still secretly wanted. It caused my hands to twitch around Big Guns' reins, so tempted to reach for her. To yank her onto my saddle, slam my mouth down on hers, and kiss that grin off her face.

She would probably think there was something wrong with me if she knew what I was thinking. I was a prince, a gentleman, after all. I wasn't supposed to want to be so...*rough.* I wasn't supposed to want to kiss her so hard and long that she almost passed out in my arms.

I needed to look away from Esmeralda so I could quickly bury the thought into the corner of my brain I refused to peer into. So, I dragged Big Guns around and rode slowly to the three poles near the edge of the forest to tie the horses to.

"Kai. Hey, wait." I heard Bucky push into a trot before they appeared by my side again. "Are you giving me the silent treatment now?"

Damn it, she shouldn't be allowed to have such beautiful eyes that she practically wielded as a weapon of mass seduction.

I swallowed hard. "No."

"Did you let me win on purpose?"

I had no idea. Honestly, I hadn't actually been that focused on the race. Not knowing what to say, I stayed silent.

"Hey. You better not have let me win on purpose."

"Or what?" I asked blankly.

She took a breath to answer. "I'll push you off Big Guns if you did."

A little taken aback, I glared into her playful, wide-eyed stare of conviction. Then down to the gap between us. "Your arms aren't long enough to reach me."

I nudged Big Guns into a trot with the heel of my boots, rushing ahead of Esmeralda and questioning what the bloody fuck possessed me to say that.

But when she shrieked an outraged laugh behind me, knowing I'd done that—made her laugh—felt really fucking good.

CHAPTER 11

Kai

Esmeralda walked ahead of me up the dozen or so uneven stone steps. Up to the old, mossy platform of a watchtower that had been taken down sometime in the seventh century. It sat on the far right of the stretch of land behind the forest, bordered by a black iron railing on all four sides.

"Wow." She gasped in awe, leaning forward against the railing. "That view. It's stunning. You can see right to the edge of Pavilion City."

It took a second for me to focus on the view that I could usually spend hours looking at and not on her. "Hmm, it is."

Below the edge of the land my home sat on was a view of Pavilion City that seemed to stretch right into the horizon. It was stunning, as Esmeralda had said. A picture-perfect mix of a million shades of green forests and parks between old, traditional red-brick buildings, faint streaks of roads, and the newer high-rises that didn't take away from the skyline. They only made it sparkle with colour when the sun set behind them, something that would start happening soon.

She smiled, all glittery and awestruck, and my entire bloodstream rerouted directly and solely to my ears. "Do you come here often?"

I pulled one hand out of my coat pocket to tug at my left ear. "When I have time."

She hummed on a nod. "What else do you do when you have time to yourself?"

"Nothing in particular. I read on occasion, check on Bucky and the horses and exercise them."

She reached out and squished the fabric of my coat around my bicep like she was honking a horn. "And what about this? Did these muscles just magically appear out of nowhere?"

It didn't make sense for me to feel proud that Esmeralda was pointing it out because weight training had never been for my appearance. But that's exactly how I felt. Oddly satisfied that she'd noticed.

I couldn't help it, I flexed. Pointlessly, because my coat was too thick for anything to be seen, but I spread my shoulders to their full breadth anyway.

I cleared my throat. "I weight train in the palace gym. Every morning. Monday to Friday. Before breakfast... I swim too."

Her gaze snagged on the movement of my torso, lingering for a few seconds too long. She noticed I caught her looking and her cheeks warmed to a deep shade of rose pink. *Fuck, she was cute.*

"I see," she uttered, her voice hitching just a bit as she turned her flushed face away.

A sweet excitement rung through my chest. Something that felt a lot like hope. Which was a shock in itself because I wasn't even bloody sure what my own interest in her even was.

I tugged at my ear again. "What about you? What do you do when you're free?"

Esmeralda began explaining the million things she managed to do when she had time, though her favourite was reading. At one point, I internally questioned her sanity when she said she did maths exam papers for entertainment. Otherwise, I listened to her babble off onto random tangents.

She couldn't have been talking for more than ten, fifteen minutes when I heard the faintest sound by my right ear.

Pat.

Pat. Pat…pat…pat. Pat. Pat.

I squinted up at the grey sky as the raindrops hit my coat, cheeks, and hair repeatedly. A low growl gathered in the back of my throat as I sunk into my coat. *My hoodless coat.*

The weather forecast hadn't predicted it was going to rain, so why?

I blinked. *Wait, did I even check?*

I stopped ransacking my brain for the memory when a fluttering laugh lifted from Esmeralda. She was holding out both of her hands before her. "It's raining."

Shit. She didn't even have a coat on. Just a short jumper that wouldn't keep her dry. Why hadn't she bloody worn something more substantial?

"Come on." I grabbed one of her outstretched wrists. "We have to go back now."

"What? Why?" she complained as I dragged her to the stairs.

"Because it's raining, and you don't have a coat on."

"But I like rain. And I'm not cold."

I picked up pace as she stepped onto the grass behind me. "You won't like it when it's pelting you in the face as you ride. And you will be cold if you get wet." And there was no way was I going to witness her shivering from the cold again. The thought didn't sit right with me at all.

"But Kai—"

Somewhere in my mind I knew I had no business dictating what she could and couldn't do. But I couldn't bring myself to deviate from protecting her. All I cared about was her being warm and dry and safe.

She protested about leaving so soon. But I charged directly to where the horses were tied around the metal poles with a one-track mind of getting us back to the palace.

I let go of her hand to untie Bucky's reins then turned to help her up. "Come on. Let me—"

There was no one behind me. *I was talking to fucking air.*

The only trace of Esmeralda was the zip-up hoodie she'd abandoned over Bucky's saddle.

It took me less than a second to pinpoint her, sneaking her way back towards the middle of the open land as the rain came down harder.

How had she gotten so far already? I clenched my teeth. *Why is she wearing a white top?*

If the fabric were to get wet like that night in the garden…if it clung to her skin and…

I ground my teeth together harder as every nerve in my body started vibrating, building up a current of static energy that warmed me all over but concentrated most in my lower region.

I had to get her to the palace before my dick reacted in a way that would embarrass me in front of her and give me an uncomfortable ride back on Big Guns.

"Esmeralda," I called out.

She twirled around on her feet. Her wrists were crossed over and resting atop her head which jutted her breasts forward in that tight, *tight* top. The buzz in my blood intensified with such a hard jolt it winded me for a second.

It was insane. I had never felt anything like it before. Such a strong pull to a woman that without even having touched her, just the sight of her—fully-clothed—was messing with me.

In the rain too. *I hated rain.* That alone should have ebbed even a potential hard-on.

Not with Esmeralda apparently.

"Come back," I said urgently.

With a huge, mischievous grin on her face, she shook her head.

My hair and coat were getting damp. The feeling of the rain of my hands was making my neck prickle in disgust. I'd be having an uncomfortable ride back if her top got any wetter, and she wanted to play games?

I flung Bucky's reins around the pole again and stepped towards Esmeralda twirling around like I hadn't just told her to get her fucking arse over to me. "Esmeralda, I'm serious." She tossed a beautiful, riling laugh over her shoulder. "I'll leave you here."

"Okay, bye," she sang.

I took a few more steps in her direction at the instruction of the raw, provoked feeling emulsifying with the heat in my blood. "Do you think this is funny?"

She nodded. "I do. You should really see the glare on your face right now. It's honestly the best."

Why was my mouth twitching?

I was irritated, aroused, and wet. Her lack of cooperation was infuriating. But her teasing and amusement were contagious. The urge to smile along with her was ridiculously strong.

I resisted the feeling because I didn't want to encourage her. *Or maybe I did actually.*

"I will come over there and get you myself if you don't come here right now, Esmeralda."

Her eyes widened and I worried I'd taken her little game too far. That I'd freaked her out with my tone or creeped her out with my threat. A panicked need to apologise rose inside me.

But then her gaze fell to my feet before flying up to my eyes. Flickered, like she was skittish prey. But her parted mouth curled up in a way that turned my pulse slow and erratic all at once.

She took a sure step back. "Then come get me."

A near-silent groan vibrated up my throat as base excitement flashed through me. A string of throbs rippled down my spine and legs making my suit trousers feel tighter around the zip.

It was wrong. I shouldn't have felt it. But it was there, it was real, it was raw. It was sure.

My focus zoned in on Esmeralda even as a part of me was panicked by the rising primal feelings I'd always tried to suppress. But she took another step back and I forgot about being worried and fell into the clutches of the craving that should have been locked up in tight chains.

I'd be careful, I told myself as I took slow steps towards her. I'd be careful not to scare her. I would never hurt her. She had nothing to fear. *I had nothing to fear.*

"You're not going to catch me if you walk that slowly, Mr Perfect Prince," she teased.

"Fuck," I hissed to myself and pushed off my back foot into a quick jog. She yelped a shocked sound and scrambled around. It turned into

an adrenaline-pumped laugh as she ran away from me.

"Am I still too slow?" I rumbled when I was a few paces behind her.

With a quick glance over her shoulder, Esmeralda screamed a laugh. And her panic, her joy, it was every reason I let her keep running for longer than I needed to. Just to keep the chase going.

Just enough before I curled my arm around her waist.

"Kai," she shrieked through a breathless laugh, spinning me with the force of her movement.

The sound of her screaming my name was so fucking perfect. It made me think of a dozen other ways I could make her cry my name just like that. *Not that I should have been thinking those things.*

"Kai," she laughed and struggled in my arms as I dragged her back and lifted her off her feet.

"Game over," I rasped by her ear. "I got you."

"That—" Her voice came out breathy. "That wasn't fair."

"What wasn't fair was you making me chase you in the rain," I said, a lightness to my voice.

She looked sideways up at me through narrowed lashes and my heart slammed to a stop before restarting again. Her mouth curled up into the softest smile. And fuck, I couldn't take my eyes off it as warmth spread over my skin.

What if…what if I dipped my mouth and kissed her?

But I couldn't just kiss her without her consent, that was madness. Instead, I forced myself to remember we were still standing in the rain. That thing I was supposed to despise. Not to mention that Esmeralda's top was growing more than just damp.

"Time to go," I muttered and swung around with Esmeralda still dangling in my arms. I strode across the stretch of land towards the horses with purpose.

"Wait. Aren't you going to put me down?"

I grunted. "And have you run off again? No."

She was grinning when I flicked a quick glance down at her. "I won't run. I promise."

"I don't believe you."

She let out an overexaggerated huff, dropping her head back against my shoulder. She tilted her face away from the sky and nearly buried into the crook of my neck. "You're such a buzzkill."

Fuck, she made me want to laugh.

A genuine laugh. Not the practised, polite one I'd mastered over the years.

Instead, I allowed myself a small smile. Until I put her on her feet next to Bucky. Then I glared at her while I wrapped her in her wet jumper and helped her up onto the saddle.

To my odd satisfaction, my frown just made her grin harder.

CHAPTER 12

ESMERALDA

Kai just chased me in the rain!!

MARIYAH

EXCUSE U?!?!?!?!?!?

MARIYAH

Like 5 yr old kid chased or primal play chased???

Kai

"**A**nd coffee for the beautiful princess," Pierre said as he placed a white mug of coffee on the island countertop in front of Esmeralda.

"Thank you, Pierre." She grinned at him, tugging at one sleeve of her pale grey jumper.

He winked. "Anything for you, Princess."

There was something wrong with my left eye. It wouldn't stop twitching as I watched my childhood friend blatantly flirt with

Esmeralda while Nur and I were right there with them.

I thought I liked Pierre, some of my oldest memories were of us running around the palace corridors every time he came to work with his uncle, Nur. But having watched him stand unnecessarily close to Esmeralda for the last ten minutes, I was beginning to question our friendship.

I had this absurd urge to shove his face away and yank Esmeralda's stool closer to mine.

"Are Your Highnesses both warm and comfortable now?" Nur asked after giving Pierre more than a few fed up side-glances.

"Yes, thank you, Nur," Esmeralda said, and I nodded in agreement.

"I must admit though, Prince Kai." Nur arched his brows. "When Michael came running down to the kitchen to tell us you had gotten caught in the rain, I was surprised."

"Honestly, same," Pierre said. "You usually check the forecast before you go for a ride."

News always travelled at the speed of light when my equerry, Michael, was the first to know about it. There was nothing he could keep to himself. And he was the one who first saw me and Esmeralda when we walked through the garden doors soaked from head to toe.

I cleared my throat, shifting in the stool seat. "I checked," I lied. I couldn't remember if I had, which probably meant I hadn't. "The rain was forecasted for later, so I assumed we would be fine."

"Ah." Nur nodded.

"A part of it was my fault too," Esmeralda added with a cheeky smile. "I like rain, unlike Prince Rain-Is-Evil over here, so I wanted to stay outside longer."

"Ah, our princess likes the rain, huh? It's so romantic, isn't it?" Pierre said, leaning his elbows on the counter perpendicular to Esmeralda so he was eye-level with her.

The thought of Pierre seeing Esmeralda in the rain didn't sit right with me. It didn't sit at all. My chest burned like there was a swarm of vicious wasps inside, desperate to get out and sting him.

"I guess so," she chuckled. "But rain is very much a luxury in the heat of Jahandar's long summers, so rather than shying away from it, everyone enjoys it when it does rain. So, I've grown up loving it."

"That makes sense," Pierre replied.

"You will all probably think this is weird, but it's a common—not custom, but just a habit I suppose many people have made—to go out for ice-cream when it rains. I have never seen an empty ice-cream parlour on a rainy day in Jahandar." She eyed her mug. "So, I was honestly sort of craving ice-cream after being in the rain."

Nur let out a light laugh, while Pierre grinned. "Really?" She nodded, and he stood upright. "Then how about I take you out for ice-cream today? We could go after dinner. Just us."

I stiffened in my seat.

Pierre and Esmeralda. Alone? Eating ice-cream. *Alone?* By themselves? Her with him? *Alone?*

No, no, no. I didn't like that. But unable to logically explain aloud why I didn't want her to go with him, I could do nothing but grind my teeth together.

"I would love to Pierre," she said but smiled sadly. "But I sent my main security, Shehryar, with Prince Arsh and the children, and it'll probably be late by the time they get back after eating out. I don't think Sher would be very happy if I went out without him."

"Are you sure? I'm sure we could work something out with the security that stayed behind."

"He might be okay with that…or maybe we could go another day when Shehryar is here?"

I glared thoughtfully into the golden, crystal-clear liquid in the mug before me.

I must have gone mad. She had made me mad. That was the only explanation as to why I was considering such a suggestion. Esmeralda had messed with my head so badly I'd gone insane.

First the game of chase in the rain. And now *this*.

I rarely ate ice-cream in the summer, Neves forbid *ever* in the middle of winter. I was always cold enough as it was.

But if she went with *me*…

"I could take you." Three heads whipped around to me, and I realised I had said it aloud.

Fuck.

I cleared my throat. "My security team are still around. If we let Shehryar know where we're going, I'm sure he'll be fine with it."

She sat up in the stool, her expression as bright as a light. "Really? Are you sure? They won't mind?"

"Hmm, I'm sure."

"Wait, what?" Pierre looked around baffled.

"That sounds like a wonderful idea," Nur added cheerfully. "We'll leave dessert off the menu so you can go straight after dinner."

"I'd like that," Esmeralda said, her glittery gaze sinking heavily into my chest.

Besting Pierre felt good, but knowing my suggestion put that look on her face? *That* felt fucking epic. Made me feel like the biggest, most powerful man in the world.

"Dude," Pierre exclaimed at me. "Did you just steal my date?"

I nearly scoffed. As if I was going to *ever* let him take her on a fucking date.

Damn...since when had I been this possessive?

"I think I ate too much," Esmeralda groaned.

She dropped her head back against headrest, sitting in the other window seat. She clutched her belly with both hands between the flaps of her dark green coat. Her expression of discomfort was lit up by the streetlamps we passed on the road as we headed back to the palace.

I grunted. "You didn't have to finish the entire sundae."

Thanks to the suggestion of the head of my security team, Rocco, and Gary, my personal driver and bodyguard, Esmeralda and I went to a small, family-run ice-cream parlour a half hour's drive from the palace straight after dinner. A dinner that was just for us two in the end.

Thankfully, ice-cream wasn't the only thing they had on the menu, so I opted for a small stack of pancakes, while Esmeralda ordered a sundae. I was honestly surprised she managed to finish it. But she was obviously suffering the repercussions of eating the whole thing.

"But it was so good." She sighed. "I don't think I've ever had mint ice-cream that tasted that good before. I should have asked for the recipe."

"Or we could go again."

Her head lifted off the headrest with a blink of surprise. I was probably looking back at her with the same amount of surprise. Crap, I didn't think before I spoke.

"We can?"

I tugged at my ear. "Hmm. If you want."

A grin blossomed on her mouth, crinkling her eyes. "I do." Then she groaned, rubbing her belly like it protested at that remark. "But let's not talk about going again yet. Not yet. Please."

A huff of laughter lifted from me at her overdramatic act. I looked out the window as I shook my head, pressing my fist to my lips to cover the lingering smile. *Cute.*

When the back of my head prickled, I glanced back at her. Her eyes were huge and round as she sat completely still. I shifted in my seat uncomfortably. "What?"

"You…" she said on an audible breath. "You just laughed."

Flames burst through my face, knotting my brows together. I rubbed at my ear. It wasn't as if I had committed a crime, but for some reason, I felt like I had been caught red-handed.

"No, I didn't," I grumbled.

"Oh my gosh, you did." Her lips stretched from ear to ear. "You did. You laughed!"

I tugged at my ear harder. "I didn't," I growled.

"Grumpy Kai laughed!" She chuckled as she practically bounced on the seat. But then she slumped with a pained groan, one hand on her belly.

A jerk of panic cleared away my embarrassment. I leaned towards her, clutching her shoulder as I looked right at her face. "Are you okay?"

She flashed a twisted smile. "Yes. Just too full. Laughing hurt."

I shook my head. "You shouldn't have eaten the whole thing, Esmeralda."

"But it was so good. I'll be fine once I walk it off. Five palace floors should do the trick."

Five palace floors or... *There was a park nearby.*

Shit, I had lost it. Me? In a park? On a cold winter night? Never. *Never before at least.*

"Gary," I called, angling my head to the driver's seat in front of me.

"Yes, Your Highness," he replied without taking his eye off the road.

"Can you take us to Pavilion Central Park?"

"Uh." Gary unsurprisingly sounded confused. "Of course. I'll inform Rocco of the change."

"We're going to Central Park?" Esmeralda echoed with excitement on her face.

The frown on my brows grew heavier. "I can't have you complaining the whole way back to the palace that you're in pain."

Apparently, I'd rather brace the cold. *The things this woman had me doing for her.*

As expected, it was bloody freezing in the park.

Our breaths instantly turned to vapour, the grass was blanketed in a thin layer of frost, and there wasn't a damn soul around us. Besides us, there was my security team as we walked between rows of lamps, casting shadows between naked, spindly trees dotted around the path.

But while I was shivering in my thick parka coat with my head buried in the faux fur hood and my gloved hands shoved deep into the pockets, Esmeralda was gleaming with delight. No bloody gloves on her hands, and her coat flapped around her jeans-clad legs because she'd left it open.

Why wasn't she cold? *How was that even possible?* She was from a hot state.

"Isn't this lovely?" Esmeralda sighed happily.

She caught my side-glance of disgust and burst into a chortle. "Oh, come on," she said, bumping my arm with hers. "What is it exactly that you don't like about the cold?"

"There is absolutely nothing to like about the cold."

"Yes, there is." Her swaying steps had her knocking into me again. "Like the crisp smell of a cold morning. The look and feel of snow. Gathering around a cosy fireplace with a book and a hot drink. Oh, and of course, the wind against your skin and in your hair. Doesn't it make you feel like you're soaring high in the sky with the birds, free and wild?"

I couldn't have felt more horrified by what she described than I did. "No." She threw her head back and laughed. "No. Cold mornings are miserable. Snow turns to slush and ice and makes everyone's lives difficult. Fires are lit to mitigate the cold, so they aren't a reason to like the cold. And wind is the bane of all existence. It makes your mouth taste of blood and your face burn until it feels like it's going to fall off, not to mention it slowly kills off all your extremities too."

"Wow," she mouthed slowly. "So much hate for the cold, Mr Perfect Prince."

"You asked. I answered."

A gasp cut through her husky giggle, interrupting my stride. I pivoted to face her where she'd stopped. "What? What's wrong?"

"Books." She blinked round eyes at me. "I promised to finish reading that book with Pierre after dinner. How could I forget? You don't think he's waiting for me, do you?"

My jaw locked tightly as the green burn of frustration made itself known in my chest again. I didn't like that she was thinking about the plans she had made with him when she was with me.

"No," I said, feigning calm. "He most likely forgot himself, so I doubt he's waiting. And he was in the kitchen when we made our plan, but he didn't remind you of it."

"I guess. He didn't say anything, did he? But still, I will have to make it up to him."

She walked past me, and with a deep, calming breath that didn't really quell my frustration with my best friend, I followed her. But I couldn't stay quiet.

"He was flirting with you. In the kitchen."

"Hmm? Who? Pierre. Oh, I know. But he doesn't mean it. He's just being playful, so it's fine. And I don't really think I'm actually his type. And he's not mine."

Don't ask. Don't ask. Don't fucking ask.

"What's your type?" *Dammit, Kai!*

Her lashes fluttered as some unreadable emotion passed over her face. Then she stared ahead to the lamp-lit path, the smallest smile tugging on her mouth. "My type? I, uh…" she muttered, appearing both shy and amused. "Tall, dark, and handsome I guess."

I frowned.

How tall? Over one-hundred-and-eighty-four centimetres? Jahandar used imperial measures, so six-foot? Under? A specific height?

And dark what? Dark-haired? Dark-skinned? Dark eyes? Dark personality?

And what was handsome? She wasn't being very specific. A lot of men fit the description of tall, dark, and handsome. Without meaning to sound full of myself, even I fit the bill.

Esmeralda's eyes slowly travelled over my body, lingering on my shoulders, skipping up to my hair, then slipping down to meet my gaze. She flicked her head away, the corners of her mouth twitching.

I narrowed my gaze on that cheeky smile she was trying to hide. "Are you taking a jab at me?"

She hooted up at the sky and my cheeks flamed. *Fuck, she was.*

"No." She shook her head. "I wasn't taking a jab at you. If I had been then I probably would have said my type was…tall, royal, and grumpy."

My face fell and she laughed again.

"Prince Kai?"

I stopped and turned back. Rocco with his warrior, two-metre frame stood in a fitted black coat, his bald head shining. He had his phone in one hand and Gary lingered behind him.

"Is everything okay, Rocco?"

He tilted his head. "Shehryar rang and requested that we ensure Princess Esmeralda is back in the palace before half ten—"

"Shehryar said what?" Esmeralda exclaimed.

"So, if we want to get back on time, we will have to leave now."

Esmeralda growled. As in, well and truly growled from deep within her chest. "Sometimes he's so— Rocco, did you by any chance remind him I'm not sixteen anymore and I have no curfew to adhere to?"

Rocco rubbed the smile off his mouth with his fingers. "It was not my place to say, Ma'am. But he was adamant we come back as soon as possible."

She huffed loudly. "I'm sorry about this," she said to me.

"Don't apologise. He's worried about you." I nodded to Rocco. "Let's get going then."

My hand moved on its own, settling on the small of her back to guide her around.

Maybe it was just me, but she seemed to walk closer to my side on the way back to the car.

I stopped a few steps behind Esmeralda outside her bedroom back in the palace as she turned to me in the corridor, her coat draped over her arms while I still wore mine.

"You didn't have to walk me here, you know," she said. "But thank you. For today too. I had fun. Though you paid for my ice-cream, so I'll have to pay you back for that."

My scowl was automatic. "No, Esmeralda. It was my treat."

"But—"

"No. And you won't mention it again."

Her eyes narrowed. "That's both chivalrous and very annoying of you, I hope you know that." She tipped her chin up. "Fine, but I will return the favour one day, and you'll let me."

I probably wouldn't, but I didn't tell her that.

"Good night then."

I nodded. "Good night."

She turned to the door. I stepped back. We both stopped. I waited. She remained still. And I wondered. Was she thinking the same thing as me?

Would we meet again tonight?

Suddenly, she spun around. "I, uh…if you can't sleep…"

I swallowed. "The kitchen?"

Her smile was so obviously relieved. "Well, after eating all that food…"

"Somewhere else then?"

She nodded, her teeth scraping her bottom lip. And I was hooked on the sight of that little tug.

"Esmer—Princess!"

We both startled. A huffing, glaring Shehryar came storming down the corridor towards us.

"Urgh, he appeared," Esmeralda groaned. She turned halfway to the door, and whispered, "I'll meet you at the end of the corridor in an hour's time. See you." Then she disappeared through, leaving me to awkwardly wish a good night to her suspicious, green-eyed private secretary.

CHAPTER 13
Esmeralda

I was floating high above the clouds. Drugged on a heady feeling of elation having had beyond the best time with Kai.

The hours I spent with him felt like a blissful dream. So good, that at times I worried they really were just a figment of my wild imagination. That I would wake up and find myself sprawled in a cold bed in the middle of the night with nothing but the realisation that none of it had been real.

Because honestly? Some moments were so surreal it truly felt like my imagination was getting the better of me. Moments that injected me with dose after dose of hope he might—not immediately, but maybe soon—reciprocate my feelings.

Now I was filled with the kind of giddy delight that stole away any sort of tiredness or worry.

After a walk around the palace where Kai showed me a few places I hadn't been, we ended up on the ground floor of the library, where all the tables and chairs were along the back.

Kai was sitting in the chair on my right while I was sitting atop the table surface. He looked sexy in his navy hoodie, loose grey pyjama bottoms, and glasses combo. With a book in his hand and his strong, thick thighs spread, he ever so slightly brushed the side of my bare calf.

"I haven't heard of half of these fables ever," I said, flicking through the red bound book in my lap.

"I doubt most of Touma's citizens have either," Kai said, nodding at the book. "They are old, pre-Zorro's Rebellion fables that were lost with the people who told them, so they're not very common to hear anymore. They're not the most interesting of stories either."

"No, they are not." I chuckled, skimming over a fable called, *A Bag of Sand.* "I think I preferred the book of Post Rebellion fairy tales."

I glanced behind me to pick up the previous bound book I had been reading, but the number of books that were piled around the table took me by surprise. "Wow. I didn't realise we'd pulled this many books from the shelves."

Kai nudged his glasses up his nose with a finger. "Not we. *You.* You were handing them to me while you were babbling away."

My spine shot straight as a defensive blush tore through me. "I don't babble!"

The dimple in his right cheek made the quickest of appearances. "Yes, you do."

"I do not. I just…"

His expression hardly changed but amusement shone in his blacker than black eyes so damn bright, I would've had to be blind to miss it. "Babble," he offered with a raise of his brows.

I scowled, but I could feel my mouth betraying me. "No. I just talk quickly. And if my *talking* was bothering you so much, why didn't you tell me to be quiet?"

"I never once said that it bothered me."

Right. He hadn't.

I struggled to swallow around that acknowledgement, and I didn't know what made me do it, but I knocked his thigh with my leg. "Still, I don't babble."

His lashes dipped to his leg or mine and up to my face. "You do." He nudged my leg with his thigh.

His touch sent a sledgehammer through my chest, but I knocked him back. "I don't."

"You do." His dimple made an appearance against the late-night shadow on his jaw as he pushed my leg again.

He was smiling, soft and small. His eyes glowing like stars. And maybe it was more of a smirk, but it was real and natural and effortless. Stunning.

And for me. *Or at me.* But for. *Me.* His first real smile.

First a laugh and now a smile. Are you sure this isn't a dream, Esmeralda?

I was almost tempted to pinch myself to test if it was or not. I opted for the better option of knocking Kai's leg again. *Nope, he was real.* Real, and warm, and rock-solid, and perfect. "I don't."

Kai let out a breathy huff and kept his sturdy leg against mine, searing his imprint into my skin permanently. "Okay, you don't."

There was a moment. One, ten or a hundred seconds where our stares mingled. By the end of it, my cheeks were aching from how hard I was smiling.

Kai was the first to break away, clearing his throat. "I'll put some of the books away."

"I'll help." I shuffled forward on the table as he stood up from the chair.

"No, it's okay."

"But—"

"Stay seated, Esmeralda."

There was no arguing with his tone, so I pressed my lips together and shuffled back on the table. But as he put a few books away at a time, I got to watch him to my heart's content.

For nearly seven years I'd had a crush on this man. I'd watched him intently from the other side of ballrooms and royal events. I thought I knew him. His stoic calm and elegant charm. The exact curve of his smile. The deep sound of his laugh. But the last few days had made me realise I didn't know him the way I thought I did, not entirely at least.

While that side of Kai—my Orange—might have sparked my attraction for him, it was learning the other side of Kai that turned that spark into a blazing fire.

The one who glared so ferociously and grumbled his hate for the cold. The one who despised rain but hadn't abandoned me in it, twice. The one who rescued animals, who laughed and then tried to pretend he never had, who blushed so adorably and was as equally awkward as he was domineering.

It was a little scary how quickly and intensely I was falling for him all over again. But at the same time, it felt so good too. Like soaring high in the sky and free-falling all at once.

Kai leaned past me to grab a few books, surrounding me in his warmth and enchanting, woody scent. For barely a moment, but it was enough to make my head cloud over and spin.

Gosh, if only he knew how much I…

I like you.

Just as Kai stood upright, he froze. Completely still. The only movement came from the quick flicker of his eyes behind his glasses to me. His shocked, wide eyes.

I froze as cold realisation splashed down my back.

No…no…no, no, no!

I sucked in a sharp breath.

Had I said that aloud? No, please. I hadn't said that aloud, please.

But no matter how much I wanted to hope that I hadn't, there was no other plausible reason for the raw surprise on his face.

A dam broke inside me. Of panic and fear and embarrassment. The explosive heat of it was so overwhelming that before I could even think to laugh it off as a joke, the urge to run swamped me.

I jumped off the edge of the table, stumbling as I landed on shaky legs. I spun back around, and Kai had only turned his head to look at me, his expression the exact same. My panic soared.

"I, uh," I muttered hoarsely and took a step back.

I wanted to deny what I'd said, but I could barely hear my own thoughts over the racket behind my ribcage. I couldn't figure out how to deny it, so I shuffled back away from him one step at a time.

"I, uh…I'm tired, so I'm going back to my room. Good night."

I whirled around, barely managing to stop myself from sprinting out the library.

The moment I was in the palace corridors, I ran. So fast.

ESMERALDA
MARIYAH!!

ESMERALDA
What do I do?????

ESMERALDA
I ruined everything!!!! Again!!!

MARIYAH
Woah woah woah what happened???

MARIYAH
Im sure nothing is ruined baby!!

MARIYAH
Just tell me everything from the beginning

CHAPTER 14
Esmeralda

"**H**ello."

I shrieked, almost tripping over my own feet as I spun around to face whoever had found me, clutching the book in my hands close to my chest. I saw the quickest glimpse of bright hazel eyes before their owner doubled over with a loud laugh.

"Prince Arsh," I gasped. "You scared the life out of me."

Kai's uncle stood tall, his lean chest shaking with soft chuckles. "I can see that," he said. "But didn't you hear me approaching? I wasn't exactly sneaking up on you."

"No," I mumbled. "I was reading."

"Ah, you were lost in your own little world. If I'm honest, I almost missed you standing here. Why are you hiding in the corner?"

My cheeks flamed. "I—I'm not hiding." *Why not just tell him you're lying, right?*

"Oh, now I'm curious." He leaned against the bookcase, ankles and arms crossed over, and raised his brows. "Why are you hiding? And who from?"

So, I was hiding on the second floor of the library by a tall bookcase. But I didn't think I could be blamed for that after my awful, blurted confession to Kai less than twenty-four hours ago.

Other than one awkward moment in the large entrance hall of

Chakham Palace after the morning conference, I had successfully avoided him all day. And I planned to continue to avoid him until the thought of facing him didn't make me break out in hives.

"Does the reason your hiding," Prince Arsh said in my silence, "have anything to do with why you didn't take the empty seat next to Kai at breakfast? I thought you would have jumped at the chance to sit next to him."

I held still as an answering blush rolled through my face.

"Ah." Prince Arsh shifted to stand straight. "So, you're hiding from Kai."

I gulped nervously.

"What happened, Esmeralda?" he asked softly.

Just like that, my face twisted up and a pained sob poured from me. "The worst possible thing, Prince Arsh," I cried, scrunching in on myself. "Last night, I blurted out my feelings to him randomly and then panicked and ran away. Literally! Just ran from the library without any explanation." He pursed his curling lips together. "Don't laugh. It's not funny."

He shook his head, rubbing his mouth. "I'm not. I'm not laughing." But he sounded like he was.

"Prince Arsh," I whined and dropped my forehead against the side of the bookcase. "I'm not even sure what's worse. The fact that I blurted out my feelings or that I ran after."

"I don't think it's as bad as you think it is."

"I'm so embarrassed I think I might die if I'm anywhere near him."

"Okay, it's really not anything to die over." I lifted my head. "So you told him how you felt about him and ran away, so what?" My face fell. His grin widened. "I know you feel embarrassed now, but I promise you, it probably worked in your favour."

"How? You seem to be forgetting the part where I ran from him. He probably thinks I'm a freak now."

"Oh, I can tell you with full confidence he doesn't. Though he was a bit annoyed."

"See."

Prince Arsh shook his head once. "No, not because of your confession. He seemed annoyed at you."

My shoulders sunk. "How is that any better?"

He chuckled lightly and shook his head again. "Esmeralda, my dear, you're not understanding what I'm saying. Kai was annoyed because you chose to walk around the table and sit next to Fay at breakfast instead of in the empty seat next to *him*."

I didn't believe him. "You don't know that."

"Yes, I do. Esmeralda, he's been watching you all day."

My stomach swooped low. There was no way that was true…

"I can see you're not convinced, but it's true. He couldn't take his eyes off you. Everywhere you went he was watching you. I half expected him to chase you when you left him in the hallway earlier."

I didn't want to hope. But I was. "Are you sure?"

He ruffled my hair affectionately. "Yes. Trust me, I know my nephew. So, I wouldn't let this little blip keep you from facing him if I were you."

My shoulders relaxed as I eyed Prince Arsh. "Thank you, but… why are you helping me?"

His smile turned lop-sided and mischievous. "Because I'm a romantic at heart and an absolute sucker for young love." He shrugged. "That, and it's been a while since anything interesting has happened in my quiet life, and I'm a nosey old man who wants to be involved in it."

I grinned. "Fair enough. But I'm not sure I'm ready to face Kai just yet."

"That's okay." He rested his hand atop my head. "Though, he hasn't left his office since we returned, so you probably don't need to hide so earnestly from him."

KAI

> What does it mean when a girl says she likes you but then runs off after?

CANDY

> hahahahaha

PIERRE

> who who who who

CANDY

> she realised how ugly you were

PIERRE

> do I know her

TREVOR

> said it to the wrong person

ZAIN

> Or she panicked?

PIERRE

> tell us who she is

KAI

> Forget I asked

Kai

Esmeralda was avoiding me.

I might not have been so annoyed by that fact if it wasn't for what happened last night. Confused, yes, maybe even a bit upset, but not frustrated beyond belief.

Hadn't she meant what she said to me? *What had she even meant by what she said?*

She liked me? Liked me how? Like, *like* liked me? Or just liked me as a friend?

How was I supposed to know when she hadn't even bothered to explain before running off? And I'd been too shocked to even react, let alone stop her and get an explanation.

She'd left me with a hundred thundering emotions that made my ears burn for hours after before I exhausted myself thinking and fell asleep. Realisation, confusion, pleasant surprise, disbelief.

Hope that she might be attracted to me like I was discovering I was to her.

But I couldn't ask her when I couldn't *fucking* find her.

I tried not to look for her. But after two hours of shuffling through new policy plans, not taking in a single word I was reading, I couldn't take it anymore. I needed to find her and get answers.

Looking on every floor was the only option she'd left me with.

From my unsuccessful trip to the kitchen, I headed straight for the library. Only to find Uncle coming down the stairs that led to the first-floor entrance before the main entrance corridor.

"Kai!" Uncle Arsh said cheerfully. "Where are you off to, boy?"

"The library." Upon realising something, I backtracked a step. "Were you on the first floor just now?"

"Up the second floor on the balcony, yes. I was. Why?"

"Did you see Princess Esmeralda there?"

"I did. Why? Are you looking for her?"

"Yes." I resisted the urge to tug at my ear as I tried to think of a legitimate reason. "There was something—this thing she mentioned…"

Uncle raised his brows. "This thing?"

"Yes." I shuffled from foot to foot. I was shit at lying. "I wanted to ask her more about it."

Thankfully, Uncle didn't seem fazed by my rubbish answer. "Of course," he said cheerfully. "Well, she's still there. On the second floor, between the wall shelves and middle bookcases under the last window on the left. Right in the corner where your mother keeps the romance books."

That was…*specific*. Not that I was complaining.

"Thank you."

"Of course. See you at dinner. Oh, but go quietly. She was lost in a book, and I accidently scared her by being too loud."

I nodded and headed straight for the stairs, climbing them two at a time.

Esmeralda

Someone cleared their throat behind me. Loudly.

I looked up from my book for the second time in ten minutes, hesitant to turn, but I couldn't pretend I hadn't heard them. So, I closed my book and wheeled around.

And regretted it instantly.

I suddenly found myself standing before a huffing, raging bull only to remember I was dressed in bright red from head to toe.

That was how it felt coming face to face with Kai's broad, heaving chest before my eyes automatically flicked up. I was caught, captured, caged by his furious ink black scowl.

Oh shit.

My heart and stomach launched forward from a slingshot then collided with my bones and slammed back into place. I barely managed to suck in a breath before my lungs seized to function and my muscles turned to ten-tonne blocks of lead.

What was he doing here? *How did he find me?* He hadn't been looking for me, had he?

He looked irate. And sexy with his hair ruffled and his tie pulled loose. But mainly irate.

Shit.

Before I could think of a way to escape, he clamped a hand tightly around my arm just above my elbow and stomped past me, yanking me with him.

"Kai," I gasped, stumbling sideways.

He dragged me around the bookcase, pulling me into the corner of the floor-to-ceiling wall shelves and around to face him. He crowded me in, forcing me right up against the books. I had to tilt my head all the way back to look up at the frustration etched all over the hard plains of his face.

I squeezed the book against my chest like it was a safety blanket and gulped. "Hi," I managed. "Is there, um, something you needed from me?"

His eyes flashed and his brows scrunched tighter together. "Esmeralda—" he growled from somewhere deep within his throat but immediately cut himself off with a hard clench of his teeth.

Something dangerous, warm, and bubbly sparked in my belly that made me want him to finish whatever threat he'd been about to issue. But at the same time, I valued my life.

"Why have you been avoiding me all day?" he eventually said.

"I haven't been avoiding you." I looked everywhere but directly into his eyes.

"You have and you are."

There was a gap on my right between Kai's large body and the bookshelves, big enough that I could slip through and make a run for—

Kai's hand shot out level with my shoulder, turning his arm into a barrier that cut me off from my only escape route. "*Don't.* Even think about it."

The hairs on the back of my neck stood on end as I stared wide-eyed up at him. Partly in shock that he'd known what I'd been thinking. But mostly because his growled warning jabbed me right in the belly with a sharp jolt of excitement. So warm and delicious that my thighs locked together.

There was several moments of tense silence, then: "What did you mean last night?"

The dreaded question.

Even though I knew it was coming, my face heated in embarrassment. I cringed and squeezed my eyes shut, turning my head away from him.

I couldn't have been hoping for the floor to swallow me up for more than a few beats before I felt the roughened pad of two fingers brush my chin gently. My lashes lifted as Kai guided me to look at him. I fell right into the endless darkness of his eyes, softer than before yet still unyielding.

He dipped his head closer. "Tell me, Esmeralda. What did you mean when you said you liked me?"

I pulled in a breath, trying to find my voice. "I meant." I gulped. "I meant that I…like you…in *that* way. I'm attracted to you. Emotionally and uh, physically."

Kai's shoulders sunk on an exhale. "You are?"

I blinked. *Wait. He sounds relieved.*

His fingers slipped away from my chin. "Since when?"

Ah, damn. I have to explain that too?

"Um…" I winced a little, my cheeks stinging hot all over again. "Since I was sixteen…"

It took a moment for comprehension to pass over his face but when it did, he reeled back. "What? Since you were sixteen? But that was…"

I nodded, wincing harder. "Like seven years ago. I've had a crush on you for seven years. Well, nearly seven years. I was technically almost seventeen then. At Kareem's first coronation anniversary party. You were with Fay and the twin princes of Prio, and it was the first time I noticed how attractive you were—*are*.

"But I wasn't just physically attracted to you, I liked the way you acted—I mean, just the way you were. Although spending time with you over these last few days, I realised that wasn't completely you. And the more I got to know you, the more I realised I was so much more attracted to *this* version of you. My feelings for you grew and I… well…you know what happened after that…"

The silence was piercingly loud after my unnecessarily detailed explanation. I wanted to disappear into thin air. I was ten-times more embarrassed than I had been about a minute ago.

When he finally moved I almost flinched, barely able to look at him. "Why didn't you tell me?"

"I never really found the chance to. And I was younger than you—I *am* younger than you, and it's never bothered me, but it probably would have bothered you…and others."

He winced like he just realised that our six-year age gap would have made things weird if I'd confessed when I was younger. "Plus, I doubt you would have taken a confession from a teenager seriously anyway. Especially considering you were with Meg then too."

His jaw visibly clenched and unclenched, and I didn't like it. It wasn't jealousy, I just didn't like the pained look on his face that her name put there at all. She was clearly his ex-fiancée for a reason.

For so long, Kai quietly contemplated what I said, and layer upon layer, the fear and anxiety built up inside me. Heavy weights sunk through me as doubts crept in.

Was he thinking of a way to let me down gently? Was this the end of my chance? Had I ruined our friendship? Had we ever really been friends? Would he ever talk to me again after this?

Kai sighed, running a slow hand through his hair. "I don't know what to say."

I shook my head quickly. "You don't have to say anything. Really. I wasn't telling you to hear anything back from you. I just wanted you to know. But if it bothers you, you can just forget about it. We can act like it never—"

"No," he said instantly. "No, it doesn't bother me. And I'm not going to act like it never happened. I'm just…*surprised*. Nothing you did ever gave away what you felt, so I'm surprised. That's all."

"Are you sure? Because we really can pretend—"

"Yes, I'm sure, Esmeralda." He shuffled closer, his brows slipping low. "If anything, what bothers me is that you have been ignoring me."

I pursed my lips together sheepishly. "I wasn't ignoring you. I was avoiding you."

"Either way, I didn't appreciate it. I would rather you have talked to me in the morning than driven me mad with frustration because I couldn't get a hold of you. You can't do that again."

I nodded because he was right. I'd let panic get the better of me and acted childishly. "I'm sorry. I was just embarrassed."

"You have nothing to be embarrassed about." He visibly hesitated with a hard swallow. "I'm…glad you told me." He rubbed his left ear between a finger and thumb. "More than glad."

More than glad? What does that mean?

"No more avoiding me, Esmeralda."

"No more avoiding," I echoed in quiet agreement.

More than glad was a good sign, right?

CHAPTER 15
Esmeralda

couldn't sleep that night.

Not that I managed to sleep very often but I never usually felt restless. Not like this.

I kept tossing from one side to the other in my bed, trying different breathing exercises to silence my circling thoughts, but nothing worked.

I couldn't stop worrying about the whole situation with Kai.

He said he was more than glad I told him about my feelings for him, and I couldn't lie, my mind was conjuring up theories and fantasies about him possibly feeling something towards me. But I was scared that maybe I was taking it all wrong and being too optimistic.

I wasn't even sure I wanted to see him to confirm either one. That was why I was suffering through my restlessness in the darkness of my room instead of wandering the palace corridors.

Eventually, the sound of rain pattered against the balcony doors and windows. I threw myself out of bed, desperate to feel the cold droplets against my overheated body.

I didn't bother donning a jumper over my grey silk short-sleeved shirt and shorts pyjama set. I simply pulled on a pair of white trainer socks and scurried out the room.

Raj's familiar face greeted me down by the garden doors.

"Can I convince you to at least put a coat on, Your Highness?" the night guard asked as he unhooked the ring of keys from his tunic belt.

"You can try. But I think I'll still skip the coat."

He sighed overdramatically. "Princess, you're going to get me in trouble again." The keys jingled in his hand as he pushed a long silver key into the lock under one handle.

"Trouble?" My brows furrowed. "With whom? And why?"

He stretched his arm for the top lock of the other door. "Prince Kai is worried that you'll get ill if you keep going out in the rain."

Had Raj inferred that? Or had Kai said that to him?

"Well, we both know Prince Kai worries way too much," I said with a haughty smile as Raj stepped back. I wrapped my hand around the dull silver handle. "And just because he's a grumpy weirdo who doesn't like rain, doesn't mean I should have to—"

"So, I'm a grumpy weirdo now?"

I gasped and flew around in the direction of the voice.

Whatever uncertainty I had moments earlier about wanting to see Kai or not evaporated now that he was in my vicinity. There was no doubt that I would never not want to see his gorgeous face.

Kai pulled the hood of his dark burgundy hoodie down and swaggered slowly towards me, running a hand through his floppy hair. From behind his black-framed glasses, his stare was intense and bright.

"I thought I was a buzzkill?" he said, stopping near my side.

He remembered that? I pressed my lips together, fighting a smile. "You still are a buzzkill, and a grumpy weirdo too now."

He glared down at me, but it was entirely playful. Then he looked over my head to Raj. "I told you not to let her go out in the rain again, Raj."

"I did try to stop her, Prince Kai. Her Highness is just very stubborn."

My mouth opened and closed in spluttering shock before I bristled and stood to my full height. Which, uh, wasn't much in comparison to the two men. "First of all, you didn't try to stop me, you unlocked the door for me immediately."

Raj chuckled and flashed a mock sheepish grin. I jabbed a finger into Kai's chest—solid, broad, warm, perfect, *perfect* chest. "And I am outraged that you dared to scheme behind my back to try to stop me from going out in the rain. How could you?"

"Very easily." His expression lacked any emotion, but his eyes glinted with mischief. It was so damn sexy I couldn't even attempt to feel frustrated with his highhanded behaviour.

"Well," I said with a huff. "I'd like to make it clear right now that I don't intend to listen to either of you."

I grabbed the doorhandles on both halves of the arched door and yanked them open. Raj grunted and Kai growled a low sound of hatred as a chilly dampness and steady pattering sound flooded the space around us. But I smiled, relishing the way the cold stroked and pinched my bare skin.

The moment I tried to step outside though, Kai wrapped a hand around my wrist and held me back. "No," he rumbled, sharp and commanding. "You are not going outside like that, Esmeralda."

I tried to tug my wrist from his hand. Futilely, because his grip was unbreakable. "I'm dressed enough, Kai, and I'm not cold anyway, so—"

"Twice was pushing your luck. A third time and you really will get sick." I shook my head. "Keep the doors open, Esmeralda, if that is what you want. But you're not going outside. Please."

I dully heard footsteps behind me, but I kept my frown on Kai. I lasted about ten seconds before I sighed heavily. "Okay. Fine. I won't."

I dropped my arm by my side once he let go of it, but I stayed forever aware of my pulse tattooing the shape of his fingers on my skin in the silence that followed.

"What's wrong?" Kai asked. He was leaning back against the door, facing me, with his brows knotted. "You're so quiet. You were quiet at dinner too."

I nipped nervously at my bottom lip. He pulled off the door. "Tell me, Esmeralda. What's wrong?"

I sighed. "I'm just…nervous about something."

"Nervous about what?"

That was the part where I was supposed to brush it off like it was nothing. But I didn't want to. Still, I struggled to find the right words.

"I've liked this guy for nearly seven years, and I told him I liked him, and he said he was glad that I told him, but I can't brush off the feeling I didn't do it right and now I feel nervous."

Understanding washed across Kai's face. He stared down at his black slippers. "You didn't believe him? When he said he was more than glad you told him?"

I was a little too desperate for answers to be surprised he was going along it. "A part of me did—*does*. But a part of me doesn't know what to think. I'm scared what I think isn't what he meant. Or what if he said it just so things wouldn't be awkward?"

"He didn't. That's not why he said it. He..." Kai sighed and combed a hand through his hair. "Maybe it was the wrong thing to say, but he's not the best at expressing himself."

Taking a moment to process the hope his words gave me, I rotated to face him fully. "Then what was he trying to say? Why was he more than glad to hear my confession?"

He was quiet for so long that I began to doubt he'd answer. Then, "For the same reason he's been walking around for the last hour or so, looking for you. And the same reason he's here. Because he might hate rain, but the moment he heard it, he came straight here hoping he would find you."

There was no way I could misinterpret what he was trying to say this time. It hit me right in the guts with a powerful, sweet blow, that almost had my knees buckling.

Kai felt something for me.

There was no single name for the feeling that crashed through my veins with reckless abandon. Immense relief, explosive happiness, an unbelievable urge to throw myself at him and latch on for dear life. That, everything, and so much more, flooding my chest until it hurt.

He took a small step towards me, and my heart kicked harder. "But in comparison to your seven years, he wasn't sure if his few days was enough. He wasn't sure if you would think he was being insincere, so he didn't tell you."

I felt lightheaded and breathless, but a delighted smile blossomed on my mouth. "Even if he said it had been twenty minutes, I would have believed him."

He frowned, moving closer yet. "You shouldn't," he whispered back. "You should expect more. You should expect him to prove himself to you first."

I was running solely on a high as I followed his lead and closed the last of the gap between us. "Then how about we test him now." I wet my lips with a quick flick of my tongue, my gaze dipping to his wide, firm mouth. "What would he say if I asked to kiss him?"

Heat flared through his irises, turning them dark before his lashes dipped. It was almost like I could feel his stare grazing my lips. I parted them on a breath and his lashes snapped up, piercing me with a hot, intense look that made me feel like I hadn't taken a breath at all.

The silence was long and loud. Not in an uncomfortable way, but in a scorching, tense, make-it-or-break-it way that pulled us closer together yet kept us apart too.

Then he said, "Wouldn't you need a stepladder to do that?"

Something around me went *pop* like a bubble bursting.

Kai's dimple appeared deep in his right cheek and with screeching understand, my confusion shattered. It gave way to embarrassed shock that made my jaw collapse to the floor.

A deep, raw, loud sound erupted from Kai's mouth as he slipped back away from me.

I might have appreciated that this grumpy prince, who'd denied that he'd chuckled in front of me last time, was laughing so hard his chest was shaking and his eyes were crinkled if I wasn't so offended and embarrassed. Even if a small part of me did find it funny too.

I clapped my lips together and slammed both hands against his chest; he barely even swayed. "You asshole," I cried.

He captured my wrists in his hands, holding my palms to his chest. I squirmed and struggled, shoving and pulling at his hoodie with no give whatsoever as I threw a few insults at him. But laughter weaved its way between my words.

"How could you make fun of my height when I was being serious?"

He grinned. A toothy one that made my heart flutter. "But you are small. I don't think you even come up to my shoulder. Not by a few centimetres. So how could you reach?"

I choked on a shocked noise. "Oh, that's it. I'm shoving you into the rain you hate so much for that!"

Kai's smile collapsed immediately. I leaned my weight back, getting ready to shove him with all my might but I was suddenly the one being swung around.

I slammed back against an open door, not hard enough to hurt, but the surprise impact knocked a gasp from me. Dizzy, dazed, and breathless, it took me a moment to recalibrate my position.

Kai was all around me. Everywhere. In my space, surrounding me. In my lungs, sweet, woody, and enchanting. His face right above mine, his parted lips inches away. And my wrists? He had them in his hands, pinned to the door just above my head, arching my body into the curve of his.

For an eternity, or a few seconds, we stayed just like that. Nothing said. Nothing done. The only thing that could be heard was our breaths and the softening rain. The tension that held us captive was blazing so hot, I couldn't feel the cold air anymore.

Kai's hands squeezed around my wrists as his gaze levelled on my mouth again. "Do I still have permission to prove myself?" he rasped.

My heart stuttered. "Yes."

There was no sudden rush to mash our mouths together, but my pulse went mad with anticipation when Kai brushed the tip of his nose ever so gently across mine. He dipped his mouth and for the life of me I couldn't tell if I froze or met him halfway.

But when our lips touched… Seven years of imagining, dreaming, hoping for this moment and it was so much better than I could have ever even contemplated.

Fireworks, butterflies, violins, a shower of petals, blinding heat. Everything exploded inside me simultaneously and I swear I died for a second. But I came back to life when Kai moulded his mouth firmly around mine. Kissing me slowly with skill and warmth that anchored me to him.

I melted and sunk back against the door, letting him take my mouth however he wanted. I gave back what he gave and memorised the shape and warmth of his soft lips.

I didn't feel him let go of my wrists, but I felt the solid steel beam of his arm curve around my back and drag me flush against him. Our mouths separated for just a moment, but his palm cupped my cheek, and my hands found his shoulders, gripping them for leverage, pulling him down and closer.

With a gruff, rolling sound, he pressed his mouth heavily against mine, pushing my head back, bending my body over his arm so I had no choice but to rely on him to hold me up. I gasped at his sudden forcefulness, sparks scattering all through me.

But Kai abruptly pulled back. "Sorry—sorry, did I hurt you? Are you okay?"

I whimpered at the loss of him, clambering up him like a tree in an attempt to pull his mouth back down to mine. "No, no, I'm good, so good. It was perfect. Why did you stop?"

He drew me up, his dazed eyes flickering all over my face. "Are you sure?"

"Yes."

It was either a mad surge of power driven by adrenaline or the advantage of surprise, but I urged Kai back, and he stumbled, slamming into the other door with a grunt. I crashed into his chest, his hoodie scrunched in my fists, and giggled breathlessly when I looked up at him.

Gosh, he looked gorgeous pressed up against the door with his cheeks flushed a faint pink. His glasses sat wonky on the bride of his nose, shock widening his eyes.

"Sorry," I purred, pushing myself up onto my tiptoes, rubbing my front up against his hard body. Looping one arm around his neck, I pinched the frame of his glasses between my fingers and pulled them

off his nose. "But you stopped." His hot stare sunk to my chest as I pushed one arm of his glasses down the V-neck of my silk shirt, letting them hang there. "And I need more."

Without giving him the chance to answer, I crushed my lips against his.

He groaned, low and long, and the sound vibrated down to my core, turning me liquid and hot all over. His hand went to the back of my head, scrunching my hair tightly in his fist, holding me still as he kissed me back with just as much force. I moaned under the sensation.

Desperate to taste him, I skated my tongue out. But instead of meeting his lips I brushed against something warm and wet. *His tongue.* Just as he flicked it out to plead for entrance too.

We both gasped at the touch, and a bullet of arousal shot through my belly. My legs shook under me, but Kai crushed me against him, and we scrambled into a frenzy.

We latched onto each other, blazing greed taking the place of sweet affection. Pulling and pushing at each other. His tongue claimed mine. My lips tugged at his. His hands in my hair. My hands on his body. Hungry and needy. And it was so good. So fucking perfect.

I was swollen and throbbing for him. Silk teased the hot, sensitive skin of my inner thighs. And against the softness of my stomach, I could feel something hard pushing into me.

Kai was hard. For me. From kissing me.

A heady breath shuddered out of me as I pushed myself closer against his erection. Kai hissed a breath into my mouth and pushed back. But just as quickly as he did, both of his hands settled on my waist, and he shoved my hips away. The next thing I knew, I was pressed against the door, he was standing in my place, and the gap between our wanting bodies was way too big for my liking.

"Kai," I panted, reaching for him as my heavy lashes lifted.

With glazed eyes, he shook his head quickly. "No—no. We can't. I can't. Not like this, Esmeralda."

I nodded rapidly, tugging at his hoodie. "We can. Just like this."

"No. I'd be taking advantage of you, Esmeralda," he croaked, his face twisted.

His comment sobered me. I cupped his cheek with one hand, getting him to look right at me. "No, you wouldn't be," I said softly. "I want this. I want *you*. I've wanted you for so long, Kai."

"Exactly." He sighed, pressing his cheek into my palm. "You have liked me for so much longer when what I feel for you, Esmeralda—it's nothing I've ever felt before—but it's new and I'm still figuring out what it is. And I would feel like I was taking advantage of you if I…" He shook his head. "I cannot do that. I won't disrespect you like that. You deserve better. You deserve more."

He was being so sweet and considerate, but I still wanted to argue. "Yes, I've had a crush on you for longer, but Kai, technically my feelings for you are new too. Because the one I really like is *this* you. And I didn't know this you existed five days ago."

He smiled a tired little curl that was annoyingly sexy. "Still, Esmeralda. It's different. You know it is."

All the steam behind my argument faded away, and I slumped back against the door in defeat. "Okay, fine." I pouted through a smile. "But know that I'm damning you for being a noble prince right now."

His dimple peeked out by my thumb. "I don't think a noble prince would have a princess pinned to a door in a palace hallway where anyone could see them."

Shit, that was right. We were by the open garden doors, where anyone could have walked past.

Wait, where was Raj?

"He slipped away a while back," Kai said as I peered around us.

"Oh. I didn't notice." I shifted awkwardly. "You don't think he saw us, do you?" As much as I was used to having guards around me seeing every detail of my life, there were some things that I would rather they didn't see.

"No." Kai shivered, a little frown tugging his brows down.

"Are you cold?"

"I am now." He stepped back from the door, taking me by the hand. "Let's go somewhere else."

I grinned cheekily. "Where? Your bedroom?"

He scowled a warning. "No."

Well, it was worth a try.

CHAPTER 16

Kai

The next day was an important day.

It was the final conference of this year's Peace Celebrations—the Business Initiative Effort—that I had planned with Uncle, Fay, and a large team of civil servants and event planners.

The whole day ended with a soiree at the centuries old Pavilion City

Hall. But instead of focusing on the older CEO of the international bank, Reynold-Notts, speaking to me, I was standing in the middle of the grand room, focusing on something past his shoulder.

Through the crowd of hundreds of people in dressed-down suits—ties and blazers gone—and simple, elegant dresses, between staff holding silver trays with tall flutes of drinks. Not to the dessert table against the furthest wall like everyone else, longingly wondering if it would be socially acceptable to go for another mini apple pastry or square of chocolate cake. But to where this pint-sized crown princess was talking to a middle-aged lady and my brother, Fay.

Esmeralda. *My Esmeralda—was I allowed to call her that yet or was it too early?*

She was wearing a dress in Jahandar's national colour—a dark rose red—with matching pointed heels. The flowy skirt, sitting below her knees, was embroidered in the traditional Jahandar style of flowers and vines climbing up the fabric. It's fitted sleeves ended above her elbows, and the bodice hugged her breasts in a way that wasn't revealing, but I was having obscene thoughts of palming her over the fabric. And sat across her neck above the wide, curved neckline was a simple, elegant gold chain, matching the dangly earrings and bracelet she wore.

She looked beautiful. Stunning. Perfect. So damn distracting.

Whatever Fay leaned into her and said made her chuckle. She pushed at his shoulder playfully and I felt a pang of jealousy that it wasn't me in his place. When she tucked a lock of curled hair behind her ear, my fingers twitched around the thin glass in my hand. I wished I could play with her hair again like I had done last night in the hours we spent chatting after that mind-blowing kiss.

Seven years she'd liked me from afar, and I didn't know how she'd done it. I was struggling to last a day away from her. I wanted to be right next to her. Touching her in some way.

"What are you looking at, Your Highness?"

I shot straight and right out of my reverie as the older CEO glanced over his shoulder to follow the direction of my stare. He looked back at me with a massive grin on his face. *Shit.*

"Is the dessert table calling your name?"

I released the breath I was holding in and smiled. "You caught me," I said, feigning embarrassment, and the man chuckled.

"Caught you doing what?"

"Ah, Prince Arsh," the older CEO gushed.

I stepped back to let Uncle insert himself next to me. He'd taken off his black suit jacket like so many others and had a glass in his hand.

"I was just telling your nephew he should head over to the dessert table he's been eyeing instead of being shy like everyone else here."

Uncle chuckled and slapped a hand on my shoulder. "Morro is right. Go for it, Kai. Don't be shy."

If they both insisted, who was I to say no? Although I didn't intend to go to the dessert table directly.

With a polite thank you and smile, I headed around Uncle and the older man, placing my untouched glass on a passing staff member's silver tray. My path aimed straight for Esmeralda.

She spotted me coming towards her just as I passed her older brother, King Kareem, in conversation with the Queen of Prio and another man. Her eyes grew larger, and her sudden skittishness sent a surge of excitement rushing through me. She was trying to tame an excited smile. It wasn't quite working, and damn if I didn't find it absolutely adorable.

Leaning into Fay, she whispered something right in his ear.

It was probably wrong that I felt viciously jealous of my own brother. So much so I wanted to shove him away so her lips weren't touching the shell of his ear. I knew it was irrational, but still. I felt it.

Fay nodded at whatever Esmeralda said, his hand going to the spot between her shoulder blades. He leaned in and said something back in her ear. Jealousy bit down around my chest harder and ground its teeth together, but the burn came hand in hand with something smoky and dark.

Because Esmeralda kept her gaze on me the whole time.

Her eyes gleamed in an audacious challenge and a beckon that made me feel warm and alive inside but riled me too. She was obviously planning something. I could feel it.

With a wink in my direction, she said something to the older lady she and Fay were with. Then she spun on her heels, walking quickly away from me, a soft swing to the full curve of her hips.

Throbbing heat roared through my veins.

She wanted me to follow her, didn't she?

She drowned my doubts when she threw a glance over her shoulder, daring me to come after her. And my excitement skyrocketed.

I knew what this feeling was. The heady thrill. The aggressive need to hunt her. To catch her and put her in her place. I knew because I'd spent more nights than I could count researching what it was in an attempt to figure out why I felt it and how I could control it.

I had always been too scared to act on it. Told that wanting to be rough was wrong, therefore too anxious of anyone finding out what I wanted. Even by accident.

With Esmeralda, I knew I had to be careful, but scared? No, she didn't make me feel scared of the feeling. And maybe that was scarier.

I would've thought with my previous toxic relationship that I would've struggled to open up to Esmeralda or even admit that I was attracted to her. But I didn't. I hadn't. *I trusted her.*

So, I chased her. I bypassed Fay without even acknowledging him and followed Esmeralda with purposeful steps that I tried to keep casual. But the faster my heart pounded, the faster I walked.

Out in the corridors of the City Hall, I caught Esmeralda's hair whip around the corner to my right. I headed the same way, trying to act cool as I walked past the presence of security watching me.

The red of her dress swishing out of sight was a trigger that made me feel wild. I was possessed with the need to get to her. Thankfully, I had a natural advantage over her.

I was taller, my strides were bigger. And she was in high heels.

It didn't take me long to catch up to her. She gasped and attempted to zip around the corner as fast as she could, but I snatched her by the arm, and we went around together. I spun her back to the wall and curled my arm around her waist, dragging her body to mine.

She slammed into me, her hands clinging to my biceps, my legs bracketing hers. Her stomach cushioned my half-erect dick. Big eyes locked with mine. Lips parted. Chest heaving. Shaking.

Or maybe that was me. Because I was aroused in a way I really shouldn't have been in public.

Cupping the back of her head, I angled her back to take my kiss. She moaned as I lavished her mouth with barely restrained control, giving her the attention I hadn't been able to give her all day.

I couldn't say how long we kissed, only that we kissed with tongue and teeth like our lives depended on it. But not once did that silk thread of control snap. Even in our drugged state, we both knew we couldn't go back to the hall full of hundreds of people with an after-sex glow on our skin.

That wasn't to say when the kiss faded into a string of long-second pecks that my mouth wasn't stinging, and Esmeralda's lips weren't swollen and bright red.

Her hands found my ears to trace, and my arms cinched around her waist, hugging her close. I dropped my mouth into the crook where her neck met her shoulder and pressed a string of kisses to her warm skin as I drowned myself in her scent.

She smelt so ridiculously good. Sweet like a peony rose, with a mellow fruity undertone. It was addictive. I could have kept my face buried in her neck for hours. But with one more kiss, I forced my head up and let her hand guide me until our foreheads were resting together.

"Hi," she whispered after a moment.

"Hi," I rasped back, rubbing the length of her back with one hand.

"I missed you."

I felt myself smile and didn't try to fight it. "I have been at the same event as you all day."

"Yes, but you've been so far away all day. So, I missed you."

It was a struggle to remember why I'd been frustrated earlier when she was being so cute. But I managed to pull back and arch a brow. "Is that why you've been giving me teasing glances all day?"

She bit down on her bottom lip, trying to hide a cheeky smile. "Teasing glances?" She widened her eyes innocently. "I don't know what you mean."

"You know exactly what I mean, Esmeralda."

"Do I?" she purred and grazed her nails down the back of my neck, causing me to shiver.

I pressed my forehead against hers and closed my eyes. I took a slow, deep breath and clung onto her hips with a vice-like grip that probably left marks. She didn't seem to mind, and I couldn't bring myself to let go. "We're supposed to be behaving," I whispered.

She brushed her nose across mine. "You're the only one who wants to behave. I just want you."

My cock and heart throbbed in sync, but I shook my head. "Not here. Not like this. And not yet."

"So damn stubborn," she muttered and slumped against me, relenting.

I lifted my head and pressed my lips to her forehead. "I am, but it's for you."

"I know."

I kissed her forehead again. "We should go back."

She hummed, looking up at me contently. "One more kiss."

I cupped her cheeks in my hands and obliged her demand, giving her an extra one just in case. "There." I brushed my thumb across her plump bottom lip. "Are you satisfied, Babble?"

She blinked, but I didn't realise what I had said until her eyes went wide and her cheeks screamed with colour. "Babble?" she stuttered.

One side of my mouth pulled up. "It suits you."

She knocked me in the chest in an adorable outburst. "No, it doesn't. How many times do I have to tell you, I don't babble."

I let her shove me back and chuckled as she stormed away before pushing my hands into my suit trouser pockets and following her.

I liked it. *Babble.*

It suited her perfectly.

For the rest of the soiree, every time our eyes met, her cheeks went bright red, and she glared at me. It was a challenge and a half not to burst out laughing in adoration every time she did.

CHAPTER 17
Esmeralda

"**I** wish your father would trim his beard. He looks awful, he does."

If I clenched my teeth any harder, I was going to shatter them all. But I couldn't laugh. I was sitting in Kareem's direct eyeline and if he caught me acting any less than a perfectly decorous crown princess, he would destroy me for it after. And I had been doing so well to keep him off my back since arriving in Touma.

But the older woman sitting among her family in the lower pew in front of me was killing me.

On her right, Fay snickered into his fist while the adorable Adam remained engrossed in his parent's speech. But on her left, Kai shifted awkwardly, and Prince Arsh sighed again.

"Gigi, please," Kai grumbled for the twelfth time in fifteen minutes. *I'd been counting.*

"Mother," Prince Arsh murmured from the other side of Kai. "Could you perhaps listen to your eldest son talk for five minutes without commenting?"

"What? You know I'm right. It's Formation Day for Neves's sake and he looks like an ogre."

I tried to bite back my laugh, but it fluttered from my grinning mouth anyway.

Gisselle Rumina Touma—the happily divorced, retired Queen of Touma, and King Rami and Prince Arsh's mother—with cropped white hair that put her diamond tiara to shame and an attitude to match, hadn't stopped nit-picking at her children since the ceremony had started two hours ago.

She'd snuck into residence at Chaukham Palace while we had all been at the Business Initiative soiree last night in Pavilion City Hall. Like the badass dowager queen she was, she casually made herself known at breakfast, shocking her family with her early appearance.

Her live commentary had been my highlight of Formation Day— the first official ceremony of the Peace Celebrations. It marked the day the first seven monarchs signed the Declaration of Independence and Peace 874 years ago to form the modern states and monarchies. Exactly 363 days after the end of The Great Rebellion of Zorro.

The service was being held in the Public House attached to the back of Westcombe Palace in Central Pavilion City. The long, gothic, stone building with a high vaulted ceiling and low hanging, black iron chandeliers was stunning, and seated over two-thousand people.

All the monarchs were sitting in high-backed chairs on a wooden stage, draped in a red carpet. It ran between the staggered pews at the front all the way down to the huge, arched entranceway, where crowds of people watched the ceremony on big screens outside.

Media crews lined the walls and I hoped with everything in me that my laugh had gone unnoticed by them, because it didn't go unnoticed by the people in front of me.

Four heads turned back to look at me and I froze as a hot blush crept through my face.

Prince Arsh grinned at me with pure amusement that glimmered through Fay's hazel eyes too, while Kai's gaze made my heart pound like it always did. But it was the Dowager Queen's narrow stare that made me sit straighter.

They were the same hazelly colour as her two sons', but for some reason they felt inquisitively sharper. Wrinkles lined her eyes, mouth, and forehead, but she looked good for her seventy-something years. Even if she was a little intimidating in the same way a headmistress was with her thin lips pressed firm, her arched brows raised in question, and her chin tipped high.

I shifted on the bench awkwardly. "Apologies," I whispered.

The older lady kept me under the scrutiny of her stare for a few uncomfortable seconds longer after the others turned away. I exhaled slowly and finally tried to focus on what Kai's parents were saying.

"…a new world, a new beginning, a second chance," Queen Leila said, turning the page of the papers laid on the podium before her, a beautiful crown sitting atop her coiffured raven black hair. "That is what Formation Day marks. And though we may have changed greatly since the days of our foremothers and forefathers as individuals, as communities, as nations, but most of all as a world, by no means can we ever forget what the declaration stood for. Together, we must remind ourselves of its importance. For when we come together, stand together, and remember together, our alliances grow ever stronger. And stronger alliances make for better cooperation, better communication, and a better Neves for everyone. So, I ask everyone to rise together please."

All the kings and queens seated behind King Rami and Queen Leila slowly stood as the two stepped back from the podiums. Chairs scraped the wooden floor when over two thousand people rose with them. I placed my hand flat over my heart in the same way everyone else did.

"Mesha ki uri Cheiftan! Azaad jahan Neves! Zakoon el raha!"

There was a quick collective pause. *"Long live our rulers! Long be free Neves! For ever have peace!"*

After a luncheon with all two thousand plus attendants of the Formation Day ceremony, a private gathering was held for royalty, government and council officials, and their families in the Grand Hall of Westcombe Palace. So, the historic room, once used as a ballroom, was packed to say the least.

But amongst all the glitzy people, laughing and chatting, Kai and

I managed to stick together. Eventually, we found ourselves tucked near the curving entrance staircase where Fay joined us.

Fay bumped my arm, his hazel eyes shimmering as he nodded his head to his left. "I think Gigi's taken an interest in you, Esmeralda."

"Gigi?" I echoed as I followed the direction of his nod.

"He means our grandmother," Kai said just as I found Dowager Queen Gisselle's stare on me.

"Oh." I straightened instinctively and gulped, offering her a smile. Her eyes flickered all over me like I was being judged for a contest I hadn't known I'd entered. She flicked her head away. I was pretty sure I didn't win first place. Or second. Maybe not even tenth. "I hope that's not a bad thing."

Fay opened his mouth to answer, but it was Kai's voice I heard. "It's not," he said firmly.

"Are you sure? I didn't offend her earlier, did I?"

"You didn't. I'm sure. She doesn't think badly of you."

"Kai's right," Fay added. "She doesn't. She liked that you laughed at her joke." He smirked at his older brother. "And I'm pretty sure she sent me over here to make sure Kai wasn't boring you to death. He might be Gigi's favourite but even she knows how dreary his personality is."

I chuckled as my gaze went from a mischievous-looking Fay to Kai, awkwardly rubbing his left earlobe as he obviously fought not to frown. The two brothers couldn't have been more different.

If Kai was dreary then Fay was a charmingly arrogant bad boy meets smouldering prince.

He was a year younger than Shehryar, and as well as being the second prince of Touma, he was also a well-known artist which only added to his charm. He had his father's hazel eyes, his mother's slim, elegant features on a square-jawed face, and raven black hair that fell to his chin, though he'd tied it back for the event. He wasn't as tall as Kai and Adam, but he was definitely the prettier brother.

"He's not boring me," I said. "If anything, he's probably getting tired of listening to me *babble*."

Kai's eyes lit up and his dimple made a long-second appearance.

"I'm not. You know I couldn't."

"Well," Fay said, dragging the word. "Kai is known for having a social battery that lasts about twenty minutes maximum, so don't be offended if he makes a run for the nearest exit to recharge."

"That's not true," Kai grumbled, tugging at his ear.

Fay and I chuckled, but we were interrupted by a woman's husky voice. "I thought I'd find you lingering here."

I whipped around and stilled.

The woman was stunning. Tall and slim like a model and wrapped in a sandy-coloured dress, with distinct red eyes, but her long, straight hair was a deep brown, suggesting she was only half Crimson Cast. She looked oddly familiar.

"What are you doing here?" Fay spat viciously.

"I was invited like everyone else, Fay. You might recall that my dad won the council leadership elections in Finlark this September gone." She sighed. "Oh, relax Fay. I'm allowed to say hi to my ex-fiancé after all these years, aren't I?"

And then it hit me.

Meg. She was Meg Fletcher. Kai's ex-fiancée.

My gaze went to Kai next to me. He was frozen in place, his face painfully pale. My insides twisted in discomfort, caution ringing loud and clear.

I stood tall and moved closer to Kai, pressing my arm to his in silent support. Meg's eyes travelled over me, and she smiled vacantly. "Hi," she said, seemingly harmlessly.

"Hi," I replied, and that was it. She acted as if I didn't exist after that. All the hatred rolling off her in thick waves was directed solely at Kai.

"You're not going to say hi to me?" she asked him, her tone sharp.

"No," Kai rasped quietly. "I'm not."

Lasers beamed from her irises. "Wow. You've grown an attitude since we last spoke, haven't you?" She cocked her head. "What happened to the sweet boy who was in love with me?"

My hands balled to fists as vexation churned inside me.

I didn't instantly dislike very many people, but I *hated* her. I hated the way she was patronising Kai.

"He opened his eyes," he said, his tone firmer this time.

Meg chuckled, elegantly arching a brow. "You're still as cute as ever."

I felt Kai shift against me. "Leave."

Colour touched Meg's pale cheeks, but she quickly hid her surprise behind a sickly-sweet smile. "At least give me a chance to catch up with you. I want to know how the Perfect Prince has been doing."

"No," Kai bit out. "Leave. *Now.*"

It was disconcerting how quickly her smile dropped and was replaced with flames of loathing. She opened her mouth, but Fay stepped forward. "I think it's time you left. Or we'll have your father escort you out in front of everyone."

Her demeanour changed again, and it was as if someone else was controlling her with a flick of a switch. She gave a big, over-the-top smile. "Oh, there's no need to get Dad involved, I'm going." She waved her hand around. "I'm too busy to attend any of the other events with him, so this was my only chance to see how you were doing. I'm glad to see you're doing well, Kai. Until next time."

Meg didn't bother bowing, just fluttered her fingers and strut away straight for the main entrance door, leaving behind a bleak tension.

"Fuck," Fay hissed, running a hand over his hair. "What was her father thinking, bringing her with him here? Is he mad?"

I faced Kai, searching the hollowness that painted his face. "Are you okay?"

He nodded, barely. "Hmm."

He was lying. He wasn't okay.

But he was a prince, and we were in public. He had no choice but to pretend he was.

And neither did I.

CHAPTER 18
Esmeralda

When we returned to Chaukham Palace that afternoon, while the reigning monarchs left for another walkabout in the city, Kai quietly disappeared.

For the first forty minutes or so, I didn't look for him. But I became restless. I was worried about him. He didn't have to tell me anything, I just needed to know he was okay, so I went searching for him.

Michael, Kai's equerry, found me in the corridors blindly searching for Kai's office. He kindly informed me that Kai wasn't even there.

"He went to the gardens? In the cold?" I asked in surprise.

Michael grinned boyishly. "Shocking, I know, but true. He was taking a walk with Prince Arsh."

So, I headed outside, but I only found Prince Arsh. He was talking to a dark-skinned, teddy-bear-like man with a big belly by a large white marble fountain that sat in a broken circle of trimmed, evergreen hedges.

"Esmeralda," Prince Arsh said when he saw me coming between two hedges towards them. "Where's your coat?"

"Why is that the first thing everyone says to me?" I said then turned to the man. "Hello. I don't think we've met before."

"Hello, Your Highness." He bowed over his big belly. "I'm Bruno, the head gardener."

"It's nice to meet you, Bruno. You and your team have done a lovely job with the gardens."

"Why thank you, Your Highness." He beamed. "But we can't take all the credit. Prince Arsh, Her Majesty, Queen Leila, and Prince Kai have all had their inputs too."

"Oh, really?" I glanced hopefully at Prince Arsh, flicking at my nails restlessly. "Talking of Kai, Michael told me he was with you."

Prince Arsh nodded. "He was. He's in the glasshouse now. Would you like me to take you over?"

"*Please.*"

He jerked his head to the left. "Come on then. I'll be right back, Bruno."

With a nod to the head gardener, I followed Prince Arsh to the western side of the gardens. He took me through a few hedge archways until a long glasshouse appeared at the end of a short path.

"Fay said you were there when Meg approached him," Prince Arsh eventually said.

"I was." I looked up at him. "Was Kai okay—when you were with him?"

"He was…quiet." He sighed and rubbed his jaw slowly. "Has he told you anything about his relationship with Meg?"

"No. But I don't want to know if he doesn't want to tell me. I just want to see that he's okay."

Prince Arsh offered me a smile as we came to a stop in front of the tall, misted door. "I don't know where he is inside, but I haven't seen him come out so he's still in there." He ruffled my hair like I was a little child. "I'm sure he'll be glad to see you."

"Can I ask you something?" I heard myself blurt before he could turn away.

"Of course," he said, slipping his hands into his trouser pockets.

"Why did you never marry?"

It wasn't a question I should have been asking. It was none of my damn business. But for some reason, I needed to know. Thankfully,

Prince Arsh didn't appear offended. In fact, he looked amused.

"Well, part of my reason was to spite my asshole of a father who tried every method under the sun to get me married to a girl of his choosing." His smirk lifted higher. It was obvious who Fay inherited his bad boy flare from—definitely wasn't his parents. "*But.* I also never found anyone who looked at me the way you look at my dear nephew."

He left me with a wink, and I smiled at the empty spot he'd stood in for a few moments. Then taking a deep breath, I faced the misted door of the glasshouse.

Inside, it almost felt like I'd been transported back home to Jahandar. The climate was warm, the scent of soil and humidity filling the air. A variety of tropical plants and trees were spread between twisting gravel paths, and it was all tied together by the distant sound of trickling water.

I followed the path that headed right but took a detour halfway when I heard the repeated scrape of metal against a stone surface. Through the purple leaves of a tree draping above the path, I spotted Kai's raven black hair. A quiet sigh lifted from me in relief.

He was sat in front of a rectangular raised bed with his side-profile to me. His large body was folded on a low wooden bench that could probably seat two but still looked a touch too small for him. His crisp suit had been replaced with dark green overalls and scuffed brown boots. And in his orange-gloved hands he held a grassy, potted plant while several more were dotted around him.

Instead of interrupting him, I watched him for a quiet minute, admiring the relaxed droop in his shoulders as he gently worked the plant out of its pot. He was oblivious to my presence, and as much as I wanted to be by his side, I didn't want to disturb his peace and quiet.

Sometimes, a moment alone was just what someone needed, and I could appreciate that was probably what Kai had wanted. So, once I'd had my fill of him, I turned away.

"Esmeralda."

My feet came to an instant stop. I guess he hadn't been so oblivious after all.

I swivelled back around and fell straight into the muted darkness of his stare. "Sorry," I muttered. "I didn't know where you were and Prince Arsh said you were here, so I just wanted to see you."

He shook his head. "Don't apologise. I'm the one who disappeared without a word. I should have told you where I was going. I'm sorry."

"Well," I stretched the word teasingly. "You did lose it when I disappeared on you, so…" He gave me a weak smile and it felt like a small reward. "But you're forgiven, Mr Perfect Prince. You needed time alone and I get that. I just wanted to see you were okay, so I'll leave—"

"Stay."

His quiet plea tugged at my heartstrings until I was being pulled to him. He took one orange glove off and held out his hand, helping me down onto the bench next to him.

"I have a condition to staying though." I leaned over to pick up the small hand trowel pushed into the soil in front of us. "I want to help you plant."

Without a word, he stood up and headed off to the left. He came back with another pair of orange gloves. "I couldn't find a smaller size, but they'll keep your hands clean."

I thanked him and took them. "What do you need me to do?" I asked once I had them on.

"Could you make three holes about fifteen centimetres apart?"

A peaceful silence fell between us as I started digging with the small trowel and Kai prepared another plant. But me being me, I couldn't keep quiet for long around him.

"You didn't tell me you're into gardening."

Kai patted a handful on soil over the base of a twig-like plant. "I don't know if I can claim to be *into* gardening, but I help out when I have time or when I need a break."

I leaned into him. "You look sexy in dirty overalls."

His mouth twitched but he frowned across his shoulder. "Behave, Babble."

I chuckled, but the weight of Kai's stare sobered the moment. "Aren't you going to ask me about her?" he mumbled. "Why our engagement ended?"

"No," I said softly. "I cannot say I'm not curious, but whatever happened, I can tell it wasn't good. I'm not going to make you talk about it if you don't want to." I sat a little straighter. "But—I would like to say that I have never disliked someone as quickly as I did her. The way she patronised you made me want to throw a brick in her face."

His dimple made a faint appearance. "You wouldn't be the first to say that."

"I don't normally swear, but she was a B—I—T—C—H."

"She's a narcissist," he said, distracting himself with the plant he'd already buried. "She was always nice until it didn't suit her, and then she was…cruel and manipulative. And it took me too long to realise it was a form of abuse."

Dread curled all over me, leaving an icy sensation on my skin. I sat immobile as Kai picked up the plant next to him and gently eased it out of the pot.

"The counsellor I saw after our engagement ended told me emotional abuse isn't always obvious at first, because abusers have a way of making you believe it was a one-off or it was just all in your head. And you believe it, because the person you're in a relationship is supposed to care about you. So why would they be trying to hurt you? That's what you try to convince yourself…and that's how it was for me too."

"The first few months I was dating Meg were…great," he explained, staring absently at the soil. "I was twenty-two and she was twenty-four. I had finished university, and I was trying to grasp my duty as a prince, and she was just starting out in a news station. But we were there for each other and whatever free time we had, we spent it together.

"But she started changing. She started verbally abusing me. Belittling the things I liked. Humiliating me in front of her friends as a joke. Making me feel like I was treating her badly. And I believed her, even if a part of me wasn't sure it was true." He turned his hollow gaze to me. "Because when someone is constantly telling you you're a bad person you start thinking it too."

A bitter prickling sensation crawled through the back of my nose. "Did anyone see what she was doing to you?"

He nodded. "No one knew details, but everyone around me knew something was wrong. Father, Mother, Fay, Gigi, and Uncle Arsh, even my friends, they all tried to talk to me and convince me to rethink my relationship with her. I could hear them, I knew they were right, but Meg had me pressed under her thumb so hard, I didn't know how to get out. And instead of trying to end things with her, I proposed to her."

"Why?"

He shrugged a shoulder. "I don't know. I suppose a part me was trying to prove her wrong for claiming I wasn't serious about her. And the other part stupidly hoped she would change if things between us progressed."

"She didn't..." I whispered. A thick lump was blocking my throat.

"She didn't," he echoed and took a long pause. "Six months into our engagement, I caught her bullying Adam when I invited her over for dinner. He was fourteen." Kai's face screwed up in resentment. "I will never forget how scared he looked. But seeing her treat him the exact way she had been treating me, I realised that I couldn't do it anymore. She was never going to change, and I couldn't spend the rest of my life with someone who could hurt a child.

"I was so angry I nearly threw her out the palace. Father and Uncle stopped me, but the next day her father came to us, and we agreed on a settlement. The end of our engagement would be announced as a mutual decision, but Meg was to cut all ties with me immediately.

"It was a few days later that Adam told me she'd been horrible to him before too." A dampness filled Kai's eyes and what was left of my heart broke into a million sharp pieces. "I hated myself for letting him get hurt. I hated that I hadn't stopped her. I had been so weak because of her—"

I all but threw myself at Kai, wrapping my arms around his neck and crushing him in a hug as a few tears slipped down my face. "It wasn't your fault. It was *never* your fault," I cried.

Everything hurt. Every corner of my body. In equal parts anger and pain. For everything Kai had been through. All the hurt and abuse he'd had to deal with. No wonder he reacted the way he had when he thought I'd hurt Adam in the library. It was all because of her.

How could she? *How dare she.* I wanted to scream at her and expose her to the world as a disgusting, narcissistic, abusive bitch for ever daring to make Kai feel so small.

My tears wouldn't stop. They flowed harder and angrier with every passing second. Especially when I realised for nearly half the years I spent admiring Kai from afar, his smiles and laughter had been hiding so much pain. And then I was angry at myself for never noticing he was hurting.

With some adjustment, Kai pulled me onto his lap, so I was sitting sideways on his thighs. And like a clingy koala bear, I pressed closer as he wrapped his arms around my waist.

"Shh, don't cry. Esmeralda, please. I'm sorry. I'm sorry for upsetting you," he whispered, pressing a gloveless hand to the back of my hair.

"Why are you apologising?" I blubbered with an angry tug at his overalls. "And I'm angry. I'm angry *for* you. At her. What she did—it was never your fault, and I hate that she made you think that."

"I know. I know that now, I do. So don't cry for me, please." He squeezed me gently and pressed a kiss to the side of head. "I don't like seeing you in tears, Babble." *Kiss.*

He landed several more kisses, soft and sweet, against my hair. Eventually my tears dried, and my breaths evened out, leaving only silence as he rubbed my back in long, languid caresses.

"How are you feeling?" he murmured into my hair.

Well, I practically bawled like a baby in front of the guy I liked, so…embarrassed.

Plus, my eyes felt heavy and tired, hopefully my mascara hadn't run, but my face was definitely blotchy and red. Otherwise, I was pretty sure I had exhausted my emotional capacity for the moment, but I had to admit, I felt better. It had been so long since I'd let myself cry like that.

"I'm okay," I mumbled, untangling myself from around him. "But I probably look awful."

He cupped my jaw with a lop-sided curl on his mouth. "A little pink, but not awful. Never awful. You're beautiful, Esmeralda."

"A little pink" didn't sound beautiful to me, but that wasn't important.

"I hope you know that she never deserved you," I said resolutely. "You were always too good for her, and she failed to treat you the way you deserved. You deserve *everything*, Kai. The entire universe. And I will do my utmost best to give it to you for as long as you'll have me."

His brows plunged into a frown. "*For as long as I'll have you?* What does that mean?" His gloveless hand slipped up my back to cup my nape, firmly. Dare I say possessively. "I understand this thing between us is new, but I don't like how you have so easily assumed that I will grow bored of you. Because I won't. So don't say something like that again."

Woah…well…fuck. There went my heart all over again.

It filled so much that it exploded and merged with the molten rush of throbs between my legs, scorching me inside out.

How was this man so flipping hot? His touch. His voice. That look. His confident claim. Did he have any idea the kind of effect his words had on me? On the direction of my thoughts?

Hint: they involved a lot of moaning, screaming, thrusting and maybe some spanking, and a bed. In fact, there didn't need to be a bed.

I gulped slowly, rubbing my thighs together. "That was very sexy. But also a little…assertive too."

Something wary flickered through his eyes. "Would you rather I wasn't? *Assertive.*"

"No." My mouth curled as I spread my hands over his jaw. "I like it."

I might've initiated the kiss, but with a gruff sound, Kai took control immediately, licking the shape of my bottom lip. He tugged me back by the hair and wrapped his tongue around mine. Slow, yet forceful, making me hunger for his warm, male taste as he kissed the fucking life out of me.

I was panting for air, my head foggy, by the time he was done with me. He'd stolen all my strength and sense from me. And I loved the feeling. I loved his kisses.

Kai groaned as his glazed eyes flickered all over my face. "Babble," he rasped through gritted teeth. "Don't look at me like that."

"It's your fault for kissing me like that, Mr Perfect Prince," I purred with a smirk, pressing myself close to him; he made me feel so sexy and powerful.

He inhaled slowly and deeply like he was fighting for control. But his stare dipped to my stinging lips as he traced them with his thumb. "Say something else. Ask me something else. Before I do it again." I opened my mouth instantly, but his lashes snapped up faster. "*Don't ask me to do it again.*"

Dammit, how had he known? I pushed my mouth into a pout.

I wasn't sure if I was impressed he could read me so well or annoyed with his level of restraint. A level I could never achieve. But that only made me want to tease and frustrate him more so his restraint would snap, and he would take it out on me.

I'd let him punish me however he wanted. Because that was what I wanted. *More than anything.*

"I wasn't," I said, tipping my chin up. "I was going to ask for your number. So, the next time one of us disappears, we can message each other instead of searching the whole palace for one another."

Maybe a few suggestive messages would help me in my "*frustrate-him*" mission too.

CHAPTER 19
Esmeralda

By the time night came that day, Kai and I had already exchanged well over a hundred messages. Most of which had been after dinner while we sat opposite each other in a seating room set up with an eighty-inch TV screen and several game consoles.

Squished onto three sofas, Kai, Fay, Adam, Prince Arsh, Princess Dabira of Shah, her brother—the King's three teenage children, and I had spent a few hours competitively playing video games.

I spent half the time sending Kai frisky messages. Then pretending I couldn't feel him furiously raking my body all over with his eyes, while struggling to contain a bratty, breathless smile.

That being said, I hadn't played many games one on one with Kai, so when we met outside my room just over an hour after we all dispersed, I dragged him back to the same room to play.

We were sitting on a makeshift mattress on the carpet against one dark blue sofa that we had made using a blanket and the cushions of the other two sofas. The dark curtains were drawn and the chandelier on the ceiling remained unlit, but the two lamps on either side of the sofa and the TV screen brightened the room more than enough.

"*Player two defeated*," emanated from the large TV in a low, overexaggerated male voice.

I giggled as my character did a victory roar on the huge screen while Kai's character lay flat on his face in the retro street fighter game. For the fifth time in a row. I dared to glance at him.

He was glaring at me through his black-rimmed glasses so

furiously his brows practically touched. I was sure I could hear his teeth grinding together with how tight his jaw looked.

"I don't want to play anymore," he grumbled, dropping his controller on the blanket over our laps.

I laughed again and Kai glared grumpily at the TV screen, tugging at his ear. *So fucking cute!* I pushed the fluffy grey blanket off me, scrambling onto my knees to face him fully. "Do you know how adorable you look when you pull at your ear, all grumpy and embarrassed?" I cooed.

He gave me a frustrated side-glance as he crossed his arms over his chest, pulling his grey hoodie taut.

Grinning, I shuffled a little closer to him. "Don't be mad, Mr Perfect Prince. We can play again, and I'll go easy on you this time. Hmm?"

The crevice between his brows deepened as his lashes dipped. I followed his gaze.

From the black cotton of my shorts that had ridden up to the very top of my bare thighs. Over the matching cropped T-shirt, stopping where the buttons were strained across my chest—I *might* have purposely chosen the set I knew fit snuggly.

His tongue pushed against the inside of his cheek before his eyes clashed with mine again. Hot. Angry. Hungry. *Perfect*. Exactly what I wanted.

I quirked a brow, resting my hands on either side of my knees, knowing the pose would push my boobs together. "Is there something distracting you, Mr Perfect Prince?" I purred.

"You know *exactly* what has been distracting me, Esmeralda," he said. I widened my eyes in mock innocence. His arms came loose from across his chest as he glared at me, and excited prickles burst all over my skin. "Did you think sending those messages was funny?"

"Funny?" I echoed. "No." I reached out and put a hand on one bulky shoulder of his and swung my leg over his thighs, straddling his lap. "I wasn't aiming for funny."

"You're being a brat, Esmeralda," he growled, his hands finding my waist and clamping down hard.

Maybe that one word wasn't supposed to arouse me as much as it did, but it was everything dark and sensual inside me that I hid behind the act of a polite, only-fucks-in-missionary princess. It was my escape. My freedom to act how I wanted and be punished for it without losing a sense of control.

Yet all the playfulness I felt was pushed to the back of my mind when something conflicted and anxious painted over Kai's face before he squeezed his eyes shut.

Curling one hand around the back of his neck and cupping his cheek with the other, I leaned into him. Cradling him with my entire body. "What's wrong, Kai?" I whispered.

He circled his arms around my back, holding me close. "Don't think that I don't want you, Esmeralda, I do. So much." He pressed his forehead to mine. "But if you ever thought I was using you as a distraction because of today I..."

I smiled to myself. "I mean, considering *you're* the one who's making us both wait because *you* wanted to respect my feelings, I don't think I could mistakenly think you were using me, Kai. *Ever.*"

He huffed an amused sound. "And you have made it your mission to drive me mad because of that decision since," he growled lightly. "And it's working, Babble. It's fucking working, but..."

"But?"

"But I need you to understand you were right." He drew back enough to look me right in the eyes. "I *can* be assertive. But I want to be—more so." He visibly swallowed. "As much as I want to be gentle with you, I want..."

He squeezed me closer, but he didn't say anything, seemingly struggling to admit what he wanted aloud. I could have filled in the gap for him, but I didn't. It felt important to let him say it himself.

I brushed a reassuring thumb across his cheekbone as he opened his mouth again. "I want to be rough with you, Esmeralda. More than just rough." He looked right into my eyes. "I want to be something like a...a dominant to you. But I know not everyone likes that, or they think it's weird or wrong, and if you don't want that, if you don't want me to be, I won't be." He shook his head. "*Ever.* I would never do anything you didn't like, Esmeralda. Nor would I *ever* hurt you."

Maybe it was the way he said it—quick, worried, almost apologetic—but I had a feeling Meg was the one who had made him feel that way. That it was wrong or that he needed to be sorry for what he liked, which wasn't true. And I hated that so much.

I captured his mouth in a kiss, heavy but quick. "I want you to dominate me, Kai," I said against his lips. "And I know you would never hurt me, but you don't have to *worry* about hurting me either. We can discuss our limits, and we can have a safe word too. Something obvious and easy to remember, and something we can both use too."

"*Monkey*," he muttered after a few moments, searching for agreement.

"*Monkey*," I echoed, smiling widely. "I like that. Easy to remember and obvious."

A comfortable silence fell between us. All soft smiles and softer stares. But softness wasn't what I wanted from Kai anymore. Especially when I could still feel the bulge of his dick.

I cocked my chin playfully. "Aren't you going to touch me now, Mr Perfect Prince?" I purred, squeezing his shoulders as I edged a little forward on his lap. "Or are you hesitating, because truthfully, you're all talk and no walk. Only able to play half games with me."

He narrowed his eyes, ominous heat flaring through them and spurring thrill through me. "You know." I rolled my hips on a sigh; he was rubbing right against my clit through our clothing. "Kiss me but won't fuck me. Chase me but won't capture me." His fingers dug deliciously hard into my waist.

"Call me a brat." I smirked. "But don't have the guts to *tame* me."

His hand came out of nowhere. As vicious and fast as a snake as he clamped it around my throat and dragged me to him. I gasped in shock, a molten ache of wanton delight ripping through my core.

That was all it took. *One. Fucking. Touch.* And there was a puddle in my sheer thong.

"Just because I haven't," he whispered so deceptively unassuming that the hairs on the back of my neck stood on end, "doesn't mean I can't, Babble. So, watch what you say."

With a hard thudding in my chest, I quirked my brows. "Then prove it. Because I don't believe—"

Kai mashed his mouth over mine, squeezing on my throat lightly as he took full advantage of my surprise. He thrust his tongue right into my mouth, his lashings bordering on base and bruising—the complete opposite to how a prince was meant to kiss by the standard of society and fairy tales. But I took it with a moan of gratitude, wrapping myself around him as if he was my source of life.

He mapped my bare thigh with a pawing hand and slipped under my shorts. His callused palm rubbed my skin to gooseflesh before he squeezed my arse cheek. Hard. Needy moans lifted from our throats, and I drank his as eagerly as he drank mine. But then he stole his mouth away from me.

"Tonight will only be about you," he panted, straightening his glasses. "Is that clear?"

Hopelessly wet and voracious, I nodded. At that point, I would've agreed to damn well anything he had said.

"Turn around and put your back to my chest."

I might have been a brat, but I was also eager to please, hungry for praise and affection. So, the moment he let go of my throat, I was scrambling off his lap to do as I'd been told. The TV screen went black just as I slumped back against the secure warmth of his chest.

Within seconds, he lifted his knees and spread his legs. He swiftly hooked my bare thighs over each of his thighs, the soft cotton of his pyjama bottoms rubbing against my hot skin. My feet didn't quite touch the makeshift mattress under us, leaving me suspended, but the helpless feeling of being completely at his mercy only turned me on all the more.

He cupped my chin in his palm, gently tilting my face up to him. "Are you okay?"

I nodded. "Yes. Are you?"

"I am." He stroked my jaw. "Promise me you'll use *'monkey'* if at any point you want me to stop."

"I promise. But promise me you will use it too, Kai. And if I ask for something you don't want to do, then you will tell me."

"I promise." He touched his lips to mine so softly it was more of a caress than an actual kiss.

But. The Kai who stared down at me a breath later knew nothing about softness or hesitation.

This Kai held himself like a powerful king, but his expression belonged to a man of the shadows. Dark and authoritative. Eyes aglow with lust. Piercing and wicked.

This Kai didn't like being messed with. *But I had done just that.*

Maybe I was beginning to regret it…only a little.

"This entire time, Esmeralda," he said, holding my chin up high so I was looking right at him, "all I wanted was for you to be sure that I cared about you before anything more happened. But did you think holding back didn't frustrate me too? That it didn't kill me every time I stopped?"

I sucked in a breath as I felt the first stroke of his fingers up my inner thigh, but when I tried to look, he squeezed my chin, holding me still. "Answer me. Did you consider how I was feeling?"

"No," I croaked.

His fingers slid higher, blunt nails taunting my skin with embers. "What did you do instead?"

I couldn't think as his touch skimmed the edge of the cotton right between my legs. "I—I teased you." I tried to wriggle my hips to get his fingers where I needed him—

Slap.

I heard the light sound snap around us at the same time I felt the sweet sting of it zip up my clit and electrify my belly. My entire body jolted as a choked sound was torn from me.

He glared down at me, velvet dark and threatening. "Don't. Move."

"Kai," I sobbed, clinging onto his wrists to anchor myself.

"Did you like that?" he asked, soothing his thumb over where he had spanked me.

I bit down on my lip hard and nodded. And just as quickly, his fingers came down on my clit again. I mewled in shock. Another, and my thighs shook. Again, and my lungs twisted to knots.

Slap. Slap. Each one harder and meaner.

Slap. Slap. Slap. Each a spiking needle of stinging pleasure that made me cry out and squirm.

Panting heavily, Kai dropped his hand from my chin to my throat, pinning my head back to his shoulder. He soothed the throbbing heat between my thighs with light strokes of his fingers, while his heart slammed against my back as hard as his bulging dick was digging into my arse.

"Are you going to act like a brat again, Esmeralda?" he growled in my ear, his breath assaulting my skin with a rush of prickles. "Are you going to tease me with *filthy* messages when we're in a room full of people and then pretend as if you're not trying to make me hard on purpose?"

I shook my head as much as I could, dazed and teary-eyed. "No—no. I won't. I won't—I'm sorry."

"You're sorry? Really?" He scoffed. I nodded quickly. "Then prove it, Babble. Show me how sorry you are. Pull your shorts and underwear to the side so I can see your pretty little pussy."

I quickly went to work to do as he said, hooking two fingers under my shorts and thong and dragging them to the side. Showing myself to the both of us.

Swollen and bare except for a tamed, little triangle of hair, and fucking soaked already.

I was too greedy for his reaction to feel any embarrassment over being the only one exposed.

"Fuck," he groaned, low and long. Desperate to see his face, I tried to glance up at him, but he growled and tightened his hand on my throat. "No. Keep looking at yourself as I touch you."

He didn't have to tell me twice. I watched like a hawk as he slid his middle finger over the swollen bud of nerves at the crest of my sex and down between my wetness. Slow and testing. I went taut as warm pleasure fluttered through my belly.

"You're so fucking swollen and wet for me," he said with a sigh as he repeated the same movement.

His mouth landed on my neck, licking and kissing, as he rubbed my clit with more pressure. I moaned loudly as the sensations fused inside me and curled my free hand back to find purchase on his hair.

Without warning, he pushed a broad finger inside me, and my mouth opened on a silent sound.

"So tight, Babble," Kai groaned thickly as he dragged his finger slowly out. "So sweet." And pushed further in. "So beautiful." *Out.* "So perfect." *In.* "You're perfect, Esmeralda." *Out.*

He took my lips in a heavy kiss and nudged another finger into me on the thrust in. And the stretch, the friction, his reach, the rub of his palm on my clit were arrows of pure ecstasy through my belly. I whined into his mouth, reeling as his tongue lapped mine. But he took his fingers out and—s*lap.*

The prickling sting in my clit ricocheted up my spine and exploded behind my eyes. I yelped from the force and Kai swallowed it greedily. He licked it up and demanded another with a sudden shove of his fingers back inside me. *Out. In. Out. Slap.* Another hard spank to my dripping cunt. And another. *Harder.* Again. *Harder.* Once more. And then he thrust his thick fingers back in.

I cried and sobbed into the cage of his mouth, thrashing and shaking. On the verge of passing out.

In an instant, Kai released my mouth, and I collapsed against his chest, nothing but a trembling mess. Too dizzy and teary-eyed to see him clearly. *Until I did.*

Black eyes dilated behind his glasses, drugged on raging power and lust. Brows knotted. Skin a little damp. Hair mussed by my hand. He was stunning. Feral. Dishevelled. Just looking at him made my muscles and thighs clench up as the sweet pressure built in my lower belly. I sobbed his name.

He groaned. "You're clenching on my fingers so hard, Babble. Are you going to come for me?"

I nodded shakily. "Yes—yes. I'm close. So close."

But just as the orgasm was about to soar through me, Kai took his fingers out, and the promised climax crumbled all around me. I gasped, shocked and disappointed as I rocked for friction I couldn't find. My inner muscles clenched frustratedly around air.

"No, Kai," I cried, my face scrunching in on itself. "Why did you stop?" A heavy, almost amused breath shook out of him. "Kai, *please*." I blindly reached for his hand as if I had the strength to push him back down to where I ached for him. "Please. I want to come. Make me come, Kai—"

His eyes instantly narrowed in warning, and my words evaporated. "You're not in control here, Babble," he said firmly. "You do not get to make demands. If you want me to *let* you come, then you ask me for it." His gaze went heavy and hot. "You *beg* me for it like a good girl."

I shuddered as his dark command stroked over my lips. "Please, Kai," I whispered or moaned or something in between. "Please let me come. Let me come on your fingers like I've been wanting to for years. Make me give it to you. Please, I'm begging you. Make me yours, Kai."

With a deep, possessive growl, he claimed my mouth and pushed his fingers back into me. I let out a heady moan, lifting my hips to the thrust of his fingers like the shameless girl I was. He rubbed me exactly where it made me writhe right to the peak of the orgasm I craved.

Only for him to pull them out before I went over. *Again.*

I thrashed and screamed in frustration, the agony of denial something beyond words.

Kai clamped his hand over my mouth. "Shh, shh, shh. You scream, and the guards will come running."

"Kai," I sobbed, pulling his hand down. Angry tears filled my eyes. "Why did you stop again? Why won't you let me come?"

He shuddered on a deep groan. "Fuck, Babble." He snaked a hand around my throat. "If you look at me like that, I really won't let you come. I'll keep you on the edge all night long."

A whimper slipped through my wobbling lips. I tossed my head from side to side. "No—*please*."

He huffed a mean laugh. "So adorable." Then muffled my whine with a kiss. "I can't get enough of you." *Kiss.* "All flushed and frustrated." *Kiss.* "This pout." *Kiss.* "It makes me want to keep edging you." *Kiss.* "Keep spanking your dripping pussy until you cry." *Kiss.*

"Would you like that, Babble?"

I bit on my bottom lip to stifle a moan and shook my head. *Slap.* I groaned as my sensitive clit stung so fucking sweetly under his hand.

"Don't lie to me," he warned, rubbing light circles around the aching bud.

"Yes," I choked out. "I want it. I hate it. I hate that you won't let me come, but I want it—I love it."

"You love it?" He pushed his fingers back inside me in an easy, wet slide. My stomach bottomed out and I gasped. "Is it good, Babble? Could you take more?"

I contemplated lying but found myself nodding. "Yes. I could—I can. But..."

He pumped his fingers faster, and I struggled for an answer. I was unable to do anything but pant and rock my hips desperately, rubbing my clit harder against his palm and my arse against his erection. I was so wet, a filthy, absurdly erotic sound echoed around us with every movement.

"But," Kai echoed breathlessly, "I want to see you come, so, come for me, Babble. *Now.*"

It was like he had full command of my body. Because he gave the instruction and moments later my climax exploded through me like a shockwave, pulling my body up and as tight as a bowstring. I knew I opened my mouth, but I didn't realise I was screaming until Kai's hand locked over it.

He kept rocking his fingers inside me, riding me through the high for an eternity and a half. My thighs gave one last shudder before he pulled out of me. I sighed and melted in bliss. But when he lifted his sticky fingers towards his mouth, I froze, my respiratory system failing to function entirely.

With smouldered, hooded eyes drilling into mine, he pushed both digits into his mouth, sucking and licking my wetness off them. "So fucking sweet," he moaned between a lick.

There were no words, not in modern Anglish or any regional language or even in an ancient tongue, that could justly describe how fucking sexy Kai looked licking me off his fingers. Everything inside me disintegrated at the sight into nothing but pockets of raw, intense, breath-taking arousal.

He pulled his fingers out of his mouth, and I scrambled to cup his face, mashing my lips to his. Like I weighed nothing, he lifted me so I was straddling his lap again and locked his thick arms around me.

"Are you okay?" he murmured with so much care and affection I wasn't sure if the intense-to-soft switch was sweet or funny. "Did I hurt you?" *Kiss.* "Was it too much?" *Kiss.* "I got carried away."

I leaned back so he could see me grinning. "It was perfect, Kai." The flicker of worry in his eyes disappeared. "So perfect. I loved every moment of it." Landing repeated soft kisses to his lips, I trailed one hand down his hot, hard chest over his hoodie. "But it isn't over."

Just as my hand brushed his erection poking furiously against his pyjama bottoms, Kai clamped his hand over mine and yanked it back up. "No." He shook his head, a crease forming between his brows. "I said this was only going to be about you, Esmeralda. That was it tonight."

"But I want to touch you." I twisted my wrist in his hand. "I want you to feel good too, Kai."

"I got my pleasure from seeing you come. I don't need anything else."

"That's a lie." I huffed, growing frustrated with how stupidly strong his grip was. "And even if it isn't, I want to give you more." Remembering my other hand was free, I reached for his hard-on, but he grabbed it instantly and yanked it up too. "Kai!"

"Esmeralda," he growled in warning, but it only made my bratty side do a happy dance again.

My mouth twitched as I shuffled forward on his lap until his cock dug into my thigh. I rocked and ground against him, fanning the frustration in his eyes into a blaze. He growled a low sound that I felt in my belly. But with my wrists in his hands, he couldn't do anything but take the movement of my hips. *And I gave.* I gave until he couldn't take any more.

With a raw, feral noise, he released my hands and shoved me onto my back on the makeshift mattress without so much as touching me.

His hands slammed down on the blanket either side of my head, and my heart went *thud, thud, oh fuck.*

Kai was furious. Frowning furiously, huffing furiously, aroused furiously. Just plain furious. He hovered over me on his hands and knees. A big bear, both hungry and provoked.

I couldn't tell if he wanted to beat my arse or eat my arse. *I wouldn't mind either.*

"That's enough, Esmeralda," he said, baring his teeth at me.

I was a cat that got the cream, my lashes heavy and body purring with desire. My mouth curled on its own accord as I wrapped my hand around one of his thick wrists, corded with restrained power.

"If you really don't want this." I pulled his slipping glasses off with two fingers, "say *monkey* and I'll stop." I lazily folded one arm down. "Otherwise, you'll have to take your pleasure from me if you want me to behave again." His glasses rolled off the tip of my fingers onto the blanket. "Use me, Kai. And I promise, I won't act like a brat again... *tonight at least.*"

With a rough sound, he slammed his lips on mine, fucking my mouth with his tongue as deep as he could. He left me so weak and shaking, I couldn't even protest at the loss of his heat over me as he sat upright, leaving his glasses by my head.

"Your shorts and underwear must be sticky, Babble," he said casually, skimming his hands up my thighs to the waistband of my bottoms. "Should I take them off?"

I nodded, eagerly lifting my hips for him. He smoothly tugged down the damp cotton and lace and threw them to the side. Then his hungry eyes were desperately licking at my body, up the curves of my legs to my most feminine place between, and it made me feel like the sexiest seductress.

Slowly, teasingly, I spread my legs for him as if I'd never known embarrassment in my life. As wide as I could for him to see all of me. *His to use as he pleased.*

"Just look at you, Babble," he groaned, cupping his dick over his pyjamas; my mouth instantly went dry. "Shamelessly spreading yourself for me." I was so mesmerised by the way he rubbed himself, I didn't realise he reached for me until I felt his thumb spread my pussy apart. I moaned, arching up from the cushions. "So fucking wet for me."

He took a moment to tuck his hoodie up under itself, exposing his sturdy yet lean waist. I couldn't take my eyes off that delicious V on his lower stomach, a trail of black hairs arrowing down under his bellybutton into his trousers. But my gaze dropped when he shoved them down.

Grey. His boxers were grey and fucking delicious against his golden skin tone. The imprint of his hard cock angrily pushed against the fabric, so big, thick, and long, and unashamedly wet over the crown.

Fuck. My thigh muscles locked in place as saliva pooled in my mouth. But I waited, anticipating the moment he pulled his boxers down his hairy, muscular thighs to sit with his pyjama bottoms.

To my disappointment, he didn't.

"I want to see you," I breathed, reaching for him with shaky hands. "I want to feel you raw, Kai."

He shook his head, his brows furrowing. "No. I don't have a condom, Esmeralda. And I won't take any chances that might lead to an accident. Not even a slim one. I won't turn us into a scandal."

My heart fluttered at the protective timbre in his voice. "It's okay, Kai. You can go raw," I said, rising up on my elbows. "Condoms aren't a hundred percent, so I have an implant too." I lifted my left arm. "And it's kept me safe from scandal for two years now."

His expression turned dark and fierce. "I should be glad that it's kept you safe. But thinking about *how* you discovered that is only making me angry."

I grinned when I realised what he meant. "Jealous are we, Mr Perfect Prince?" I purred. Laying back down, I brushed the hem of my cropped shirt up. I skimmed over the gold piercing in my bellybutton and exposed my stomach to him. "Maybe you should mark me as yours with your cum then."

His eyes flew up from my bellybutton piercing and crashed into mine, lust storming through them. "You have a filthy fucking mouth, do you know that, Babble?" he growled and lowered his mouth over mine. "And one day soon, I'm going to enjoy stuffing it full so you can't use it."

One instant, we were moaning, groaning, and kissing ravenously, sealing those promises. The next, Kai was upright and yanking his boxers down to hover with his pyjama bottoms above his knees.

And well…it became clear he had big dick energy for a reason. *Because he was big.*

Jutting tall and proud from a trimmed patch of dark hairs, long and thick and veiny. He was swollen at the head and glistening with pre-cum. So perfectly, deliciously male.

He cupped his balls and gave them a squeeze before he dragged a slow fist up and down his cock. He groaned, and my eyes flickered up from his hand to the twist of pleasure on his face and down again. I was desperate to sear every sexy detail of him jerking off into my mind.

I moaned for more, scrunching the blanket in my fists to resist the urge to touch myself. With a heavy sigh, he stopped. I whimpered in protest, but suddenly his hands were under my knees, pushing them down to my shoulders. He practically folded me in half, lewdly exposing me to him.

I was still trying to figure out what had just happened when I felt him move. I looked down and he was lying on his stomach, lowering his face to my pussy. "Oh, fuck," I gasped as a ten-tonne weight of anticipation landed on my chest, crushing my lungs under it.

His ink black eyes twinkled smugly. "Did you think I would give you what you wanted so easily, Babble?" He hadn't done anything other than speak and my body was already shaking. "You will get my cum after I get another orgasm."

There was no teasing and testing like when he first fingered me. He opened his mouth and pressed his tongue full and flat over my aching clit. I cried out under the breath-taking sensation, my legs fighting the grip of his hands. Stars flooded my vision before I squeezed my eyes shut.

"Eyes open, Babble," he growled, and the vibrations shot right up my spine.

The moment I lifted my lashes, Kai was lapping my pussy with his tongue again. He teased circles around my clit, flicking over it with purpose, sucking until I shook. He licked hungrily between my wet cunt and groaned praises and promises into me as he palmed my breasts. And I watched the entire filthy performance, fighting to stay sane but failing to do anything but feel.

But he didn't let me come. He edged me. Once with his tongue. Once with his fingers *and* tongue.

On the third time with his mouth, tears rolled down the sides of my face as I twisted in agony.

"I thought I told you, Babble," he panted against my inner thigh, his hands keeping my knees apart. A smirk sat proudly under his dimple. "If you want my cum, you need to come first. But you didn't."

"You didn't let me!" I shrieked as I thrashed and clawed at his bulky shoulders and hoodie.

He bit on my inner thigh and sucked, grazing my skin with his late-night stubble and rubbing my wetness around his mouth back on me. I cried out in pleasure and pain and frustration. "Kai, please," I whimpered. "Please let me come. I can't anymore, let me come." He sucked harder and I choked on a gasp. "*Please.* I—I'm sorry." He released my hot, throbbing skin from his mouth. "I won't be a brat, I'll be good. As good as you want. So please. I can't take it anymore."

He stared at me for a long moment, looking drugged and wild. Then he let go of my knees and crawled lazily over me. "That's a big promise, Babble," he said, wiping away a tear from the side of my eye with his thumb. "But do you mean it?" I nodded furiously.

With one more swipe of his thumb, he sat up, grabbing his glasses as he did. He rubbed the back of one hand over his mouth as he put his glasses back on with the other. Then his fingers were slipping around each of my ankles.

"If you really mean it, Babble, promise me you'll be my good girl," he said, lifting my legs up against his torso so my ankles framed his face. It was so hard to focus on what he was doing and saying at the same time. "Come on, Esmeralda. Promise me."

"I'll be your good girl. Always."

He pressed a licking kiss to one of my legs and clamped a thick arm around my thighs, holding them together. He jerked my body down the blanket to his. "Again."

"I want to be your good girl, Kai," I moaned.

He shuddered, but I was so focused on his beautiful, damp face that the rub of his hard cock surprised a gasp from me. My gaze flew down to between my legs.

Kai wasn't pressing down my wetness to push into me. He'd slipped his thick cock between my thighs, sliding against my clit as he inched forward until his hips were pressed flush to the back of my legs. And maybe I should have felt disappointed that he wasn't fucking me, but I couldn't help but moan at the sensation and sight of him between my thighs, leaking pre-cum over me.

I squeezed my legs together to cushion his erection, loving the slight flinch that tugged at his mouth. He wrapped his other arm around my legs as he dragged his hips back, gliding so easily from between my wet skin. My whole body tightened up in ecstasy as his length rubbed against me.

"Fuck, Esmeralda," he groaned against my ankle, thrusting back between. "You feel…"

"Perfect," I finished for him.

Neither of us could speak after that. We could only moan and groan and pant loudly as I squeezed my thighs together and Kai thrust between them. Faster and faster until wet skin was slapping against wet skin, his balls smacking against me. It felt as incredibly delicious as it sounded.

We weren't interested in play a leisurely game of pleasure anymore. We were running a race to the finish line desperately, riding and urging each other on. My hands touched Kai wherever I could reach, scratching at his exposed lower stomach, his knees, his arms, while his mouth lapped at each of my ankles, nipping and licking as his fingers dug into my thighs. But not even for a second did I take my eyes off his nor he off mine. Maybe that was why the pleasure built so damn fast.

"Kai." I panted, writhing and rocking urgently with his thrusts. "I'm—I'm—*please.*"

"Come," he growled huskily.

I shattered into a million pieces within seconds, so hard that my mouth opened on a silent scream as my back flew up from the blanket. I trembled so much for so long but then I sagged just as quickly.

With a few quick, shallow thrusts between my thighs, Kai followed me over. His groan vibrated through my entire leg as he sank his teeth into my skin and spurted in long, warm jets over my belly. When his hips finally stopped giving little jerks, he slumped forward, completely weak, sweaty, and spent. *So fucking beautiful.*

In the perfect, panting silence that followed, Kai carefully dropped my legs around either side of his body and collapsed over me. One forearm landed on the blanket by my head while his other hand cupped my cheek. "Are you okay?" he rasped, wiping away the dampness around my eye.

I nodded tiredly. "I am." And curled my arms around his shoulders. "Are you?"

He pressed his damp forehead to mine and nodded. "I am—I am, I just…I need to know I didn't hurt you. That these tears aren't bad tears."

I squeezed him close. "I'm not hurt," I whispered. "And these aren't bad tears, Kai." I stroked a hand down the back of his hair repeatedly, slow and soothing. "You were so good." *Stroke.* "So perfect, Kai." *Stroke.* "And I wanted everything you did to me." I pressed a light kiss to his lips and the tension seeped out of his shoulders. "You made me feel so good, I can't even begin to explain—"

He moulded his lips around mine, swallowing my words, with a kind of need that made my heart clench and warm in my chest. It was passion that wasn't heated but was an entirely different form of affection. Just as intense and raw and blinding, and still unbelievably incredible.

"One more," he whispered against my lips. "Come for me once

more, Esmeralda." *Kiss.*

I blinked. *Wait—what?*

He lied.

It wasn't once more. It was twice more.

CHAPTER 20
Esmeralda

My eyes shot open with a hard snap of my body when a loud sound shattered my sleep. Fear stampeded through my heart, and I blinked and blinked, trying to figure out where I was.

Pillow, mattress, blanket. A bed. And a black wall of warmth and muscle.

Said wall moved and I numbly realised I had one arm around it and a leg tucked between it. It instantly drew me closer with a heavy barrier over my waist until I was wrapped in a protective circle. That was when I finally thought to look up.

Kai.

I was in Kai's arms, completely safe and secure. He was squinting and scowling drowsily through the dim room at something over my head, his hair effortlessly mussed.

"Bloody Neves," an awestruck male voice said from behind me. "You have got to be kidding me…"

"Fay?" Kai said, his voice so rough and deep I felt the vibrations in my belly.

Kai lifted his arm off me, patting his hand searchingly above our heads. He picked up his glasses, and I tipped onto my back to look at Fay, dazed and confused as to what was going on.

Fay stood in the open doorway with light streaming in from the corridor. His wide eyes flicked between me and Kai, but my gaze narrowed on his clothes. Where were his pyjamas? Why was he dressed up in the middle of the night? *If three AM counted as the middle…*

"What the fuck, Fay?" Kai growled at his brother, leaning up on his elbow. He dropped his other arm protectively over my torso. "What was that for?"

Fay blinked his surprise away and quirked a brow. "*What was that for?*" he echoed, then scoffed and shook his head, looking somewhere between disbelieving and amused. "Dammit, Kai. This whole time! And you two have been snuggling in the TV room, bloody *sleeping.*" He gave a stunned chuckle. "I knew something was going on, but you have some fucking explaining to do, asshole."

I stared blankly at Fay, then glanced to the eighty-inch TV opposite us, and down to the cushions Kai and I were lying on.

Apparently, somewhere during our quiet chattering as we cuddled after all those mind-blowing orgasms, we fell asleep instead of going back to our rooms.

I blinked. *Hold on…we fell asleep?*

Kai and I had been sleeping? As in actually *sleeping.*

Warm understanding landed on my torso with the grace of a feather but the weight of an elephant. My gaze searched for Kai's, and I found him looking at me, reflecting back the realisation I felt.

We had fallen asleep together. Just drifted off while talking.

I didn't know about Kai, but I couldn't remember the last time I had just *drifted off* the way most people did. Not since I'd stopped sleeping eight years ago after Mother passed away.

Every night since, sleep had been a temperamental mistress that needed coaxing to come to me. She hadn't willingly taken me in so long that sometimes I forgot sleeping every night was a normal occurrence for the majority.

But with Kai, sleep had wrapped me in her arms so tightly it was almost like I hadn't spent nearly a third of my life fighting her moody arse. Actually, I didn't think I'd ever slept so well before.

Kai's throat bobbed slowly as his glazed eyes searched mine. His slow smile was so damn beautiful, I couldn't help but return it.

The only other person in the room cleared his throat loudly, not quite bursting the bubble around me and Kai, but still poking through. "Are you two done giving each other googly eyes?"

We weren't done but Kai reluctantly dragged his gaze to his younger brother, and I followed suit. The way Fay was knowingly smirking made me blush. I wasn't naked, but I pulled the blanket up closer to my chin as if I was, feeling shy. He must've noticed because he laughed.

"If you're not decent, hurry up and get decent before I tell everyone I've found you and they come running," Fay teased.

"Why would you tell everyone?" Kai asked as he pushed himself up, making sure the blanket stayed tucked around me.

"Because we've all been bloody looking for you both for the last ten minutes, that's why."

"Looking for us?" I echoed, rising onto my elbows.

"Yes."

That was when my eyes dropped to his clothes again.

He wasn't in pyjamas. He was dressed in a V-neck sweater and chinos like it was…

A hard jab of alarm made me bolt straight up and glance at the two sets of windows. The red curtains were still drawn but glimmers of sunlight peeked through the sides.

Already morning.

"What time is it?" I heard Kai ask and I apprehensively glanced back to Fay.

He smirked. "It's past nine. And you lovebirds didn't show up at the start of breakfast."

No…

Gone was my contentment, leaving dread and fear to curdle my insides until I felt nauseous. Because if I hadn't turned up for breakfast then…

Kareem.

Kai

I resisted the urge to shift awkwardly on the sofa as my mother, Queen Leila, clasped each of my hands in hers. She swallowed me up in the bottomless gaze I'd inherited from her.

"Did you sleep with her, Kai?" she asked in a dead serious tone.

My eyes went wide as spluttering coughs erupted from my mouth. I quickly pursed my lips together to hold them in. "What?" I croaked, heat swarming my face and ears.

I didn't know if I could call what Esmeralda and I did "sleeping together." But *perfection*? Fuck yes.

Just thinking about it—I shouldn't be thinking about it. I risked a hard-on in front of my family, but I couldn't help but think about it.

Last night was the first time I'd ever let go like that. Just given in to the side of me that demanded submission and wanted to dominate instead of trying to lock away the feeling.

I'd still been fucking scared at first. I had worried that Esmeralda would see how rough I wanted to be, and it would make her uneasy. But gosh, how bloody wrong she'd proved me.

Her assurance and trust completely freed me from every fear and concern. She purposely riled me, not pleading to be dominated but demanding it like a punishment-hungry brat. And fuck, her every reaction had been as if I was giving her everything she'd ever wanted. I completely lost my mind in pleasuring and punishing her. *But* I wasn't going to tell my entire family that.

Fay, who'd called them all to the TV room after Esmeralda left in a rush, was snickering into his fist, while next to him Uncle Arsh was grinning from ear to ear. Adam was blushing and smirking down at the floor. Our father, King Rami, was sitting on one of the other sofas with our grandmother, Gigi, now that the cushions on the floor had been returned.

Father tried to hide his smile by stroking his trimmed beard sprinkled with white. "Leila, honey," he said, his hazel eyes dancing with amusement. "You might want to rephrase your question."

Gigi grunted next to him and quirked a thin brow at me. "Oh, I don't believe she needs to, Rami. Leila got it spot on. Your son has been rolling in the sheets with Princess Esmeralda."

Shit, shit, shit. There was no point denying it when my face gave away the truth of those words instantly, burning hot with embarrassment. I could feel the skin melting off my bones.

"Look at his face," Fay hooted as his whole body shook with laughter and Adam chuckled with him.

I scowled at my siblings and pulled my hand from Mother's fingers to tug at my ear. At least Uncle and Father had the decency to try to hide their chuckles, but Gigi grinned at me, looking bloody impressed with herself. So much for being her favourite if *this* was how she exposed me.

"Oh, stop it," Mother said to them all, her softly curved brows pinched together. "Rolling in the sheets or not, you all know that isn't what I meant." She glanced back at me, her light wrinkles smoothing out instantly. "Ignore their teasing and tell me, Kai. Did you really fall asleep with her?"

Mother's hopeful question softened the amusement wafting through the room and everyone went quiet, patiently waiting for my answer.

It was no secret among my family that I had struggled with sleep since a young age, and it had only gotten worse as I grew older. For some reason, my thoughts never went quiet enough for me to fall asleep for long periods of time or several nights in a row. Nightfall only ever made my mind run faster, jumping from thought to thought, worry to worry, and rarely ever stopping for a breath.

But with Esmeralda's body wrapped all around mine, there was nothing I thought about other than how good and soft and sweet she felt against me. And how I could imagine lying in bed with her every night for years to come.

I swore I only closed my eyes for five minutes, but the next thing

I knew, Fay was crashing through the bloody door.

I didn't bother trying to tame the small smile forcing its way onto my mouth and tugged shyly at my ear. "Hmm." I gave a slight nod. "I fell asleep with her."

There was a split-second of silence then delighted chaos broke loose.

"Oh, this is wonderful." Mother gleamed, watery relief filling her eyes.

"Well, I never…" Father said in awe while Uncle was doubled over in laughter.

"Marry her," Gigi stated. "Put a ring on that girl's finger today and marry her tomorrow."

I felt heat rise through my face again, but it wasn't the bad kind this time. It was surprise that Gigi was telling me to marry Esmeralda so quickly, a heavy satisfaction at the realisation that my family liked her, and a new excitement at the thought of a possible future with Esmeralda. And it was fucking scary because I had only really known her properly for a week, but…

My Esmeralda. My Babble. *My wife…fuck, fuck, fuck, I liked that.* I liked that more than I could say.

"Look at him," Fay said, laughing again. "He's fucking thinking about it!"

"Fay! Language," Mother rumbled, and Fay snapped straight. "And Gigi, he can't marry her just like that." Gigi arched a questioning brow. "Well, I suppose not unless…" Mother turned to me. "Do you *want* to marry her? Are you even dating yet? Does she know how you feel about her?"

I nudged at my glasses. "I—we like each other, but I don't know if we're *dating* yet."

"Bloody Neves," Father muttered, glancing at his grinning younger brother.

"Who cares about dating? Just marry her," Gigi said like her word was law.

"What did I tell you?" Uncle Arsh said to Father. "*What did I tell you?* And you doubted me. Now you owe me. A hundred Sterlings was the bet, and you better pay up, Rami."

Mother swung an outraged look to Father. "You made a bet on our son?"

Father's eyes widened in horror. "Uh—what? What? No. No, not at all, my love. It was Arsh."

"What?" Uncle Arsh exclaimed.

Mother started railing off at the both of them without so much as taking a breath between her words and they dropped their heads in shame. Even Gigi added a few smug words of support for Mother. Fay and Adam grinned, obviously happy that it wasn't them being told off for once. I had to admit, even I found it amusing. At least until the conversation swerved back to me.

"The point is," Mother said, "that none of us should be interfering in Kai's relationship with Esmeralda whether that is making *bets* on them or anything else." She elegantly cleared her throat and faced me, motherly authority painting her face and posture. "That being said, Kai, there are condoms in the palace infirmary. Please be sensible and use them."

I fought the urge to groan in painful embarrassment but couldn't help a wince. Because as open as my family was about sex, this conversation was going in a direction that was simply plain awkward.

"That really wasn't necessary, Mother," Fay said with a face of disgust.

"Leila, dear," Father said with a chuckle, "I think that's enough. He's a grown man, not a teenager."

"Forget the condoms," Gigi announced with a flick of one nimble hand. "Get her pregnant and she'll have no choice but to marry you."

My mouth fell open, Mother gasped, I think Adam choked on a cough, and Father and Uncle Arsh called out, "Mother," in perfect sync. Fay was the only one cackling hysterically.

Gigi sniffed and haughtily tipped up her chin. "What? I said nothing wrong. And anyway, all those romance books you read, Leila, are exactly like that."

It was Mother's turn to blush as all eyes turned to her, but she held herself tall and regal and without shame. "It works in romance books,

Gigi. *Not* in real life."

A full-blown discussion broke out as to whether it would be acceptable for me to get Esmeralda pregnant or not so she would have to marry me as if I wasn't even sitting there.

I wasn't sure what surprised me more. That everyone in my family was talking about my marriage to Esmeralda as if I had already proposed to her. That Gigi wanted five great-grandchildren from me.

Or that I kept picturing Esmeralda waddling around Chaukham Palace by my side, her belly big and round with our child, while I held a little girl with her mother's eyes and smile on my other hip.

Fuck. What had she done to me?

CHAPTER 21
Esmeralda

"How could you be so bloody *stupid*?"

I flinched at Kareem's vicious tone, shrinking into myself. I didn't dare lift my gaze up from the dark red carpet where he was pacing in the middle of his bedroom.

My heart was pounding at the base of my throat, my hands clenched in fists. I was fighting the trembling fear pouring through me by focusing on the pain of my nails digging into my palms.

"Look at me when I'm talking to you!"

My head reflexively snapped up and I stood tall. Shoulders down, back straight, chin ninety-degrees to the floor, hands clasped in front of me. *The perfect posture.*

Face blank. Mouth shut. Silent unless spoken to. *The perfect princess.*

My older brother glared at me through his flaming eyes with his hands on his hips. "What did I say to you before we came to Touma?"

"That I wasn't to cause any trouble," I uttered as evenly as I could manage.

"Exactly," he hissed, and that one word lashed at me like a whip. "So, what are you bloody doing disappearing off with Prince Kai and running around the palace *half-naked*?"

A pained blush of mortification burnt my cheeks at the way he spat out the words like they felt dirty on his tongue. "It's not what you're assuming. I fell asleep—"

Kareem scoffed. "Oh, it's not, is it?" His scrutiny tracked down my body and he threw a hand towards me. "Then explain to me why you're wearing nothing but a T-shirt that clearly doesn't belong to you with love bites all down your legs."

Humiliation stung wet and hot at the back of my eyes. I scrunched the front of the black T-shirt that fit me like a short dress in one hand, glancing down at myself.

I was wearing Kai's T-shirt. The one he'd hurriedly grabbed from his room when he went to get a damp towel after he saw my pyjama shirt had his spend on it. He'd carefully dressed me in it too, and I'd felt so comfortable and safe then, wrapped in the soft fabric and his scent.

Kareem's accusation made the T-shirt feel coarse and scratchy against my skin. Like I was wearing something that was burnt and shredded and dirty. *I felt dirty.* And humiliatingly bare.

The fabric that swallowed me up last night suddenly felt too short. Too exposing even though I was wearing my pyjama shorts underneath. My legs felt cold and naked, and I was so painfully aware of all the marks Kai had left on them that I was fighting the urge to crouch down and wrap my arms around my legs to hide the hickeys. When the previous night I had wanted him to leave more on me.

I didn't regret it. Last night. I wasn't ashamed of what I'd done with Kai. But I wished Kareem had never seen me like this. I wished I had gotten to my room instead of bumping into him not even ten seconds after I rushed out the TV room. I wished I hadn't seen the shock and anger flash through his eyes like a still image film before he told me to follow him through gritted teeth.

I wished that last night's ecstasy and joy hadn't become another reason for Kareem to hate me.

"How many times do I have to remind you that your actions reflect on me?" Kareem bit out in my silence. I rapidly blinked back tears as my tongue swelled in my mouth. "You are my *heir* for fuck's sake! Do you think it looked good that I had no idea where you bloody were?"

I watched his feet take two aggressive steps towards me until I could feel the heat of his rage coming off his body in brutal waves. "Do you know how embarrassing it was to have everyone realise that my heir was using the Peace Celebration to *mess around* with Prince Kai instead of doing her duty?"

My gaze flew up to his as a painful jerk ricocheted through my chest. *No…*

I could take every complaint, accusation, and scold Kareem had for me. I could take the hurt every time he referred to me as "his heir" and not *his sister.* But my whole body screamed in protest at the way he belittled what was between me and Kai. No. I wouldn't let him do that.

"I wasn't messing around," I said, my words coming out rushed and quiet. "We weren't—"

"Look at yourself, Esmeralda," he snapped. "You can't tell me you weren't fuck—"

"I like him," I sobbed as loudly as I could before Kareem soiled what Kai and I had done.

I choked on a breath as liquid fire pooled in my eyes, turning Kareem's face into a blur. "I like him," I repeated, pinching my thigh in hopes it would make the tears go away. "I like him, and he likes me too. And we—we did—but it was more than what you're making it sound like." I swallowed the salty heat in my mouth. "We fell asleep, Kareem. *I* fell asleep with him."

Kareem's face slowly came back into focus. To no surprise, the anger in his eyes remained unchanged.

"Do you think the media would care about your *feelings,*" he asked, sounding misleadingly calm, "if someone leaked that you were running around the palace half-naked after sleeping with him?"

I bit down on my trembling lip, keeping a sob of frustration behind the barrier of my teeth.

It was always that. The media. The world. People. *What would they think? What would they do? What would they say?* It was always about them with Kareem.

I understood why. He was a young king. Everyone had been so

sceptical of his ability to rule when he was coronated seven and a half years ago, so he worked tirelessly to prove them wrong. That didn't mean it didn't hurt that it was never about me. But I knew it never would be. What I wanted and felt were the last things he cared about. He barely even tolerated me.

Kareem swayed back, standing cruel and tall over me, appearing so big despite his lean frame. "Stay away from him, Esmeralda. The last thing I need right now is to deal with a scandal because of you."

The world seemed to tilt and break under my feet. I was shaking my head desperately before he'd even finished his sentence, panic gnawing through my chest. "No, Kareem, please." My voice cracked as I struggled to breathe. "*Please.* I like him—I—I fell asleep with—"

"I don't care, Esmeralda," he roared.

"I know you don't care," I yelled back.

I didn't know where the shout came from. Maybe from all the frustration, sadness, and anger that had been building up over the years from his neglect. But I shocked myself as much as I shocked him.

I pressed the back of my hand to my mouth as a sob retched from me. The tears I'd been fighting to hold in finally escaped. It took me a few moments, but I forced myself to breathe, to steel my shoulders, and swiped away any evidence of the dampness on my cheeks.

If I was finally going to confront Kareem, I refused to do it while falling apart.

"I know you don't care," I repeated. "You're not even listening to what I am saying."

"I fell asleep with him, Kareem." I patted a hand to my chest. "*Me.* I haven't slept properly since Mother… But I fell asleep with Kai because he…"

Kareem's eyes narrowed and I swallowed slowly, letting my hand fall limp by my side. "Because he made me feel safe," I whispered. "He makes me feel safe and protected. And wanted. He makes me feel cared about." I shook my head. "And I haven't felt that in years."

My gaze blurred over. "You *hate* me, Kareem. You have since Mother told us about Father, and—" I cut off my words and bit down on my bottom lip until it stopped trembling. "I know things haven't been easy for you, I know things only got harder when you became king, but I was a child. I was scared and confused, and I needed you. But instead of seeing how I was struggling when everything I knew turned out to be a lie, you punished me every day for something that wasn't my fault."

Tears seared down my cheeks, but I didn't have the strength to wipe them away. "You were so cruel and bitter, and I never blamed you for it because you were angry. But you hurt me so much. I became nothing to you. Unless it came to duty. And I have tried so hard to make sure you are satisfied with my work, because hoping for you to care about me again is pointless. But nothing I do is ever good enough for you. You still act like you wish I didn't exist.

"Sometimes at night I used to wonder if—if that was the only way I could make you happy." I struggled for a breath over the pain squeezing the life out of my heart. "If I just ran away and disappeared from your life. Or if I just stopped existing entirely."

I choked on a sniffle of shame from hearing those words. I had never admitted them aloud before. Not to Mariyah, not to Shehryar, or to his mother, Mama Katiya. I barely even acknowledged the thoughts myself. But when Kareem made his hatred so obvious, when he made me so miserable and lonely every day, sometimes those sorts of thoughts became inevitable.

Kareem's eyes might have widened, but a new stream of tears flooded my vision before I could properly see. "I wasn't brave enough to do either," I whispered, "but sometimes I wondered if you were." Someone made a soft, shaky sound, I didn't know who. "I wondered if one day you would tell me you'd had enough and wanted me gone. Or that you might expose me to the world."

"I am constantly scared of messing up in case that's the last straw. But I wish it wasn't like that. I wish I had my brother back. I want Jahmal to feel like a home again." A huff of broken amusement slipped from my lips. "But it's never really been my home, has it?"

I used both hands to scrub away the wetness running down my cheeks, seeing properly for the first time the blank look on Kareem's face. I didn't know why I thought he might make a different face.

Silence filled the room as I took a few moments to gather myself.

"I have never asked you for anything before. I know there's nothing you want to give me, and I know you'll probably hate me even more after this, but *please*. Don't make me stay away from Kai. That's the only thing I'll ever ask for." I clutched my hands to my chest, clasping them together. "*Please*. He means so much to me. I—"

I'm falling in love him.

Those words felt dangerous to admit out loud. Like Kareem might use them as a weapon against me.

"I can't be without him. Please. I'm begging you. I don't need anything else."

Kareem might have flinched, or I might have imagined it, but a stillness fell between us. He didn't move or speak and neither did I as I silently pleaded him not to be so cruel.

Then just like that, he turned away, showing me his back as he ran a hand over his hair. "Shehryar or Katiya should be in the corridor for you." There was a hoarseness to his voice that I couldn't read. "Go to your room and change."

I took a step towards him. "But—"

"Someone will bring breakfast to you." His words were final.

That was it. The conversation was over. He wasn't going to give me an answer, he was just going to dismiss me as always. But this time something broke inside me with a painful crack.

Hope.

The last of my hope that the brother who had always given me the bigger half of the chocolate bar he'd snuck from the kitchen was still somewhere inside this man.

He wasn't. *I didn't have a brother anymore. Maybe I never had.*

My body went limp, broken and lifeless. I was giving up. I was done banging my head against a wall with no breakthrough. There was no point trying to talk to this stranger anymore.

Somehow, I managed to make my way to the door. "I apologise, Your Majesty, for causing you trouble," I said, almost making myself shiver with how empty I sounded. "It won't happen again."

I closed the door behind me and turned away. Shehryar's massive body appeared before me with Mama Katiya hovering next to him. Both of their expressions were filled with concern.

I lasted three seconds before I collapsed against him on a broken cry.

CHAPTER 22

Kai

KAI

Did you reach your room okay?

KAI

I'm sorry I should have come with you

ESMERALDA

Hey sorry I just saw your mssg

ESMERALDA

I did and its okay xx

ESMERALDA

Did your family say anything?

KAI

Not really

KAI

Can we talk after you eat breakfast? x

ESMERALDA

Sorry Mr Perfect Prince

The moment Esmeralda sat down next to me at the dining table for the first private lunch in several days, I knew something was wrong.

There was no shine in her big, greyish-brown eyes. No colour on her cheeks, not from make-up and not from her natural glow. Neither was there any truth to the tight smile she gave everyone.

She sat too stiff and straight as she ate. She answered too simply as she conversed, and her laugh didn't sound right to my ears. She didn't react when I pressed my thigh against hers under the long oak table, trying to get her to look at me so I could see what was wrong. She didn't even look at me.

It troubled me so much I couldn't remember if I ate anything of the three courses.

After lunch was over, she left the dining hall lagging behind everyone else. I followed her to where Shehryar appeared to be waiting for her further down the corridor.

"Esmeralda," I called out just as she reached her hulking private secretary.

Her back visibly stiffened, and my heart plummeted. *No, don't react like that, Esmeralda, please.* The tight look Shehryar gave me as he pulled his huge shoulders wide only made my mind whirl harder.

"Prince Kai." Shehryar's pale green gaze briefly darted past my shoulder. "Now is not a good time."

My gaze fell to the back of Esmeralda's head anyway. I wasn't going anywhere until I had spoken to her. I needed to know she was okay. I needed to know it wasn't because of me.

"Esmeralda, look at me. Please," I said softly, taking in the small, unusually delicate sight of her.

"Prince Kai," Shehryar warned firmly in a way that might've been considered rude, but I didn't care what he said. Neither could I fault him for being so protective of Esmeralda. "That's enough."

"Sher," Esmeralda said quietly. "It's okay."

She slowly, rigidly turned. A painful web of cracks tore through my chest as I saw the sad dampness coating her eyes she was trying to keep at bay. Fierce protectiveness exploded inside me with so much intensity, it was agony.

Someone hurt her. Someone hurt her. Someone hurt her.

Was it me? Was it something I did?

I was shaking from the effort not to snatch her up into my arms and take her away where I could talk to her alone, and hold her, rock her, soothe her, anything she needed from me. To sit her down somewhere and get on my knees and apologise for whatever I might have done to upset her.

The longer her eyes flicked timidly between my shoulders and gaze, the stronger the feeling got.

I couldn't stop my hand from reaching for her smaller one, gripping the fitted, dark green jumper dress she wore with black leggings. I gently nudged at the side of her palm until her fingers hesitantly opened, letting me slip mine tightly around hers. I gave her hand a squeeze.

"Come with me for a minute. *Please.* Then you can go back to your meeting with Shehryar," I said.

"What meet—" Shehryar started then suddenly stopped. He avoided my gaze as he scrubbed a hand over his mouth, wincing all the while.

I glanced immediately down at Esmeralda, and the way she grimaced and dropped her head was a solid blow with an iron fist to my stomach.

She'd lied about the meeting. There had never been a meeting.

My head spun as hurt and fear burned through my chest. *It was because of me.* She was hurt because of me. That's why she'd lied. So she didn't have to see me. Because *I* hurt her.

"It's my fault," I croaked as I swayed back from her. "Isn't it? I did something wrong. I messed up."

Her lashes flew up and she shook her head. "No. no, Kai, you didn't do anything. It's not you."

I wanted to wrap my arms around her and crush her to me, but my fists were ten-tonne weights by my side that wouldn't stop trembling. "Then what is it? Why are you upset?"

She slowly closed her eyes, squeezing them shut until her face scrunched into a pained frown. "Kai, I—I..."

"Go," Shehryar said quietly, reminding me he was still there. Both Esmeralda and I glanced to him. He nodded to the side, his piercing eyes locked on Esmeralda. "Go talk to him. I'll cover for you."

Esmeralda stared silently at the view of Pavilion City below us, sitting close to me on the bench. Though I kind of forced her to when I pulled our entwined fingers into my lap.

We'd ridden on Bucky together through the forest and come to the stretch of land on the other side.

Really, I should have taken her somewhere warm to talk. I hated that we were outside. But this was the only place that guaranteed Esmeralda and I could talk alone without any disturbance. So, there we were. Sitting on the lone bench by the old watchtower platform. Her head rested against my shoulder, and I pressed my lips to her hair and closed my eyes, breathing in the sweet scent of her.

It was disturbing how happy she'd been the last time we'd been here, and how quiet she was now.

We sat in silence for five, maybe ten minutes, then she finally said, "I bumped into Kareem on the way back to my room."

I slowly lifted my head, not quite understanding why she'd mentioned her brother. Then it hit me, and my body went rigid.

Kareem was the reason she was upset.

With the way my own family reacted, it hadn't occurred to me that Esmeralda's brother might not have reacted in the same way. Plus, she had said before she didn't get on with him. Had him finding out she'd spent a night with me made her relationship with her brother worse?

I gulped as worry churned through me. "Did he say something to you?"

"He did," she muttered and lifted her shuttered gaze to mine. "But it's more what he didn't say."

Her chin started wobbling first, though she bit down on her bottom lip to hide it. But her face crumpled, and tear flooded her eyes, slipping straight down her cheeks like she could no longer hold them in. And every droplet was a hammer to my glass heart, shattering it to a million pieces.

"Esmeralda," I choked out and reached for her.

She met me halfway, wrapping her arms around my neck as I pulled her into my lap, her legs draped on one side. I squeezed my arms tightly around her as she pressed her face into my shoulder. The quietest little whimper lifted from her, and I buried my face in her hair, cradling and protecting every part of her as agonising emotions tore me apart.

Esmeralda cried almost silently as I held her, trembling against me as I stroked her hair and kissed her temple repeatedly. These weren't the loud, angry tears she'd shed when I'd told her about Meg. They were tired and sad and hurt, and they wrecked me. They made my raw heart bleed, but they made every cell inside me erupt in an aggressive sort of rage.

I wasn't a violent person, but I wanted to find King Kareem and bruise every inch of his body. One punch for every tear that fell because of him. For all the hurt he'd caused her when he should have been protecting her. I didn't give a shit that he was the King of Jahandar. If he had been in front of me right then, I was sure I had enough anger in me that I would have done it.

Yet with every passing second, a part of me became more and more convinced that her pain was somewhat my fault too. *I ought to have been more careful.*

"I'm sorry," I said into her hair. "I should have taken you back to your room last night. I shouldn't have—I didn't think—"

Esmeralda lifted her head. Her lashes were wet, her warm golden skin pink over her cheeks and nose. She was no longer crying, but her face was damp and her eyes still forlorn.

"Don't apologise," she mumbled. "Stop apologising."

I slipped my hand from the back of her neck up to her cheek and wiped at the wetness on her skin with my thumb. "But a part of it is my fault, Esmeralda. Kareem didn't like that you were with me—"

"Kareem doesn't like anything I do, Kai," she said, shaking her head weakly against my palm.

I ground my teeth together, imagining myself grinding his face to a pulp. "But why?" I probably wasn't supposed to ask that question, but I had to know. It didn't make any sense to me that her own brother didn't like her. There was nothing about her not to like. *She was perfect.*

Her lashes flickered before she dropped her gaze down to the zipped front of my coat. The wind fluttered through her long, wavy hair. "I don't know." Her voice cracked and everything inside me detonated all over again.

I dragged her closer and silently watched her try to drag in slow, shaky breaths. There was nothing I could say that wasn't a bunch of insults at her brother, and I knew she didn't need nor want that.

"We were close when we were little," she said on an exhale, "even though he's eight years older than me. We did everything together. We were inseparable." Her voice went quiet as her eyes filled with tears. Nothing had ever made me feel so helpless before, because I couldn't do anything other than hold her tighter and listen.

"Then Father passed away in a boating accident, and I was only six. I didn't really understand what was going on other than he was gone, but things became difficult for Mother. I hardly saw her that first year after, and Kareem started growing distant too. Especially after he was proclaimed the future Prince Consort."

I remembered the accident Esmeralda was talking about, probably more than she did.

I was twelve when it happened, and the news of the King's death was horrific. It was my first experience of death, the first funeral I attended with Mother and Father too. I remembered giving my condolences to Kareem—who was only two years older than me—though I didn't recall seeing Esmeralda. And I watched on the TV months later when it was officially announced that in accordance with Jahandar's hereditary line of succession, Kareem was to become Prince Consort.

As Prince Consort it meant that Kareem, as the next in line, had to rule alongside the Queen once he reached the age of twenty-one until the crown was officially passed down to him. It was a concept that Prio and Shah had too. We had it in Touma too, but our line of succession wasn't hereditary.

"I ended up spending most of my days with Shehryar and Mama Katiya, his mother and my governess, but there were days where I used to silently follow Kareem around just so I could spend some time with him. But then—" She stopped. Something flashed in her eyes, maybe panic, but she dropped her lashes too quickly for me to be able to understand the look properly. She held still and silent for several beats after.

"Then one day, he no longer had the time nor the patience for me anymore. I was ten," she said, her voice shaking. "I think it was the pressure of everything, and when we found out Mother was ill after the expedition to Dale…" She gave a watery shake of her head and my chest twisted painfully. I tugged her close in a tight hug, pressing her cheek against my shoulder.

I remembered that too.

The late Queen of Jahandar's visit to a military camp in the southern mountains of Dale had been all over the news when it became known that her and several other soldiers and military officers had caught a degenerative illness. The world's leading scientists discovered it had been caused by contact from a one-of-a-kind, poisonous plant. But they didn't find a cure or an antidote quick enough. Thirty people had died as a result, including the Queen.

I couldn't pretend I knew the pain of losing one, let alone both parents, so I didn't know what to say. I just pressed my cheek to her forehead, hoping to comfort her even a little bit.

"I know he was scared and worried, but it was like he completely forgot that I was scared and worried too," she mumbled, the wind almost stealing away her watery words. "And when Mother passed away, he completely shut me out.

"The night of her funeral, I sat outside his bedroom and waited for hours, and when he finally came, he told me get up and go back to my room. He said I was going to be the Crown Princess and I couldn't act like a child anymore. He didn't even look at me as he said it."

There wasn't a name for the feeling that washed over me. It was like nails of fire through my heart and a stampede of water buffalos charging angrily through my blood, shaking me down to the bone.

I couldn't believe Kareem had said that to her. She couldn't have been more than fifteen when the Queen died. She *had* been a child. *How the fuck could he have said that to her?*

She sniffed and scrunched in closer against the padding of my coat. "Everything after that became about image for him. And I understood. He had the pressure of the world on his shoulders, but nothing I did was good enough for him. He found fault in everything I did. He still does.

"This morning when he saw me in your T-shirt all he cared about was what the world would think if they found out. He didn't care that I fell asleep with you. He didn't care that I like you. All he cared about was me causing a scandal. And now he wants me to stay away from you."

Everything inside me turned ice cold. "What?"

She pushed against me to sit up, scrunching my coat in her fists. She shook her head firmly as tears streamed down her face. "I won't. I won't stay away from you. I don't want to. I can't."

Agonising understanding tied a rope around my chest and my face twisted. *That wasn't the end of her sentence.* And I held nothing against her for it, but that didn't mean it still didn't rip me apart.

I cupped her face in both of my trembling hands, her cheeks hot and wet against my cold skin. She immediately let out a retched sob. A damp pressure built at the back of my eyes.

"I don't want him to hate me even more, Kai," she cried, pleading me to understand.

I yanked her to me, pressing her face against my shoulder and my lips to her cheek. I kept my mouth there as I hushed her and rocked her, not knowing what else to do. My mind whirled to find something to say but it was coming up blank. *What was I supposed to say?*

I had no idea what to do. No clue how I could fix this for her. For us. I didn't want this thing between us to be the reason she was suffering at her brother's hands, but neither was I strong enough to let her go. I couldn't. I couldn't lose her. I wouldn't.

"Esmeralda," I rasped against her skin. "I'll—we'll figure something out. We will. I promise. We—we can talk to him. I'll talk to him. So don't cry. Don't worry. Please. *Please.*"

My voice lacked any conviction, because as I sat there holding her, I had this sickening feeling in my stomach that there was nothing I could do to fix this.

It was out of my control.

ESMERALDA

I'm sorry I'm staying in my room
tonight

Her message came that night once everyone had gone to bed. I read it and I understood it. I understood why too. But I went down to the library anyway.

I sat in her favourite corner and picked up a book from the shelf and waited for her.

Just in case she came and proved that my anxiety over losing her was for nothing.

She didn't come. I understood why.

My heart broke anyway.

CHAPTER 23
Esmeralda

The next day was Cannon Day, the official day The Great Rebellion of Zorro ended. Marked and remembered by the cannons that signalled the last battle along the shores of Prio.

In Touma, the Cannon Ceremony was held in the afternoon, so the morning was left free for the annual royal scavenger hunt. All the seven families were in attendance at Chaukham Palace, with the royal children and palace staff's children getting ready inside for their own mini hunt.

Prince Arsh had been in charge of planning the hunt and had decided to change things up. Instead of mixing everyone up into teams, he wanted to do a "royal family versus royal family" game.

To my complete, absolute delight—*not*—I was on a team with Kareem and Shehryar.

Awkward wasn't even the right word to describe the atmosphere between me and Kareem. It was suffocatingly silent as I did my best to stick to Shehryar's side and avoid all interaction with my brother.

We were trudging around the side of Chaukham Palace where rose bushes roped up the red brick between windows when Shehryar sighed. I glanced sideways to look at him, only to find myself staring into Kareem's shuttered gaze.

My heart jumped and I immediately turned around to where

Shehryar had stopped. He was scowling as he glanced between me and Kareem. "What's wrong?" I asked.

Shehryar shook his head, his permanently shadowed jaw shifting. "I can't do this," he said. "With all due respect, Your Majesty, Your Highness, if this is how you intend to play the entire time, then I would like to drop out of this team now."

Panic swooped low in my belly.

He wouldn't. *He couldn't.* He couldn't leave me alone with Kareem.

An apology softened his pale green gaze, but Shehryar stood tall and stubborn. "You can't keep using me as a buffer," he said to me before his attention flicked to Kareem. "Your Majesty too. It has to stop. Because someone will notice that something is wrong, and it'll be too late to pretend that everything is fine." He stepped towards Kareem, holding out the red envelope in his hand with our next riddle inside it. "So, I think it would be best if I left."

I watched the silent exchange between their hands. Then my frantic gaze was all over Shehryar as he moved away. "Shehryar," I croaked pleadingly.

He gave me a twisted, remorseful look. "I will be waiting at the start with Prince Arsh and the others if you need me," he said and bowed his head in a quick greeting.

My feet jerked me towards him. "Sher, please," I whispered with a desperate shake of my head. He winced but turned away, striding back the way we had come. All I could do was watch him go as shock and anxiety filled my lungs instead of oxygen.

How could Shehryar do this to me? How could he leave me with Kareem? Nothing good could ever come of me being alone with him. He knew that. So why?

In the dragging moments I stood with my back to him, Kareem didn't say a single word. It made me more and more reluctant to turn around and face the reality of my situation.

I was picking at the hem of my cropped, lapel collar jacket wondering what to do when someone cleared their throat. Every muscle in my body turned to immovable ice blocks. But there was only so long I could stand there pretending *he* wasn't trying to get my attention.

Taking a deep breath, I forced myself to turn slightly, sneaking a quick glance in Kareem's direction.

The stranger in my older brother's skin was looking at me as he scratched his cleanly-shaven jaw. Forget what had happened, I couldn't look him in the eyes because of how casually he was dressed.

I could count on one hand the number of times I'd seen Kareem wearing jeans since he'd turned twenty-one and become Prince Consort. Paired with old white trainers and a worn-leather aviator jacket, he looked like a completely different person. I was struggling to recognise him.

"We should carry on working on the riddles," he said like this was politics and not a game.

I glanced in the direction Shehryar had gone and gave a slight shrug. "It doesn't really matter if we solve them or not. We're probably too far behind to catch up with the others anyway." Twenty minutes of the hour-long scavenger hunt had passed already, and we had only solved three riddles.

He was quiet for several moments, then, "People will ask questions if we quit now."

My shoulders sunk in disappointment and a sharp ache stung in my chest as if I couldn't have already guessed that was what he was going to say.

"Yes. People," I mumbled, closing my eyes over the prickling dampness that filled them.

I didn't think the silence could grow any more suffocating, but it did, and it made me feel sick down to the stomach. I wished I had my phone with me so I could call Shehryar and beg him to come get me. But phones were prohibited during the scavenger hunt, and I had a feeling—

"You used to like solving riddles."

I blinked down at the evenly cropped grass under my scuffed pale blue trainers, wondering if my ears were playing tricks on me. There was no way the Kareem I knew could have spoken to me so… softly. I lifted my gaze to find him watching me with some unreadable expression.

"I did," I heard myself say eventually. "But I haven't had anyone to tell me any in a long time."

He was the one who used to tell me riddles. When I'd been too little to solve them, I used to bribe him with my toys for answers. By the time I'd been able to solve them, he'd stopped telling me any.

Kareem glanced down at the red envelope in his hands. He flipped open the triangular flap and pulled out the little square piece of paper with the typed riddle on it. *"I'm a snake who's sick of my skin,"* he read aloud. *"I dig, I chop, and I snip. But look up high and you'll find I'm home to four legs and a long neck. Spotted and spouted and all. Find me and the next riddle is yours."*

Kareem raised his brows in question. "So? What do you think it is?"

"I don't…I don't know." I wasn't talking about the riddle. I had no idea what was going on with Kareem. Was he really going to tell me the riddles like we were kids again and solve them with me? Did that make me angry or happy? Relieved or frustrated? I had no idea. I felt almost numb.

"*'Four legs and a long neck'* and *'spotted'* sounds like a giraffe to me. Though I don't know why it's *'spouted'.*" He frowned a little at the paper. "But *'a snake who's sick of my skin'*?"

Maybe I was using the riddle as an excuse to avoid having to decipher what this interaction between us was, but I replayed the words in my mind repeatedly, stuck in my awkward stance.

Then it hit me. "Snake's shed their—" I said just as Kareem said the exact same words.

We stopped at the same time. He blinked at me. I looked away first, feeling embarrassed.

He cleared his throat. "So snakes shed their skin, but how is that related to *'I dig, I chop, and I snip'*?"

"Gardening tools," I mumbled upon realisation. "They're what you do with gardening tools. The riddle is a homonym. Shed has two meanings."

"Not shedding skin, a gardening shed. We're looking for a shed with some sort of giraffe inside."

I nodded, small and awkward. "There are three sheds in the palace gardens. But only one is used for gardening tools. It must be that one."

Kareem returned my nod with the same level of stiffness. "Do you know the way?"

We walked with a one-metre gap between us in dead silence as I led the way back around to the gardens. We were hollered at by Raven's team as they rushed past us, and Kareem chuckled at the King's joke. But when they disappeared through an arched hedge, silence fell again.

"How did you know this was the only gardening shed?" Kareem asked as we came up the side of the glasshouse. There stood a wooden shed with a slanted roof, about thirteen-feet wide and twenty-feet long.

"Kai—" I replied but faltered, my shoulders going stiff. "I mean, *Prince* Kai showed me once."

My stomach churned uncomfortably. Talking about Kai in front of Kareem felt like talking about something taboo or forbidden. And just the mention of Kai's name brought back the agony of Kareem telling me to stay away from him.

Without another word, I turned the knob on the wooden shed door and stepped inside ahead of Kareem. Stained workbenches lined the two long walls under four square windows placed at equal intervals, and metal shelf units stood in the middle, forming a rectangular path around them.

I walked down the right side of the shed, scanning the workbench. But I was so hyperaware of Kareem's quiet steps on the other side of the metal units that I couldn't take anything in other than a general blur of empty plant pots and small garden tools.

"How long have you and Prince Kai been close?"

I flinched to a stop. Through the seedling pots sitting eye-level on the metal rack, I stared at Kareem's back, my heart a frightened bird in the cage of my chest. But the moment he put down whatever he was fiddling with, I whipped my head away so fast my neck clicked, and my vision spun.

Why was he asking about Kai? It felt like a trap. Like he wanted me to say something that would give him a reason to condemn me further.

"I don't want to talk about Prince Kai," I said quickly.

There was a rustle of movement behind me. "I'd like to know."

His near-emotionless statement sent anger and bitterness spiking through me. None of which I had felt yesterday, but they arrived with vengeance right then, curling my hands to tight fists.

After all the hurtful things he'd said, after he'd shut down my attempt to tell him the full story and told me to end it with Kai, what was the point of asking anymore?

"Why?" I spat out bitterly before I could put a lid on the words boiling in my throat. "So you can determine how big of a scandal I've caused and how badly it will hurt your name?"

The silence that followed was loud, ringing, and cold. It was a knife through my anger. I fisted my jacket hard to the point my fingers ached as panic leaked through the cut.

What was I doing snapping at Kareem and making the situation worse? I didn't need to give him another reason to get angry, nor did I want to have another argument. I was already tired as it was.

"I apologise, Your Majesty. I shouldn't have said that. Please forgive me."

No answer came from him, so I kept my back to him and forced myself to search the workbench for the answer to the riddle.

"Kareem." His soft voice stopped me in my tracks again, and his greenish-brown gaze pinned me where I was. But I couldn't figure out what the little notch between his furrowed brows meant.

"Don't—don't call me *Your Majesty* when it's just us," he said, the rough lilt to his words sounding...*pained*?

My mind was an empty space of whirling numbness that couldn't understand why he was looking at me or speaking like that. This wasn't the Kareem I had spent so many years of my life trying not to infuriate. I didn't know who he was.

It became hard to hold his stare, so I let my lashes shield me from him as I tried to get a grip on my thoughts. Then lifted them again.

Then flicked them to my right and stilled. I blinked and blinked again, my lips coming apart. "I—I found it," I said quietly.

Tucked against a big plant pot along the back wall, sitting two shelves above my gaze was the face of a ceramic giraffe sitting atop stubby spotted legs. Its shiny pink tongue was licking the corner of its mouth, its eyes were wide and animated, and a semi-circle handle curved up behind 3D ears. Tucked against the tail-shaped waterspout were two red envelopes like the one in Kareem's hands. One labelled "ten" and the other "five."

Kareem huffed a breath that could have passed as a laugh, but I wasn't sure. I hadn't heard him laugh properly in forever. "Damn on Neves, that is creepy. How did we miss it?"

The flicker of tentative amusement that darted through my chest almost made me smile, and that shocked the fuck out of me. *Me? Smiling at Kareem? What the fuck?*

He swiped our fifth envelope off the shelf, being careful not to knock over the empty plant pot next to it. He held it up to show me, a bright look in his eyes. Then he flipped it over to open it. But before he pulled the paper with the riddle out, he stopped and found my gaze again.

"I want to win this year," he said firmly.

I searched the confidence steeling his face. But I ended up getting distracted by the little ache in my chest as I studied him.

My brother had aged a lot in the last eight years. Not that he looked much older than his thirty-one years, but he looked…tired. Like he'd seen and experienced too much too quickly, and it had turned him a little rough and worn on the outside. His square jaw was always set a little too firm. Shadows that spoke of late nights working sat under his eyes. His warm golden skin, a few shades darker than mine, lacked its childhood glow. And his once full cheeks were now hollowed, showing chiselled cheekbones that bordered on harsh, softened only by his short, loosely styled hair.

Maybe it was realising that or something else, but the knot of wariness in my belly loosened.

"Me too," I mumbled, flicking at my nails.

He shifted on his feet with a hesitant bounce then turned his hand to look at his silver wristwatch. "We have thirty-five minutes to solve seven riddles, including the last one."

I gave a small shrug. "We'll probably need ten minutes for the last one."

"That leaves twenty-five for the rest."

"Four minutes per riddle."

He winced a little. "It's a big palace."

"We might have to run."

"It's not impossible."

"It's not."

A weird silence stepped into the conversation as something wary but warm painted on Kareem's expression. My cheeks smarted and I quickly dropped my lashes. With the way Kareem cleared his throat, I was sure I wasn't the only one freaking out at how civil that conversation was.

"We should probably get started then," Kareem said and fiddled with the envelope. He read, "*One: two: three: four I declare a titles war. Five, six, seven, eight—shh!—find me—shh!—before—shh!*"

The riddle sent us rushing to the library but figuring out what the "one: two: three: four" meant took us past our four-minute limit. It was Kareem who said it might be a reference for a location, and with a bit of guess work we realised it was *first floor, second row, third shelf, fourth book.*

Riddle six took us to the larder room in the kitchen. On the way, we passed a group of children excitedly searching for the answer to their own riddle. The girls and boys whined and grumbled as Kareem mock scolded them for trying to cheat by asking us for help. A small smile touched my mouth as he spoke to them. Though my heart hurt for the little girl who had hoped every day for years that her brother would ruffle her hair affectionately the way he did as he sent the children off.

By the time we worked out riddle eleven, Kareem and I were running around with nearly as much excitement as the children, sure we were on target for a possible win. I couldn't say it was like we had gone back to the way it was when we were children, but it was definitely the best our relationship had been since.

We were siblings again, not King Kareem and Crown Princess Esmeralda. Albeit siblings who had drifted apart, but still.

"I see it. I see it!" I called out to Kareem, grinning as I pointed at the red envelope. It was tied to a low branch on a cherry blossom tree on the far eastern side of the gardens. "And there's two! Number nine. Someone hasn't been here yet."

Kareem came running over from the other cherry blossom he had been frantically searching, but I was already climbing onto the wooden bench under it. I took a wobbly step onto the armrest for added height to untie the string from around the letter marked with a big gold star.

"Esmeralda, be careful," Kareem rumbled, suddenly appearing before me.

Two tugs on the string and the last riddle slipped into my fingers. "I got it." I flashed the side with star on it to him above his head. Once he helped me down, I handed him the envelope. "Quickly, read it, read it, read it."

Kareem tore open the envelope. "*I live on my back and face the sky. Day and night. Stuck in my place, frozen in time. I have kept a thousand kisses secret in my lifetime and collected the tears of a million clouds. Sound too vague? Well, change your perspective and think. For I am the lion above the kings and queens, and you measly ants will get nothing more from me. Other than the pretty yellow prize. If you can find me, that is.*"

My upper lip lifted in confusion. "What?"

Kareem let out a baffled puff of air and read it again slowly. And then again and again, but we were both coming up blank for any ideas to where the riddle led to.

"What always faces the sky?" I asked, trying to comb out a tangle in my wind-ruffled hair.

"Everything that is outside and inanimate," Kareem said with a wave of his hand around us.

"Somewhere where you would go to kiss in secret."

Kareem widened his eyes. "I don't know why you're looking at me for an answer. You're the only one who's been kissing someone recently out of the both of us. Where did you go?"

An indistinct sound fell out of my hanging mouth as my face flushed in embarrassment. I was too shocked to even process what I was shocked over. That he was bringing up Kai so casually or that that was the closest thing to a joke I'd heard from Kareem, like everything else, in *forever.*

"We didn't *go* anywhere specific," I squeaked, flinging my hands out.

Kareem waved the torn envelope around. "Okay, okay, forget that. Why does it say, *'change your perspective and think'?*"

"It's a place that lays on its back and faces the sky, so maybe we're supposed to do the same. Maybe lie on the bench and say what you can see?" Kareem handed me the envelope and flopped onto his back on the bench with a grunt. He hooked one leg over the armrest. "What do you see?"

"What you'd expect to see. The sky, clouds, trees."

"You can't stand on those, Kareem. Look for somewhere you can stand and kiss someone."

"I don't know." He threw a frustrated hand up. "There's only the palace. The balconies or the rooftop terrace."

"What's the *'lion above the kings and queens'?*" I asked, brows furrowed in thought. "Isn't there a lion on Touma's crest?"

"Touma's crest?" Kareem echoed, and I looked up to find him squinting at something. Then his eyes popped. "The crest…I can see the crest on the rooftop."

I twirled on my feet and followed the direction of his stare. And damn, he was right.

Touma's shield-shaped crest with a golden lion sitting atop a column in front of a big, sprawling tree could be seen from where we were stood. Stuck to the front of the small building on top of the white terrace rooftop that had two flag poles sticking up high out of it.

I sucked in a breath, realising something else. "You can kiss someone in secret on the rooftop. It's always facing the sky too."

"The prize is on the rooftop."

There was no second-guessing our deduction. Kareem was scrambling up and we were running back through the garden, yelling excitedly at each other.

"But how are we going to get up there?" Kareem said from my side just as we reached the single door entrance on the right side of the palace. "We don't know the way."

"I think—I think I know one way up," I said, eyes darting around the palace's red, gold, and off-white fairy tale interior before I was running down the left corridor. "Kai took me once."

"You *have* kissed him on the rooftop!"

Heat sliced through the cold pinching my cheeks. "He didn't kiss me there. He just showed me."

I might have heard Kareem scoff in disbelief, but I was too focused on trying to remember the route Kai had taken me. Considering I only took one wrong turn, I'd say my memory served me damn well.

"Fuck, I hate running." Kareem huffed behind me as we rushed up a narrow staircase to the metal door at the top.

I giggled breathlessly and grabbed the long door handle, shoving the door open. I squeaked as I stumbled out, almost tripping face first onto the ground. A hand on my arm jerked me back upright.

"Careful," Kareem warned.

"Where is it?" I quickly scanned the cream-tiled rooftop with a matching columned balustrade wrapping around the entire area.

Kareem pointed ahead of us at the same time I noticed a bright yellow teapot sitting on a small stool in front of the building with Touma's crest on it. "There! That's it."

"I'll get it." With a burst of excitement, I ran right for it.

"Wait, Esmeralda!"

A loud bang stopped me in my tracks. My attention snapped ahead to the left where the second door that led up to the terrace had flown open.

Kai stepped onto the rooftop, his thick, raven black hair gorgeously messy, his parka coat pulled up to his chin. He spotted me as Pierre and Adam came out from the doorway behind him.

My gaze flicked to the plastic children's teapot and back to him.

Kai's eyes moved behind me then settled back on me, narrowing just a bit. I felt my mouth stretch into a big, giddy grin.

"You're too late. It's ours," I declared loudly.

Next to Kai, Pierre chuckled. "I don't think so, Princess. That prize is ours."

Shaking my head, I looked to the teapot. I was closer to it than they were, but they were all taller and had bigger strides, could probably run faster too. But I was overdosed on excitement and adrenaline, and there was something about knowing I was up against Kai that made me feel even more competitive. *Nothing* was keeping me from getting the teapot before them.

Without a second thought, I pushed off into a run.

"Kai, run," Adam shouted.

Shit, shit, shit. Kai was fast. But I couldn't, wouldn't let him get it first. I had to get it—I had to.

A jump was possible. The stool wasn't taller than my waist, so the possibility of diving over it was there. I would probably hurt myself and it was technically just a game, but—

Apparently, the prospects of getting injured didn't scare me, because before I knew it, I was throwing myself up and forward through the air as if I was trying to tackle someone to the ground. My hands clapped around the teapot, gripping hard and tugging it to my chest. But then the hard tiles were in my face and my mind screamed at me to tuck and roll too late.

I crashed into the ground, only just breaking my fall with one hand. Something made a painful cracking sound, and something slammed into my chest, knocking all the air out of my lungs.

"Esmeralda," two voices shouted out. One louder. One closer.

I gasped and wheezed for air I couldn't seem to find as I rolled onto my back. My head spun, my ears rang, and my gaze was a disorientated blur. I felt a thud next to me before someone bent above me, their frantic hands hovering over my aching body.

"Esmeralda. Esmeralda." Kai's voice whispered over the noise in my ears. "Shit, Esmeralda."

I blinked rapidly to refocus my gaze and I slowly found Kai's wide, worried eyes right over my face. Gosh, he was so gorgeous it hurt more than the fall. I smiled up at him, or at least I tried to. "Hi, handsome," I croaked.

His mouth opened and closed once, twice. "Dammit, Esmeralda." He sighed heavily, and his brows furrowed. "Are you okay? What were you thinking?"

Before I could answer, Pierre and Adam appeared behind Kai and someone else crashed down to the floor next to me.

Kareem.

My brother's eyes were huge and round as they darted all over me. "Are you—are you okay? Are you hurt? Can you move? Does anything hurt?"

"I'm okay. I'm fine, I think. Nothing hurts." Not yet at least. "I just hit myself in the chest when I fell."

"Can you breathe?"

"Yes. Yes, I can." I made a weak attempt to sit up, and two hands went to my back, helping me up. One was Kai's. The other belonged to Kareem.

Kareem suddenly had my shoulders in his hands and turned me slightly towards him. "Are you mad? What were you thinking? You could have seriously hurt yourself." His voice grew progressively louder with each sentence.

I pursed my lips together sheepishly. "I just wanted to win."

He shook his head furiously. "You stupid girl," he said but it didn't sound mean or vicious. He sounded part amused, part annoyed, and mostly worried. "Don't ever do that again, okay?"

"I won't. I won't." A slow smile slipped over my mouth as I remembered I still had the teapot in my hand. "But we won." I grimaced a little as I lifted the cracked toy, broken on one side and dented on the other. "I hope this doesn't belong to one of the children."

Laughter echoed around me, but I didn't get to see who it came from.

I was abruptly pulled against a lean, warm body. Strong arms locked around me as my chin was squished to a shoulder.

I froze. Not going cold but burning hot and numb as a familiar scent and tightness sent memories crashing through my mind. Old giggles and whispered jokes. Secure hugs I'd missed so much.

"Dammit, Esmeralda." Kareem chuckled, his arms tightening around my shoulders. "Yes, we won."

Kareem…Kareem was hugging me.

Wet heat prickled my eyes, blurring Kai's face, as emotion crashed over me like a tsunami.

My brother was hugging me.

With my arms flying to clamp around Kareem's torso, I buried my face in his neck, hugging him back.

Now I hurt.

But it felt so fucking good.

CHAPTER 24

Esmeralda

"You didn't tell me you were a nurse as well as a chef," I said down to Pierre as he held my bare foot in both of his hands, pressing and rubbing his thumbs into my ankle.

Pierre grinned up at me from the small black stool in front of where I was sat at the edge of a hospital bed in the palace infirmary. "Any pain?" he asked, moving my foot from side to side.

I shook my head. "No, no pain."

"Good." He gently lowered my foot to dangle by his knee then took the other one in his hands. "And I would've told you if I'd known it would impress you this much, Princess." His grin turned lop-sided and flirtatious. "You're looking at me like I'm irresistible right now."

I rolled my eyes, unable to stop a smile from blossoming. "No, I'm not." I nodded my head to the right. "I'm just avoiding looking at those two angry bears."

Pierre's chest shook with laughter as he glanced over his shoulder to Kai and Shehryar, standing side by side. Both were leaning against the white countertop and wall-cupboards. Their arms were crossed over their chests, biceps bulging under their jumpers as much as the veins on their foreheads were, and frowns consumed their faces. It was entirely comical and not at all intimidating.

Shehryar shifted his weight upright, his glare piercing into me.

"Of course, we're angry. What you did was reckless and insane, and you could've seriously hurt yourself, Esmeralda."

"Ooph, he dropped your title. That means you're in serious trouble, Princess," Pierre teased then leaned in close to me. "If it makes you feel any better, I thought your dive was epic." He winked. I grinned. "Any pain by the way?" I shook my head.

"Don't encourage her, Pierre," Shehryar snapped.

"Gosh, look at her beautiful smile." Pierre sighed as he lowered my foot down like he hadn't just aggravated Shehryar further. Shehryar grumbled something under his breath about knocking teeth out. "I'm gonna be the one who needs medical care if you keep looking at me like that."

I was halfway through rolling my eyes when a slight clatter came from where Kai and Shehryar were.

Kai was standing like Shehryar, his hands balled into fists by his side as he glared furiously at Pierre. With the way he rolled his clenched jaw and the way his fingers kept shifting by his sides, it seemed like he was getting ready to attack his best friend. My heart started squealing in my chest, because that wasn't anger in his blacker than black eyes.

Kai was jealous. He had no reason to be, but he was.

"Oh, it looks like the other bear has something to say now," Pierre joked. I had no idea if he couldn't see Kai's jealousy or if he was being purposely obtuse. Either way, I giggled.

When Kai looked at me, flooding my heart with adoration for him, I flashed him a big, loving grin. The dark aura around him wavered as he huffed out a breath, but his frown remained stubborn. Though at least he looked more adorably grumpy than he did murderous.

Once Pierre gave me the all-clear with some instructions on what to do if anything started hurting or bruising by the end of the day, he left me in the infirmary with Kai and Shehryar. I barely got a breath in before Shehryar burst into an angry rant about how dangerous what I did was—though he hadn't even seen it. I quietly nodded and apologised until he eventually ran out of steam.

"Don't do that again," he said softly. "Please, Princess."

"I won't. I promise, Sher."

He put a hand to the back of my hair and leaned down to press a kiss to the top of my head. "Good." He pulled back and checked his wristwatch while turning to Kai. "You may have half an hour with her, Prince Kai. Then I need her back to get ready for the Cannon Ceremony. I would appreciate it if you could accompany her up to her room."

"Of course," Kai said with a firm nod.

Shehryar bowed and exited the room, leaving the door half open behind him. Then it was just me and Kai and a warm silence full of fuzzy awareness.

"Hi," I whispered, my lips curling up timidly.

"Hi," he rasped as he swaggered over until he was standing between my legs.

His gaze caressed all over my face with a delicacy that made my skin tingle. I dropped my head further back to let him check over me completely the way it seemed like he needed to. A sigh slipped out of me when he brought his hands up to cup my face, and my lashes fell shut.

I had missed his hands on me so much. I'd missed the warmth of his huge body, and the sweet, enchanting scent of him too. *I'd missed him.* And we'd only been apart for one night.

The weight of his mouth landed on my forehead first and he inhaled deeply. His body sagged towards me on his exhale. Then he kissed the bridge of my nose so gently. The hollow of my left cheek, and my right cheek. He dipped his head and kissed the thudding pulse under my ear, then dropped his head lower and inhaled again, sending a sweet shiver skittering all over me.

"Kai." My shaky hands clung onto his biceps as my lashes fluttered.

He moved back up, swift and easy, tilting my head higher as he slanted his mouth heavily across mine. He tugged at my lips with a near-desperate greed, yet his hands were so gentle on my face. I could feel it in the tremble of his fingers how careful he was trying to be and gosh, it was so sweet, but I didn't need careful. *I just needed him.* So I kissed him harder, dragged him down closer, and after a moment of hesitation, he reciprocated.

"You scared the life out of me, Babble," Kai panted, resting his forehead on mine.

"Sorry." I gulped slowly, knowing I had much more than just that to be sorry for. "And I'm sorry for not—I mean, last night—I said I wasn't going to stay away from you but—"

His arms immediately squeezed me closer, and he shook his head. "No, don't apologise. It's okay. I understood why, Esmeralda. You had a lot to think about, and I..." He let out a sigh. "It hurt. But only because I knew there was nothing I could do to fix it for you."

A crack split through my heart, filling me with regret. "I'm sorry. I'm so sorry for hurting you, Kai."

But he smiled, soft and small and genuine, as he stroked his thumb across my cheek. "Don't be sorry, Babble. It hurt because you were hurting. Because I care about you so much, Esmeralda. And I'm not sorry about that. I won't ever be. You shouldn't be either."

Forget that he'd just spoken the hottest, sweetest words possible, it was the burning sincerity in his eyes that stole my heart's ability to function properly. It hiccupped and sobbed and screamed, pumping bubbles and achy heat through my veins instead of blood. And that breathless feeling wiped away the rest of the world and all its problems.

All I could see was Kai and how beautiful his heart, his mind, his soul were. And he was mine, and I...

I was in love with him. There was no question about it.

Slipping a hand around to the back of his neck, I pulled him back down to me, mashing my mouth to his and showing him exactly what he was making me feel. All the love, happiness, trust, everything, until I felt satisfied just pressing soft pecks to his hot, swollen mouth.

"Kareem was asking me about you," I whispered. Kai's fingers slowed as they combed through the side of my hair. "But—I think it was a good thing."

"Really?" My nod put a relieved smile on his mouth. "I'm glad. I'm so happy, Esmeralda. For you. But for us too."

My mouth stretched. "I like it when you say *us*."

His gorgeous dimple appeared deep in his right cheek. "Me too."

And then he kissed me.

Somewhere during that kiss, the metal hinges on the door whined behind Kai. We pulled apart, both glancing over, and my heart slammed against my ribcage.

Kareem stood in the open doorway having abandoned his jacket. "I apologise for interrupting like this," he said quietly. "I just wanted to see how you were doing."

Kai looked down at me, an uncertain question in his eyes. I smiled at him, giving his hand by my knee a reassuring squeeze, though honestly, I didn't know how I felt about the situation.

Now that the scavenger hunt was over, I had no idea where Kareem and I sat.

Kai understood, albeit reluctantly, and leaned down to press a kiss to my temple. "I'll wait at the end of the corridor for you."

Kai and Kareem exchanged bows on his way out. Then my brother faced me.

The relaxed atmosphere between us from before? Gone. Now it was just bloody awkward.

With a capital A.

The hairs on my skin stood on end as he came towards me, and I didn't know where to look. I couldn't tell how this was going to go and that scared me so much. At least before I had known Kareem would try to condemn me at every chance he got. I'd always been able to brace myself for the known, but it was harder to prepare for the unknown, and I had no idea who this Kareem was, what he was thinking or why he'd hugged me. Not that I wanted him to take it back.

"Did Pierre examine you?" Kareem asked, his voice quiet and tentative.

"Hmm, he did," I mumbled, only able to meet his eyes for bursts of a few quick second.

"And your hand?"

"It's fine." I turned my left palm up, brushing my thumb over my skin. "There were just a few light scratches, but he cleaned it with antibacterial wipes."

Kareem cleared his throat. "May I see?"

I hesitated, but I lifted my palm up for him. I just didn't expect him to take my hand in both of his and gently rotate it, looking intently over my skin.

"Does it hurt?" he asked, pressing the pads of his thumbs into the base of my palm.

My hand? *No.* My heart? *Yes. So much.*

Like it was being beaten by a hundred different emotions. And none of them were relenting.

I shook my head, swallowing around the growing lump in my throat. "No."

"Okay." He let go of my hand and I missed the rough warmth of his skin immediately. "I know there's still the Cannon Ceremony but try to take it easy. And—if at any point you feel any pain, make sure you say something to Shehryar...*or me.*"

"Even if it means people will notice something is wrong and ask question?" I asked once I found my voice. It was part accusation, but I supposed I was also testing this unknown version of him. I needed to know, whatever his answer was.

He grimaced but it was such a quick twitch of his mouth that I would have missed it if I hadn't been watching him so closely. "Your health is more important, Esmeralda."

My ears were so used to hearing how other people's thoughts and opinions mattered more than I did that it took them a while to register his words. But there was no hiding that he meant what he said. I felt it in my gut.

The tears came fast and hot and so did the ache of relief in my chest. But I blinked rapidly down at my hands, refusing to cry.

That was all I had ever wanted. To know that I was still somewhat important to him. That he still cared just a bit about his little sister even if—

"Esmeralda, I—"

My attention soared to the tight scrunch on his expression, his eyes appearing glazed and uneasy. He opened his mouth, but nothing came out. Then he closed it again and with a resigned sigh, he swayed back. "I'm—I'm sure Prince Kai is waiting for you and I'm sure you need to get ready for the ceremony, as do I, so I'll leave now. Remember what I said about taking it easy."

It was obvious that wasn't what he had wanted to say but I didn't push him to tell me. I just nodded and watched him leave with one last glance over his shoulder.

It was going to take a lot more than one scavenger hunt and an awkward conversation to fix eight—no, eleven years of a broken relationship no matter what either of us said. Too much damage had been done, putting miles of distance and hurt between us.

Even if I wished one hug and a smile could fix it all as if it had never even happened.

CHAPTER 25

Kai

It was past midnight when I stepped into my bedroom again after nine hours of celebration.

It was bliss to finally hear absolute silence instead of screaming crowds and the constant chatter and laughter of too many people. Of course, I couldn't forget the cannons. I could still hear the echoes of seventy-five blasts ringing in my ears.

Not that the Cannon Ceremony had been bad or anything, but it was the noisiest celebration and Fay was right. In big crowds and lots of noise, my social battery depleted at the speed of light.

Finally being back in my space was a relief. Removing my contact lenses and taking a much-needed shower was a bigger relief. But the biggest relief came when I left my room and found Esmeralda coming down the corridor, only for her to flash me a stunning grin and run right into my arms.

Absolutely nothing would ever beat the relief of having her near me, her warmth and sweet, peony rose scent filling every cell in my body, and knowing she was safe and happy again. *And mine.*

I wasn't sharing that joy with anyone tonight. Even if the night guards and palace staff were discreet and mindful of giving us privacy when they saw us wandering around together.

Without letting Esmeralda out of my arms, I practically dragged

her back into my bedroom, loving the way she chuckled into my chest.

"So, this is your secret lair," Esmeralda said as she walked into the middle of my room.

I closed the door behind me—and locked it—as my gaze trailed over her small frame while hers trailed the space. I swallowed hard, wanting heat wafting down my body.

Her and her fucking pyjama shorts and tops were going to be the death of me. Though tonight she was wearing a black jersey jumper over the plum-coloured silk that complimented her warm golden skin tone perfectly, with her long, slightly damp hair draped down around her shoulders.

"Can I snoop around?" she asked, throwing me a wide-eyed glance over her shoulder.

I hummed my assent and nudged at the frame of my glasses. As she looked around in fascination, I lazily made my way over to the foot of my wooden-framed, four-poster bed.

My room wasn't much different from the one she was staying in. Same blood red carpet, corniced ceiling with a big, gold and crystal chandelier. There was one scenic painting, one of Bucky, and one of my other two horses dotted around the walls, all three of which Fay had painted. The doors to the right of my bed led to an ensuite and walk-in wardrobe, and where Esmeralda had a vanity in the top corner, I had a wooden chest of drawers matching my bed with a big rectangular mirror above it.

She made her way over to said chest of drawers, peeking at the products I had meticulously set in their right places. She went straight for the black, square-shaped glass bottle of cologne and brought it to her nose. Her lashes dropped as she inhaled deeply, and the moan she let out after should have been fucking illegal. It was low, honest, and so unashamedly lusty. Or maybe the lusty one was me.

I felt like a teenage boy who had brought a girl to his room for the first time. I was already horny from seeing her in my space, but her moan was like a lit match against my petrol-soaked body.

I was so lost in my lust for her that it took me a moment to realise she was pulling open a drawer, not going for the top one but the second one. The one where I had hidden her—

Panic shot up my spine. "Wait," I called out, my body jerking towards her.

She gasped, her mouth gaping wide. *Fuck.* Her head turned slowly and that perfect O on her lips turned into a big, accusing grin, her eyes glittering with bubbling amusement. *Double fuck.* Hot blood swarmed my face. Before I could come up with an excuse, my hand was moving up to tug at my ear on its own accord, giving away my secret.

"Mr Perfect Prince," she said, laughter lacing her words. "Why is my black *thong* in your drawer?"

Her hand dipped inside and out came the black lace thong she'd been wearing the night in the TV room, dangling on the tip of her index finger. She shook it accusingly at me like a pendulum.

"I…" I cleared my throat, rubbing my treacherous fingers over my mouth. "I just…"

"You just…" she repeated mockingly. "Picked them up that night and forgot to send them back with my shirt the next morning? So you were keeping them in your drawer to give to me later?"

The corner of my mouth twitched but I kept the curl hidden under my fingers until I had it under control. I pushed my hands into my black pyjama bottoms and stalked over to her. "I could ask you the same thing." She widened her eyes innocently. "I don't recall getting my T-shirt back."

Her lips spread impossibly wider, and she cocked her chin like an audacious little brat. "That's because you're not getting it back. That T-shirt is *mine* now."

I ground my teeth together as her claim on my clothes sent throbs of possessive desire raking down my front. "Then these…" My voice came out low as I slipped the lace off her fingers, tracing my thumb over the detailed design before I blindly dropped them back in the drawer. "Belong to me now." The quiet clap of the drawer shutting matched the last syllable of my sentence.

The colour on her cheeks deepened as arousal washed over her face, turning her greyish-brown eyes murky and hot. I could see her scheming thoughts playing out in her stare, and I could pretend I was going to be strong, but we both knew I'd give in to whatever game she was planning.

"But," she said, giving me a fake little pout, "that's my favourite pair."

"Is that supposed to make me want to give them back?" I tried to sound as unbothered as I could.

"Then how about a trade?" she purred, leaning into me until I could feel her body heat. "The thong in your drawer…for the ones I'm wearing now?"

I nearly choked on a groan. My eyes automatically flew down to her thighs, to the secret space between I wanted to bury my face in again. My cock gave an angry jerk in my boxers, refusing to lose to my salivating mouth and trying to stake first claim on her. It didn't matter who got her first, I'd keep taking her on rotation—hands, mouth, and dick—all night long if she let me.

The soft rub of her thighs together jerked my gaze back up to hers, and even in my drugged state, I registered that I wasn't the only one about to explode. Esmeralda's pupils were so dilated they ate away her irises and her skin was flushed all down her neck. But that sultry smile of hers…*fuck*.

I took a slow, needy step towards her, nearly pressing us flush together. "Don't tempt me, Babble." My voice came out hoarse and sounding like I was demanding she do the exact opposite. *Tempt me. Tempt me. Don't fucking stop tempting me, my beautiful Babble.*

Her smile widened and she pushed up onto her tiptoes, circling her arms around my neck. My hands naturally slipped under her jumper, finding her hips to anchor myself to. "Then you shouldn't have tempted me first by stealing my underwear, Mr Perfect Prince."

I huffed a laugh into her mouth as she pressed her soft lips over mine, cinching my arms around her as I kissed her back. It wasn't rushed or desperate and yet there was still a dizzying hunger controlling our slow swipes and licks.

When we pulled apart for air, I gripped the hem of her black jumper and pulled it up over her head. Throwing it over my shoulder, I stepped back to get my fill of her. *Fuck…*

There was no cropped, buttoned shirt tonight. Just a flimsy vest top in the same plum colour as her shorts. If it wasn't for the pale pink bra I could see peeking out from under the black lace straps, one slight pull on the silk would have had her ample breasts spilling out onto display.

I was throbbing everywhere humanly possible with arousal, too addicted to the sight of her to care that I was blatantly ogling at her chest. Until my mind supplied me with the image of that dive she took in the morning and then my gaze was searching all over her for another reason entirely.

"Are you really not injured anywhere, Esmeralda? At all?"

"I'm fine. *But* I guess if you're worried..." She moved past me. I blinked in confusion, taking a second to turn and watch as she swung her hips over to the door. I was about to ask where she was going when she suddenly spun on her socks-clad feet to face me.

"I could ask Pierre to check me over once more and then come back here," she said with a casual shrug. "I heard he was staying the night for the Memorial Service tomorrow. I'm sure he wouldn't mind if I told him that you wanted him to give me a *thorough* examination."

Who knew if that was the sound of her unlocking the door or the sound of something cracking inside me at the thought of Pierre touching her all over. *Again.* I had no idea, but my body went rigid with something red-hot.

Having to put up with it the first time while he flirted with her had turned my insides green with envy, but this, oh this was something ten times more ferocious. My desire was now tainted with jealousy, turning it into something dark, a little mean, and a whole lot of demanding.

"Don't even think about it, Babble," I snarled through gritted teeth. My pulse hammered brutally through my head, heart, and erection. "He's not coming anywhere near you again."

Excitement ignited in her eyes, but her lips parted on a shaky inhale. Even so, I heard the twist of the door handle behind her as she opened it just a slither. She didn't say anything. She didn't have to. That bratty, impudent look dancing in her hooded eyes said it all.

Try and stop me.

Her challenge set me off. I was charging towards her before I fully registered I was. She squeaked and clambered around, tearing the door open wider. *But it was too late.* I was right behind her before she could get one foot out the threshold of my room. I hooked an arm around her waist and yanked her back against my chest. She shrieked something that sounded a lot like my name.

I kicked the door shut behind me and locked it then headed straight for my bed. She landed with a gasp when I dropped her on the charcoal grey silk sheets and tried to scramble onto her hands and knees in a useless attempt to escape me. Grasping her by the hips, I yanked her back to where I stood at the edge, slamming my hard dick right between her thighs.

She choked loudly on a gasp, and I groaned, fighting to keep my eyes open as pleasure coiled through my belly. I ground myself against her in long, hard rocks, and she pushed back against me, our clothing doing nothing to lessen the delicious feeling. My dick begged me to give in and fuck her right then, but the dominant beast in me demanded repentance from her first. *And he won.*

I leaned over to thread one hand into the back of her hair, pulling her upright until her back was pressed to my chest. Her whimper was loud as I moved my hand from her hair to her throat, holding her head to my shoulder. She curled her arms back to cling onto my hips, keeping me in place.

"Kai, please," Esmeralda panted, trying to turn her head to look at me. "Fuck me."

I grunted mockingly into her ear. "After telling me you would let Pierre thoroughly examine you?" I growled, watching her lashes flutter and her mouth open wide. "I don't think so, Babble. You don't get to make me jealous and then beg to have your pussy pounded. It doesn't work like that."

She whimpered a protest, and I silenced her by slipping my index and middle fingers into her mouth. "There is no point whining now." I was careful not to push my fingers too far back as I stroked her tongue, but she moaned and clamped her lips around the digits, sucking them

in deeper.

I shuddered on an exhale, pressing my jealous dick harder against her shamelessly grinding arse. "Only good girls get what they want," I rasped, dragging my lips over the shell of her ear. She gasped around my fingers. "But you've been a bad girl, Babble. And bad girls only get spanked and edged and teased until they're crying and begging for mercy. Isn't that right?"

She went still, her eyes wide as a muffled whimper left her stuffed mouth. The mixture of arousal and panic on her face turned me on so much I felt the literal burn of it in my eye. I smirked down at her, and she started shaking her head, more flustered sounds coming out of her.

A near-silent laugh fell off my lips and I pulled my fingers from her mouth. Before she could voice a protest or an apology, I captured her parted lips, looting her of words with my tongue. When I released her, she slumped weak and shaking against my chest, her eyes so glazed and hooded she looked like she was about to pass out. And the rush of power to my head made me feel possessed.

"I'm—I'm sorry," she said through her panting.

Fuck, she was so unbelievably beautiful. "I know," I whispered, stroking her jaw with my thumb. "But the only place my dick is going is in your mouth until I'm convinced of it, Babble."

She nodded, small and eager. I rewarded her with one last kiss before I unwrapped myself from around her, helping her turn to face me. I undressed her quickly, dropping her silk pyjamas at my feet and taking a breathless moment to appreciate the near-naked sight of her. All the dips and curves of her slim, hourglass figure.

She was a little soft around her belly where that sexy, gold piercing dangled from her bellybutton, her hips accentuated by the graspable dip in her waist. Her arms and legs were slender, but her thighs were still supple and full. And the sight of her pink lace lingerie set, so fucking pale in colour against her warm golden skin, was more arousing than the seductive plum of her silk pyjamas.

The see-through lace sat high on her hips, two pieces of ribbon rather than any actual fabric, and the bra was no better. The cup barely covered her nipples, tempting me to set them free from their confines. So, I unhooked her bra with a clumsy flick of my fingers and pulled it off her. I groaned my pleasure at seeing her exposed dark brown nipples, already puckered and ready to be teased. I couldn't help but run caressing thumbs over them both, making her shiver deliciously.

Her thong didn't go on the floor with her other clothes. It went straight into the drawer of my bedside cabinet. I didn't care that she witnessed me taking her underwear this time.

When I moved back towards her, she was on her knees at the edge of the mattress, grinning teasingly up at me. "I'm going to have no underwear left if you keep taking them."

"That doesn't sound like a problem to me," I said, and she giggled sultrily.

"I want to see you naked too. Please."

There was no way I could deny her when she asked like that, so I stripped out of all my clothes, tossing them on top of hers before I straightened my glasses. The way her eyes flamed as she looked at me was hot enough to keep me warm on even the coldest of days. *Without a coat.* And then she fucking moaned, long and low, and if that wasn't the biggest ego boost in the entirety of Neves then I didn't know what was. She made me feel like ten times the man I was.

That was why I silently let her look her fill, standing tall and perfectly still—*admittedly, I was flexing a bit*—as she practically licked all over my hot, damp skin. From my broad shoulders down my muscular legs to my hard cock, wet around the swollen tip and jutting right at her.

"How are you so beautiful?" she whispered. "It shouldn't be allowed. It could kill someone."

My grin was unstoppable, the heat in my cheeks untameable, and the urge to kiss her fucking unquenchable. I cupped her chin and tipped her mouth higher to receive it. "You're one to talk, Babble," I muttered against her lips. "You should see yourself right now."

She smiled at me, and my heart ached at how precious she looked. It gave me a moment of pause. "Are you really okay, Esmeralda?"

"I'm not hurt," she said, squeezing a small hand around my wrist.

"I promise, Kai."

"If it's too much, use our safe word. Or give me two taps on my legs or arms, okay?"

"Okay. But don't forget that safe word is for you too, Kai."

Shit, she was so... I barely managed to get in a quick nod before I was taking her mouth again with gratefulness and a desperate kind of urgency. She knew acting like a dominant was still new for me, and her reassurance, her confidence and trust in me meant *everything*.

"Eyes on me as you suck, Babble," I said as I lifted my mouth from hers.

She nodded and brushed a soft peck to my lips as I let go of her chin. I straightened and she moved up with me, caressing her hands up over the rippling muscle on my abdomen. Ever so slightly grazing her short nails through the even dusting of dark hairs on my firm pecs.

She set her mouth on the stubbled underside of my jaw, kissing and licking her way all over my neck, stealing more than one shudder and sigh from me. The scrape of her teeth over each of my flat nipples forced rough moans out of me, but it was the licking kisses below my bellybutton that left me trembling with need. I could barely get my erratic breaths under control.

Fuck. Was now a good time to mention that nobody had done this to me in nearly five years?

But then her hands were on my thighs, clinging and digging in, as she slid back on the duvet and lowered her mouth to my dick, and those words met a swift death. I carefully took her hair in both of my hands and held it back from her face. And then she parted her supple, swollen lips.

Her first lick over the wet tip of my dick was explosive. The second down the side enough to kill me. But I desperately clung onto consciousness as pleasure wound my body tight. I wasn't going to die before I had the chance to see my Babble's bratty mouth stuffed full of my cock.

"Fuck, Esmeralda. Lick the head again," I growled through gritted teeth, fisting her hair harder.

She did. With the flat of her tongue, then round and round in teasing circles. Then down the full length of me, and against the sensitive skin of my balls. Watching me, learning my reactions as she got me wet all over with her saliva.

It was anybody's guess who moaned louder when she pursed her lips around me, both of us lost in the pleasure of giving and taking. Then inch-by-inch she eased me into the wet heat of her mouth.

She pulled back a few and I gasped, nearly doubling over her as the threat of coming undone in under ten seconds hit me like a speeding truck. Delight and lust and something like pride danced in her eyes as she blinked up at me, and fuck, it pissed me off. *It turned me on.* I loved that look in her eyes, but it riled me too. This was supposed to be her punishment. *But it felt like mine instead.*

Gritting my teeth, I pushed her head down just enough to force her to take those inches back into her mouth. "Keep sucking, Babble. Or I'll never forgive you at this rate."

She whimpered and doubled down on sucking me off, steadily building up speed and suction, scraping her nails over my thighs, arse, and abdomen, massaging my balls with one hand until she had me panting. She preened under every groan, gasp, and whispered praise I gave her and moaned as I let one hand roam around to pinch and pull at each of her pebbled nipples.

When she started getting comfortable, I started using her hair to guide her, but it wasn't enough. Fuck, it wasn't. I wanted tears running down her face. I needed to hear her gag on me.

"Can you take me deeper?" I rasped, caressing a thumb across her hollowed cheek.

With the subtlest of nods and without so much as even a flicker of hesitation, Esmeralda slowly swallowed every inch of my throbbing dick. Until her swollen lips just brushed my skin at the base, painted in trimmed dark hairs.

Her breath heaved quietly and mine completely halted. Trapped in my lungs so fucking blissfully as my balls tightened, only to break free in a loud groan when her throat convulsed around my length.

"Fuck, that's it, Babble. Such a good fucking girl." I bared my teeth down at her as I watched her beautiful eyes fill with tears, her

cheeks going pink as she struggled to keep the whole of my dick in her mouth. But she did. And it was gorgeous. *She was gorgeous.*

She held herself there for a few seconds, then she pulled back, gasping the moment my dick slipped from between her lips. Saliva strung over her chin as her mouth hung open, the liquid lust in her eyes threatening to spill down her cheeks. Not even the best artist in the world could have replicated the stunning picture she painted.

Something wild and possessive roared through my blood, tearing apart any sanity left in my mind. My hands moved reflexively under the consuming feeling, shoving her head by the hair until her parted lips pressed against the side of my dripping wet cock while my other hand flew up.

I leaned over her and swung back down, smacking her over one pert arse cheek thrust up in the air behind her. Not as a punishment, but as the fucking reward she craved and deserved.

Esmeralda choked on a cry, her body jerking from the impact and her nails biting so damn hard into my thighs it hurt so fucking sweetly. Probably hard enough to leave little marks. *Her marks on me.*

I groaned my delirium as the vibrations of her cry lingered through my dick. Just like the faint pink stain of my handprint on her arse. *My mark on her.*

Pulling on her hair, I drew her head back to look at her. Part of me was checking I hadn't pushed her too far, but the other part wanted to memorise every expression she made.

I ran my fingers gently over her swollen mouth and flushed cheeks. "You're stunning, Esmeralda."

The glow in her eyes grew headier. "A—again." She aligned her mouth with my cock.

There was no doubt that she meant both the spanking and deep-throating. I huffed out a single chuckle, smirking as I cupped the underside of her chin with my free hand. "Open up."

She obeyed and I slowly slid home. Holding still for three seconds, sliding almost fully out, hitting the back of her throat again, then pulling out all the way. I shuddered as she gasped and landed two hard smacks on her arse as a reward before shoving my dick back into her mouth.

I only managed to do it a few more times before the pleasure felt too much like an impeding orgasm. But there was no way I was coming before she did. Or in her mouth. Right then, at least.

The moment I dragged her mouth off my dick, I moved her around, turning her arse to me. I pressed a hand between her shoulder blades, pushing her chest down to the mattress so her derriere stuck higher in the air and—

Slap. I landed a hard spank on one of her arse cheeks. She was still crying out when I slapped the other cheek too, the vicious sound ringing through her breathless shriek.

"Are you going to fucking try to make me jealous again, Babble?" I gritted out, palming both my hands over her backside.

"No," she cried, her head thrashing from side to side as she fisted the silk-covered duvet in her hands. I spanked her arse cheeks in quick succession. "I won't! I won't!" *Slap.* "I promise." *Slap.* "I'm so—rry." *Slap.* "Kai!" *Slap.* "*Please!*"

She wasn't begging me to stop. She was begging for more.

Rubbing a hand over her smarting skin, I said, "Say '*thank you*' after every spank, Esmeralda. Loud and clear."

Slap. "Thank you," she mewled. *Slap.* "Thank you!" *Slap.*

After her tenth "thank you," I was so overdosed on arousal that my mind was a complete fog. I had to shake my head to see straight before I smoothed my hands over her reddened arse.

"Fuck," I moaned, watching her arousal drip down from her swollen cunt onto my bedsheets. "You're fucking dripping, Babble. Is that how much you like being spanked?"

All I got was a whimpered sound from her and a hard quiver of her thighs. I chuckled, feeling prouder than I should have for stealing my chatty Esmeralda's ability to speak, but all I wanted to do was keep her silent and drugged on the pleasure I wanted to give her.

I stroked two blunt fingers between her drenched pussy lips, coating them in her wetness. Before shoving them right into her to the knuckle. She cried out with a shake of her body, and I wished I could've seen the face she made right then. Instead, I held her down with a hand around the back of her neck and pumped my fingers hard and fast. Her cunt made delicious, filthy wet sounds.

"Tell me, Babble," I rasped as I moved my hand on her neck into her hair. "Who makes you feel so good you can't fucking speak or move or breath?"

"You," she sobbed. "F—uck, Kai. *Please, please, please.*"

I pulled on her hair, forcing her to move back and upright. "Who's good girl are you?"

"Yours." Her new position let her ride my fingers, and fuck, did she grind on them hard like a needy little brat.

I yanked on her hair, tipping her face all the way up to the ceiling, giving me a glimpse of her damp cheeks and gasping mouth. "Who's the only person who gets to *thoroughly* examine you from now on?" I growled, swaying closer to her to get a better look at her beautiful, teary face.

"You, Sir!"

I froze. My fingers froze. Time froze.

Panting, I blinked and blinked again. It took my mind a moment to catch up with why my cock was suddenly pulsing so fucking much it almost outpaced my heart.

"What—what did you call me?" I managed with a croak.

Esmeralda's lashes fluttered nervously as she gulped for air. "I…"

I pulled her back the rest of the way to me and quickly snuck my arm around her shoulders, cupping her chin in my hand and turning her face up to me. "You called me *Sir*," I said, searching her shy gaze. Her wet lashes dipped, and I gave her chin a stern shake. She lifted them swiftly. "Say it again."

Her eyes widened and she took a hesitant breath. "Sir," she whispered.

The groan that rolled up my throat was raw and primal, shoved out of me by the hard jerk my dick gave. She wasn't the only one dripping all over the bedsheets anymore.

"Again."

"Sir."

I groaned a chuckle and kissed her hard and quick. "I like that. I like that a lot."

She smiled against my lips. "You'll be my Sir then?"

"Fuck, yes, Babble," I said, kissing her again. "Yes, I'll be your Sir." *Kiss.*

"Then, can I ask for one more thing—Sir?" I gritted my teeth as my balls tightened to the point of pain and nodded. "I like it when you praise me, but I want you to degrade me too. Call me your cum slut. Your good little whore. Your filthy brat. Anything you want. You don't have to hold back."

Fuck, fuck, fuck. My mind should have warred against the idea of degrading her like that, but arousal spiked through me so hard, I saw stars.

I slammed my mouth down on hers, kissing her hard and sealing that deal. Because I wanted it. Fuck, I wanted it too.

"Then what does my good little whore want from her Sir?" I panted hoarsely, stroking my thumb across her jaw. "My mouth or my dick?"

"Both," she purred cheekily.

I fought the urge to smile. "Don't be a brat, Babble. Which one do you want *first*? And answer quickly, or I will pick and then that's all you'll be getting all night long."

"Your dick. Please—*Sir.*"

I took my glasses off and dropped them on my pillow before changing our positions. Gently pushing her onto her back in the middle of my bed and climbing over her.

She sighed when I pressed my mouth to the softness of her belly, breathing in her scent. I kissed and nipped and sucked on her skin, making her squirm and whine. A trail of pink blotchy love bites followed my mouth up to her breasts. She watched me, biting on her bottom lip, as I blew teasingly over one tight nipple. Her lips pulled apart on a silent sound, and I was almost tempted to lean up and fill her mouth with my tongue again. *Almost.*

Instead, I drew her nipple into my mouth, moaning into the pillow-softness of her breast pressing into my face and sucking. I pulled her into my mouth in harsh tugs, rolling the peaked bud between my teeth. She groaned and clawed at my head and shoulders as if she was trying to get me off her, and yet she arched up into my mouth at the same time, pleading for more.

I did the same to her other nipple, turning it hot and raw with a red tinge like its twin, and my beautiful Babble was shaking almost violently. She mouthed my name as she blinked her unfocused eyes up at me, nothing but a soft breathy sound coming out.

A groaned chuckle slipped out of me as I leaned over her. I pressed repeated nipping kisses to her lips and at some point, her trembling hands came up to cup my face. "I have condoms in my drawer, Esmeralda," I whispered. "I can use them if you've changed your mind."

"I haven't. I want you raw. Now, Kai. Please, Sir."

There was nothing more I could say so I kissed her and adjusted my weight over her as I slipped a hand down between us. I lined my erection against her entrance, rubbing the tip between her wetness. She sighed as she sunk back into the duvet. Her stare engulfed me, doing something tight and achy to my chest that nearly pulled a broken sound from my throat.

Fuck. Maybe it was the sex, maybe it wasn't, but it felt like…

I was falling in love with her.

"Esmeralda," I rasped, easing the head of my dick into her. "You're so beautiful."

"So are you," she whispered, drawing me closer to her with her arms and legs.

Our eyes stayed locked as I slowly sunk into her, her mouth opening wider and my breath turning more and more ragged with every inch. And it was so painfully intimate, like nothing I had ever experienced before. Like I was baring my soul to her, and she was doing the same for me, and we were tearing them apart so we could entwine them together into something new.

When her inner muscles clenched around me, I was sure she felt it too.

I pressed my forehead to hers, trying to find my breath. And sanity. "You're so big, Kai," she uttered.

I groaned, closing my eyes, and tried to convince my overexcited dick to relax for a second. "Don't say that, Babble, or I won't last more than a minute."

I sensed her grin as her fingers stroked the tightness from my jaw. "I wouldn't mind."

"But I would," I gritted out and opened my eyes. "I'm not letting my first time after five years end so quickly. Especially considering it's with you."

Her fingers stopped. "What? Your first time—"

I didn't let her finish her sentence. I dragged my hips back until I almost slipped out of her and snapped them forward, thrusting all the way in. Esmeralda gasped, surging up under me, and threw her head back against the duvet. I didn't know what lingered through me longer, the pleasure in my belly or the sharp sting over my shoulders under her nails, but I didn't want either feeling to leave me. *Ever.*

I growled and dropped my mouth to her neck, sinking my teeth right into that spot where it met her shoulder as I did it again. She cried my name and my eyes rolled back. Again, and she pulled at my hair. I moaned and did it again. Again and again and again. *Drag. Thrust. Drag. Thrust.* Harder. Faster. Deeper. Filling her, kissing her, biting her, licking her, memorising her as she marked me, cried for me, met me thrust for thrust, kiss for kiss. And it was so fucking good.

"Fuck," she sobbed, rocking her hips up into my thrust. "It feels so good—you feel so good, Sir."

"Esmeralda," I groaned and clamped my mouth over hers, silencing her for the sake of preserving my wavering stamina. Fuck, she was ruining me. So perfectly. Irreversibly.

It didn't take long for her breaths to turn quick and shallow, her pussy pulsing around my dick. I gritted my teeth as white threatened the edges of my vision, but I anchored a hand around the back of her neck, her hair tangling between my fingers and clinging to her damp skin.

"Fuck, Babble. Say it," I growled between my teeth, plunging so fast and hard the mattress shook under her. "Ask me for it." I slipped a hand under one of her thighs, squeezing and dragging her leg higher over my hip, spreading her further for me so I could reach deeper, rub her clit harder. She cried for me louder, her mouth opening wider. "Don't you *dare* take it without asking."

"Kai," she choked out, her drugged eyes crinkling in a desperate plea. "Please—I can't—I'm…let me come. Let me come. *Please let me come.* Please may I come, Sir?"

I slammed into her on a vicious growl. "Give it to me." *Thrust.* "Come for me like a good little slut."

I kept my rhythm going, grinding against her clit the way she needed me to, watching her flushed face twist, her hands clambering all over me to find the perfect grip.

And then she soared. Eyes wide, her mouth releasing a broken cry, nails clawing over my back, and her pussy. Fuck, her pussy clamped around my cock so hard the pleasure of it cut off my airway.

I tried to last. I really did. I tried to grasp onto control, tried to breath, tried to think, tried desperately not to chase the relief begging to be freed. But I failed to do anything but thrust into her like a wild beast the moment her body melted just the slightest, driving her deep into the mattress.

"Please," she whimpered, one her hands finding my cheek.

That was it. I couldn't hold back any longer. I came undone with a loud groan of her name, sensation pulsing through my belly and head as my hips jerked against Esmeralda's pelvis.

It felt like it went on forever. I'd never come so hard or so long in my life. My body was desperately trying to give her every ounce of cum in me like it was trying to prove I was hers.

"So handsome." Esmeralda's soft voice cut through the ringing in my ears. A sweet, soothing call that made my body lose all its strength. I collapsed on top of her, making a feeble attempt to roll off but she banded her arms around my shoulders, keeping me there.

I should've worried more that I was crushing her. I didn't. I curled my arms around her and buried my face into her neck, only then registering that it wasn't her who was shaking. *It was me.*

"Are you—are you okay?" My voice came out muffled against her skin.

"I am so much more than okay, Kai," she whispered, stroking a hand over my damp hair. "I'm great. So good. Are you?"

"I am. I am." I kissed my way up her neck and over her jaw to her smiling mouth, lifting my weight off her as much as her arms would let me. "You were so perfect, Esmeralda." I searched her soft, sated stare. "Did I—was it good for you?"

Her mouth stretched into a tired grin. "I think the answer to your question is quite obvious, Kai."

I smiled, brushing a lock of hair off her forehead. "Even the spanking? It wasn't too much?"

She kissed the bridge of my nose. "No. It was everything I wanted." She smirked. "And I really like your thing for biting. You're like a sexy vampire with your pointy canines." I huffed a laugh. "More importantly though—are you sure you haven't done that in five years?"

"I'm sure," I said, grinning. She didn't make it sound like something I should be embarrassed about. She looked amazed. And then absolutely mischievous.

"Want to do it again?"

Considering how hard I had just come, I shouldn't have been able to feel heat surging through me all over again. But my dick defied the biology of man and was ready to have her again.

CHAPTER 26
Esmeralda

"**H**ello?" I said into my mobile phone, eyeing the black court heels I was wearing against the blood red carpet of my bedroom.

"Esmeralda…dude," my best friend, Mariyah, whisper-groaned on the other end of the line. "What time is this to call, man? And my ringtone scared the fucking life out of me too."

I winced, glancing at the digital clock on the bedside cabinet from where I sat at the edge of my bed.

10:17 AM flashed in red across the rectangular screen, which meant it was five-thirty-ish in Raven. *Not* exactly an appropriate time to ring someone, but she was my best friend, so that etiquette didn't apply to her.

"Sorry, it's early, I know," I said. "I had some time before I head down to the car with Shehryar for the service, so I thought I'd try my luck."

"Well, you're in luck." She yawned. "Lilly, Drew, and the kids are here. And my dear nieces and nephew think it's great fun to wake Aunty Mari up before six o'clock every morning to play trucks and dolls—*and* ask questions I don't have answers to—so I was already half awake anyway."

I smiled at my lap, picking off a piece of fluff from my black, princess-style coat. "How are they all?"

"The kids are great, as curious and adorable as always. Lilly's good too—excited. And I'm still not sure if my brother-in-law was crying happy tears or sad tears. They're having another baby."

"Oh," I cooed happily. "Girl or boy?"

"Dunno yet. I think they want to keep it a surprise this time though."

"Well, tell them I said congratulations."

"I will, I will. When we're watching *'Aunty Mari's princess friend'* on TV for the Memorial Service," she said, and I grinned. "So, why did Aunty Mari's princess friend call so early in the morning? Something big must've happened otherwise you would've just messaged me."

My smile turned smug and coy at the same time as heat warmed through my face and belly, memories of last night flooding my mind. Not that I needed the memories. The sweet aches lingering through my muscles wouldn't let me forget the way Kai railed me into his bed all night long.

"I, uh…" I swallowed down the giddy feeling soaring through my chest.

Mariyah gasped down the phone. "Esmeralda…you didn't…"

I let my silence speak for itself. But even if I had wanted to say anything, the massive grin on my face left no room for words.

"You little slut!" A giggle jumped from my mouth. "You fucked TRG!"

I threw my head back and laughed up at the ceiling. "You can't call him that!"

"Dude, Orange as his nickname went out the fucking window the moment you told me you called him *'tall, royal, and grumpy'*, so TRG is here to stay, okay?" I rolled my eyes, laughing. "And don't try to change the subject. Tell me. Did you fuck him?"

I nibbled on my lip, trying to tame my beaming smile. "I mean… technically, *he* fucked *me*. But—"

Mariyah squealed so loudly I had to pull the phone from my ear, her excitement for me sparking my own happy laughter. "Yes! Yes! Yes, yes, yes," she said, and I could perfectly picture her fist pumping the air. "*Finally*. Six years of pining paid off. I'm so happy for you my gorgeous, gorgeous girl!"

Everyone needed a friend who hyped up their every achievement the way Mariyah hyped mine up. I loved her so fucking much. She was my friend equivalent of a soulmate.

"Thank you—I think."

"So—so is this it? Are you two like official now? Because if you tell me you're still *'figuring it out'*, I swear I'm gonna come to Touma and smack both of your asses."

"I mean…" I fiddled with the belt of my coat. "Neither of us have really *asked* what we are, but with how things have been between us the last two, three days, I don't think there's any question about it. He's so…" A longing sigh slipped from my mouth as a sweet ache clamped down on my chest. "He's better than anything I could have ever asked for, Mariyah."

She made a giddy sound on the line. "I can literally feel how much he cares for me in everything he does, and I…" I swallowed the lump of happiness in my throat. "He feels like *it* to me. Like there could never be anyone else other than him. Not even a book boyfriend, Mariyah."

"Oh, Ezzy," Mariyah cooed through a heavy sigh. "You love him."

I nodded to myself as the words sunk into my every bone. "I do." I had for a while now. And maybe it wasn't supposed to happen so quickly, but it was too late to rewind the clock. Not that I wanted to. I hadn't been blind to what was happening. I'd chosen to let it happen. I'd wanted it to happen, and there was no other way it was meant to be. Loving Kai had been my fate and my choice.

"Kyah!" she squealed. "Oh my gosh, this is so cute. You're so cute, Esmeralda!" I giggled. "This has to be the *best* royal love story ever. Oh my gosh, I can't. I think I'm gonna die from happiness."

"Okay, okay," she said once she stopped cheering and I stopped laughing, then her voice went low and suggestive. "What about the sex? Was it good?"

Good was the understatement of the century. I still couldn't believe how fucking amazing it had been considering Kai admitted that he hadn't had sex in nearly five years. He didn't say it directly, but I realised that meant he hadn't even been sleeping with Meg towards the end of their relationship. That stupid, narcissistic, abusive bitch.

But that was a secret he'd entrusted to me, and I couldn't tell it to Mariyah. I wouldn't tell anyone.

I licked over my lips slowly. "It was life-changing, Mariyah."

She cackled loudly down the phone as I heard a faint thumping sound like she was smacking something. Probably her pillow. "She didn't say insane, she said fucking *life-changing*. Oh shit, I'm dead!" She tried to tame her laughter. "Damn. Crap. I think I woke the kids up." She went quiet for a second. "Shit, they're really awake. Ez, quickly. Give me details without giving me details."

"Uh." I chuckled, thinking of what to say. "So…turns out he is in fact a soft Dom." My best friend gasped, muttering something that sounded like '*no way*'. "And I uh, accidentally called him *Sir*. And then he *Sir-ed* the fuck out of me all night long."

I swear Mariyah's shriek of laughter was so loud, it probably could've been heard from outer space.

Kai kept me close to his side as we walked through Chaukham Palace's kitchen that same evening after the Peace Memorial Service at Westcombe Palace.

We found Fay, Adam, and Shehryar in conversation with Pierre and head chef, Nur, around the big metal kitchen island towards the back. Half full mugs and plates covered most of the countertop as if they had been eating like they'd been starved all day. I didn't blame them.

The luncheon after the service had been a hall of too many people and too little portions, especially the elaborate, deconstructed apple crumble for dessert. And the hour and a half of mingling with emergency service and Army personnel after hadn't helped with the tired and hungry situation.

When the five men spotted us, they stopped what they were doing and blatantly stared at mine and Kai's intertwined hands. A blush assaulted my cheeks.

It was the first time Kai and I were holding hands in front of anyone during the day. And if it wasn't proof of what I'd said to Mariyah on the phone, I wasn't sure what was.

Maybe we hadn't talked about what we were to each other, nor had we discussed when we would officially tell people, but last night had clearly changed something between us. And this was our silent declaration we weren't going to hide that we were involved with each other.

Shehryar stopped shaking his protein shake mid-air, his eyes narrowing on Kai like an overprotective brother judging his little sister's boyfriend for the first time. Kai's siblings, Adam and Fay, smirked at me, Adam more subtly than Fay. Nur grinned like a proud grandfather under his silvery moustache, and Pierre was trying to play the part of the heartbroken second male-lead who didn't get the girl.

No one said anything as Kai pulled out the last available navy stool for me next to Adam and then stood beside me as close as he could, while Nur, Pierre, and Shehryar stood on the opposite side.

"Tea or coffee, Your Highnesses?" Nur asked.

I requested black coffee, Kai opted for jasmine tea, and Nur headed off past the island to make them. That was when Pierre finally spoke up.

"So, this is how it's going to be?" he muttered, though his ruby red eyes danced with mischief. "I thought there was something between us, Princess." He gestured between me and him then pointed to Kai. "But now you're choosing him? Were you just playing with my heart this whole time?"

Fay chuckled quietly, while Shehryar shook his head, taking a sip of whatever disgusting flavour of protein shake he was drinking, probably banana. Kai, though, radiated feral rage as he shifted even closer to me, so that he was standing on the rounded base of my stool.

It was comical and unbelievably cute. I found myself struggling to hold in an adoring giggle as I leaned into my jealous bear's side. I felt Kai shift above me, but I kept my smile on Pierre.

"I'm sorry, Pierre," I said, playing along with a light sigh. "I don't think this thing between us would have ever worked out. It's not you. It's me." I tipped my head back to grin up at Kai. "I'm completely infatuated with the way this handsome prince frowns at me."

Kai blinked at me, his eyes widening. Then his brows furrowed, his cheeks going pink as his hand came up to tug at his left earlobe. He looked away, appearing shy and embarrassed.

I nearly doubled over from the overdose of adorable that stabbed me right through the chest. *How and why was he so fucking cute?*

"Why the fuck are you blushing?" Fay hooted hysterically. Pierre and Adam chuckled along, but Shehryar tried to hide his amusement.

"I'm not," Kai grumbled, scowling viciously at his brother as he tugged at his ear again.

I pressed my lips together, but a snicker still slipped out between them loud enough for Kai to notice. I leaned into him, grinning so hard my cheeks hurt, but he just scowled down at me. Even if it did turn more playfully grumpy than embarrassed. It was beautiful.

"Well," Pierre said. "I suppose if frowns are your thing, Princess, then you're with the right man. No one frowns harder than my friend—for no apparent reason too."

We all chuckled at Kai's expense, and he grumbled and growled incoherently under his breath until I swivelled the stool around and wrapped my arms around his torso. It only took a few seconds for his dimple to make an appearance in his cheek as he hugged me back tightly.

Fay muttered something about the sight of us being sickeningly sweet, at which point Nur returned with my coffee and Kai's tea before leaving again. Adam saved his eldest brother from any further teasing by changing the conversation, mentioning the upcoming release of an improved re-make of one of the old-school games we had played in the TV room a few nights back.

"I already have a copy of the game," I announced proudly.

"What? How?" Adam practically leapt off his stool towards me.

"I'm friends with Andreas, the CEO of Cork, and he sent me an early copy for my birthday."

"For your birthday, huh?" Fay echoed.

Pierre smirked. "Just asking, but how good of friends are you?"

I felt a dark aura crowd me from my right. Giddy delight bubbled inside me as I sighted the frustration flaming through Kai's narrow eyes.

"We're just friends," I said, more to him than anyone else. His nostrils flared but he gave me a single, reluctant nod. It looked more like he was sulking. "Kai." I stretched his name. "I mean it."

"Andreas Price is a forty-five-year-old happily married gay man," Shehryar deadpanned.

Kai invented a new measure of speed with how quickly his head snapped from Shehryar to me. I laughed so hard and loudly, I nearly fell off the stool. He caught me and kept me upright, but he did *not* look impressed that I'd purposely let him believe otherwise about Andreas.

Fay grunted and smirked. "That's what you get for acting like a jealous prick." Kai glared at him.

"Do you have it with you? The game, I mean," Adam asked with a childlike hope to his tone.

"I do actually. Andreas sent me a download code on my Connect, which I actually brought with me."

Adam's eyes lit up. "Could we play? Please."

"I don't see why not. There's plenty of time for a few rounds before dinner, isn't there?" He nodded eagerly. "Let me go grab it from my room then."

Adam looked like he was about to say something, but Fay spoke over him. "Sure thing, Esmeralda." His eyes went to Kai. "We'll meet you down in the TV room, okay?"

With the way Kai shifted like a child who knew he was about to be told off I was almost hesitant to leave him alone with them. But I agreed and hopped off the stool, squeezing Kai's hand before I left.

Once I passed the tall, metal shelves full of pots and pans of all sizes, I glanced back over my shoulder. Adam, Pierre, and Fay were crowding a wary-looking Kai while Shehryar finished off the last of his protein shake without moving from his spot.

"So, are you officially dating?" I heard Pierre ask.

Kai's answer was too quiet for me to decipher but—

"You haven't asked her to be your girlfriend yet?" Fay exclaimed. "What the fuck are you waiting for? Permission from the King?"

Kai, Shehryar, Fay, and Adam were only just coming down the opposite end of the corridor with what looked like big bags of crisps in hand as I rounded the corner, my handheld console with me.

They made it to the door first, and Kai stepped away from Fay to wait for me. His relaxed expression made me a little curious as to what they'd said to him in the kitchen after I left, but I held my tongue. He pressed a kiss to my temple when I reached him.

"Could you stop with the lovey-dovey shit please?" Fay teased with a smirk. "There are children here." He thumbed at his youngest brother, pushing the door open. "Adam cover your eyes."

"I'm not a child," Adam grumbled, following Fay in.

They both froze a step inside the TV room, going dead quiet.

"Why did you stop?" I asked, moving inside and between them.

My attention shifted to what they were looking at as Kai came up behind me and Shehryar gently pushed his way to my side. It took a moment to register what I was seeing, but I did a doubletake, my eyes nearly popping out of their sockets.

Oh…woah…what?

Standing by the back of the dark blue sofa that faced the eighty-inch TV screen was Prince Arsh.

With Mama Katiya. In his arms. Half turned towards us.

Their eyes were bright and glazed, their cheeks flushed, lips red and swollen. Prince Arsh's suit shirt was rumpled, and Mama Katiya's twisted bun was coming loose low on her nape. As if…

As if they'd been kissing. Or making out. *Intensely.*

"Get. Your. *Fucking hands.* Off my *mother.*"

A cold static crept through the hairs on the back of my neck as Shehryar's low voice draped over the silent room like a dangerous cloud.

It was the exact same tone he'd used when he'd caught the man who had been stalking me in my second year of university. A voice that came from somewhere deep and protective within his chest, promising murder without hesitation. A dark, incensed side of him he didn't show very often, but once he did, it could never be forgotten. Especially the wild rage in his pale green eyes.

He still wouldn't tell me what he'd done to my stalker. But I never saw that man again.

And if he was protective of me then he was ten times as much with his own mother.

"Shehryar," Mama Katiya warned as she swivelled away from Prince Arsh to face us. One of Prince Arsh's hands lingered around her lush hips as he stood tall and calm by her side, not bothering to straighten his shirt.

"I said get your hands off her. Now," Shehryar growled. "Or I'll rip them off your arms."

"Sher," I whispered in panic.

"Shehryar," his mother snapped at the same time, her curved brows dipping into an outraged scowl. "Don't you dare threaten Arsh."

She used his name. Fuck, she used his name. *Just his name.*

"Arsh?" Shehryar echoed, and Mama Katiya's stern expression wavered. But she tipped her chin up, confirming exactly that. *It was Arsh.*

Someone on my side swore quietly.

Prince Arsh stepped forward without dropping his hand from Mama Katiya's hip. "Shehryar—"

"I wasn't fucking talking to you," he snapped, jerking towards them.

The ferocity of his movement made me flinch, but a strong barrier curled around my waist and dragged me swiftly back. I looked back up over my shoulder and Kai's eyes flickered all over my face, a worried furrow sinking between his brows. I shook my head, so he understood I was okay.

"You're being rude, Shehryar," Mama Katiya said, "and that is not how I raised you."

"Well, how did you expect me to react, Mum?" Shehryar threw a hand in Prince Arsh's direction. "He's a *prince*!"

Her spine straightened. "I'm aware of that."

"Then what are you doing with him?" He stalked towards Prince Arsh. "Is he threatening you? Is that it?" He went nose to nose with the older man. "Because he thinks he can get away with it because he's a *prince*."

Despite Shehryar having five inches on Prince Arsh's six-feet and at least an extra fifty pounds of muscle, Prince Arsh didn't shrink away. He stayed calm and quiet as he met Shehryar's gaze head-on.

"Shehryar, stop this right now." Mama Katiya tried to move between them but neither man moved.

"I understand you're angry finding out like this," Prince Arsh said, his deep voice feeling almost like a salve on the tension straining the atmosphere. "But I do not think less of your mother for being a member of staff. I care for her, Shehryar. A lot."

"Do you honestly expect me to believe that bullshit?"

"It doesn't matter whether you believe it or not, because we're getting married!"

Shehryar and Prince Arsh's heads flew around to Mama Katiya at the same time, someone choked next to me, and my jaw collapsed to the floor.

"You're…what?" Shehryar croaked.

"You said you hadn't decided yet," Prince Arsh said in quiet surprise.

"Yes, well, I've decided now," Mama Katiya stated firmly. "And I want to marry you."

"You can't—you can't marry him." Shehryar shifted to face her. "You don't even know him."

From the side of him, I saw his mother slip her hand into Prince Arsh's. "I do."

I winced as Shehryar shifted back from them. It was as if the realisation he felt settled over the entire room. "How long?"

"Shit," Fay whispered, and I numbly felt Kai shift behind me.

"How long has this been going on?" Shehryar asked again when neither of them answered.

"Four years," Mama Katiya said.

Dead silence echoed like a piercing ring through the room.

"So what?" Shehryar rasped. "He's just been stringing you along for four years? And now you suddenly believe him when he says he wants to marry you?"

His mother's shoulders fell, her beautiful, elegant features softening as she shook her head. "No, Sher. Arsh isn't the one stringing me along. I'm the one who asked him to wait, because *I* wasn't sure. *I* wasn't ready. And because I knew *you* were going to struggle to accept it."

"You think *I'm* struggling to accept it?" Shehryar grunted mockingly. "And what about the rest of the world? You're a maid with a *bastard* son!" He spat out the word so bitterly, I flinched.

"Don't call yourself—"

"There is a law in every state forbidding your marriage to a prince, Mum, and that hasn't changed in hundreds of years. No one has wanted to change it, so what makes you think they suddenly will now?"

"Because," Prince Arsh said, "I have written up a proposal for its change. And Rami, as well as King Kareem, are backing my proposal. And if they are, then the others will too. Because you're right, Shehryar—it is an outdated law we need to scrap, and I will fight to get rid of it."

Mama Katiya gave Prince Arsh a soft smile, and if that wasn't what I felt for Kai in Prince Arsh's eyes for her, then I had no idea what it was. *He loved her. And she loved him too.*

"You can't believe what he says." Shehryar shook his head in disbelief. "Mum, you can't believe what he says—*tell me you don't believe him.*"

She sighed. "I can't tell you that. Because I do believe him. I trust him completely."

"What?" he said viciously. "The same way you believed *Dad's* empty promises too?"

Silence. Shocked, hurt, angry silence.

I couldn't believe he'd just said that. This wasn't Shehryar. He wasn't normally so cruel and vindictive. But anger and shock did bitter things to people, and he wasn't immune to their effect.

Mama Katiya blinked away her pale expression and stiffened her shoulders. "I've moved on from what your father did, Sher," she said calmly. "It's about time you did too."

The silence that followed was heavy before Shehryar spun around and charged towards us, raking both his hands through his hair. I was so stunned, I couldn't move, but Kai tugged me back against his chest in time to take me out of Shehryar's destructive path on his way out.

I glanced at the empty doorway then to Mama Katiya. Her sad gaze was filled with tears that wrecked my heart. "I'll go talk to him," I croaked.

"No, my dear. Let him go. He wouldn't have left if he wanted to talk."

It was fair to say playing the new game was entirely forgotten after that.

CHAPTER 27
Esmeralda

I sighed for what felt like the millionth time as I stopped outside Shehryar's bedroom door an hour and a half after his exit.

I knew he was in there. I had no idea, though, if he wanted to talk, hence why I had a plate of chocolate cake from dinner in one hand.

There was nothing that softened Shehryar quicker than an offering of chocolate cake, especially when he was angry. That, and I'd been told by the other staff he hadn't been there for dinner.

Lifting my hand, I rapped on the door twice. "Sher. It's me. Can I come in?"

No reply came for what felt like forever, but as I went to knock again, the door slowly opened. Shehryar loomed in the threshold of his room wearing the same black jumper-chino combination he'd been wearing earlier. He looked somewhere between exhausted and frustrated, his hair spiking in different directions as if he'd been yanking at it for hours.

Without saying anything, he stepped back, and I made my way into his room.

His bedroom was on the same corridor as my stylist, Rose, Mama Katiya, and Sully—Kareem's private secretary and valet. It was smaller than mine but still spacious with the same red carpet and cream walls as most of the palace, and an ensuite bathroom.

"Pierre told me you didn't have dinner, so I brought you some chocolate cake," I said as he closed the door behind me. I smiled and held out the covered plate for him. He took it and muttered a thank you, then trudged over to the top corner where his bed was and put it on the bedside cabinet.

He plonked himself on the edge of the mattress, combing a hand through his hair, and my heart twisted at how troubled he looked. I quietly made my way over and sat down next to him.

"How are you feeling?" I asked.

"Fucked in the head."

I leaned into the side of his sturdy frame, trying to offer comfort as he stared blankly at the wall ahead of him. It took me a moment to figure out what to say. "He loves her, you know," I mumbled, and Shehryar's jaw visible tensed. "And not just a little bit, he loves her a lot. You should've seen the way he comforted her after you left."

"That's not the point, Esmeralda."

"Why isn't that the point, Sher?"

"Because love isn't enough. Love is *never* enough in our world."

I sat upright as my brows bunched together. "That's not true. Love is always enough. What more could you want for her than someone who loves her?"

His piercing eyes flashed to mine. "*Respect*, Esmeralda. And with Prince Arsh she will never *ever* get that respect."

"You doubt that he respects her just because she's palace staff?"

"It's not about him respecting her." He shot up from the mattress, pacing away before he turned back to me. "It's about the rest of the world not giving her the respect she deserves *because* of him, and the fact that you don't understand that is exactly my point."

I reared back from the impact of his bitter tone before a swirl of anger had me standing from the bed too. "What is that supposed to mean? That I don't know what it's like to be under the scrutiny of the rest of the world? Because you of all people, Sher, should know that I have lived with that fear and anxiety for years."

"That isn't what I meant, Esmeralda." He sighed, scrubbing a hand over his face.

"Then what did you mean?"

He threw a hand out. "It's different for you! You might be judged for your actions and mistakes, but Mum will be judged for simply being her. They're not going to treat her story like some magical fairy tale. They'll scorn her for not coming from a wealthy, educated family. They'll accuse her of seducing her way into a higher standing and they will never let her forget it!"

I swallowed slowly, unable to find the words to deny what he'd said. He was right. Even if times and opinions had changed, there were some people in the world that still held old views on marriage among the elite classes. And unfortunately, they would judge Mama Katiya and label her as a woman *not* of "good stock"—forget about how degrading that was to women anyway.

"You don't know that, Sher," I muttered, but the words fell flat. "People don't *all* think that way."

He gave me a weak shrug. "You're right. Maybe not everyone will care, but the people who matter in this world will. The people in your circles will never accept her." He jabbed a finger at me. "And that's where she'll spend most of her time if she marries Prince Arsh. And that's *if* he can convince them to scrap the law forbidding their marriage in the first place. But what if he can't? What then? Is he going to keep her on the side as a mistress? Tell me then, Esmeralda, should I be happy seeing my mother being toyed with by *another* rich man just because he claims to love her?"

My blood ran hot in my veins as I squared up under his anger. "No, Sher. Of course, you shouldn't be, but Prince Arsh would never do that, Mama Katiya wouldn't let him. But don't you think she's considered all of that already?" I gestured towards the door. "I doubt she's spent four years only worrying about her son's feeling. She must've pictured every scenario possible, but she still wants this because she trusts Prince Arsh to be there with her every step of the way.

"And why shouldn't she? He is literally willing to fight the world for her, and you know how hard it is to change an old law. But he already has support for it because that's how much he wants it. For

Mama Katiya, not anyone else. And as her son, your job is to be there for her and fight for her happiness, not make it harder for her by pointing out the obvious."

The vein in Shehryar's jaw ticked as he stood there glaring at me. Someone else might have been intimidated by the huge, angry sight of him, but I'd known him too long to take his anger at face value. He was only acting like an animal stuck in a trap because he was worried about his mother.

"You weren't there, Esmeralda, when the man who fathered me turned his back on her and let his fucking grandfather threaten her when he found out her four-year-old son was his heir's flesh and blood. Because she was the housekeeper's daughter who must've seduced his grandson and got pregnant on purpose for money. You didn't lie in bed with her and pretend you couldn't hear her crying every single night for years after because of every empty promise my fucking *dad* made to her about marrying her and claiming me as his own. Until she finally realised he never would."

He took a step towards me, a self-depreciating curl pulling up one corner of his mouth. "You weren't there when I went to confront my father and was reminded by his *wife* that I was nothing but an unwanted *bastard* who would never have any claim on him."

It was hard to tell what made me feel worse, the invisible claws sinking into the skin upon hearing *that* word again, or the wrecked look in Shehryar's eyes. "You never told me you confronted him."

"What was I going to tell you, Esmeralda? That I was humiliated in front of his entire family? That he watched his wife throw money in my face before his staff escorted me out his fucking mansion? Because according to her, what else could a bastard want from his rich father other than money?"

"Stop that," I croaked, a faint burn searing the back of my nose. "Stop calling yourself that."

He grunted, a cruel look turning the angular lines of his face harsh. "Why shouldn't I? It's true, isn't it?" I shook my head quickly, but he just laughed, and the hollow sound grated at my heart. "Come on, Esmeralda. Don't be naïve. I'm a by-blow in the world of old money and royalty, and do you know how they treat bastard children? Like scum, Esmeralda. Because to them that's what we are!"

"Shehryar!" My voice cracked like a whip between us.

I dragged in a broken breath, struggling to find any air as my lungs felt as if they were collapsing in on themselves. Everything inside me was burning, falling apart and cracking as his words attacked me at my weakest point. With the way Shehryar stilled, I knew he realised what he'd done. *What he'd said.* But it was too late.

He'd cut into my biggest, deepest scar, and now it was bleeding open.

"Esmeralda," he croaked. "I didn't mean—"

I put my hand up to silence him. "You meant exactly what you said, Sher." He shook his head, looking every bit chagrined and regretful. I dropped my trembling hand to my side. "And the thing is you're probably right. But do you remember what you always used to say to me? *You can't let your past define you.* So, what are you doing right now, Sher?"

He scrubbed a hand over his face then scrunched his hair in his fist. "Mama Katiya was right," I said. "You haven't gotten over what happened, and you're not only hurting yourself, but you're hurting her too. Because Shehryar, how can you accuse the world of judging her when that's exactly what you're doing to her—and to yourself—right now?"

Swallowing down the growing lump in my throat, I turned away, but his hand clamped around my elbow immediately. "Esmeralda, please, I'm sorry. I didn't—"

I shook my head. "I'm not the one you need to apologise to."

Without glancing back at him, I tugged my arm from his grip and left his room, closing the door on his distraught expression.

I knew he hadn't meant it. I knew he was sorry for having said it. But that didn't mean it hurt any less as I stood there staring at the closed door, his words spinning in my head like a cruel taunt.

Like scum, Esmeralda. Because to them that's what we are… Like scum, Esmeralda. Because to them that's what we are… Like scum, Esmeralda. Because to them that's what we are.

What. We. Are.

We. We. We. We…

"Esmeralda?"

I jumped at the sound of my name, spinning out of my dark reverie to face the owner of the voice.

Kareem stood a few feet away from me, and the emotional exhaustion I already felt suddenly grew into a ten-tonne weight on my shoulders. I didn't have the energy to brace myself against the mess that was mine and my brother's relationship. Though, honestly, we'd barely spoken since my visit to the palace infirmary on the morning of Cannon Day.

Despite my tiredness, I instinctively straightened my spine and tried to conceal my emotions. I didn't do a very job though because a little crinkle appeared between Kareem's brows as his eyes searched mine. I couldn't help it, I tensed under his worried scrutiny. It wasn't natural. I wasn't used to his concern, only his contempt.

He took his hands out of his smart black trousers, shifting as if he was going to move towards me but then seemed to think better of it. "Are you—are you okay?" he asked, awkward hesitation filtering through his voice. "You don't look—I mean…you're pale…"

I swallowed, trying to get my shoulders to ease but I couldn't. I physically couldn't relax around Kareem. So I tried to smile, but it felt more like a grimace. "I'm fine, thank you. How are you?"

"I'm—yeah, I'm okay." He scratched his jaw with one set of fingers. "I take it you were with Shehryar. Was he okay? Prince Arsh told me he didn't take the discovery of Katiya's relationship with him very well."

"No. He didn't take it well. He's worried and angry, but he just needs time to process it." Kareem nodded and I rolled my bottom lip into my mouth. "How long have you known?"

"Since Shah's New Years Eve party." I blinked in surprise. "He approached me the morning of the party and told me that he wanted to marry Katiya but that he needed my backing for his Change of Law proposal first to make that possible."

"And you agreed?" The quiet disbelief in my tone was obvious, because honestly, I couldn't believe it. I would've bet my entire fortune that Kareem would have been opposed to the change.

"I did." He lifted one shoulder in a barely-there shrug. "I had no reason not to agree."

It sounded like he was trying to mean something else with what he said. Not that I had any idea what that something else was. But then Kareem's brows dipped, and I forgot about figuring out what he was trying to tell me.

The twisted look on my older brother's face was new and confusing. Maybe regret, maybe sadness, maybe unease, maybe grief. Maybe a combination of all four. But it had the same effect as when I'd seen him dressed so casually for the scavenger hunt. It made me really see him, the tired look in his eyes and the years he'd aged. And it did that same tight thing in my chest again.

"Esmeralda…" He shifted on his feet. "Can we…can we talk?" His eyes bore into mine. *"Please."*

I couldn't recall agreeing to Kareem's request to talk. I barely remembered leading him to my room afterwards. But that's exactly where we were. Sitting on either end of the velvet chaise between the window and balcony doors, facing my neatly made bed.

In silence. Awkward fucking silence for the last five minutes.

It was torture of the worst kind, waiting for Kareem to say something while I stared at my lap and twiddled my thumbs. I was struggling to control the nervous bounce of my leg as anxiety spun through me, tearing apart my insides with brutal force. It was making me sick to my stomach.

"I'm sorry."

The room turned more silent than death itself. All the buzzing background noise, the soft rustle of our clothes, every single breath just stopped. And then there was nothing but my own heart going *thump, thump, thump* in my ears—the only sound or movement that proved I was still living and what I'd heard had actually been real.

Kareem had apologised. *To me?*

I numbly revolved my head in the direction of my older brother, bracing myself to catch his gaze. But I found him frowning down at the space between his slightly spread legs, his forearms braced loosely on his thighs. His whole posture looked tired and uncertain.

Kareem sighed heavily then scrubbed a hand over his face. "Sorry doesn't even cut it. But I don't know what else to say. I've ruined so much so badly."

The chaise seemed to wobble underneath me, and I clung onto the edge of the seat cushion for dear life. *Was I hearing him correctly? Was this really happening?*

A bleak look hollowed his face. "Do you…do you really believe I hate you enough to harm you?"

I dropped my head, unable to look at him, and winced. Unable to answer him.

I hated that he remembered I'd said that. It was a worry that came from a lonely, hurt place in my mind that I had never wanted anyone to know about. It was a dark side of my thoughts that battered and bruised me more than Kareem's words and actions themselves had. And I hated the power they had over me when my emotions were wound up so tight. But they were there, and sometimes they were so loud and destructive no matter how hard I tried to silence them.

I *had* thought Kareem hated me enough to hurt me. I wasn't sure if I *didn't* anymore.

"Esmeralda," he croaked, and the back of my nose began to sting with guilt and sadness. "I wouldn't." His voice cracked. "I would never—I couldn't do that."

"But you do. You hate me, Kareem," I whispered to my lap, my voice thick and watery.

He didn't reply. But that was more of a truthful answer than any words could have given me.

The sting in my eyes turned liquid and hot as pain filled the cracks in my heart. I clamped my eyes shut, trying to hold it all in, but no amount of tensing stopped my body from trembling.

"I don't hate you, Esmeralda."

For some reason, his earnest whisper only made my chest squeeze tighter. The dampness slipped between the fan of my lashes.

"I don't hate you," he repeated. "But I don't blame you for thinking that I do." He paused. "I have been horrid to you. The worst I could possibly be. And you were right. I pushed you away and hurt you when I should have been there for you. You were a child and you needed someone, but I—"

Kareem sighed so heavily, so painfully, my wet lashes fluttered open.

"I was so angry." He hung his head. "That night when I found Father's letter for you at the bottom of Mother's drawer. What I read— what he had done when Mother had been sick, I was so shocked. I felt…betrayed by him. Like the man I had respected and known him to be turned out to be nothing but a fraud and I…I couldn't believe Mother had let him get away with it. I couldn't believe she had covered for him, and I was furious."

Regret turned his eyes glassy. "I wasn't thinking straight when I went to confront her, and when I saw her laughing with you in the sitting room, it tipped me right over the edge. I didn't stop. I didn't think. I didn't consider you." He shook his head weakly. "But you should never have had to find out like that, and I will always regret how I handled the situation, Esmeralda."

The memory brought a fresh wave of tears to my eyes, blurring my vision. Until one by one they trailed slow and searing down my cheeks and dripped off the edge of my trembling jaw.

And I let them fall. For the little girl who'd had the carpet ripped out from under her feet so violently, tripping her into a never-ending hole of darkness.

The one who'd been cuddled with her mother on the sofa, giggling over an old memory when Kareem had come charging into the room. The girl who'd been scared by the rage darkening her older brother's face as he glared at her—something she had never seen him do before. The one who'd felt confused as he waved the paper in his hand, demanding their mother to tell him what it was before he asked the questions that sent the girl's blood running cold.

Is Esmeralda not your daughter? Did Father cheat on you when you were sick?

I was ten. I was a child. But I wasn't stupid. I was old enough to know what he meant even if I didn't understand what he was saying entirely.

My life was a lie. My mother wasn't my real mother. I wasn't a real princess.

I was nothing but an unwanted bastard child. Born from betrayal.

"And the worst part is I took it out on you as if it was your fault," Kareem croaked, dragging me out of my head and back into the room. "I shouted at you like you had any idea what had happened, and I treated you like you had some part in Father's actions."

A whimper broke through the seal of my lips when he reached out and dragged the back of his fingers across my cheek, wiping through the stream of tears. "You weren't. You never were." He did the same to my other cheek. "But I was so blindsided by my anger at Father, and without having any way of talking to him about it, I directed that anger towards you.

"I convinced myself I hated you. That every memory I had with you was tainted. That by loving you like a little sister I was somehow part of what Father had done. And that made me hate myself because I felt like I had betrayed Mother." His face scrunched in on itself. "Mother told me again and again that you were innocent in all of this, but I didn't listen to her. For my own conscience, I thought I needed to make it clear that you meant nothing to me.

"So I did. In every way I could."

Sliding towards me on the chaise, he cupped my wet cheek in his palm, and it was only then I realised his eyes were brimming with unshed tears. "I was wrong, and I should never have turned my back on you. But by the time I came to accept that, it was too late. I had already destroyed the light in your eyes."

A sob wretched from deep within my chest as I squeezed my eyes shut, everything in me burning, screaming, raging at how we'd ended up like this, why it had taken us so long to try to fix it. Because the knowledge that I was Father's mistake might have broken me but losing Kareem had hurt me so much more. He'd been my ally, my partner in crime. *My best friend.*

"I couldn't take back everything I had said and done, no matter how guilty I felt. I didn't know how to. And with Mother falling ill and me becoming King, I was a mess, and I thought if I had ruined everything already, then it was better to continue to keep you at arm's length. Because you didn't deserve to deal with the wreck I was."

His mouth tipped into a self-depreciating ghost of a smile as a single tear slipped down his cheek. "I didn't realise how much worse I had made everything by treating you the way I did until I pushed you too far. But it killed me realising I had failed you in every way that mattered as your brother. I had failed to protect you. Even from myself."

"I didn't need protecting from you," I sobbed, slamming the flat of my palm against his shoulder. "I needed you to talk to me. I needed you not to push me away. I needed you not to abandon me. I needed my brother—I needed my best friend!"

"I know," he whispered, another tear rolling down his cheek. "I know. And I can't ask for your forgiveness; I can only apologise for failing you for the rest of my life."

"You hurt me," I choked out. "You hurt me so much, Kareem. And I took it all because I thought I deserved it." I gasped for air. "I was Father's mistake. I ruined the family. I didn't deserve to be a princess, and it didn't matter that Mother loved me as her own, I felt guilty around her all the time. And then she was gone, and I knew I had no right to, but all I hoped was that one day you would treat me like I was your little sister—"

I crashed into Kareem's chest as he locked his arms around my shoulders. "You are," he said into my hair. "There is no other truth, Esmeralda. You *are* my little sister. You *are* Mother and Father's child. You are the rightful Princess of Jahandar. *You're my family.* And I dare anyone to say otherwise."

With a harsh sound, I clamped my arms around Kareem's torso and buried my face in his shoulder.

The little girl in me who had always wanted to hear those words wept into his jumper until she'd cried double all the tears she'd shed silently into her pillow for nights on end. And it was enough to finally put that little girl to rest.

I was left behind with only cuts and bruises that would take time to heal, but at least now they could start healing. And this conversation had been the start of that process. A process I discovered very quickly that *wasn't* going to be comfortable.

I shuffled in Kareem's arms with a sniff as the atmosphere turned awkward and sombre after the sobbing and blubbering confessions had been completely drained from the both of us.

Kareem shuffled too before his arms loosened around my shoulders. And then slowly, stiffly we untangled ourselves. I avoided looking directly at him and I was pretty sure he did the same as we shifted on the chaise to once again create the space that had been between us.

He cleared his throat, and I distracted myself by straightening the hem of my jumper dress. "Are you—are you okay?" he muttered hoarsely.

My face was throbbing and no doubt my head was going to start hurting at some point soon, but I nodded. "Hmm. Are you?"

"Yeah—yes…I think?"

The question in his voice made the corner of my mouth twitch and I glanced over at him. His eyes went wide when I caught him looking and he quickly glanced away, only to look back at me sheepishly. He gave me an awkward little man-smile—more pursed lips than any actual curl of his mouth—that made things a little less weird.

"I should…" He gestured to the door. "I should go now. Let you rest. For tomorrow."

I nodded. He didn't move. I didn't say anything. He cleared his throat. I gulped.

"Are you—are you going to accept a painted rose from Kai? Tomorrow, I mean."

I was surprised by the question. "If he offers one, yes."

"Are you and him…you know?"

"I think so…" Kareem's brows knotted together, and I shifted. "I mean, we are, but we haven't given it a label—yet. I think he wants to change that though."

Kareem gave a firm nod. "Good. He better. I like him and I don't want to have to unlike him."

That made me smile, which made Kareem look a little bashful. "I'm going to tell him," I said.

"About me not wanting to unlike him?"

"No. About me…"

He went still. For an instant, he looked like he was going to try to convince me otherwise, but then he said, "Are you sure, Esmeralda?"

"He has a right to know, so he can decide if I'm worth the trouble if the truth ever came out."

"There wouldn't be trouble with the Change of Law Prince Arsh is proposing. It would protect you too. And if Kai thinks you're not worth it, I'll kill him."

Neither statement was true, but I just smiled at Kareem and wished him good night as he finally got up and headed to the door. Only he turned back before he opened it.

"Esmeralda," he said. "I didn't agree to Prince Arsh's proposal for the sake of him and Katiya."

"I agreed for *you*." His eyes bore into mine. "I won't allow anyone to judge you for something that wasn't in your control. I swear that to you on my life."

CHAPTER 28

Esmeralda

I shed a few more tears after Kareem left me with his dramatic last statement. Then I washed up in the bathroom, wincing at the sight of my red, puffy face in the mirror, and changed into the black T-shirt I'd stolen from Kai and a pair of cotton pyjama shorts.

After my emotional outpour, I was relatively numb as I made my way out of my room. But the closer I got to Kai's bedroom, the more I became aware of the quiet jitter of nerves in my belly.

I had never told anyone about the circumstances of my birth ever, not even my best friend, Mariyah. I didn't even dare bring it up with Shehryar and Mama Katiya—both of whom knew about the whole thing—because I feared that talking about it would print the truth on my face and people would be able to tell just by looking at me. Impossible, but a fear was a fear.

It wasn't as if I thought Kai would betray me and tell everyone if I confided in him, but I worried about his reaction. That was why I had decided to tell him sooner rather than later. Because if somewhere down the line Kai found about my illegitimacy and decided he wanted nothing to do with me, the damage to my heart would be irreversible. At least if I told him sooner, I had more of a chance of gluing some of the broken pieces back together.

At least that was what I was trying to tell myself.

Kai's bedroom door flew open the moment I knocked, and the gorgeous man filled the doorway. There was a painful twist behind my ribcage as I took him in. From the sexy permanent shadow on his cleanly-shaven jaw to the perfect fit of his dark green hoodie and black cuffed pyjama bottoms.

I printed him into my memory from head to toe as if this was the last time I would get to see him like this.

Suddenly, he was right in front of me, hands cupping my puffy face and tilting it up. I was forced to stare into his ink black eyes behind his glasses. "Esmeralda," he rasped with a sense of panic. "What's wrong? What happened?"

I buried my face into his chest and snuck my arms around his back, clasping him as close as I could. His arms locked me against him instantly, his body curling all around me in a protective ball.

Please don't be the last time I get to hug him. Please don't be the last time I get to hug him. Please don't be the last time I get to hug him.

"Was it Shehryar? Was it something he said?" I shook my head against him before one of his hands stroked up my back and tangled in my hair. "Then what was it? Tell me. Please, Babble. What made you cry? What can I do to make it better?"

Gosh, he so precious. It shredded me apart and flooded me with love for him, and if I needed any more evidence that losing him would break me, I gained it right then. It was solid enough to make me question whether I was really going to tell him the truth. But only for a moment.

I pulled my face back and Kai relaxed his hold enough to let me look up at him. I swallowed slowly. "There's something I need to tell you."

His expression went blank, but I could feel the tension in his body. Without a word, he nodded and drew me inside his room by the hand, locking the door behind me.

There was an indent on his king-sized bed where he'd been sitting, a book on the bedside cabinet and his pillow resting up against the wooden headboard. He resumed his spot there, stretching his legs out, but when I tried to sit up next to him, he frowned at me. I gasped as he hauled me into his lap, making me straddle his thighs as he cradled me close.

"Why is it every time either of us has something to tell I end up on your lap?" I muttered with a light smile.

"Why shouldn't you be on my lap?" There wasn't a single doubt in the deep timbre of his voice.

That was meant to make me feel light and giddy but instead, a heavy stone sank through me. *Would he still think so after I told him?*

My emotions were clearly displayed on my face because he pinched my chin between his finger and thumb and gave it a little shake. "Nothing you tell me could ever change that." He dipped his head to look right into my eyes. "You're mine, Babble. And I'm yours."

The back of nose started burning again, but I offered a weak smile. That was all I could offer him. The thing I actually wanted to tell him was refusing to rise any higher than my chest. But Kai didn't utter a word. He didn't rush me or appear impatient or concerned about what I was hesitating to tell him. He just repeatedly combed his fingers over the side of my hair, tucking the strands framing my face behind my ear. Comforting me. Promising me.

"I am not the late Queen of Jahandar's daughter."

I flinched when Kai's fingers halted behind my ear and blinked rapidly down at the bunched fabric of his hoodie as I braced myself for his reaction.

Nothing. He didn't move, didn't speak, I wondered if he was even breathing.

I risked a glance up at him and the shock rounding his eyes was almost palpable.

But it wasn't judgemental. It wasn't angry. Neither was it edgy. He was just surprised by the huge curveball I'd thrown at him. *Understandably so.*

He blinked a few times before dropping his hand to frame my ribcage. "What do you mean?"

I took a deep breath. "I'm not my mother's real daughter. I'm Father's illegitimate child. Born to a member of the housekeeping staff who…took advantage of his mental state when Mother was ill.”

Kai squeezed my side in his hand, but it was unclear if it was reflexive or meant to be comforting. “How do you… How long have you known?”

“Since I was ten…” I forced myself to meet his unblinking regard. “I lied the other day when I said Kareem just turned his back on me one day. It wasn’t random.”

Discomfort at recalling the story I had never voiced twined around my limbs, but I tried to ignore the feeling. “Father wrote me a letter before he passed away to tell me about my real mother. One he had planned to give me once I turned eighteen. But Kareem found it first…”

I’d memorised every word of the letter. That was how many times I had read over it. Again and again and again until the truth of my illegitimacy was carved into all of my bones. *A fake. A fraud.* A lie I knew even at aged twelve that no one could ever know about. So I burnt the letter. But I’d recited it to myself every few nights, so I never forgot the truth that had been written on it.

“And without Father there to explain himself, Kareem took his anger out on Mother. And me.”

“You were a child,” Kai said.

“I was. But I was old enough to understand Father made a mistake, and that I was never meant to have been born.”

“That’s not true.” Kai moved a heavy hand up my spine, pressing me closer into his warmth, but as if there was a pole down my back, I didn’t budge. “You know that’s not true.”

I knew it wasn’t so much the truth now that I was older. But I knew there had been far more days when that thought had been the only possible truth. Especially when Mother was no longer alive.

“I read the letter,” I continued, “but it wasn’t until Mother was in hospital after the Dale expedition that she finally told me her side of the story. That she had a miscarriage about a year or so before I was born. How she fell sick after, so Father took her and Kareem to Glossham Palace to get away from the politics in the capital. How Father went back-and-forth to keep the government in session.

"At some point, they hired new palace staff. Mama Katiya was in that group with a four-year-old Shehryar…and so was my birth mother—Linda."

"Linda saw an opportunity," I said devoid of any emotion, repeating the words that had been told to me. "Mother was ill. Father was stressed and worried, and Linda offered him comfort. He rejected her at first, but apparently, she was persistent and he…gave in.

"Mother said Father came to her the next morning and wept at her feet as he told her what he'd done. She was furious, of course— what woman wouldn't be? But they couldn't fire Linda in case she accused Father of assault, so they sent her to another palace. And two months later she came back."

"She was pregnant," I croaked after a beat. "And she wanted compensation."

"Money," Kai rasped, bitterness wisping through.

I nodded numbly. "Money in exchange for not going to the media. *One million Raal* and she said she'd be happy to—to get rid of me and disappear quietly."

Where my insides once were, there were now a million eels wriggling over each other, creating rolling waves of sickening sensation. Taking deep breaths didn't help. It just made the feeling worse.

It was miserable knowing I had been conceived from a betrayal, even if Linda had taken advantage of Father being in a bad place. I wasn't naïve to think Father hadn't known he was cheating on his sick wife. Maybe his judgement had been skewed from being in a bad mental state, but what kind of a man found comfort with another woman while his sick wife was suffering? Even if he had come clean immediately.

But worse than that was knowing that my biological mother had been selfish and unfeeling enough to put a price on my life without any hesitation. Ironically, it was the woman who was cheated on that I owed my life to. *Literally.*

"Mother refused. She didn't want Linda to get rid of me. She wanted Linda to give birth to me so that her and Father could claim me as their own."

Kai's palm spread over the back of my neck, and it was only then I realised I was sitting so stiffly my shoulders and neck were aching. He squeezed and soothed the tautness from me. For a moment, I closed my eyes and let him, easing into his touch until my shoulders slipped lower.

"Mother said she'd thought of me as a last chance to have another child. She'd had three miscarriages since Kareem had been born—none of which had been publicly announced—and she'd struggled to conceive otherwise. She wanted me. I'm still not sure I completely understand *how* she could have wanted me as her own, but that's the kind of woman she was. Loving to a fault, and completely selfless when it came to me and Kareem.

"In his letter, Father said he was wary at first, but they came up with a plan to keep Mother and Linda at Glossham Palace with Mama Katiya until Linda gave birth. They told the media it was because doctors had raised concerns over Mother's health. No one ever questioned the decision.

"Less than six months later, *Princess Esmeralda Ayla Jahandar* was born." A ghost of a smile touched my mouth. "I guess it was a good thing I had Father's distinct eye colour—there was never any question that I was his."

"And Linda?" Kai asked.

"She left the moment she received her money. But three months later, it was on local news that her drug-addict boyfriend killed her after a fight over a big sum of money she hid from him—the same money she was given by Mother and Father."

Silence slipped around us as I fiddled with the fabric of his hoodie over his shoulder. I avoided his gaze, but he kept his hand spread over my nape, his thumb on my jaw.

"With the current legitimacy laws," I mumbled, "I have no right to the title of princess, let alone a right to the throne of Jahandar as Kareem's heir."

"That's not true," Kai said right away. His thumb went under my chin and urged my head up. "Legally, you *are* their child, so you have every right to both."

"Only because the world doesn't know the truth. If they did—"

"Uncle Arsh's Change of Law proposal would protect you." He leaned closer, burying me in his bottomless irises. "I went to see him before you came. I read through his proposal. He's not just suggesting a change to the marriage laws, he wants to scrap the illegitimacy laws too. Nobody could say anything to you, Esmeralda. You would be protected."

That wasn't entirely true.

Maybe I would be protected legally, but emotionally? The strain of the world's judgement and opinions? It would be like carrying the weight of a dozen elephants using only my index fingers. *Impossible.*

What about the people I cared about? I wasn't so bothered by what everyone would say about me, but what about Kareem? All the hard work he'd put into earning everyone's trust in his authority would be destroyed. What about my parents' image? The entire Jahandar lineage? Kai?

I would forever be a stain on my family's name. And possibly Kai's too.

I didn't want that. Ever.

"Maybe I would be," I whispered, "but no one I care about would be." Using all my willpower, I uncurled my hands from around Kai's hoodie. But as I lowered them to my lap, Kai caught one of my wrists and brought it back up to his shoulder, holding it there. "If my illegitimacy came out and Prince Arsh's proposal fell through, it would hurt everyone around me. Including you, Kai."

My eyes flicked almost frantically between his glaring ones. "I haven't forgotten that you're to be Touma's Crown Prince. If ever, because of me, you wouldn't be able to—and I—I couldn't—"

"*Stop.*"

My voice evaporated as his angry growl closed around my throat; his frown was just as unforgiving.

He slipped his hand from my jaw to the back of my neck, clamping down firmly. "I hate that you're scaring yourself with a made-up scenario where I would have to pick between you and a title. But I hate more that you don't know what my choice would be." His frown deepened. "Haven't I made it obvious how much you mean to me, Esmeralda? How could you think I would pick a title over you?"

My head moved on its own accord, shaking in denial. "It's only been a week. We barely know each—"

"Nine days. Today is the ninth day you've been in Touma, and maybe we haven't been *this*—*us*—for all those nine days, but what about the nights we spent together?" He gave my neck a light squeeze. "You cannot tell me after all those hours together that you don't know me, Babble. Because if you don't know me then no one does.

"You see me and understand me better than anyone. You haven't doubted me—not once. Instead, you've trusted me with so much. Your secrets, your heart. Long before I even knew I had it.

"You waited long enough for me to open my eyes and see you too, and you will *never* understand how grateful I am for that. And now that I have seen you, you're insisting that I hardly know you?" His dimple snuck light and cheeky into his right cheek. "Don't I know what your constant babbling sounds like?"

I knocked his shoulder playfully. "I don't babble."

He let out a low, sexy chuckle that fluttered through my belly. "You do, my little Babble, and it's one of the most beautiful sounds in all of Neves."

My. My. He said "my." And shit, it turned my insides into a puddle of warm goo.

"The other one is your laugh," he added. "And I have been addicted to that for months now."

Caught off guard by his statement, I straightened mid-swoon. "What? What do you mean?"

A wash of colour drifted over Kai's cheeks. "If we're being honest tonight, then I should tell you that I saw you. At Shah's New Years party. On the balcony."

My heart hiccupped. "What? When? Where were you?"

"It was after the countdown at midnight. I needed a break from the crowd, so I went out onto the balcony. I didn't expect anyone else to be there. But you were." He rolled his jaw. "You were on the phone, and I couldn't quite hear you, but I didn't know how to make myself known. So, I didn't. But I didn't leave either."

My jaw hung loose as he stroked his fingers through my hair. "You looked stunning in that black silk dress, and it caught me off guard. I didn't understand how I had known you my entire life and only then realised how beautiful you were. I couldn't look away. I knew I was being a creep watching you, but I couldn't even move, Esmeralda. You had me captivated."

I spluttered an unintelligible sound, and he flashed me a lazy, lop-sided smile. "And then you laughed, and I...couldn't breathe. It was so loud, so unbashful, so sweet. And I loved it. I wanted to go over to you and find out what made you laugh and do it again and again so you would laugh just for me. But then you turned, and I panicked and hid in the shadow instead."

He shook his head. "But Babble, I never forgot the sound of your laugh or the way you looked that night. I thought about you for days and nights after, wondering what would have happened if I had made myself known. I lost count of the number of times I wished I had."

"And you're just telling me this now?" I exclaimed when I found my voice, giving him a hard shake by the shoulders. "Why? Why didn't you tell me sooner?"

He frowned but still looked amused. "What was I supposed to tell you? That I stood in the dark watching you laugh like a perverted stalker and day-dreamed about you for weeks after?"

I nodded vigorously. "Yes! Do you even understand how happy that would have made me? The guy I liked watched me and was thinking about me without my knowing? That was my ideal scenario."

His head reared back. "We must have different definitions of ideal."

I chuckled at his dismay then dragged him back to me, capturing his mouth in a clumsy kiss.

"But I'm glad you didn't hear what I said that night," I whispered.

"Why?" he breathed, the mint of his toothpaste filling my lungs.

"Because I was talking about you to Mariyah." I kissed the sweet, bashful tilt that blossomed on his mouth several times in quick succession. "Are you sure about this, Kai?"

"Yes. And if you ask me that again, you're going to earn yourself a hard spanking." My thighs clenched around his as his growled warning sent a bolt of heat rushing down my core. "I would never let anyone, or anything take you away from me. I will always fight by your side."

"But what if your family—"

"My family would pick you too, Esmeralda. They're obsessed with you. And if I don't ask you to be my girlfriend tonight, I am a hundred per cent certain they will ask you themselves tomorrow."

My thudding heart felt like it was going to explode trying to process what he was saying. "You want me to be your girlfriend?"

"Of course, I do. But if King Kareem is still not happy with me—"

"No. He's not unhappy with you, or with us. He told me so himself earlier. Before I came here."

Understanding melted over his face. "So, the reason you were crying…"

I nodded. "He apologised, and we had a chat. It wasn't easy, but I think we can slowly start to fix our relationship now." I smiled, lifting a hand to Kai's cheek. "And he told me he really likes you."

"So, I can give you a rose tomorrow?" His eyes were aglow as he nestled into my palm.

"Hmm." I traced my thumb down the bridge of his nose below his glasses.

"And you'll be my girlfriend?"

"Yes. If you'll still have me."

All I heard was a rush of air in my ears and suddenly I was on my back, blinking dazedly up at Kai as he hovered above me on all fours.

"You shouldn't have said that, Babble," he growled as he stroked one hand up my decolletage and wrapped it around my throat. "Because now I want to punish my girlfriend even harder for still fucking doubting me."

My heart went *yes, fuck, yes* in my chest, even though a ball of panic bounded through me.

CHAPTER 29

Kai

"Esmeralda," I called out upon spotting her in a little circle with Mother and Gigi.

I nearly missed her through the crowd of chattering royals and invited guests gathered in the gardens of Chaukham Palace, enjoying the pre-celebration appetisers and beverages being handed out by palace staff. The white clothes everyone was dressed in ready for the Festival of the Life were blindingly bright under the morning sun high in the sky.

In my opinion, it was too cold for a celebration outside. Though, throwing powdered colour around the palace corridors wasn't an option, so outside was where we had to be. I couldn't say the cold wasn't bothering me, but I was more than willing to put up with it now that I had a beautiful girlfriend to celebrate with. To give a painted white rose to as the men who'd returned from the Rebellion War did to their loved ones more than eight hundred years ago.

Maybe I was a bad son and grandson for completely ignoring Mother and Gigi, but I couldn't take my eyes off my Babble when I stopped by her side. *My girlfriend.*

She had her hair tied up. I'd never seen it tied like this. I wanted to touch it so badly. To tuck the locks framing her face behind her ears and trace the two elegant braids over her head. They met above her nape where they were tied together in a hairband, leaving the rest of her wavy hair loose in a low ponytail.

The cold breeze that fluttered the white silk of her skirt around her bare calves had turned her cheeks and nose adorably rosy. And her greyish-brown eyes glittered impossibly bright behind her long, mascaraed lashes as she grinned up at me. It was devastating.

I tugged hard at my left ear as it burned. *Fuck, why did I feel so nervous?*

"Do you intend to say something or simply ogle at her?"

I nearly jumped out of my skin at Gigi's mocking tone like she'd shouted the words. Her thin red lips were curled up in a smirk, her straight, white hair swishing around her chin as she shook her head knowingly. Mother's grin was equally perceptive, though there was a wet warmth to her ink black eyes that softened her amusement.

With my cheeks burning hot, I cleared my throat and tugged at my ear again. "Yes," I croaked. "Candy, Trevor, and Zain are here, and I wanted to introduce them to Esmeralda."

"Well, remember to actually *talk* when you introduce Esmeralda to them."

Wow. Thanks for that, Gigi.

"Though I suppose drooling over her in front of everyone is one way to announce she's your girlfriend," she added with a teasing arch of her brow. "Took you long enough though, didn't it?"

I'm her favourite grandson. Apparently.

Gritting my teeth, I yanked at my stinging ear, trying to expel some of my embarrassment as Mother and Esmeralda laughed at my expense.

Esmeralda and I had told our families that we were officially dating only a couple of hours earlier; we'd even managed a quick family chat before breakfast in the TV room. Shehryar and his mother, Katiya, had been there too. Sometime during when my over-the-top family had been surrounding Esmeralda, Shehryar and Uncle Arsh had come to some understanding too.

I had to admit, seeing the way my family welcomed her and had so quickly created their own mini fan club for her felt bloody good. They respected her and admired her and were so animated without any polite pretence. But it went both ways. She was the same with them. And it had felt so right seeing her with them. Like she was meant to be a part of my family. *Part of me.*

My only complaint was that my family had weaponised our relationship to tease me to their hearts content. *I present Exhibit A.*

"Thank you, Gigi," I grumbled, a reluctant smile tugging at my lips. "I'll remember to wipe the corners of my mouth regularly from now on." Gigi winked, damn well proud of herself, as I placed my hand on Esmeralda's lower back. "May we be excused now?"

"Of course. Go," Mother said, resting a gentle hand on Esmeralda's arm. "Go have fun."

People stared as I walked with Esmeralda away from my family and through the garden. I wasn't exactly paying attention to the curious gazes, but I slid my hand across her back to her waist, clutching her possessively.

My Babble. My Esmeralda. My person. My heart. Let them all fucking see she's mine.

She had been so brave last night, trusting me with the burden she'd held for so long. And after the way she had looked at me—a frightened little deer expecting nothing less than death—I'd be damned if I ever shied away from her in public. I wasn't going to give her reason to doubt that I couldn't fucking care less about her illegitimacy. The circumstance of her birth, that she had no control over, meant nothing to me. I'd never think less of her for it or want her to be anyone else.

Esmeralda placed a small hand flat over my chest and rubbed her thumb in back-and-forth motions over my white jumper. "Aren't you cold without a coat?" she asked.

"Freezing, and I have a thermal T-shirt on underneath," I muttered honestly, because it gave me a reason to hug her soft body even closer. "Stay close and keep me warm, please."

"Of course, Sir," she purred.

A fierce spark of lust licked through my groin. "Babble," I growled low between clenched teeth. Like the brat that she was, she chuckled and cuddled closer. There was only so long I could maintain a frown when her delight was so contagious.

Too soon we reached the arched rose trellis leading to the enclosed space my friends were gathered in. Following Esmeralda down the single stone step, I ducked my head under the naked twining twigs. Zain, Trevor, and Candy were laughing with Pierre, glass flutes in hands, when they noticed us.

"Ah, he's returned with our princess," Pierre said, grinning at Esmeralda as the other three moved over to make space for us in the circle.

"Hi, Pierre," she said, her voice laced with light laughter.

Maybe it was because the white of Pierre's hoodie, jeans, and trainers made the ruby red of his eyes appear even more starry than usual, but I wanted to lean over and poke his eyes out for daring to look at her. And why did he have to smile at her like that?

"You weren't kidding about the whole jealousy thing."

My attention shifted left to Zain, the tallest of us five, rubbing a bronzed hand over his dark beard. Sunlight glimmered off the silver wedding band on his finger. He eyed me with a curiously entertained spark in his brown eyes, sending a wave blood to the surface of my face.

A dad of two little children, Zain was the newest addition to our group, becoming our friend in university, but he was the one who could read me best. I supposed it was because we were both the eldest children of our families, him as the future CEO of his family's international hotel group.

Pierre laughed. "I told you, and you guys didn't believe me." He wiggled his brows. "The beast turned into a prince, but our prince turned into a jealous beast."

I glared at him, tugging at my burning ear.

On the other side of Pierre, Trevor chuckled and shook his head. His teasing, lazy grin left me unable to meet his chocolate brown eyes as a thousand hot pinpricks crept over my face. "My, how the mighty have fallen."

Of a mixed heritage, Trevor was what Candy called a lady-killer. Tall and well-built, he kept his brown hair perfectly coiled atop his head. But Trevor shied away from too much attention, preferring to work alone behind a computer on the billion-Sterling online gaming platform he'd created while we had still been in university.

"Are you going to introduce us or just glare at us?" Candy said, ending the two seconds of quiet.

Someone remind me why I thought I wanted Esmeralda to meet them.

I dropped my scowl from Candy's sea-blue gaze to Esmeralda tucked against me. Her smile was the only reason the notch between my brows eased and I found myself gesturing to my friends.

"Esmeralda, this is Zain Sultan." Zain bowed his head and smiled softly.

"You already know me, Princess," Pierre said as my hand drifted past him to Trevor.

"That I do," Esmeralda said with a laugh.

"Trevor Kingston," I gritted out, trying not to glare at Pierre as Trevor repeated Zain's bow and offered a slight wave of his hand. "And this is—"

"Lord Candy Hamilton, the fashion designer," Esmeralda finished, an excited pitch to her tone.

"Oh," Candy piped and flashed her the grin that had wrecked more hearts than Pierre's ruby red eyes and Trevor's killer looks combined. "So you've heard of me, Your Highness?"

"I have," Esmeralda replied, and the sight of a blush on her cheeks turned the irritated hissing in my chest to a full-on territorial growl. *Damn Candy and his stupid fucking smile.* "You're one of my favourite designers. I own several pieces from your summer dress collections of the past few years."

Candy preened under the praise and smoothly flourished over into a bow. Taking Esmeralda's hand in his, he brought it to his lips and pressed a long-second kiss to her knuckles.

"That is high praise I shall never forget, Your Highness," he said while rising. He leaned into her. "I'd love to send you the entire collection for next summer. I'm sure our dear prince would absolutely love seeing you dressed in *my* label all the time." He winked at me.

Dammit. I was used to Pierre driving me up the wall all the time, but I had forgotten Candy was ten times worse when he wanted to be. Which was more often than not.

If the three-piece white suit and bowtie he was wearing weren't proof of how eccentric Candy was, then I didn't know what was. Blond hair, dark blue eyes, and a bloated ego to go with them. Candy Hamilton was Prince Charming's rebellious twin brother. But saying that, as his friends we had seen that his arrogance was more of a bitter façade to spite his parents than it was the complete truth.

That didn't mean his bold behaviour and selfish attitude weren't irritating a lot of the time.

"I agree," Esmeralda replied while I ground my teeth to a pulp. "I'm sure he would enjoy watching your dresses fall to his bedroom floor every night."

I blinked, completely stunned by the casual way she dropped the suggestive little bomb of sass. She looked Candy head-on with a big, mock innocent smile, and the corners of my mouth twitched.

"Damn." Trevor chuckled.

"Told you," Pierre said proudly.

"So you did," Candy muttered, narrowing his gaze at Esmeralda. "Good answer, Your Highness. But I'm just getting started."

My smile fell. "Getting started on what?"

Candy waved me off. "Nothing you need to worry your pretty little head over, dear prince."

"The idiot insisted on testing Her Highness," Zain clarified with a disapproving shake of his head.

My frown grew heavier. "Candy," I warned, curling a protective arm around Esmeralda's waist. "You're not—"

Esmeralda silenced me with a hand on my abdomen. "No, let him. As your friend, he has every right to ask me questions."

"No, Esmeralda—" But she was already tipping her chin up at Candy.

Candy took a step towards her. "His favourite colour?"

Bloody Neves, he was fucking serious. And the others weren't stopping him. They all just stood there, observing Esmeralda intently. Even Pierre.

"Candy," I growled in frustration, drawing Esmeralda closer to my side.

"He doesn't have one," she answered calmly. "But he tends to wear darker colours. He looks especially delicious in black and dark green. Oh, and grey of course."

Trevor chuckled, but I was too caught up in the fact she called me "delicious." It was odd, but her kind of odd, and I liked it. I tugged at my ear.

"The name of the horse he rescued?"

"Bucky. And he doesn't like anyone but Kai—and me." Her shoulder shrugged up against my ribcage. "He's been more than happy to have me on his saddle."

My chest puffed out in pride at the way my mouthy Babble backhanded his questions like they were annoying little flies. For someone so small, she had one mighty attitude that she let loose in the most unexpected of moments. I loved it. My Babble didn't need me to defend her. She was a fiery queen all on her own.

Zain nodded in slow approval of her answer, Pierre beamed at her like an overexcited puppy, and Trevor let out a low whistle.

"Bucky let you ride him?" Candy spluttered, unable to mask his surprise. My friends knew of Bucky's behaviour—they had all been rejected by him multiple times. Especially Candy.

I pressed my mouth to the top of Esmeralda's head in a heavy kiss to hide my grin as Candy cleared his throat. "I mean yes, yes, correct. Well done."

"Any other questions?" she asked, a teasing note to her voice that made my smile grow. Fuck, I was going to kiss her so hard when I had a moment alone with her.

"I like her," Trevor mumbled while Candy stewed.

"Yes, actually." Candy stepped closer to her, intimidating her with his height. A deep sound rumbled from my mouth in warning, but he didn't bat an eyelash at me. "He loves the cold weather, but does he prefer rain or snow?"

"That's a trick question because he hates the cold. Especially rain. He would much rather bury himself in a dozen blankets than go within ten feet of a window or door while it's raining. Although…" Her dancing eyes met mine. "Never mind, actually."

"No, no," Candy insisted and waved one hand around as the other went to his hip. "Please inform us, Your Highness, what this smirk and '*although*' meant exactly."

"Candy," Zain warned, but he was struggling to tame a smile.

"It meant," Esmeralda said, tipping her chin up at Candy. "He's followed me into the rain—"

Candy didn't give her the chance to finish her sentence; his outburst was instant. "Are you bloody serious?" He angled to me. "I begged you to come to my fashion show, but you refused because the forecast said it was going to rain. My show wasn't even outside! But you followed her out into the rain? Explain yourself. Now."

"Here he goes," Trevor sighed with a roll of his eyes.

I shifted under Candy's accusing stare. "I did come to your show."

"Because it didn't end up raining! And you hid at the back away from the glass roof the whole flipping time because you said you didn't like the look of the grey clouds." Candy pointed past me. "And I was there when you rescued Bucky, and that damned horse won't let me anywhere near him, but he likes Her Highness? Why? What is there not to like about me? And I thought your favourite colour was navy-blue? But now it's *dark green*? So, you didn't like the suit I designed for you—"

"Candy," Zain grumbled at the same time Pierre smacked his palm over Candy's mouth.

"Why are you getting so emotional?" Pierre stressed, his eyes popping from their sockets.

But Candy harrumphed and turned his head away, not even bothering to push Pierre's hand away. My brows dipped as I tried to look at his face. A pouty Candy was usually a worried Candy, and when Candy was worried enough to drop his arrogant mask, then something was wrong.

"Please accept our apology for Candy's behaviour, Your Highness,"

Trevor said with a small smile. "He's known Kai nearly as long as Pierre has, and he's the most protective of him too. Unfortunately, when he gets protective like this, he tends to spout selfish nonsense."

"No, don't apologise, and please, call me Esmeralda," she said, but I couldn't take my eyes off Candy acting so passive behind Pierre's hand. "And I understand why you're protective of Kai, Candy." I felt her gentle weight sink against me. "I'm protective of him too."

A passing breeze brought a cooling silence with it as my friends absorbed what Esmeralda said.

Candy pulled down Pierre's hand from over his mouth. "She knows about…"

I nodded. "Hmm, she does."

No one said anything for what felt like a solid minute. Then Candy huffed loudly enough to make Trevor jump. "Dammit, she's so cute, I can't even be mad." He sighed. "All right. Fine." He straightened the lapels of his pristine blazer, stepped forward, and swung over into a deep bow. "Please accept my apologies, Your Highness."

"*Esmeralda*," she said and shook her head. "And I will not accept your apology because no apology is necessary. Although…" She dragged out the word in a playful way. "If you really would like me to accept something, I would love to have an exclusive dress designed by you."

He grinned at her like the last couple of minutes hadn't just happened and took her hand in his. "Only if you promise to model it at one of my shows too."

"Deal."

"Then consider it done."

The moment she gasped, she was gone from my side. Tugged away by Candy as he drew her around to stand between him and Pierre. Far away from me.

"Candy," I growled, jerking forward to reach for her.

"Oh-ho, look at this. Look at him trying to get her back." Candy's teasing forced me to stop. "Look at that face—so angry as if I took away your blankie." He fussed at me like one would do to a baby and my cheeks heated. It only made him look more pleased with himself.

"We're so damn possessive, aren't we, dear prince? So much so you can't even be away from her for even a second?"

He words rang true. My hands were opening and closing around air, unnerved by how empty they felt without having Esmeralda to hold onto. And without her body pressed right next to me, I felt like there was an icy wind biting away at the imprint of her warmth on me. I hated it. I wanted her back. Where she belonged. Next to me. *Always*. That probably made me seem like a petulant child, but I couldn't change how miserable I felt without her in reaching distance.

Trevor chuckled. "Candy, stop."

"Let her go," Pierre said. "He bloody looks like he's about to explode."

"I know. I like it," Candy said and winked at me. "Who knew this whole jealous-possessive thing would look so good on our dear pretty prince."

I ground my teeth together and rubbed at my burning ear as my friends laughed, even Zain.

At least Esmeralda didn't laugh. But the tilted-head-achingly-beautiful-smile combination she subjected me to scratched my bones with a bittersweet needle.

Having her go back to Jahandar in a few days' time was going to kill me.

CHAPTER 30

Kai

"**T**hank you for coming," I said, pulling back from Zain's hug. We stood next to his car in the palace car park to the west of the gold-painted iron gates.

"Thanks for inviting me," he said with a smile. "I'm only sorry I couldn't stay longer. But with Max ill, Alisha and I hardly had any sleep last night. I can't leave her on her own to look after the kids with both of our parents wreaking havoc in the house too."

"No, you need be with your family. Give Alisha and your parents my regard. And tell little Tara she can play in the tower the next time she comes."

Zain grunted and shook his head. "You know I haven't heard the end of that since you mentioned it her. Every night it's, '*Baa, when are we going to see Uncle Kai's tower?*'. I'm entirely sure she believes you have some Visney princess in there for her to meet." I chuckled, and his mouth turned up in a slow smirk. "Though, I guess you do in fact have a princess to put in your tower now."

Heat fanned across my cheeks, and I tugged at my earlobe. "Yeah, I guess I do."

"We're going to have to do another meet up. Alisha and Tara really wanted to meet her. Maybe dinner at our place—if Princess Esmeralda is fine with that."

Something tight gripped my stomach. "It would have to be when she's next in Touma."

"Crap, right. I forgot she has to go back. When is she going?"

"She'll be leaving on the morning of the twenty-eighth."

"Four, five days then." He eyed me carefully. "How are you feeling about the long-distance thing?"

It had always been a dull understanding that Esmeralda had to go back to Jahandar. But ever since I woke up in her arms earlier in the morning, the realisation that today was the final event of this year's Peace Celebrations was beginning to fill me with more and more unease with every passing minute. I would be counting down the days until I watched her leave after today.

I didn't want her to go. Not yet. Not ever.

"I'm dreading it," I admitted. "Not because I don't think we can do it, but because…"

He smiled in understanding. "Because she hasn't even left, and you already feel like you miss her."

"Yes," I sighed. "Though I know she has to go. She's a crown princess, she has her own work to do in Jahandar that she can't abandon, and with my upcoming appointment as Crown Prince, I know I'm going to busy too. My worry is that our schedules won't match up enough for me to go visit her in Jahandar every so often. Or for her to come here."

"Invite her to every event here and get her to invite you to events in Jahandar and then you can see each other every other week," he joked then patted a hand to my shoulder, squeezing lightly. "But seriously, Kai, don't worry. You like her a lot, and it's obvious she feels the same, so you'll make each other your priority and figure it out day by day."

He shrugged. "I won't lie, you're probably going to miss her a lot. In my experience, that part doesn't get any easier. I miss Alisha and the kids so much every time I go on a business trip, but time passes by more quickly than you think. And the moments when you do see each other in person are so fucking worth the time apart."

I nodded, holding onto his words tightly for some sense of security. He smirked at me. "With the way you were looking at her though, I doubt that time apart is going to be more than a year. You look like you're halfway in love with her already."

One corner of my mouth tugged up in something that was both a wince and a smile. "Would it be mad to say I think I'm *more* than halfway in love with her already?"

His burst of laughter was loud and short. "You're asking the wrong person, dear prince. I proposed to Alisha within three months of knowing her, remember? But. When you know, you just know. And I think you know with Princess Esmeralda."

"I do know." *She's it. She's the one.* But I didn't have to say that part aloud, because from the way Zain looked at me, I knew he already understood.

"Then that's that," he said and patted me on the shoulder again. "Give Gigi and your mother a kiss from me. And take care of our hooligan children. Let me know if they give you any trouble."

I sighed, remembering that Pierre, Candy, and Trevor were still in the gardens with Esmeralda probably collecting roses or powders in different colours to dust across the flowers. "When do they ever *not* give me trouble?"

"It's going to be ten times worse now that they know you have a jealous streak. Be prepared."

"Thanks," I grumbled, and he laughed.

With one more thump on my shoulder, he walked around the back of his black car, stopping to look at me from the driver's seat door. "It's good to see you looking genuinely happy again, Kai."

Just like that, he opened the door and ducked inside.

I watched him drive down the long straight road leading away from the palace on the other side of the golden gates and disappear from sight. The soft smile his words left me with remained stuck on my face as I headed back inside the warmth of the palace and through to the gardens.

I was by the circle fountain, water streaming from the mouths of the four lion statues, opposite the garden doors when Candy and Trevor slunk into step on either side of me.

"Here you go," Candy said, holding out a single little off-white, fabric pouch stained slightly pink in places. "I picked red by the way. To decorate your rose for Esmeralda with."

I didn't take the pouch and flicked a suspicious frown between their smiles. "Where is she?"

"Should we help you pick a rose for her too?" Trevor said casually. *Too casually.*

My feet came to a swift stop and they both swung around in front of me. I narrowed my eyes at them. Something bright danced in Trevor's eyes, but then again, his eyes never looked dull. "Where is she?" I repeated.

"With Pierre, of course," Candy said. "They were heading to the cherry blossom trees, right Trev?"

Rationally, I knew I had no reason to feel irritated upon hearing that. Pierre was my friend; he wouldn't flirt with her—anymore, at least. I trusted him, and I trusted Esmeralda too, completely.

I was discovering very quickly that jealousy didn't listen to any rational thoughts. It sparked and twisted and turned and reached its flaming arms in every direction possible without a care. And I couldn't control it, no matter how much I knew I really didn't need to feel jealous.

Trevor nodded. "Hmm. Something about getting her a painted rose, wasn't it?"

"Oh, yes." Candy snapped his fingers to point at Trevor. "He wanted to be the first to give her one."

My blood pressure skyrocketed with a hard lurch.

Fuck no. No. No! There was no way Pierre was giving Esmeralda a painted rose before I had. There was no way she could—would accept it either. *Shit, would she?*

"Hey, Prince," Candy called out. "Where are you going?"

No answer could pass through the blockade my teeth had formed as I charged past Trevor towards the eastern side of the gardens where the old cherry blossom trees were. If my ears hadn't been ringing so loudly, I might have heard the single celebratory clap of hands behind me.

"Kai!" Uncle Arsh grinned as I passed him. "Where are you…

Okay then. See you—I guess…"

I didn't stop. I couldn't stop. I had one image in my mind I wanted to destroy, but I couldn't destroy it until I had seen the reality. It was taking everything in me not to sprint to get there quicker.

The moment I shot past the first tree, its naked branches swishing with the wind, I staggard to a halt.

Sure enough, there was Esmeralda with Pierre. Stood near the big sacks of red, green, yellow, pink, and blue powder and a large washing basin full of water the palace staff had spent the early hours of the morning placing in different locations throughout the gardens.

She was laughing at something he must have said. Just as he tucked a painted rose into her hand.

She took it and lifted it up to brush a gentle finger over its petals, smiling so sweetly at it.

Every vein and artery exploded inside me, simultaneously releasing a possessive roar.

He gave her a rose first. He gave her a fucking rose first!

"Esmeralda." The sound came from deep within my throat but sounded distant to my ears.

Her head flew around, her smile widening. But it dropped just as quickly. Pierre, on the other hand, looked like a smug little fucker. Like he was silently telling me I was too late. *He won. I lost.*

"Kai," Esmeralda uttered, a little waver to her voice.

"Oh…this suddenly feels like a very couple-y situation right here," Pierre said, feigning awkwardness, "so I think it's time for me to go." He bent into Esmeralda. "I'm glad you like it, Princess."

"What?" she croaked.

With his back to her, he winked at me, and strut off with an arrogant swagger to his stride.

I didn't chase after him to demand why he'd done it, though I really fucking wanted to break his perfectly straight nose.

"Kai," Esmeralda said cautiously. "Please don't tell me you think that I—"

"You took a rose from him."

She blinked. Paused. "What?"

"You took a rose from him," I repeated, my voice hoarse. "Before I had the chance to give you one."

She tipped the flower by the stem pressed between her fingers as if she'd remembered she was holding it. "What? No." She shook her head weakly. "This is—it's—"

"I'm your boyfriend," I grated, taking a step towards her. "I was supposed to give you one first."

Her lips pulled apart then she pursed them together after a breath. My gaze narrowed. *Why was her mouth fucking twitching at the corners?* "You are, Kai."

"Then why did you take it from him?"

"I didn't." Her voice lifted several tones, light rather than defensive. "I didn't take it from him."

"I saw you. He gave it to you, and you took it."

She curled her bottom lip into her mouth, but it did nothing to hide the tug in her cheeks.

I ground my teeth together. "Do you think this is funny?"

"No." She shook her head quickly, but her smile grew wider, bigger, toothier. "No, I..."

A breathy giggle rose from her mouth before she quickly captured it in the palm of her hand, but it was too late. I heard it. I saw the unashamed delight dance in her eyes, and it poisoned my blood with another hot emotion other than irritation and possessiveness.

I quickly found myself feeling more inclined to put her over my knees and bruise her arse before taking her arse, rather than wanting to throw around accusations I knew had no deeper meaning. There was nothing between her and Pierre.

But I was still fucking annoyed about the rose, and my little brat thought it was funny.

Fine. She'd get exactly what she deserved then.

Stretching my shoulders wide, I took a prowling stride towards her. Her bottom lip trembled apart from the upper one on a breathless little rise of her chest.

"You accepted a rose from someone else before me for our first Festival of Life together." I moved another pace forward.

"No, I," she breathed out. Excitement coloured her cheeks. "It's yellow—the powder on the rose is yellow. Yellow means friendship. It's not—"

"That's not the point. You took it." I took a bigger stride, threatening to close her in against a tree.

She took the bait. She stumbled back a step, offering herself up to me, playing this game with me. "Kai, wait, I..." I edged forward. She flew back. "Kai." I moved; she moved, her hands lifting to keep me back while her dilated eyes called at me to come closer. "Kai." *Forward. Back.* "*Kai...*" Every gasping stutter of my name from her soft lips as we danced around each other only made me feel evermore unhinged.

"If you didn't take it," I rasped, my voice so thick with primal lust that I almost didn't recognise it, "why are you moving away from me, Babble?"

"Because," she spluttered, edging around the bags of colour. "Because you're chasing me."

The poisoned blood in my veins flooded my head and sunk straight to my dick, polluting the sensible voice that told me to remember we were outside, surrounded by people, three of which were royal photographers. There was nothing sensible about what that voice was telling me to do to Esmeralda.

I wanted her to run. I wanted to chase her. To capture her. To fuck her so hard she couldn't stand straight for the rest of the day without feeling me deep inside her.

"I haven't started chasing you yet," I said before I could stop myself. "But I will."

Her breath audibly hitched, and my skin burned all over. It was then I noticed the red sitting in the corner of my vision and remembered the forgotten sacks of powder beside us. One glance at them and urgent need rocked right through me.

I want to streak her body with colour in the shape of my hands as I fuck her.

To paint her for everyone to see she's mine.

Without a second thought, I shoved my right hand into the

powder and lifted a fistful of red out. The dusting sprinkled from my skin to the white of my jumper, tainting the pure colour.

"Kai," she whispered, her bright stare darting frantically between my fist and face.

"If I catch you," I growled, "I am marking you. Inside and out. And when I'm done, I won't need to give you a rose for the world to see that you. *Are mine.*"

"Kai…"

"Run, Babble."

CHAPTER 31
Esmeralda

"Run, Babble."

My body lurched to life, not with a jolt of my heart, but with the liquid throb between my thighs. I stumbled around as my brain seemingly forgot how my muscles were supposed to work, every motor neuron receiving nothing but messages of malfunctioning chaos.

I ran the opposite way to where all the noises were emanating from. Away from the centre of the gardens as roses were probably being exchanged and colours thrown around. I was running from the safety of civilisation into the dangerous wild. But fuck, I didn't want safe. I wanted the wild promise of ravaging and marking in Kai's piercing stare when he caught me.

"You're making this too easy," Kai rasped behind me, and I gasped. It sounded like he was whispering right in my ear, his lips teasing my skin to gooseflesh.

With just the right amount of panic firing through my excitement, I pushed my feet harder, sending petals scattering off the forgotten rose in my hand over the pathway. But the movement of my legs was restricted by the white silk skirt tangled around my calves. Not that that was the reason Kai's footsteps remained close and threatening behind me.

"Come on, Babble," he said without sounding even the slightest bit strained. "Faster."

Fuck, fuck, fuck. I wanted to look over my shoulder and see how close he was, but I couldn't risk losing any momentum. Instead, my eyes chased after a route of escape ahead of me, and I spotted a trail through some tall scarlet red hedges trembling in the breeze. I made a beeline for the opening, heading across a corner of lawn.

A set of fingers brushed across the side of my neck.

I squeaked as my legs threw me forward through the opening, and Kai's mocking laugh rushed up the back of my neck. "Almost had you there."

He was taunting me. A big cat toying with a cornered mouse, grazing the belly of the little creature with a single claw until it quivered in fear. He was reminding me he was in control with that touch to my neck, and he got his desired effect. I turned into a frantic mess.

I also realised my mistake of heading through the hedges.

Three walls of scarlet red shrubs surrounded me, including the one I'd come through, with a stone wall opposite forming the large rectangular space. There was a path around the perimeter that gave access to the pale wooden outbuilding in the corner with a trimmed patch of grass in the middle.

"Looks like you trapped yourself, Babble," the big bad wolf snarled behind me.

No, no, no. Yes. No!

I went straight over the grass, bounding around one of the three oval-shaped flowerbeds cut out in the lawn, hoping that I could misdirect Kai and circle back out of there.

In hindsight, it was an absolutely stupid idea sure to fail from the beginning. I was done for the moment I tried to zip around the second flowerbed back towards the opening.

He must've known what I'd been planning to do, because his hand was already out, ready to clamp around my elbow. By the time I realised it was there, it was too late to move away.

He caught me and I shrieked. He yanked me back and the

momentum threw me spinning around to face him. I crashed straight into his front as he stumbled to slow down. I tried to take advantage of him being off-balance, but he was so much bigger than me, so much more powerful. So much faster. His corded arms wrapped around my waist before I fully extended my elbows, trapping me against his hot, heaving body with no escape.

"Got you," he grated through a heavy breath, his cheeks flushed and his eyes so black and drugged on some manic sort of arousal.

"Kai." I was panting, my burning lungs and lust-induced trembling leaving me weak. But I still struggled and pushed against him, trying to force my way out of his superstrength grip.

"Oh no you don't."

He lifted me up off the grass and dragged my tingling body all up his front. The big bulge of his erection dug into my lower belly, rubbing into me so good with every step he took. But I still kicked and wriggled and thumped his shoulders, fighting his conquering while craving my downfall.

All I achieved was making myself breathless as he took us inside the outbuilding. He slammed the door behind us, shaking the whole structure, and shoved something under the handle. Darkness whirled around me as he spun me away until the light from the two small windows on either side of the door poured through. My breath vanished at what I saw.

The glow in Kai's eyes was absolutely feral as the light bounced off his irises, illuminating his cheekbones and the tight angle of his jaw. The panic that bucked through my chest shouldn't have turned me on, but a hollow ache jolted so hard through my pussy, I whined in anticipation.

He chuckled. "Are you already whimpering, Babble?"

Faster than I could form a retort, he dropped my arse on a wooden surface in the middle of the space and snaked a hand around the top of my ponytail. He crashed his mouth over mine, forceful and greedy. His tongue chasing, cornering, catching my own as he'd just caught me.

I moaned under his rough domination but pushed and clawed at him, biting his lip as he retreated his tongue. That earned me a rough growl and a hard yank on my hair, sending sharp sparks all over my scalp. I gasped, and he took full advantage, plundering my mouth even deeper.

He kept his weight heavy on me as his other hand spread over my ribcage and shaped my body up my neck to squeeze my cheeks. He held me completely still, my lips puckered and forced open.

To his smug purr of satisfaction that left me no choice but to let him take my mouth however he pleased until my body shook and the strain on the fabric of my skirt bit into my thighs.

I gasped for air when he relented on his attack and slumped into the sturdy hold of his palm at the back of my head. My vision split and blurred before combining back into one clear view of Kai's beautiful eyes, glowing and hooded as they travelled down my body.

"Look at you, Babble," he whispered huskily. "So fucking beautiful all tainted in red."

My mind struggled to catch onto his meaning. That was when I noticed the red dust all over his hand and down the sleeve of his white jumper, and I remembered his earlier threat.

He'd promised to mark me.

With a sharp inhale, I glanced down and gaped.

There was a path of red streaked up one side of my jumper. An obvious handprint over my left breast. And a trail that moved up to my neck and higher.

It was wrong. It was beautiful. It was base. It was seductive. Everyone would know exactly how he'd touched me the moment I stepped outside, but desire exploded inside me like fireworks, so bright and breath-taking. All because this gorgeous man had marked me for the world to see.

"Isn't it beautiful?" he purred into my ear, and I shuddered. My trembling hands clung onto him as he dragged his mouth across my cheek towards my chin. He lifted his head and the red on my face was now smeared all over his kiss-stung lips. "You look like a work of art. *My* art."

I nearly whimpered at how stunningly mad he looked. With my

thumb, I rubbed the colour into his lips and needily dragged him down into another feverish kiss.

He didn't let me stay in control for very long. He clamped his hand around the back of my neck, adjusting the fit of our mouths together, and kneaded my breast over my clothes with a possessive touch, no gentle attempt at seduction in sight. He rubbed the red all over my chest, spreading his mark as he licked down my jaw to my neck. I writhed against him, my gasp echoing through the panting darkness of the shed when he found the sweet spot below my ear. And sucked.

I tugged at his jumper, his hair, and clawed at his biceps, trying to push him off, but needing to pull him closer. My every moan and pant were an undeniable plea for more. Harder. Meaner.

He did just that. He pushed down on me heavier. Forced me to bow back, giving him better access to my neck as he dragged his mouth lower. And bit me again. Sucking and licking my nerves into overdrive. He groaned as he forced my thighs wider to make space for the leg he had between them.

Stretching the fabric of my skirt until I could feel it on the verge of ripping at the seams.

"Kai," I breathed, tugging at a fistful of his thick raven black hair. "My skirt—it's going to tear."

With a deep exhale, he let my hot skin slip from his mouth and lifted off enough to let me quickly adjust my legs. But he rasped, "Maybe I want it to tear," as he slid his hand on my breast down to the side of my thigh, leaving a path of faded red on the silk. The sweet little smudge of red on the tip of his nose did nothing to make him look any less than a starved beast.

Holding his palm there, I shook my head. "I'll have nothing to wear to go back outside."

"I know," he sighed. "That's the only reason I haven't torn it already."

A little indecipherable noise fell from my hanging mouth. But for the life of me I couldn't tell if it was in shock of what he said. Or because his mouth found the sensitive shell of my ear.

"Shall we move it out of the way then?"

I shuddered, tipping my head to fit his mouth closer. "Yes."

"Yes what?" he growled, his breath assaulting my nerves with a hundred prickling tugs.

"Sir." I gasped. "Yes, Sir."

He groaned a sound of satisfaction. "Better."

I swayed forward when he moved back, almost collapsing like boneless mush without his sturdy support. But I braced myself back on my hands as he took a fistful of my skirt, tugging it up my legs. When he got to my knees, he adjusted his fingers, spreading them to cup the outsides of my thighs.

Teasing and slow, he caressed up my thighs, taunting my skin to gooseflesh with every bare inch of my legs he exposed. I bit my bottom lip, muffling a moan as I stared at the faint red trail behind his stained fingers on my left thigh. It was as if I'd been lightly scored by a predator's claws, and the higher the trail went, the harder it became not to pant and arch up off the table for more.

Once Kai gathered the silk under my arse and completely out of the way, he stroked his hands over the top of my thighs, hungrily eyeing the space between.

"You wore a *white* lace thong too?" he growled, the thick words coming from the back of his throat. "But do you know, Babble—it doesn't look pure or innocent. It looks so fucking *slutty*." One thumb brushed the lace right over my clit. My whole body jerked, pleasure pulsing up my spine, but he dragged it lower immediately. "All soaked through. Your swollen pussy peeking out around it." He pressed his thumbs high into my inner thighs and pulled. Not a single breath made it out of my lungs as cool air stroked the heat between my spread pussy lips. "*Fuck, Esmeralda.* There is nothing innocent about your needy little cunt, is there?"

"Kai," I whimpered, rocking my hips towards him as more wetness trickled down to my arse.

His hand came up and slapped down over my clit. I cried out, stars blinding me for a full second. I tried to snap my thighs shut, but his hands wouldn't let me. "It's Sir," he spat viciously. "Now answer my question. You have a needy little pussy, don't you?"

"Yes," I choked out. "Yes, Sir."

He soothed his thumb over the light sting in my clit. "And who does it belong to?"

"You, Sir."

"That's right, Babble. *Me.*" He wrapped a hand around my throat, dragging me up and forward, forcing me to look right into his eyes. "It belongs to me. *You are mine.*" His hand tightened. "But you enjoy acting like a brat and playing little games to make me jealous, so I am going to remind you who you belong to right here, right now. And you're going to take it like a good girl who is sorry for what she did. Then you're going to walk out of here with my cum deep inside you and hope that your thong covers enough to keep it from dripping down your legs. Is that clear?"

My recollection of what words were and how they were used completely vanished, lost in the thick smoke of hunger his filthy words pumped into me, turning me into an obedient, mindless sex doll. Only the two most essential words formed my entire vocabulary.

"Yes, Sir."

"Good girl," he whispered and pressed a heavy kiss to my lips. "Now take my dick out and stroke it."

I sat upright immediately and reached for him, fumbling blindly under the hem of his ruined white jumper to undo his slim-fit jeans and pushed them down. He took over, dragging them along with his boxers to the middle of his thighs, while I lifted the skin-tight thermal T-shirt he had on underneath. I curled it up over his jumper to hold both fabrics high up against his abdomen.

Then I stared like I was seeing him for the first time.

The sturdy width of his hips, the delicious V, the dark hairs against his golden skin. He was so fucking beautiful, so sexy. So unbothered by how his dick hung straight towards me, thick and hard. My mouth watered remembering what he felt like in my mouth—the heat and taste of him—and bloody Neves, I would have fallen on my knees right there if I hadn't wanted him inside my pussy more.

I closed one hand under the crown of his cock in a tight fist while

I cupped his balls in the other. His heavy exhale fanned my cheek and his hands landed on the wooden surface on either side of my thighs. I watched, captivated by his expression, as I brushed my thumb over the tip, smearing his pre-cum, and massaged his balls. He groaned, the sound like oil on the flames already burning in my belly.

"Fuck, Babble." He wrapped his hand tightly around my throat, holding my face up to his. I rotated my hand, giving him a light tug, and he moaned. "Fuck, yes. Keep your hand tight. Just like that, Babble." He panted into my open mouth. "My pretty little Babble is good at listening to me, isn't she?" I nodded as much as I could with his hand on my throat and I felt his mouth curl against mine, searing my insides with pride. "Yes, she is. She *fucking* is." His mouth landed quick and heavy over mine. "Now let go of me."

I did exactly as he said, desperate need shaking through my hands. Kai quickly caught both of my wrists and dragged them behind me, pressing my palms flat to the surface, so I was leaning my weight back. "Keep your hands there," he said and grabbed each of my ankles in turn and pulled my trainers off, letting them land on the concrete floor with a thud. "Feet on the edge of the worktop. Now."

I grew breathless realising how he wanted me, but I lifted my legs, resting my heels on the edge of the worktop, letting him adjust them as he pleased. Then hooking a finger under my thong, he dragged it to the side, and released it with a gentle snap against my arse cheek.

He braced one hand on the table by my hip, gripped the root of his cock with the other, and rubbed the swollen head down between my wetness and up again, nudging my clit. I stifled a moan, biting down on my lip, as I watched. *Up and down. Up and down. Up and down.*

"Look at me, Esmeralda," Kai demanded, and I angled my chin. "Do you want to use our safe word?"

I shook my head. "No—"

The syllable was still falling off the tip of my tongue when he abruptly thrust forward.

Sliding into me. Stretching me. Filling me right to the hilt on a low groan.

A broken sound was ripped from my throat as my back arched, my eyes widened, and my fingers clawed into the table for purchase…that I never found. *Kai didn't let me find it.*

"Fuck," he half breathed, half chuckled. A twisted smirk pushed his dimple deep into his right cheek. "You're so wet, Babble, you took all of me in one go." He dragged his cock back slowly, making my inner muscles clench around every inch of him. "Such a greedy little slut for me, aren't you?"

He snapped forward again, ripping my breath and wits right out of hands as the sweet sensation of being rubbed everywhere right flared up to my head.

"Kai," I gasped, lifting one hand to anchor myself to him.

But he jerked forward on an angry, "No," and slammed so deep inside me, a blissful bolt of pain electrified my core. My other arm nearly gave out behind me, but Kai grabbed my wrist and pressed my palm back on the table. "Keep your fucking hand right there."

I choked on his name, my face crumpling in a plea under his intense scowl. But he stayed right there—hand on my wrist, a bruising grip on my thigh, jaw grinding together—as he snapped his hips back-and-forth. Thrust after thrust after mean, breath-taking thrust. And he didn't let up.

He set a vicious pace, ignoring my sobbed begging, grunting on a hard plunge every time I panted his name. He wasn't fazed when my foot slipped off, he just grabbed my ankle and put it back into place, clung onto my hip with his other hand and *thrust, thrust, thrust*. Doing his best to ruin me.

On a fractured noise, I squeezed my eyes shut and Kai's movements instantly slowed to a stop.

"No, no, no, *no*." His hand around my wrist lifted to the back of my neck and he gave me a little shake. "Open your eyes, Esmeralda. *Now*. That's it. Good girl. Keep your beautiful eyes on me."

I whimpered under the praise as he rewarded me with a quick kiss. "Kai, please," I choked out against his mouth. "Sir, *please*."

"Please what, Babble?"

He snaked his hand around my neck and down my front as he

leaned back. Pressing his hand against my lower belly, he drew his cock out and slowly pushed back in, creating an erotic, sloppy, wet sound. I gasped as my thighs gave a hard quiver under the intense wave of pleasure.

"*Please have mercy on me, Sir?*" He pushed in. "*Please fuck me harder, Sir?*" Out. "*Please, it's too much, Sir?*" In. "Or..." His gaze dropped down as he dragged out. "*Please torture my clit, Sir?*" In!

I thrashed my head from side to side. "I'll come—I'll come—I'm going to come!"

"No, you fucking won't," he growled and completely drew his cock out of me, leaving me crying on the sudden feeling of aching emptiness. His red-stained hand came out of nowhere to clamp around my chin, squeezing my cheeks. "Have I given you permission to come yet?"

"No, Sir," I stuttered, my words muffled by the way he was squishing my mouth.

"Exactly. So, are you going to come?"

"No, Sir."

"Do you want me to let you come?"

He had me held still, but I still attempted a nod. "*Please*. Please, Sir. I want to come—let me come."

His lashes fell shut for a second as he moaned, then he lowered his mouth over mine. "Be a good girl and stick your tongue out for me."

He loosened his grip on my cheeks, and I took the chance to stick my tongue out. I thought he was going to spit in my mouth or shove his fingers to the back of my throat. I wanted both. I wouldn't have minded either. But what he did was even hotter.

Kai stuck his tongue out and shamelessly licked across mine. A full-on, filthy lick, not tasting me but possessing me before sucking my tongue into his mouth for a dirty kiss. I moaned as my pulsing pussy clenched around nothing, and he groaned, deep and lusty, pressing me ever closer to him.

"Wrap your arms around my neck, Babble. Let's make you come."

"Yes, Sir."

A wobbly curl touched my mouth as I snaked both my arms around his shoulders, but it fell away on a sigh when he pushed back into me. Then his arms were sliding under my thighs, his fingers digging into my arse cheeks as he picked me up off the wooden surface. The new position was bliss, my clit rubbing right against the hot, damp skin on his exposed washboard belly.

"Oh, fuck." My entire body shuddered as he lifted me higher and pulled his hips back.

I knew what was coming. The lack of mercy in his eyes told me what he planned. But nothing could have prepared me for the way he dragged me down and thrust forward at the same time.

I swear it felt like he was hitting my stomach. So deep and so good, no sound could come out of my gaping mouth. Again and again and again. Grinding my clit against him so perfectly all the while.

My orgasm rose, coiled, and tightened in my belly at the speed of light.

"Fuck," I sobbed, pulling on the hair at the back of his head as I rode his thrusts. "*Please.* I'm going to come—say I can come. Please, Kai—Sir."

"Come, Babble," he spat through gritted teeth. "Fucking come for me."

Every noise lifting from our sweaty, thrusting bodies grew louder as we chased my orgasm. The slap of skin against skin, his groaning, my panting. And then the trainwreck of my climax hit me.

I tensed right down to my toes as my lungs shattered on a scream. Blinding heat flew through me in every direction and forget white, I blacked out for a second. Before Kai's roar dragged me back to consciousness as he came in hard, erratic jerks inside me.

My body burned and tingled and quaked as I clung to him, and he drooped into my arms. We passed a long, panting minute just like that before either of us had the energy to move or speak.

"Are you okay?" Kai rasped into my ear as he slid his hands up my back and circled his arms around me, hugging me close.

"Hmm," I hummed tiredly, dropping my forehead against his damp cheek. "I am—I—"

"Shh." His softening length slipped out of me as he lifted me closer. "There's no need to say anything. Just relax and take deep breaths. That was—that was intense, I…I hope no one heard us."

A weak giggle fluttered from my mouth. "That was. You can put me down if you're—"

"No, I'm fine." He buried his face in my hair.

"But—"

"Shh, I have you. I have you, Esmeralda. Don't worry about me. I only need you to close your eyes and rest for a moment. And I will keep you in my arms." He landed a kiss to the side of my head.

With an acquiescing lift of my chin, I nuzzled closer to him, melting into the enclosing warmth of his big, sturdy body as he lulled my reeling mind to stillness. The earthy undertone of his perspiration mixed with the enchanting sweetness of his cologne cleansed my lungs. I basked in the kisses he pressed to my hair until I lifted my head and offered him my forehead for the same soothing treatment.

I had never felt so relaxed and protected in my life, and I would never have disturbed the perfect quiet we were sharing if I hadn't felt the tell-tale ooze between my sticky thighs.

Heat fanned through my cheeks as an awkwardly amused smile lifted my mouth. "Kai."

His cheek shifted against my forehead. "Hmm?"

"Can you uh, move my thong back into place before your cum really does drip down my legs?"

I felt his body turn to stone for a second before, "Shit, I—" He carefully lowered me onto the edge of the wooden surface again and untangled himself from my limbs. Yanking his jeans back up to his toned arse, he rummaged through his back pocket and pulled out a neatly folded tissue.

"It's unused," he said as he flicked it open. "Let me clean you up."

"I thought you wanted your cum dripping down my legs?" I teased with a raise of my brows.

His own eyebrows sunk into a bashful frown. "I did—I do." He urged my knees apart as he lowered the tissue to my centre. "But that doesn't mean I want you to feel uncomfortable and sticky. I couldn't do that to you."

Squealing on the inside at his adorably sweet answer, I let him wipe the wetness between my thighs without entirely wiping away his cum after which he moved my thong and skirt back into place. Then he cleaned himself up, pulled up his boxers and jeans, and disposed of the tissue in a scrunched up black bag in the corner by the door.

And I quickly remembered why all of this had started in the first place.

"The rose was for Kareem," I said as Kai wiped my face with the unstained sleeve of his jumper.

"What?"

"Pierre didn't give me that rose. He helped me choose it, but I was decorating it to give to Kareem." Kai comically blanched. "Pierre took it out of my hand, saying there was a thorn on it, and then you showed up. Thinking back now, with the way he made it seem like he was giving it to me and your perfect timing, I think he planned it to irritate you on purpose."

The confusion, the realisation, the pure vexation, everything played out on Kai's face in real time. "Candy and Trevor," he growled, his hand in my lap curling to a fist. "They told me he was with you and I… Bloody Neves, when I find them, they're—"

"Don't," I chuckled and raised my hand to his cheek. "I just hope that you weren't at any point jealous because you thought there was ever any chance that I would betray you."

His hand on my lap leapt to my wrist. "*No.* No, Esmeralda," he said urgently. "Never. I never once thought that. I trust you completely. I only…" He huffed out a breath, dropping his head a little. "I don't know how to explain it without sounding absurd, but I…I can't help wanting you all to myself, and when another man smiles at you and makes you laugh or even looks at you…" I was pretty sure his cheek heated under my palm. "I want to wrap you in my arms and hide you from them, which I know I can't, and neither would I ever try to, but I cannot help feeling jealous when they do it so effortlessly in a way I know I never could."

"Kai." His name fell off my tongue like an aching sigh at the self-conscious vulnerability he admitted to. One that wasn't true, because all this man had to do was exist and I felt explosively giddy.

He shook his head, pressing my palm deeper into his cheek. "But I would never stop you from being friends with anyone or meeting anyone or anything else, Esmeralda. You have my word on that." His eyes did a pouty, puppy dog thing that shot through me like a heart-shaped arrow. "I cannot lie to you and say I *won't* act like a jealous oaf after, but if it's bothering you, I will stop. I promise."

I shook my head, lifting my other hand to cup his jaw. "I don't want you to pretend to be someone you're not, Kai, so if you are jealous, I want to know." I shrugged one shoulder. "Plus, it's kind of, *really* quite cute." He glowered and I gleamed. *"And*—I can use it as an excuse to remind you that you are *literally* the man of my dreams. *My Perfect Prince.* I don't have eyes for anyone else."

His face definitely warmed under my hands that time as his mouth rose shyly. Then he turned his head and pressed a long-second kiss to each of my palms and offered his lips for me to kiss.

"We should probably go back before they send out a search party for us." It didn't sound like he wanted to though.

"Probably." I pressed another peck to his mouth.

"Would you like to change before going back? I ruined your jumper."

"No." *Kiss.* "And you clearly haven't seen yourself." I kissed his smile. "And everyone else should be covered in colour by now, so I think we'll be fine if we just rub it in a bit more." *Kiss.* "Though, we might need to find a water basin to wash the sweat off our hands and faces."

My famous last words.

The moment we stepped out of the shed and ran into Shehryar on the other side of the scarlet hedges, he. Went. Ballistic.

To summarise Shehryar's rant, Kai and I gave "caught red-handed" an entirely new meaning.

CHAPTER 32

Esmeralda

It was an hour or so after breakfast the next morning when Kai and I were standing by the garden doors getting ready to head out to the stables together.

After all the exhausting celebrations, both private and public, for the Festival of Life the day before, we thankfully had a day of rest. The first of two known internationally as Peace Bank Holidays with no royal events or activities planned. It also signalled the start of my last four days in Touma before who knew when I would be able to see Kai next.

The gnawing anguish at the idea of being apart from him without knowing when I would be in his arms again was nibbling at my belly like a twitching baby mouse. Small in its strength yet, but it was only a matter of time before it grew. I would have to find a way to cage it, because with our roles in state ruling and politics, avoiding the dating long-distance set-up was impossible.

But while I was with him, I planned to enjoy my time with him to the absolute fullest. All his worrisome grumbling and adorable frowning and every other expression I could tease out of him.

"It's not *that* cold," I purposely said, fighting a grin.

The frustrated line between his brows intensified. "Yes, it is." He tugged the puffy standing collars of my dark green jacket together even though he had already zipped it up to my chin. "This jacket isn't warm enough. You need a proper coat, Esmeralda."

"You mean like the floor-length bear suit you're wearing?" I buried the toothy curl taking over my mouth behind the collar as his death glare became *death-glare-two-point-oh*. A muffled giggle bubbled from me. "Oh, come on." I lifted my chin and leaned into him. "You worry too much, Mr Perfect Prince. My jacket is fluffy and warm, I promise." I took one of his hands in both of mine and tugged at it. "So, shall we go now? You told Jorge we'd be there ten minutes ago."

He looked like was going to grumble something else but then he pursed his lips into a thin line and huffed a long exhale through his nose. "Fine. Let's go." He dropped his head and I rose up on my toes. Our mouths mashed together in the middle. "If it starts raining, we're leaving immediately."

"We can further discuss that *if* it rains."

"Babble," he warned. But I was already swivelling away with a flick of my hair, pulling him along towards the arched garden doors.

We had only made it two steps when, "Princess Esmeralda."

I came to abrupt halt, my gaze flying across my shoulder. A cold pebble slipped down through the middle of my ribcage and settled in my stomach as a pair of ice blue eyes greeted me.

"Sully," I said as I faced the tall, slim older man who'd worked as a secretary for Jahandar's royal family since before I was born.

Kareem's private secretary, Sully, hinged at the waist in a bow, then clasped his white-gloved hands in front of his navy-blue suit trousers. "I apologise for interrupting, Your Highness, but His Majesty, King Kareem, sent me to find you after you didn't answer your phone," he said, his full, neatly groomed moustache moving more than his paper-thin upper lip.

Another cold pebble fell through me. *Kareem...called me?*

Shoving my free hand into my coat pocket, I pulled my phone out and my heart did an odd wobble. There was a missed call notification on the screen with *His Majesty* under it.

Another pebble tumbled through me, knocking against my bones as it did.

Kareem didn't call me. Kareem *never* called. Not directly at least. If he wanted to speak to me, he always rang me through Shehryar. If it was official, I received an impersonal email from him. That was it. Nothing else. Never anything else.

"Oh." The sound slipped from my mouth as a breath. I lifted my head, searching Sully's poker face for an answer but not a single one of his wrinkles twitched out of place. "Is something the matter?"

"His Majesty has requested to see you, Ma'am, and His Highness, Prince Kai, in his room."

A handful of icy pebbles scattered through me, and I tensed under the light battering. Then the usual feeling of centipedes, eels, snakes, and worms wriggling all over each other inside me whenever Kareem asked to see me rose instantly.

I was supposed to feel reassured by the new hope of reconciliation these past few days had given me. But years of bad experiences had conditioned this anxious reaction and there was no off switch that could put a stop to it immediately.

I felt a strong pressure around my hand and my attention dropped to the security being offered by the callused palm pressed against mine. And up to the owner.

A fiery resolve, a promise, and reassurance all rolled into one radiated from Kai. My shoulders eased as it wrapped around me.

Maybe it was just about us? Me and Kai. Our relationship. It had to be. That was probably the only reason Kareem wanted to see the both of us. So, it was fine. *Everything was fine.*

Holding onto those three words, I smiled at Sully. "Just give us a moment to take our coats off."

"Your Majesty," Sully said into the dark wood of Kareem's bedroom door and Kareem's softened call from the inside came within seconds. The older man opened the door for me and Kai to enter.

I hadn't really paid attention to the interior the last time I was there, but the room Kareem had been given was massive. It was two connected rooms actually. A sitting room immediately through the entrance and a larger bedroom on the right, divided by a rectangular cutout in the wall. In the sitting room, there was a desk perpendicular in the far right corner, and two red velvet sofas opposite the window close to the door. There was a dark oak coffee table between them and a closed laptop on top of the polished surface.

Kareem was sat on the sofa facing the same direction as the door, looking worn and quiet. When I saw who else was there, the collapse of my heart to the floor made me stumble to a stop.

Shehryar was there. Standing with his hands clasped before his black chinos to the left of the red velvet sofa, opposite the one Kareem was sitting on. He wasn't frowning, but there was a cautious alertness in his piercing pale green eyes, his six-foot-five frame pulled rigid.

I knew instantly then something was wrong, and dread seeped through my skin as a cold sweat.

"Your Majesty," Kai said from next to me with a bow of his head once Sully closed the door.

Kareem offered Kai a pursed-lip smile and a nod. Belatedly, I remembered to bow too, but I couldn't seem to get my mouth to unhinge to speak when my brother's gaze trained on me. It was intense with something I didn't recognise on him.

"Come, take a seat, please," Kareem said, gesturing to the sofa opposite him.

Kai's gentle push on my lower back urged me forward with a promise to be there right behind me, so I moved like I was walking a plank. I went around the sofa one way, and Kai went around the other, passing Shehryar. We sat down next to each other with a slither of space between us.

Kareem straightened his hunched shoulders and rubbed his jaw with one hand. "Thank you for coming. Shehryar said you were headed to the stables, so I apologise for disturbing your plans, but this was," —he visibly swallowed— "*urgent.* I needed the three of you here."

Urgent equalled bad. It *always* equalled bad.

"Did something happen?" I managed, but to my ears, it sounded like I was ten feet under water.

Kareem's gaze trailed from Shehryar to Kai, then lingered on me before moving to his private secretary who'd situated himself next to the sofa. "Sully and I sat down for a meeting after breakfast to discuss some changes to my schedule for the first few days back in Jahandar." He turned back to the three of us. "I hadn't checked my emails for a few days, so we decided to read through a few.

"That was when I saw an email in my junk inbox. From yesterday." His jaw clenched, his eyes darkened, and dread dripped off the tip of my fingers like blood. "I don't recognise the email address, neither did they give any indication of who they were. But…"

There was a moment of pin-drop silence as he reached for the closed laptop on the coffee table. He opened it and typed something out. With a few swipes and a click on the mouse pad, a quiet voice played out.

My voice.

With a regretful wince, Kareem turned the laptop around.

Just as audio me said, *"I'm not my mother's real daughter. I'm Father's illegitimate child."*

Shehryar shifted, Kai made a quiet sound, and I…

Someone silently laughed in my face as they stepped on a trigger, destroying the warm, happy bubble around me in a violent explosion.

That night. The video on Kareem's screen was of that night. In Kai's bedroom. When I told him about my illegitimacy. Taken from the side, a blur of black along the bottom, but it was still clear it was us.

Ringing. Only ringing.

No voice. No heartbeat. No breaths. Just ringing. That was all I could hear.

A piercing scream of noise rang in my ears as my charred skin burned numb. My insides went cold as the life dripped out of every blackened pore. I sat still, completely frozen and unblinking. Because one slight move would send my ashes dispersing into the air, never to be found again.

Everything I'd hoped for—a bright future with someone I loved— gone. Just like that.

Because the one thing I had always feared and worried and fretted over had happened.

Someone had taken a video. Someone knew.

Someone had evidence of my truth.

Kareem roughly turned the laptop back to him and slammed a finger down on the spacebar.

Silence. So loud. So painful. So destructive.

"There…" Kareem croaked, scrubbing a hand over his face. "There is another recording of you two…*together.*" Bile rose in my throat in understanding as his disturbed gaze lowered from mine.

A sex tape. He meant a sex tape.

"But that is it." He shook his head weakly. "There's no demand for money, no explanation as to how or why they have these recordings, although it is clear that someone bugged the room."

Numbly, I felt Kai stir next to me, but I couldn't bring myself to look at him.

"The only thing the email says is…" He swiped on the mousepad and read, "*The prince was my target, but your half-sister did a splendid job of stealing the show, Your Majesty.*"

Silence.

"If Prince Kai was the target," Shehryar said, his voice strained, "then Your Majesty can't be the only person who received this email."

Kareem nodded. "I agree. I think, Kai, your parents might have been sent the same email."

Everything inside me came tumbling down so hard the ground underneath my feet shook.

I couldn't hear what Kai said next, nor what Kareem said in reply and in turn Shehryar. I couldn't do anything but stare at the back of Kareem's laptop, one thought ripping my heart, piece by piece.

This was exactly what I had wanted to avoid.

Someone I cared about getting hurt because of me. Because of my secret.

Now someone was trying to use it against Kai, but it wouldn't just

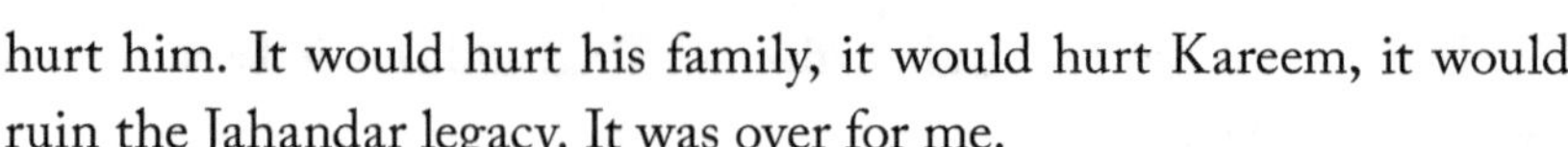

hurt him. It would hurt his family, it would hurt Kareem, it would ruin the Jahandar legacy. It was over for me.

And it was all my fault.

I was the problem.

CHAPTER 33

Kai

"Esmeralda, wait," I called out, chasing her down the corridor away from her brother's room.

She didn't stop. She didn't slow down. She didn't look back. *Still.*

She still wouldn't look at me. She didn't even wait for me before leaving King Kareem's room. She just got up and excused herself with barely a whispered word while Shehryar, her brother, and I were still in conversation.

I was falling apart in every way known to man as I pursued her. My heart, my lungs, my mind, my everything being torn every which way with more agonising emotions than I'd ever felt in one go.

Shocked by what had been unleashed. Panicked by the storm I found myself lost in. Scared out of my fucking wits at what I was supposed to do. Livid at whoever had bugged my room and recorded Esmeralda in more than one vulnerable moment. *How long had that camera been there? What if they had more recordings?* Those thoughts had me ready to kill whoever had done it.

But strongest of all was the fear of losing Esmeralda with every step she took away from me.

I pushed into a jog as she dashed around the corner. "Esmeralda, stop! Esmeralda, please."

Skidding into the corridor, I lurched into a full run, nearly crashing into her back when I reached her. I latched onto her upper arm and dragged her around, caging her up against the wall so she couldn't slip away. That was when she finally looked at me. And my heart splintered.

Her eyes were wide and bloodshot, glazed over with a distressed sort of fear that nearly tore a sob from me. Yet somehow, she looked determined too. Determined to do what though, I had no idea.

With shaking hands, she tried to push at my chest. "Kai—"

I ignored her and searched for somewhere to talk privately, quickly finding a door behind me labelled "Utility 1." Without a second thought, I took Esmeralda by the hand and spun for the cleaning room, pulling her inside and slamming the door shut behind us.

A woman yelped out and it wasn't Esmeralda.

There was a young member of general staff at the opposite end of the brightly lit room, holding the handle of a spider mop to her chest. "Prince Kai…"

"Morning, Sylvie," I said and stepped slightly to my right, making sure I hid Esmeralda out of sight. If Sylvie noticed, she didn't give it away. "I apologise for scaring you."

"It—it's all right, Your Highness."

"Would it be okay for me to use this room for a moment?"

"Oh, of course." She fumbled forward. "I just needed the mop, so I'll be out of your way now."

I offered her as much of a smile as I could manage as I moved out of the young woman's way. Sylvie's eyes darted past me, but she kept her head down and left, closing the door behind her.

In the moment of tension that followed, Esmeralda tried to twist her hand out of mine, but without glancing back, I tightened my hold on her and pulled her further into the small room.

White cupboards lined the right wall, with bigger cleaning supplies sitting in cubies along the back, but to the left there was a countertop with a silver sink on one side. I trapped her there against the worktop with my hands pressed to the surface on either side of her. But Esmeralda turned her face away as I bent into her, her lashes lowered to some spot on the tiled floor.

"Look at me," I said, my voice hoarse with anguished frustration. Her lashes squeezed together, and my desperation doubled in intensity. "Esmeralda, look at me *now*."

"Please move," she whispered and wearily pushed at my chest.

"*Look at me.*"

"Kai, please. Let me go." Her voice cracked and my heart broke all over again.

"No." I cupped her jaw in one hand. "I can't let you go." With a gentle touch, I guided her to turn to me. "You're asking the impossible of me, Babble."

She gave up resisting and finally raised her gaze, nearly killing me with the liquid desolation brimming in it. "You have to. *You have to.* This is all my fault..."

"What?" My brows knitted together. "How on Neves is this your fault, Esmeralda? You're more the victim in this than any of us."

"It was my truth—"

"Exactly!" I lifted my other hand to her cheek too, tilting her face up to mine. "It is *your* truth to tell who you wish and keep from who you wish. No one had any right to secretly record it and use it to manipulate you, when in all of this, you have done nothing wrong."

Fisting my jumper, she jostled me in a tired shake. "But they're not trying to use it to manipulate me. They are using it to hurt you!" A breath shuddered out of her, all her strength seeming to slip away. "They're trying to hurt the people I *love*. Kareem. *You*. And I can't..."

Somewhere inside me I acknowledged what she said for what it was. *My Babble loved me.* But the moment hurt too much to feel what she was saying instead of hearing what she was trying to do.

Put distance between us.

"Don't you see, Kai?" Her voice grew watery and thick. "I told you my illegitimacy would cause you trouble and look what happened. Someone is using it to threaten you—"

"Why are you acting as if I'm the only one who could be hurt in all of this?" I said angrily. "It affects you more than me, Esmeralda."

"I know that," she snapped back, pushing my hands away from

her face. And fuck, that hurt more than anything. That she didn't want me to touch her or comfort her when she was clearly distraught. "But I have been prepared for it to affect me for over a decade now. You haven't been. You never asked to deal with this—with any of my lies. It was never your problem to bear."

I framed her waist in my hands and lifted her up onto the countertop, bringing her face closer to mine. Bringing her closer to me as I nudged her legs apart and stood between them. "You are *not* a problem, Esmeralda," I growled, keeping my hands around her hips. "Neither is your illegitimacy. It makes no difference to who you are or how I feel about you. And I will never let anyone judge you because of it nor blame anyone you care about for it. Because despite what you seem to think, the moment you trusted me with your truth, I vowed to protect it for you and never let you deal with the burden of it alone. *Ever.* And that is my choice, Esmeralda."

The first heart-wrenching tear rolled down her reddened cheek as she shook her head. "You can't take on the world for me, Kai. It's bigger and louder and meaner, and people will never stop judging you because of me no matter what you say. And I can't let you choose that."

Words failed to get past my gritted teeth for a breath. "You told me you hated it when your brother always said it was about other people. And now that's exactly what you're using to try to push me away?" Maybe my accusation was a bit harsh or hurtful, but after everything, she should have been picking me, loving me, letting me protect her, not trying to break up with me.

She lowered her wet eyes. "Maybe there was some truth in what he said after all."

A spear, a knife, a sword, and a dagger flew through my heart all at once. Cutting me, maiming me, unleashing an agonising heat from behind my ribcage until it was so fucking hard to breathe.

"So, what?" I heard myself rasp. "You're going to break up with me because of something that hasn't even happened yet?" She winced, but she didn't correct me. My hands fell away from her waist, devoid of strength. "What happened to all the things you said about never intentionally hurting me? About protecting me and being there for me?" My voice clotted in my throat as the back of my nose stung. "Didn't you mean what you said?"

She bit down on her trembling lip as tears slid down her cheeks. "I did."

"Then why are you trying to leave me?"

"I don't want to leave you," she sobbed, her hands flattening around the base of my neck, pulling me closer even as she was verbally pushing me away. "But Kai—"

"Then stop this. Stop trying to break up with me."

"Kai—"

"*No*, Esmeralda. Listen to me." I fit my palms against her damp cheeks. "We're a couple. That means if you promised to protect me and be there for me, then I promised you the same thing. And I know you're scared, Babble—I am too—but you are *not* allowed to take those rights away from me. I am here for you, and I am going to protect you from whoever is trying to hurt you."

"It's not just about the videos, Kai."

"For now, it is. There's only the recording, that is it. Nothing else."

"Kai—"

"You're worried about me, Babble, but I am worried about you. Your tears, your pain, your truth in someone else's hands other than your own—it is killing me. And I will not stand for it. I won't let whoever did this get away with it."

"Kai, please."

I dropped my forehead heavily against hers. "Plead all you want, Esmeralda. I won't let you face this on your own. I will fix this for you...*because I can't see the woman I love hurt.*"

A broken cry lifted from her as she clung to me. "You can't, you can't, you can't." She wasn't talking about the videos. That I knew with certainty.

"I can. I do." I tilted her chin up. "*I love you, Esmeralda.*"

She shook her head weakly. "No, please."

A burning pressure built behind my eyes. "Don't you love me?"

She let out a choked sound, trying to turn her face away but I didn't let her. "Don't you, Babble?"

"I do," she cried. "Of course, I do. *I love you.* I love you so much—"

That was all I needed to hear to stop myself falling into a pit of misery. To solidify my resolve to hunt down whoever had done this to her. To know that I would change the world for this woman.

Releasing a breath, I captured her lips, kissing her long and slow and deep. Giving her all my love, all my heart. Every single promise I repeated to myself. *For the rest of my life.*

"I will fix this, Esmeralda," I whispered against her forehead, cradling her in my arms. "I promise you. *I will fix this.*"

She didn't quite wrap her arms around me, but she held onto my jumper on either side of my waist, her cheek resting against my shoulder. Once she settled, she pulled away, and I silently wiped away the wetness on her cheeks and pressed half a dozen kisses to her hair.

As I helped her down from the countertop, there came a knock at the door.

"Esmeralda. Prince Kai." Shehryar sounded restless. "Please open the door, I cannot wait out here any longer."

Heading over, I opened it. Shehryar charged straight to Esmeralda and engulfed her in his arms without sparing me glance. If she felt small against me, she looked like a tiny kitten in the arms of a tiger against him. But she sunk into him, burying her face into his chest.

I felt a little pang of hurt that she didn't let me hold her the way she was letting him hold her, but I repressed it under a mountain of anger and determination.

I caught Shehryar's attention over Esmeralda's head when I shifted. I held his stare. He lifted his chin in a single nod of understanding. And I left with the comfort of knowing he'd stay with her.

The moment I rounded the corner I had chased Esmeralda down, I pulled my phone out of my trouser pocket and speed-dialled my head of security, Rocco.

"Yes, Your Highness?" he answered before the second ring.

"I need every inch of my bedroom searched immediately," I hissed, keeping my voice low.

"Your bedroom?"

"Someone bugged my room and took a…" I couldn't bring myself to say it; just thinking about it made me nauseous.

I heard the softest breath of a curse on the other side of the line. "We're on it immediately."

"Focus especially on the side closest to the door, it was taken from that angle."

"Yes, Sir."

"Whatever you find, I want it brought to me immediately. And I want to know who has been going in and out of my room for the last ten days. Speak to Mini about the cleaning schedule, any maintenance, whatever, I want to know. Find out who stayed back in the palace while we were away for events. And check the CCTV footage of my bedroom corridor and the ones around it. I will come down to the security room once I've spoken to my parents."

"I'll send Gary down to speak to Mini now, and I'll take Laal and Earl with me to search your room."

"Good. I want this kept between as few people as possible until we find out who did it."

Ending my call with Rocco after he promised to do just that, I took the stairs in the main entrance up two at a time to the first floor.

"Kai," I heard my brother call when I was on the third step going up to the second floor.

Fay came towards me from the corridor to the left, dressed in an old T-shirt and loose trousers both splattered with dried paint. A squiggly headband held his hair back from his face.

"What's wrong?" he asked, wiping his paint-smeared hands on a filthy flannel.

"I need to speak to Mother and Father."

"I don't think they're in their room if that's where you're headed. They went to the TV room with Uncle and Shehryar's mother after breakfast to watch a movie, so I—"

I swore under my breath and turned around, rushing past him to head back the way I had come.

"Hey—what's wrong? Did something happen?"

I didn't answer him, and Fay being nosey Fay followed after me, demanding to know why I was acting like the world was coming to an end.

But my world was *in threat of coming to an end.*

By the time we got to the TV room, I was breathing heavily from running all over the palace. I shoved the door open and tore inside without even thinking to knock. Four sets of eyes landed on me, two with a gasp that faded away into the sound of whatever was playing on the TV screen.

"Bloody Neves," Uncle Arsh sighed, dropping his arm from in front of Katiya.

"Way to give everyone a fright, son," Father grumbled from the sofa opposite the TV screen.

Next to him, Mother sat upright, her brows scrunching together. "Kai. What's wrong?"

"Have you checked your emails recently?" I asked, moving towards them with Fay tailing me.

"No, sweetie. Not for a couple of days."

"I need you to check them." Someone turned the TV off.

"Now?" Mother said.

"Yes, now. Please. Quickly. It's urgent. Mother, *please.*"

"Hold on, hold on," Father said, all signs of easiness gone from his hazel eyes. "Slow down, Kai. Tell us what has happened first."

"Someone bugged my room and took a recording of me—of me and Esmeralda." The colour drained from all four faces at once, and Fay swore. "Gary and Rocco are searching my room and checking CCTV footage, but it was sent to King Kareem. I need to know if they sent it to you too."

"Oh no," Katiya whispered, her hand covering her mouth.

Mother quickly stood from the sofa, elegant strength fortifying her shoulders. Father, Uncle Arsh, and Katiya got up too. "Let's go to the office immediately."

CHAPTER 34

Kai

Shehryar and King Kareem had assumed correctly.

Mother and Father had been sent the email with the two videos too, just with a different message. But they weren't the only ones.

It had been sent to me as well. From the same email none of us recognised, but with a different message to the ones King Kareem and my parents had received.

"So the Perfect Prince found himself a fraud princess? What a fairy tale match."

I'd lost count of the number of times I had read the single line since I'd discovered the email after leaving my parents' office. My teeth ground harder together every time I did.

That nickname. *The Perfect Prince.* Seeing it grated at my bones. It reminded me why I hated the name before Esmeralda started calling me it. All the times it had been used to taunt me, and that made me suspicious. *It made me see red.*

I felt numb with rage as I stared at my laptop screen, sitting in my office after dinner.

A dinner I hadn't stayed for beyond the moment I realised Esmeralda wasn't there. The same way she hadn't been there for lunch. I lost my appetite to the fear of what her absence meant for us, so I left and holed myself up in my office, torturing myself with silence that I wanted filled with her voice.

Now there was a tray of untouched food at one end of the dark oak desk I was tapping a set of fingers against. The red velvet curtains were drawn over the two large windows to my back, and the crystal chandelier hanging from the ceiling glowed with a warm yellow light.

Twenty minutes. That's how long it had taken Rocco, Laal, and Earl to find the bug in my room.

It took five hours for Gary, Rocco, and I to watch through nearly all ten days of CCTV footage.

Five minutes to figure out who had been acting suspicious.

And one minute for any sympathy, kindness, and understanding to evaporate from my blood.

No one was being forgiven for hurting my Babble. No matter what their excuse was.

I picked up the glass of water on the silver tray and finished the last few sips in a long gulp. There came a heavy knock on the door directly opposite me. Like planned, without receiving my summon, it was opened.

Three sets of footsteps clicked against the solid wood floor before the door closed, and the sound of two sets of steps were softened by the thick red patterned rug spread over most of my office.

I didn't look up from my laptop. I didn't have to. I knew exactly who had entered and where they were standing. Gary by the door. Rocco just ahead, at the end of the rug. The culprit ahead of him.

"Good evening, Your Highness. You asked to see me…"

Slowly, I lifted my chin. "Good evening—*Sylvie.*"

Sylvie—the young, newly-hired member of general staff who I'd startled this morning in the utility room—stood with her hands clasped in front of her a few steps away from my desk. About the same height as Esmeralda, she kept her shoulders relaxed, but her brown eyes screamed with the guilt she couldn't manage to hide.

She knew why she was there. She knew what she had done. What I wanted to know was why. Because there was one thing that didn't make sense in all of this.

I opened the top drawer of three on my left and picked up the bug. A thin black rectangle a touch smaller than my pinkie, with two wires that had been attached to a small cube housing the battery before Rocco had taken it off to cut the feed. It had been on the wall behind the painting of Bucky hanging by my bedroom door that Fay had done for my twenty-seventh birthday. The camera almost blended into the black frame of the painting, hence why I hadn't noticed it.

It rolled off my fingers onto the wooden surface with a little clack. Sylvie's eyes dipped to it, her knuckles on one hand going white as she squeezed the other. Leaning into the high back of my chair, I gestured to the bug with a lazy turn of my hand. "Rocco found this in my bedroom."

"Really?" The puzzled look on her face was so obviously forced. "What is it?"

"You don't know?" I arched my brow. She shook her head. "Are you sure?" I gave her a moment to answer. She replied with nervous silence. "Because the CCTV footage from the corridor shows you on the morning of Memorial Day—at the same time we were on our way to the service—pulling something that looked just like this out of your uniform pocket as you entered my room."

Sylvie blanched, her body tensing before she blinked rapidly. "I—I don't know what you mean, Your Highness. I mean, I did enter you room, but I didn't—I didn't have anything with me other than a trolley of cleaning supplies. Mini asked me to clean the window, because—"

"Mini asked you to do no such thing." The ice globe caging my anger started cracking. "So don't waste your breath trying to lie to me." She twitched all over with a panicky restlessness.

"Why did you do it?" Silence. "Why did you bug my room?" Nothing but a rapid flicker in her expression as she refused to look at me head-on.

I sighed and leaned forward, pressing the pads of my spread fingers together, and touched my joint index fingers to my chin. "Okay, fine. Then tell me why you sent us those emails? What did you intend to gain from doing that?"

The edginess died away from her hands instantly. "What—what emails?"

Ah. There it was. The puzzle piece that didn't fit.

She hadn't sent the emails.

That was her first moment of honesty. And it made sense. What was the point of sending riddles rather than a demand for what she wanted in return for the footage? Only someone who had an agenda other than a material gain would have played with our heads like that.

That wasn't Sylvie. But I had a skulking feeling I knew who it was.

"Who was your accomplice?" I said, my voice darker than the deepest depths of the Pursian sea.

She quickly shook her head. "I didn't—"

"I suggest you tell me who it was unless you want to find yourself incriminated before a court in Touma *and* Jahandar for infringing on the privacy of two royal households and threatening them with illegally recorded videos. And I swear on Esmeralda's life, Sylvie..." I looked her dead in the eyes. "I will make sure you serve nothing less than a life sentence in jail, never to see the light of day again, let alone have any interaction with your brother."

She jerked a desperate step forward and Rocco swiftly moved, his two-metre frame lingering right behind her. "No, no please. Please, don't hurt Jack. He's all I have. I'm all he has—I can't—I can't go to jail, we have no one else. Please, he's only a child. I can't leave him—"

"You should have thought about that before you did all this, shouldn't have you?"

She made a choked sound, the sheen in her eyes spilling down her cheeks. "I didn't do it. I didn't send the emails. I promise—I promise. Please, you have to believe me. *She* paid me to do it. To put the camera in your room and collect the recordings and send them to her, but—"

"She?" I echoed, ice crystalising the blood in my veins as that feeling in my gut set firm.

A familiar face. Familiar actions. A hatred I knew all too well.

One that had taken me nearly a full year of counselling to realise I hadn't earned. But it latched onto my back like vile, blood-sucking leeches, trying to drain the life out of me.

It wasn't the first time I had found one still stuck on me. Put there by a person who wanted to see me for ever miserable. Using every method to hurt me for reasons I still didn't fully comprehend.

"Give me a name, Sylvie," I said in her silence.

Sylvie's lashes dipped over her eyes before she uttered a name.

I felt hot and cold as a tired hush and a murderous buzz crept over my skin at the same time.

"Your employment has been terminated, effective immediately."

"Your Highness. Please—"

"You will be placed on a blacklist of employment, and you will never work for any royal household anywhere again." I felt nothing over the tears that streamed down her face. "Rocco and Gary will escort you back to your room. You will tell them everything that happened from the beginning, after which you will pack your bags and leave with Gary tonight."

It was nearly half past ten when Gary returned to my office informing me he had escorted Sylvie home. In that time, Rocco had given me the phone and laptop he'd confiscated from her, and the NDA and contract she'd signed agreeing to every term I had given her. Once he filled me in on what she told him, we considered what to do next and by the end of it, I was exhausted.

I wanted to fall asleep and wake up to find out it had all been one big nightmare. But the impossibility of doing so was almost ironic. I was drained but I wasn't sleepy. My mind was whirling with thoughts and worries at a speed it had never quite reached before.

How could it not be when the one person who could silence my mind in the safe, warm bubble of her embrace wasn't with me? When she was the reason for every anxious thought?

I needed to see her. To make sure she was okay. To tell her I was close to fixing this mess and ask her to brush away some of the agony with her touch.

I was a mess, standing outside her bedroom. My contact lenses were dry and scratchy, my head throbbed, my furious hands had destroyed my hair, and my heart was a battered shipwreck.

I filled my lungs on a shaky breath and stepped up close to the closed door. "Esmeralda," I called into the wood. "Babble. Can I come in?"

Whether the faint noise inside was real or my wishful mind hallucinating, I didn't know, but other than that I received no answer. And that scared me. It made me desperate to see her.

"Babble, I'm coming in," I said, lifting a hand to the door handle.

I pushed it down. The door moved a millimetre. Then nothing.

It was locked. She'd locked the door. *No…*

My forehead fell against the cold wood. "Esmeralda," I croaked. "Esmeralda, please. Open the door. I know you're in there, I know you're awake, so let me in. I'm begging you, Babble. *Please.*"

Nothing. And my face twisted as a damp heat crept over my eyes.

Hope soared up my spine when I felt as much as I heard the lock click open. I shuffled back, anticipating the moment my Babble stepped out.

She didn't. It was Shehryar. His massive frame slipping with the agility of a fox out the door, shutting it quickly but quietly behind him.

"Where is Esmeralda?"

He let out a slow breath, his expression softening. "The princess is inside. She's resting."

Resting, not sleeping. Which meant she was awake. *She knew I was there but didn't answer me.*

"Move out of my way, Shehryar."

"I can't do that. You know I can't do that, Prince Kai." I stepped forward but his hands immediately went to my chest and shoulder, holding me back. "I don't want to escort you away, but I will. So please don't try to force your way in. She doesn't need that right now."

He was right, but it still fucking hurt to hear she didn't need *me.* "I just want to see her."

"I understand." His voice lost its hard edge. "But she's shaken, Prince Kai. This was always her worst nightmare and it's become a real threat, so give her a night to gather herself. She isn't shutting you out—she asked me to make that clear to you. She just wants some time to figure out the situation."

But she didn't have to figure anything out. That was my job. I had made a promise to her. Didn't she trust that I would keep it?

Even as I asked myself that, I knew that wasn't it. Esmeralda had it in her head that her problem wasn't my problem, so she didn't want me to help her fix it.

I tried to sidestep Shehryar to get closer to the door, but he flexed his elbows, keeping me back. "Prince Kai, I said—"

"I won't go inside. I only have something to say. And then I'll leave."

It didn't seem like he believed me at first, but after a heavy sigh, he pulled his hands away and stepped to the side. He stayed close like a watchful guard, but he let me move to the door.

"Esmeralda," I said, pressing my palm and my forehead to the door. "I know you're listening, so let me remind you that I promised you I was going to fix everything." I gritted my teeth for a breath. "Rocco found the bug in my room. We found out who did it. Just give me one more day to sort it all out. I promise you, I will make it like it never happened, so you don't have to worry about anything, Babble. I have it—almost. One more day. Okay? I..."

I love you.

I wanted to say it so badly. The words were on the tip of my tongue, but I bit them back. I didn't want to use the words as a desperate attempt to convince her to trust me. That wasn't what they were meant for.

"Good night..."

With what little strength I had left in me, I pushed away from the door and met the hard look in Shehryar's eyes. "If you have information, I need you to share it with me, Prince Kai."

"Tomorrow morning. Come to my office. Rocco and I will tell you."

I knew if I looked towards the door, I was going to try to force my way into Esmeralda's room, so I turned the other way and dragged my feet back down the corridor. I went to my office again because sleeping in the room it had all happened in just wasn't a feat I could achieve. Not that I managed to sleep on the sofa in my office either.

KAI
I need your help

KAI
Can I come see you tomorrow?

TREVOR
What happened? Is everything ok?

TREVOR
Should I cancel my meeting?

KAI
No don't I will come after

KAI
When is it?

TREVOR
10.30 to 12

TREVOR
But what happened?

KAI
I'll tell you tomorrow

CHAPTER 35

Esmeralda

I didn't sleep that night. It was the torture I deserved.

I listened to the wounded voice of the man I loved while he told me he was fixing the problem I had created, and I still hadn't run right it into his arms. I had left him outside on his own instead, fearing how he could be hurt because of my secret.

That either made me a coward or it meant I cared about him more than I did about myself. Nothing, however, changed the fact I was hurting him anyway by staying away, and that made me the biggest idiot in all of Neves.

But a lifetime of fear had knocked me to the floor with a winding blow and it was hard to stand straight back up. I couldn't rely solely on Kai to pull me up either. I had to stand up myself.

Saying that, one sleepless night away from him and I ached all over with exhaustion. As if my body had forgotten that I had struggled to sleep most nights for the last eight years.

The exhaustion didn't fade by lunch, but I went down to the dining hall with Kareem. I was hoping to see Kai. I wanted to apologise and hold him and talk to him. I wanted to ask him about what he'd told Shehryar in his office about the girl who had bugged his room.

But he wasn't there. And I was forced to eat and pretend everything was okay for the sake of hiding the entire mess from the royals of

Shah.

"What? When?" I asked Kai's equerry, Michael, after I found him near the palace kitchen with his pastry chef husband, Roger.

"About an hour before lunch was served," Roger answered, glancing to Michael for agreement.

"Yes." Michael nodded firmly; his boyish features turned down in a frown. "Prince Kai came to the kitchen earlier for a bottle of water and a protein bar. I don't know what he said to Pierre, but Pierre seemed tense when he told Nur that he needed to take half a day's emergency leave. They left together and Prince Kai had his own car keys with him. Oh—and Rocco, Gary, and Earl from Prince Kai's security team were waiting in the corridor."

"Oh," I breathed and received a mixture of pitying and concerned looks. "Thank you for telling me."

On my way up to my room, I pulled out my phone, tempted to message Kai and ask where he'd gone with Pierre. But the nagging voice in my head made me feel like I had no right to, so I didn't.

Still, I typed, deleted, and re-typed a dozen messages while I paced the length of my room, wanting to say something but everything sounded wrong. I couldn't start a conversation we needed to have in person over the phone. But the thought of sitting around and doing nothing made anxiety gnaw at my ribcage, so I pulled my laptop out and started researching.

Spy cameras. Hacking. Tracing emails. At some point, I opened the speech I had written years ago for this exact situation—when my truth came out and I finally had to face the world.

I was on my third re-read and edit when a steady knock came at my door. "My dear, it's me," Mama Katiya said from the other side.

Closing my laptop, I then shuffled to the edge of the bed and hobbled over on a numb foot. The warmth in her pale green gaze and motherly smile met me the moment I opened the door, untangling some of the knots in my chest. I nudged it shut and she engulfed me in an embrace.

"Dearest. What are you doing in here all alone?"

I sunk into her soft curves, every breath coming easier than the previous one the harder she squeezed me. "I was just on my laptop." A smile touched my mouth. "You smell like Prince Arsh."

"That, I—well, I..." She huffed a defeated sigh. "That is what happens when you find out the man you love has an incessant need to touch you and hug you at every chance he gets." The laugh lines around her mouth deepened with a reluctant sort of delight as she pulled back from our hug. "Now that I'm not insisting on hiding our relationship, he doesn't see the need to behave anymore. Not that it bothers me—it's very flattering actually. But I had to pry myself out of his arms so that I could come find you. One more minute and..." She cleared her throat, her eyes sparkling impishly. "Well, our next destination would have been a bed."

"Mama Katiya." I chuckled, wrinkling my nose.

"Don't you *Mama Katiya* me, dearest Princess. As if that isn't exactly what you and Prince Kai have doing too."

The abrupt reminder of the sex tape in those emails killed my grin and she winced. "Oh, sweetie, I'm sorry. That was entirely the wrong thing to say at this moment."

I managed to resurrect half my smile. "No, don't apologise. You're not wrong."

Her soft gaze scanned my face before she nodded towards the bed. "Come on. With all these men around we haven't been able to have a proper girl's chat, and I think we're long overdue one."

Sitting the cushions up against the headboard, we got comfortable on the bed and pulled the duvet over our legs. I dropped my head on Mama Katiya's shoulder, and she took my hand in hers, kneading her thumbs into my up-turned palm.

"Sher told me what happened last night," she said quietly. "Why did you tell him to send Prince Kai away without speaking to him?"

I squeezed my eyes shut as Kai's broken plea replayed in my ears. "Because," I whispered. A painful ache burned through my chest. "I couldn't face him. I felt guilty. It is my truth, but someone is using it to hurt him, and he doesn't deserve that. That's the last thing I want for him."

"And what about you? Because you don't deserve to be hurt either,

Esmeralda."

"I know, but I don't have a choice. It's my reality; I have to live with it. Kai doesn't have to. He has a choice. He doesn't have to carry the burden. But he's trying to, and I… What if he regrets it later?"

"If he has a choice, my dear," she said, turning my palm over and brushing her thumbs over the back of my hand, "then it's in his prerogative to pick whatever he wants. But it sounds to me like you're trying to make that choice for him rather than accept what he has chosen."

"But his choice—"

"Is you," she said as a soft, indisputable fact. "Prince Kai has chosen you. And from what I've heard, he has been running around like a man on a mission since yesterday doing everything in his power to protect your secret. He hid what he could of the truth from his own family too." She paused. "I was there when he told his parents the message in the email was a recording of you telling him about your falling out with King Kareem, but it had been made to seem like it was something it wasn't. He stopped me after to tell me the truth of the recording.

"Do you know what he said to me when I asked why he didn't tell them the truth?" she asked. "He said, *'because it's Esmeralda's truth to tell, and if she doesn't want anyone to know, then I will make certain that no one knows. Including my own family'.*" A burning dampness filtered over my gaze, turning Mama Katiya's face into a blur. "He isn't spending every waking hour trying to find the people who did this because he's scared of the truth coming out. He is doing it to give you back the power over your own truth."

I blinked away the liquid shame brimming in my eyes and hung my head. "I'm a coward."

"No, sweetie. You aren't a coward. You're scared. And I have no doubt that part of that fear is because you're worried about what it means for the people you love. But I think a part of you is projecting too." She brushed my hair back from my temple, running two fingers over and around my ear. "I think your fear for them is a reflection of how scared you are for yourself. But you find it easier to worry about others, because that is what you have been doing for so long. Whether out of guilt or obligation, I don't know, but you're trying not to put yourself first. So, worrying about Kai is your way of coping with how you're feeling."

There was no holding back the tears as the truth of her words ripped the veil off me, leaving me exposed, raw, bleeding out. I searched desperately for words to deny it, hide it. *But she was right.*

You're not allowed to cry. Be grateful for what you have. Don't complain, you're not even a real princess. Duty first, always. Your feelings don't matter. Don't give him a reason to kick you out.

You were never meant to be a part of this family, so just shut up and keep your head down.

I'd lost count of the number of times I had told myself those things, training myself to put my feelings last. I was convinced my circumstances meant I had to accept what I was given and not ask for anything more. That I wasn't allowed to be scared or show hurt or complain. I had accepted Kareem's cold treatment without any objection for over a decade for exactly those reasons.

Guilt for being my father's mistake, doing my best to play a role I wasn't meant to have been casted for. Penance for ruining a family—I was the reason Kareem and Mother drifted apart.

But I had always been scared about what would happen if my illegitimacy came out.

It was just hard to worry about myself when I had spent so long convincing myself I wasn't worth worrying over. So, I worried about keeping it a secret for the sake of not hurting those around me.

It was easier to push Kai away than it was to admit I was terrified of what the world would say to *me.*

Mama Katiya gently curled her arm around me, cupping the side of my head as she guided me into the crook of her arm. "You don't have to hide that you're scared, my dear, and you certainly don't have to bear it all by yourself either. That's the great thing about family and loved ones. You're allowed to rely on them for support when you need it."

"When I fell pregnant at nineteen, my parents supported me in a way I could never have imagined. They weren't disappointed in me nor were they hurt because of me, they guided me and protected me, and when Shehryar was born, they were the happiest I had ever seen them.

"That is not to say I wasn't still terrified of what people in my community were whispering about me. But if I had listened to them, then I wouldn't have tried to do better for myself and gotten a new job. Queen Amaya wouldn't have become my closest friend. And I wouldn't have been lucky enough to raise my son alongside a beautiful, bubbly little princess, who gave me just as much love as she gave her own mother. Because Amaya was always your *real* mother, Esmeralda."

She pressed a heavy kiss to my head and a new, different flow of tears rolled down my cheeks. "And if anyone gave me the choice, I would go through those four difficult years all over again just to end up exactly where I am right now." She shrugged against me. "And well, it seems the joke is on the people who judged me, because now I'm boinking a prince who's desperate to marry me."

A surprised, watery giggle spilled from my mouth. "My point is," she said, swiping at the dampness on my cheeks with her fingers. "In this world, there will unfortunately always be people who have something to say about things that are not any of their business, and while it's absolutely fine to be scared, the only person who suffers if you let that fear dictate your life, is you. You are better off claiming who you are, so they cannot use it against you."

Tucking a finger under my chin, she tilted my head up higher. "It is your choice who you tell. But it is also your choice how you feel and think about your own truth." She shook her head. "It has never made you dirty or unwanted, Esmeralda. It has never changed the fact that you *are* a princess. It doesn't change the beautiful young woman you are now. And it certainly hasn't changed that Prince Kai is head over heels in love with you. So don't let it change what you want with him."

Her words slowly cleared the cloud of fear distorting my thoughts, and with a sniff, I nodded.

"As for the people who only understand rubbish, outdated laws," —she waggled her eyebrows— "my handsome fiancé has a Proposal of Change they can shove down their useless mouths."

My lips spread into a small grin. "Are you officially engaged now?"

"Oh." She flicked her hand in their air. "We've been secretly engaged for the last two, two-and-a-half years." My brows flew up. "He gave me a ring too. I told him we had a few hurdles to jump over before we could marry, but he insisted I keep it because he would knock the hurdles down for me. And that's exactly what he's been preparing to do." A distant, happy look filled her crystal green eyes. "I should probably wear it now, but I'm considering proposing to him myself first before I do."

"I think he would really like that," I said, already picturing it in my head.

She huffed. "The arrogant man would be so smug about it. But he deserves it after everything he's done for me. And maybe I'm also trying to make up for the fact I asked him to hide our relationship for longer than I should have.

"I thought I was waiting for the right moment to tell Sher, knowing how he felt about his father, but I think I was also a little bit scared of what people would say about me too." Her lips tipped to one side in a gentle smile. "It's not the easiest fear to get over, is it?"

"No, it's not."

"But. It's also very liberating to take what you want too." She raised her brows in question. "So, my dearest—what do you want?"

The answer was simple.

I wanted Kai.

CHAPTER 36

Esmeralda

Kai hadn't returned to the palace by dinner, but Fay told me he was still at Trevor's house with Pierre. I was relieved to know he was with his friends and not by himself, but despite wanting to, I hadn't messaged him to ask when he would be back. I chose to wait for him instead.

I was sitting up against the headboard of my bed, the black t-shirt I'd taken from Kai in my lap, when the first, light patter of rain started. The curtains were drawn over the windows and balcony doors, but my gaze immediately jumped between them.

As the quickening drum of the droplets hit the glass, something in my gut clicked into place, flashing a symphony of lights through me.

I had been waiting for the right moment. *This had to be it.*

I swiftly moved to the edge of the mattress and pulled Kai's T-shirt over my head. It fell down over my pyjama shorts as I stood up. Not bothering to waste a second more with slippers, I left.

I didn't rush as I walked down to the garden doors, but I didn't exactly take my time either. The same way I wasn't nervous, but there was a restless jitter in my hands I couldn't seem to stop. But when the arched doors came into sight, a calm certainty settled over me.

I was in the right place.

The night guard I'd seen most nights, Raj, wasn't there. It was a young black man who looked at me as if I had told him to hit me when I asked him to open the garden doors.

"Your Highness, I, uh…without seeming to overstep, Touma's winter showers are cold and you're, uh…" His eyes dipped down my bare legs to the white socks on my feet and back up to my face. "A coat might be better to, uh—I mean *if*, Ma'am, you're sure you want to go outside."

"I'll be fine without a coat."

"Uh…okay." He unhooked the keys from the belt loop of his crisp black slacks and unlocked both sides of the arched doors.

The cold, wet air flew across my bare skin when he pulled one side open for me. He shuddered as I stepped straight into the light shower.

Goosebumps sparked all over my arms and legs when the raindrops splattered against me, soaking into the soles of my socks, and sucking the anxious heat right out me. I made my way over to the tall, black lamp lighting up the bench beneath it. The same one Kai had found me sitting on that second sleepless night.

"You shouldn't be out here."

My ribcage exploded upon hearing the deep, clear voice behind me, giving my heart the freedom to clatter around my body.

The wet undersides of my socks were glued to the gravel path and yet I spun around so easily as if I was skating on ice to face the man of my dreams. *Maybe if he forgave me, the man of my future.*

Kai had the hood of his jumper pulled up over his hair, but there was enough light for me to see the wide-eyed expression of hope and longing behind his glasses. My heart ached and sobbed and leapt out of my chest and right into his hands.

He was here. There in the rain and cold he hated so much. For exactly the same reason I was.

Despite everything, I felt my lips curl into a small smile. "I think I should be the one saying that considering you hate the rain, Mr Perfect Prince."

His shoulders dropped instantly, the relief almost palpable as his expression melted and twisted before his head fell forward. For a man so big and sturdy, he suddenly looked so small and fragile. A ceramic doll who'd only just teetered away from a fall that might have shattered him.

All because of me.

Remorse punched me right in the throat. I moved swiftly to stand right in front of him. "Kai—" My voice cracked, everything I had wanted to say forgotten as if I hadn't spent hours planning it down to a T.

He lifted his chin, showing me the liquid in his eyes. "You're not leaving me?"

I couldn't get words past the lump in my throat, so I frantically shook my head.

With a fractured noise, his arms shot out, scooping me up off the gravel path from around the waist and crushing me against him. His face fell into the crook of my neck, my arms curled around his shoulders, latching on just as tight. He was so warm under the dampness of his clothes, shaking as he sighed into me. I buried a hand in the back of his hood, squeezing my eyes shut as I lowered my face into his shoulder. Basking in the dull feeling of all my broken pieces merging back together.

"I'm sorry," I croaked. "I'm so sorry, Kai. I'm sorry. I'm—"

He shook his face against my neck. "No, no, Esmeralda—"

"No, let me say this." I curled my fingers deeper into the fabric. "I was an idiot."

"No, you were not."

"I was. I was. I pushed you away and hurt you all because… because I was scared. For you but for me too. But I didn't know how to admit I was. I didn't think I was allowed to be. It was my fault—"

"No," he growled sternly. "It wasn't your fault, Esmeralda. Ever. Any of it. You have to stop saying that. You have to stop *thinking* that."

"I'm trying." My voice cracked as tears filtered over my eyes. "But it's hard not to when that's all I have ever thought."

"I know," he whispered and gently thumped his forehead against mine. I let my eyes fall shut as he held it there. "I understand. But that is why I want you to be honest with me about how you're feeling.

Because I want to be there for you. Whenever those bad thoughts become too much. I don't want you to keep them to yourself. I want you to tell me so I can fight them away. And you can tell me anything, my little Babble, and I will *never* judge you for it. I promise."

My bottom lip quivered, and even with the cold droplets of rain hitting my skin, I felt the burning streaks of tears roll down my cheeks one by one.

"I'm scared." The words shook off my lips barely above a whisper.

Kai's moulded his lips over mine. So soft, so secure, so sweet. Swiping away half my fear just like that as if it had never even existed in the first place. "I know," he said against my mouth before planting another kiss to my lips. "But I'm here, Babble." *Kiss.* "I promised you I would fix it." *Kiss.* "And I almost have." He met my gaze. "I found out who sent the emails."

I couldn't tell if my heart stopped entirely or bucked even harder. "Who?" I said, holding my breath.

His eyes drooped apologetically. "Meg."

It took me a moment to catch on, but when the name clicked into place, I tensed.

His abusive ex-fiancée. She was behind this? Why? How?

"She met Sylvie at Westcombe Palace on Formation Day," Kai explained as if he'd heard my questions. "It must have been after she approached me while I was with you and Fay. She convinced Sylvie to meet her the next evening where she offered her a big sum to plant the bug."

Bitter frustration bunched Kai's brows, and anger slowly curled around my stomach. "I don't know how much Shehryar told you of what I told him, but Sylvie planted the bug while we were away for the Memorial Service. She downloaded the feed daily and emailed it to Meg. Sylvie said she never watched the entirety of any of it, though even if she did, she signed an NDA and she will be under tight surveillance for the next few years. One suspicious move and she knows she will be serving a thirty-year sentence without any chance of bail or parole, or early release."

The assurance didn't ease my worry. All my concerns were for him.

"But what about Meg? I know you were at Trevor's house, but you didn't go to see her, did you?" I hoped for the life of me the answer was no. Because if he had gone to face his abusive ex while I had been hiding like a coward in my bedroom then I was going to punch myself in the face.

Thankfully, he shook his head. "No, I spent the whole day at Trevor's house. Pierre called Candy and Zain there too. We spoke about what to do, and they were with me when I called Meg's father." He gave me a light squeeze. "I'm sorry I didn't send you a message to tell you. But if I had, I would have abandoned everything to see you, but I knew you needed some time to yourself. So, I didn't."

"I wanted to message you too," I admitted, moving my hand into the hood of his jumper to cup his jaw. "But I didn't want us to have this conversation over the phone, so I didn't."

He nuzzled against my palm. "One more day, Esmeralda. That's it. And I promise you this nightmare will be over." Anger turned his expression stern and dark. "I'm going to go see her tomorrow and deal with her as I should have done years ago."

"Alone?"

"Yes. I have to do this on my own."

Just the thought made my insides lurch up in rebellion. "That's not fair," I said, my brows bunching together. "You dealt with my problem for me, but you're going to deal with her on your own? No. I don't want that. I'll go with you."

"No, Esmeralda. I'm used to her hatred, but I don't want her directing it towards you. Besides, it's not the first time she has done something like this."

For the first time, the cold droplets landed like spikes of ice against my bare skin and damp clothes. "What?"

A bitter, ghost of a smile touched his mouth, ironically displaying that beautiful dimple of his. "She enjoyed making me miserable while we were dating, and she still does. Since our breakup, she has tried endlessly to hurt me for her own satisfaction."

My heart ripped in two, but fury screamed through me at the

same time. "How many times?"

"My family only know about the first time it happened, but she's attempted to defame me multiple times," he answered quietly, and the scream grew ten times louder. "I brushed it under the carpet, sometimes by myself, sometimes with Trevor's help, because I didn't want to give her the satisfaction of thinking that she had gotten to me, that she still had control over me.

"But I realise now that I only let her get away with it all, and now she has taken it too far. She made the biggest mistake of her life the moment she asked Sylvie to bug my room. She hurt you in the process of trying to hurt me and I cannot—I *will not* let her get away with it."

Pressing his palm to the back of my wet hair, he tucked me into a tight hug against him. I silently curled my arm around his neck and squeezed him back.

The beautiful, precious man had decided by himself that he was going to protect me and fight his own battle too. My Kai was a softie, but on this, I already knew nothing I could say would make him change his mind. He sounded stubbornly determined.

But there was no way I could let him do that. After what he'd just told me? *No fucking way.* I didn't want him facing that narcissistic bitch all on his own. He was more than capable of doing so, that I had no doubt of, but I wanted to fight by his side.

With him. *For him.*

"Aren't you cold?" I whispered into the warm dampness of his cheek.

"No." He kissed my temple. "I have you to keep me warm."

I nuzzled against him. "Have you slept?"

"I can't sleep without you, Babble. And the thought of sleeping in the room it happened in makes me sick to my stomach. I can just about go in there to get a change of clothes."

And just like that the thought solidified inside me.

I was going with him tomorrow whether he liked it or not.

"Let's go to bed, Kai."

CHAPTER 37
Esmeralda

Kai slept with me in my room that night. Tucked around me with his face buried between my breasts as I cradled him close. I eventually fell asleep too listening to his gentle breaths.

I awoke when the pillow sunk under my head and a succession of heavy kisses landed on my forehead. "It's time to wake up, Babble," a deep voice purred against my skin.

I reluctantly blinked my eyes open and was rewarded with the sight of perfect, naked man-chest before Kai leaned back and flashed me a gentle smile. "Good morning," he whispered.

"Morning," I croaked.

He pressed a long-second peck on my lips, and it dully occurred to me that the scratch of stubble on his jaw was gone. He stood, giving me a full view of his tall, deliciously naked body and I forget entirely what stubble even was. The only thing he was wearing was black boxers as he lifted the white towel in his hand and scrubbed his wet hair. I couldn't take my eyes off his perfectly full arse as he walked away to the clothes draped over the velvet chaise between the windows.

"You already showered?" I asked, rolling onto my side to watch him pull on charcoal grey trousers.

He turned around just as his butt slipped inside the waistband, and I didn't know where to look. His hands pulling at the zip and button or his refreshed face. "Hmm. I went to the gym, but you were still asleep when I returned, so I asked Michael to bring my clothes and toiletries here."

I spotted the black bottle of his cologne, among other things, sitting on the vanity alongside my stuff. As much as I liked the sight of our things together, watching him change was only reminding me of what he had planned today.

"Esmeralda?" He adjusted his thermal undershirt, walking towards me.

"Are you going to see her now?"

"No," he said and sat down at the edge of the bed. "I'll be going after lunch when her father is there too. But there is nothing to worry about. It will be fine."

Of course, it was going to be fine. I was going to be there with him to make sure it was.

Kai, Pierre, and the two giant ex-marines from Kai's security team, Rocco and Gary, were standing by the entrance door, all in conversation until they heard the clack of my black, red-bottom heels.

Four heads whipped around to look at me as I walked down the entrance hall stairs with Shehryar following one step behind me. I saw the way Pierre's mouth went slack, but Kai had my full attention as his eyes popped. They quickly narrowed into a glower that took over his face.

Shehryar and I joined the rough circle they were standing in, and Pierre let his ruby red gaze openly skate over me. "Wow," he said with playful exaggeration. "Talk about making an entrance."

A little smile touched the corner of my mouth because I *had* been aiming for a little dramatic flair. I wanted everyone to know I was ready to win a war today, hence the statement red-bottom heels. I had kicked my confidence up a few notches too by wearing a jumper and a matching calve-length, silk pencil skirt in my favourite colour—a dark forest green.

I turned to Rocco and Gary. "Shehryar will be coming along for his peace of mind and my security. I hope that's okay."

"Of course, Your Highness, that's perfectly fine," Rocco said, and he almost seemed glad to see us. "We'll give him a rundown on the way."

"No," Kai growled. "You're not going, Esmeralda."

"Yes, I am," I said at the same time Pierre said, "Yes, she is."

Kai lifted his glare to Pierre. "What? Don't look at me like that. You won't let me go with you, but if Esm—I mean, Princess Esmeralda says she's going, then she damn well is."

"No, Pierre, I can't—"

"I'm going, Kai," I said clearly. "You're not doing this on your own. *You can*, but I don't want you to." I stepped up close to him, taking his fist in the hand and carefully prying his fingers open. "This is *our* problem Kai, not just yours or mine, so we're doing this together. I am going with you."

I slipped my fingers through his and clamped down on the back of his hand, holding his furious stare. He shook his head down at me, again and again until the action looked weak and wavering. Then he closed his eyes and sighed. It was quite obvious what that meant.

"Princess for the win," Pierre whispered smugly, giving me a wink.

Kai's lashes snapped up on a grumpy glare, but it softened as he turned to Shehryar and held his hand out for my coat. "Thank you," he said when Shehryar handed it to him.

"I'm not col—" I started, but the fierce warning in Kai's narrow eyes shut me up instantly.

He swung my coat over my shoulders, and I silently and obediently shoved my arms into the sleeves.

I stood directly behind Kai on the stone step of the red-brick country house as he rang the doorbell.

It had taken an hour to get there, and with each passing minute, Kai's body language had grown visibly more rigid, though he tried to hide it. And it hurt, because I didn't know what to do to reassure him without seeming like I was trying to coddle him. So, I pretended I didn't notice instead.

The chime of the bell echoed from inside the large house for some seconds before the door was opened. Kai's hand around mine tightened and I squeezed back as an older woman bowed her head in the entrance and gestured us in; clearly she'd been expecting us.

We headed inside and Shehryar, Rocco, Gary and another on Kai's security team, Earl, followed behind us. Like planned the other two from the security team stayed outside.

After closing the door, the lady, who was quite possibly a housekeeper, led us through the white, modern hallway and said, "They're in the back sitting room."

"I told you not to invite any of your friends over without telling me, Dad. I swear if—"

"Sit down, Meg. *Now.*"

Kai's hand cut the blood flow through mine as the voices of his ex-fiancé and an older man leapt out of the open doorway ahead of the older lady. His response to simply hearing her was a red, hot poker being traced all over my skin, leaving an intense, angry heat in its wake. I couldn't even begin to describe the urge it gave me to hurt her.

Despite his reaction, Kai walked us straight through into a minimalist sitting room. The only features I registered were two white leather sofas, the three bi-fold doors that showed off the rolling hills beyond it, and the silence of the two occupants that followed our entrance.

Unlike her classy get-up at the luncheon gathering on Formation Day, Meg was wearing a pastel blue T-shirt, the designer label, *Decay*, printed across the chest, and black leggings. Her hair was in a ponytail and her face was make-up free. Annoyingly, she still looked pretty, but I found her stumped expression wonderfully satisfying. And the not-so-subtle way her lips thinned as she straightened her spine almost had me grinning.

Oh, she did *not* appreciate being caught off guard. But I didn't appreciate her abusing such a beautiful, soft-hearted man—*my man*—

so her discomfort served me great amounts of pleasure.

With a low scoff, Meg Fletcher plastered a big grin on her face from where she stood by the bi-fold doors. But fiery hatred flashed like a beacon in her eyes, directed solely at Kai and not once trailing to me. "Oh, look what the rats dragged in today. Now this should be interesting."

"Meg," the older man snapped, his thin, salt-and-pepper brows lurching together.

I had only interacted with Head Councillor of the Eastern Region of Finlark, Beau Fletcher, once during the course of the past two weeks, and only for a few fleeting minutes. That had been before Kai told me what Beau's daughter had done to him. Maybe it wasn't the older man's fault how she behaved, but I couldn't see him in the same decent light as that day anymore.

The tall, sturdy man bent over in a bow, his face wrinkled in a wince. "I apologise, Your Highnesses." He gestured to the sofa besides Kai. "Please have a seat."

Without a sound of acknowledgement, Kai pulled me towards the sofa and let go of my hand to undo the two buttons of his black overcoat. We sat down together, barely an inch between us. I tipped my knees in his direction, and as if it was a pose we had sat in a thousand times before, Kai placed his warm hand just above my right knee, his forearm lying across my lap.

Possessive. Protective. Secure. *Seeking.* Like he needed to know I was right there the whole time.

Meg arched her brow at her father as he sat down on the sofa opposite her. "You knew he was coming?"

Huh. It was funny how she was talking as if Kai was the only person in the room. Rocco, Gary, Shehryar, and Earl were hovering in the corridor, so she didn't know they were there. But I was sure I was entirely visible sitting next to Kai.

"*He,* is a prince," the older man bit out. "Now sit down."

She plonked herself down on the edge of the glass coffee table in front of Beau, disrespect dripping from her every pore. "What happened to never wanting to see me again, Mr Perfect Prince?"

My body flashed hot and cold as a bucket of irritation poured down my spine. But as I bristled, Kai's hand clamped around my knee, mooring me to him. It dully occurred to me that he'd possibly also put his hand there because he could sense my growing anger and was trying to calm me with his touch.

"The statement still stands true," Kai said with quiet calmness. "But you have gone out of your way to prod and provoke me, so now I have to forgo what I said—just this once."

"Oh, come on. Dad just rejoined politics after a three-year break. I'm allowed to turn up to one event in support of him, aren't I? Or do I need your permission for that too because this is getting ridiculous. You're so hung up on this grudge you have against me for something I apologised for, it's a bloody joke. Isn't it time to move on, Mr Perfect Prince?"

Oh, that was it.

"It's *Your Highness*," I said firmly, and Meg finally spared me a glance. "And you will not refer to him as anything else hereafter. If we're having a conversation as adults, then at least have the decency to act with some respect instead of speaking like an ill-mannered child. It's embarrassing."

I created a new world record for the loudest silence ever. I had never experienced anything like it. Neither had I ever felt so triumphant in such tension before, which in any other circumstance, my mouth would have tasted like I'd eaten a hundred bitter gourds.

All I tasted was oozing satisfaction at Kai's quiet intake of breath before his stare landed so heavily on the side of my face it felt as if he was touching me. And the rising flush of fury on Meg as she visibly shook was the cherry on top. I'd hurt her fragile ego, and now she would—

"That's rich coming from you, *Princess*, considering the secrets you're hiding are an embarrassment to the entire State of Jahandar."

Well…that was easy.

Beau Fletcher's head sagged forward as he let out a deep sigh of shame. He didn't know exactly what was in the recordings, but Meg had as good as admitted she was behind them. It was what we had needed from her. But my stomach still dropped knowing she held my secret over my head.

The fear of it getting out hadn't vanished overnight. I doubted it ever would fade entirely. But with what Mama Katiya had given me to think about, it was a little easier to sit there and face it. To stare the biggest, scariest monster in my closet right in the eye, knowing Kai was waiting for me behind it.

I could face my fear for *us*.

"Is that enough for you, Councillor Fletcher?" Kai said.

"Yes." The older man scrubbed a hand over his face. The corner of his eyes drooped in disappointment at his daughter. "You can confiscate everything you want."

"Rocco," Kai called out.

"On it," Rocco's reply came instantly from the corridor.

"What? Confiscate what?" Meg demanded, shooting up from the glass table.

Shehryar slunk into the room and the footsteps of Rocco, Gary, and Earl moved back down the corridor. The sound of the front door opening filtered through, followed by shoes on the wooden staircase we'd passed coming in.

"What's going on?" Meg glared daggers at Kai. "What the fuck did you do?"

Shehryar stepped forward, his face impassive but his huge shoulders were pulled back and wide, ready to react. "Give me your phone, Miss Fletcher."

Her attention dipped to the smartphone that had been lying face down on the glass table the whole time. She quickly snatched it up. "I don't think so."

"Give him the phone, Meg," her father said.

"What business does he have with my phone?"

Councillor Beau swayed up from the sofa. "Give him the phone," he roared, his pale face turning red.

Meg's brows flew up to hairline, but Beau Fletcher wasn't done.

"You have brought this upon yourself. Paying someone to put a camera in Prince Kai's bedroom? What were you thinking? You have committed treason against two royal households!"

"Put a camera in his room? Is that what he told you? And you believed him?"

"Do not lie, Meg. The maid confessed everything. Prince Kai has proof that you met with her and paid her and sent those emails, so you can't lie your way out of this." Beau shook his head, so worn and fed up. "And I cannot clean this up either. I will *not* clean it up like I did every other time you created trouble. Because you haven't changed like you promised me you would."

She threw her hands up in the air. "Okay, I did it. I paid the maid—Sila or whatever her name was—to bug his room. There? Are you satisfied? But it was just a joke, Dad. I was just messing with Kai as a *joke*. You're taking it completely out of proportion, and that's not fair."

My mouth hung open as my mind strained to keep up with the baffling human being before me. The more she spoke, the more convinced I became that Meg Fletcher really wasn't okay, and her father had failed her by covering for her instead of trying to get her the help she so obviously needed.

Beau opened his mouth on an exasperated breath, then seemed to give up as he faced Kai with the fallen shoulders of a broken man. "Do with her what you please. I will not intervene."

"Dad, come on." But Beau ignored her, and Meg scowled at Kai. "Does it make you happy turning my own dad against me? All because of a joke. You're unbelievable."

Curling his hand around to the small of my back, Kai guided me up from the sofa with him. "Give Shehryar your phone."

Shehryar didn't wait for Meg to offer it up. He was as agile as a viper as he grabbed her wrist and snapped her arm straight. The click of her elbow cracked off the white walls, and she shrieked, her palm reflexively opening. The phone fell right into Shehryar's waiting hand.

"What the fuck?" she cried out, holding onto her forearm. "You nearly broke my arm!"

"You should've listened when I asked the first time," Shehryar said, his voice lethally quiet, as he shoved Meg's phone into his back pocket. The fact he had even acknowledged her spoke volumes to me. His anger had crossed the border from bodyguard into brother territory.

"You think I'll stay quiet about this when Touma's royal guard just assaulted me?"

"I'm Princess Esmeralda's personal guard," Shehryar said and shrugged one shoulder. "And nobody saw me do anything."

Meg searched for backing from her father, but when he kept his whole body turned away from her, she gritted her teeth. "My phone. *Now.*"

"No." Shehryar stepped back.

It wasn't obvious if she followed his movement or if she lunged at him, but Shehryar reacted as if she had done the latter. Catching her by the wrist, he dragged her around and slammed the side of her face against the glass of one bi-fold door. He kept a hand around the back of her neck, not squeezing or hurting her, just holding her still and restricted.

"Let go of me. Let go," she screamed. "Get him fucking off me!"

"Your Highness?" he drawled, not taking his eyes off Meg.

Councillor Beau spluttered forward next to me, his frightened gaze flying between Shehryar and me. Silently pleading me to help his daughter but I wasn't going to make that decision by myself.

I tipped my head up to Kai. "What do you want Sher to do?"

Meg's huffing and the guards moving up and down the stairs filled his silence as his jaw locked and unlocked a few times. "He can let her go."

"Did you hear him, Sher?"

"Yes, Ma'am," he answered and released the raging woman.

Said red-faced troll swung around almost toppling herself over with her unnecessary aggression. Slowly, Kai lifted his shoulders and dragged himself forward towards her, holding his head up high. But Meg made the mistake of charging at him with murder stamped across her entire person.

"Sher," I growled quickly, and Shehryar's hand shot out, roughly guiding Meg back.

"Don't fucking touch me," she roared, swatting his hand away.

"Stay exactly where you are, Miss Fletcher."

She had half a brain to realise she was better off doing as he said, but she threw a vicious glower in my direction. It was cut out of my vision by Kai's broad back as he stole in front of me. Shielding me.

"I could post those videos online and ruin you both in seconds," Meg spat.

"You don't have access to any videos," Kai said blankly. "And you won't ever after your trial."

"Trial? For what?"

"For treason. And for everything else your father couldn't bury entirely."

Beau was slumped on the sofa, scrubbing a hand over his face. "You're lying," his daughter said.

"All the evidence has been documented and is ready for use in your trial in three weeks' time. After which you will be transported to Zestan Prison off the coast of Raven where you will serve your sentence."

I couldn't see her face, but her voice portrayed her shock. "You can't—you can't do this to me."

Kai shifted forward. "You had a member of staff bug my room. You filmed Esmeralda and me together." His tone darkened with each statement. "You sent it to our families. And you tried to take something from Esmeralda that was never yours to take. So, I *can* and I *have* used everything in my power to pay you back in kind, because I am done.

"I put up with your bullying and hatred for years, letting you get away with everything you did and said to me. But after what you did to Adam, you should have known that I would never stand for someone I care about being hurt by you. But you decided to hurt the woman I love, and that was the biggest mistake you could have ever made."

I was so mesmerised by Kai's rough, threatening voice that I

couldn't take my eyes off his back. I didn't bother moving out from behind him to fit myself back into the conversation.

"You did it for my attention and for your own entertainment, and now you will pay with the rest of your life. You will never have the power to hurt anyone you deem weaker than you ever again."

In my head, I could hear a crowd of a million Esmeraldas screaming and cheering for Kai for finally getting the justice he deserved. In real life, Rocco walked into the room behind me not giving anyone the chance to say anything after Kai's mini power speech.

"Your Highness, they're here," he announced.

"Bring them in," Kai said.

"Who did you call?" Meg asked as Rocco left. "You can't just bring anyone to my house." *Uh, it's your father's home, actually.* "You can't come in here and threaten me and throw accusations around that aren't true. You might be a prince, but this is illegal. And you're *not* above the law."

"No. *I am the law.*"

Wow... I felt that in my stomach.

A quick succession of heavy footsteps into the room drowned out the irate sound Meg let out. Three tall women slipped around us towards her, one of them striding ahead of the other two. Wearing black cargo uniforms, they were most definitely *not* ordinary police officers.

"Miss Meg Fletcher," the black woman with a cropped afro said, lifting her badge for Meg to see. "I am S.I.2. Sergeant Lamar of the Royal Defence Division, and you are under arrest for four accounts of treason against the royal households of Touma and Jahandar, as well as multiple accounts of assault, and several charges related to organised drug parties. You have the right to remain silent, but anything you say or do can and will be used against you in court."

"Bloody Neves, you took their TVs too?" Pierre said with a scoff of disbelief. He dropped his car keys on the marble countertop of Trevor's kitchen island and shucked his jacket. "Why?"

After Meg's arrest, which, other than a few hissed swear words, was rather civil, Kai wanted me to go back to the palace with Shehryar, while he went to see Trevor. I refused to go anywhere without him, so, while Rocco, Earl, and one other guard stayed behind to speak to Head Councillor Beau and follow up on Meg's arrest, Gary drove Kai, Shehryar, and I to Trevor's parents' place. A massive two-storey house in a quiet, suburban area of Pavilion city where each multimillion-Sterling house was gated and sat on its own bit of land.

Trevor's portion of the house was connected to the side of the estate. Candy and Zain had already been waiting for us with Trevor in his classically designed, open-plan living area.

It wasn't what I would have expected for a tech and gaming genius, but it was really nice. A blue, country-style kitchen in one corner, a white, rustic wood dining table with matching chairs next to it, and a spacious sitting area with a wall-mounted TV and three brown leather sofas.

Shehryar and Trevor helped Gary and the other guard unload all the laptops, tablets, a single monitor, and computer, as well as four TV screens from the two cars. Pierre had arrived just in time from the palace to witness the mess.

"Because our prince is a petty bastard," Candy said, throwing a blue-eyed wink to Kai. He made his way over from the kitchen with two big bowls of crisps and chocolate-covered pretzels. Zain trailed behind him, holding a tray of black mugs filled with tea and coffee.

We were sitting around the dining table, Trevor at the head of the table, frowning between Meg's phone and laptop with a small black device plugged into it. He had Beau Fletcher's two phones in front of him too. Kai sat in the seat next to him, I sat on Kai's left, and Shehryar sat on the other side of me. Gary had opted to stay outside with the other guard.

"I'm not petty," Kai grumbled as Zain came around to me first. "Trevor told me to take everything."

I quietly thanked Zain and took a mug of black coffee from the tray while Candy placed the bowls down on the table and took the seat opposite me.

"Everything of *hers*. Meaning her phone, tablet, and laptop," Trevor deadpanned. "Not everything in the house."

"See? Petty," Candy teased and chucked a pretzel into his mouth.

"Good," Pierre said, slumping into the chair next to Candy. "Be petty. You're allowed to be petty."

Kai scowled. "I wasn't being—"

"Also, I'd like some tea too, if you're still offering to make it."

Zain rolled his eyes from across the table as Shehryar took a mug. "I already made you some."

Pierre put a hand over his heart and fluttered his eyelashes. "You know me so well."

"I wasn't being petty," Kai grumbled, louder this time. "They're smart TVs. I was being safe just in case Beau knew… You can login into an email on a smart TV. Or plug in a USB stick."

The atmosphere sobered up as Kai glared at his mug of tea. My heart didn't exactly ache, but it did a dull clench for how deeply he'd thought it all through. I reached over, taking the hand hanging between his thighs and entwining my fingers through his. The crease between his brows melted away as he glanced at me, and I smiled. He didn't smile back, but he lifted our hands and pressed a long, firm kiss to the back of my hand that launched a soft flutter of butterflies inside me.

"Bloody Neves, I'm so fucking single," Pierre whisper-groaned at the same time Candy asked, "Are you planning to give it all back to Beau Fletcher once Trevor's done?"

"Only what he needs for work," Kai answered, his thumb absently brushing across my skin. Zain finally took his seat next to Trevor with the last mug on the tray.

"Can we smash the rest?" Clearly, Candy had been contemplating the option hopefully for a while because the question fired off his tongue with an almost childlike excitement.

"You're not smashing anything inside my house," Trevor declared.

"Who said anything about doing it inside?"

"No."

"You could donate the TVs to an orphanage or a shelter for the homeless," Shehryar said, giving Candy a disapproving look over the rim of his mug.

Pierre lifted his mug in agreement, but Candy rolled his eyes. "Thank you for chucking a bucket of guilt all over my idea."

"You're welcome." Candy narrowed a distasteful gaze at Shehryar.

"How about we donate three of the TVs—assuming one needs to go back to Beau—and smash her laptop, phone and tablet?" I suggested.

"I vote for Princess Esmeralda's idea," Pierre said.

"You can vote, but it isn't going to change the fact you're not smashing anything," Trevor said.

"Oh," I mumbled, my shoulders sagging. Candy's idea had sounded fun.

Trevor's gaze flicked up once, twice, and lingered on mine. Then he threw his head back and sighed up at the ceiling. "Dammit." He huffed and straightened up. "Okay, fine. Give me an hour and then you can smash her phone. But *only* her phone, okay?"

Pierre laughed, Candy gaped, Zain smirked, and I grinned at Trevor. He gave me a reluctant smile back that lifted into a smirk as he directed it to Kai. "You realise you're never going to be able to say no to her, right?"

My cheeks went hot, and my grin wavered shyly. "I know," Kai said, but not even the slightest glimpse of his dimple appeared in his right cheek. His face remained soft but impassive, his eyes bright and quiet at the same time, and it poked at me uncomfortably.

I couldn't tell if he was sluggish from slipping down from the adrenaline rush after everything that had happened or if his mind was reeling instead and his emotions were everywhere.

But I was going to find once we were alone.

MARIYAH

Dude it everything okay?

MARIYAH

You haven't messaged for two days.

CHAPTER 38

Kai

After smashing Meg's phone, we ended up staying for dinner with Trevor's parents, which Zain's wife and children joined us for too. So, by the time Esmeralda and I walked through her bedroom door it had just gone eleven and the entire palace was in bed or getting ready for bed.

She came back out from the walk-in wardrobe, having hung her coat up and abandoned her heels, but I was still standing exactly where she'd left me. By the velvet chaise that I had draped my coat across, staring at nothing in particular until she sauntered over.

She was giving me that look. The one she'd been giving me since we left Beau Fletcher's house. Like she was summoning her telekinesis powers to read my mind, but she couldn't figure out what she was seeing, and she didn't like that.

The thing was, I couldn't tell what I was feeling myself. Only that the closer she came, the harder the beckoning behind my ribcage became.

She rose on her toes, snaking her arms around my neck, and I sagged against her small, soft body, encircling her around the waist. She kissed me, tugging my lips between hers at a sweet, leisurely pace. With a groan, I sought out her tongue, but she forced me to keep to her slower rhythm.

She still tasted like clementines and cream. It reminded me of how she sat in Trevor's parents' living room after dinner, peeling the orange fruits with Zain's daughter tucked right up against her while Zain's son sat on her lap. The little girl had been mesmerised by her. So had the boy as he demanded to be fed his share of broken segments covered in squirted cream. Esmeralda had played on the girl's princess obsession and made both children giggle endlessly, and I…

My gut had felt like a ball of dough being pulled and stretched. Even though it had left me wheezing, it had felt so right too as I'd pictured Esmeralda with *our* children.

Now the thought was buzzing round and round in my head again in a new form.

I want to put a baby inside her. I want to put a baby inside her. I want to put a baby inside her.

But it strummed at strings that were making me feel angrier, needier. Agitated. Driving me to grapple at Esmeralda, filling one hand with her pert arse and holding her flush against me.

"Kai," she panted, taking her lips away. An animalistic sound vibrated in my throat as I chased after her, but she lifted her chin and my lips landed against the underside of her jaw. One whiff of her sweet, peony scent, and I was burying my face into her neck like a starved brute. She sucked in a breath, quivering on her legs as she fought her instinctive impulse to squirm.

"Kai," she whispered against my cheek. "What's wrong?" Her question might not have cut through the fog playing games with my mind had it not been for the waver in her voice.

I lifted my mouth to her hair but failed to loosen my grip on her. "I don't know, I just…I don't know."

It wasn't the answer she wanted, but I couldn't give her anything more. My emotions were birds freed from a cage, flying all over the place at once. I could just about hold onto a few of them.

I was happy that this nightmare had been dealt with. Relieved that I'd faced Meg and won. I was in awe of how powerful and fierce Esmeralda had been by my side, *in my defence.*

But I couldn't bring myself to celebrate.

It wasn't technically over yet. Not until after the trial within a few weeks, even though it was just a legal formality. Meg *would be* charged. But I was still uneasy. And irritated.

I'd lost nearly three days with Esmeralda because of this mess. I didn't blame her one bit, but fuck, it made me so angry thinking about all the memories I could have made with her. Now it was hitting me repeatedly like a sledgehammer that she was leaving the day after tomorrow and I wasn't ready.

I hadn't even managed to take her on our first date yet. That was somewhat ironic though. Because in truth, I was ready to get down on one knee and ask this beautiful woman to stay with me and let me love her for the rest of our lives. To make me her husband and let me give her a family.

That was why my agitation and irritation were so heightened. I knew she was endgame for me, but I hadn't gotten the chance to prove I could be endgame for her. What if she went back to Jahandar and realised she wasn't really in love with a needy, jealous recluse of a prince like me?

The anxiety was unforgiving. It made my teeth ache, my hands twitch, my temple throb, and my heart sweat with how fast it was racing. *Was this what withdrawal felt like?*

"Kai." A gentle brush of her fingers across the back of my neck and I was falling out of my head and right back into her arms.

She squeezed her palm around my nape, and I don't know what it was about the touch, but the words came surging out of my mouth as a croak. "I love you."

Her mouth didn't move, but her eyes smiled so tenderly. "I love you too. So much." She pressed a quick kiss to my lips. "Let's go shower."

I found it oddly therapeutic watching Esmeralda through the bathroom sink mirror wipe her make-up off with soaked cotton pads before splashing her face with water. By the time she turned to me with fresh, glowing skin, a beautiful, natural pinkness in her cheeks, my twitchy symptoms had faded into a relative easiness.

Relative being the key word. Because she gripped the hem of my jumper and a hot knot formed with a hard pull low in my middle.

"Arms up, please," she demanded.

It was adorable how she tiptoed and struggled as she took my jumper and thermal undershirt off. Once she threw them aside, she tracked slow, admiring fingers over my abdomen and through the dark hairs over my chest. My heart jackhammered under her palm, but my hands settled on her hips, pulling her jumper from her skirt with a one-track mind.

I want to put a baby inside her. My baby. Our *baby.*

I dropped her jumper onto the patterned tiles and in the same breath, spun her by the shoulders to face the mirror. Round eyes reflected back at me as her lips parted breathlessly. *Fucking stunning.*

Skirt, bra, panties. I stripped her out of everything that hid her naked curves from me, then let her stand with her back to me, watching through the mirror as I took off my trousers and boxers. The moment we were both naked, I wrapped my arms around her and drew her back against my chest.

Our first skin on skin contact in nearly three fucking days.

I groaned into her hair as embers flew across my skin, mapping the way she fit against me and collecting where the top of her arse cradled my thickening length. She made a hitched noise and for a single moment, she pressed back into me. But then she tipped her weight forward against my arms.

"Kai," she said huskily. "Shower."

I squeezed her back closer to me. "Later."

"Kai." There was an amused bounce to her tone as she smiled through the mirror. "Patience."

She wanted me to be patient? How? I was an addict, and she was the temptation I couldn't possibly ever give up standing naked and within reach. And I was supposed to resist when every inch of me was weeping to have her, feel her, taste her?

She stepped past the mirror, tugging me by the hand to the shower along the back wall. Of course, I didn't complain, but…but if I had to be patient, it was only fair she felt my frustration too…

It was childish. But the possessive, clingy agitation weaving through me needed her to feel the exact same helpless need and

obsession I felt for her.

Her black and white ensuite bathroom had a big, sleek, modern shower against the black-tiled wall. Open on both sides, there was only a glass, wall-to-floor panel keeping the sprays at bay.

Esmeralda pulled me under the large, square showerhead and kept her back to my chest while the warm water soaked us for a minute. Then she picked up the pastel purple bottle of shampoo and turned to me. "Did you use my shampoo in the morning?" she asked, flicking the lid open.

"Hmm," I said, nudging the lid back closed and taking the bottle from her. I leaned over and swapped the shampoo for the mint-coloured bottle of bodywash and put it in her hand.

"You don't want me to wash your hair?"

I shook my head, pushing my wet hair back from my forehead. All I wanted was for this shower to be over so I could take her in seven different ways. And that would just be the start of it.

She flipped the lid open and drizzled the whitish-green liquid across my chest and shoulders.

I lifted my arms and turned which way she asked as she lathered the soap all over my top half. I bit back my groans and growls every time her wet breasts and pebbled nipples brushed against my burning skin. But when she tried to pull me back under the shower spray to wash off, I didn't budge.

"My legs," I said, my voice as thick and hard as the heavy length between my thighs.

Esmeralda wasn't shy when it came to sex, but her face flushed beet red the moment her gaze dropped to my legs. It was adorable. It turned me on. It made me want to fucking tease her.

I stepped forward, crowding her against the wall to her back, and picked up the bodywash to squirt some on my thighs. Her lashes dropped…and rose. I arched a brow as I waited. And with a delicious little gulp, she slowly got down on her knees. *Fuck yes.*

I bent over her, bracing my hands on the wall and protecting her from the shower spray, as she looked up at me. Eyes so big and beautiful. So fucking greedy and eager and hungry. My dick throbbed and twitched towards her parted lips as she rubbed over my thighs and down my legs. Not once did she dare touch my hard cock, but she couldn't resist a few lingering peeks.

"Done," she croaked, placing her hands on her thighs like such a pretty, obedient little slut.

My legs were shaking, my dick was leaking like a broken tap, and I was a thousand per cent sure if I took her hair in my hands and told her to open her mouth, Esmeralda would take my length to the back of her throat and swallow every drop of my cum. But I wasn't done with her yet.

Taking her by the hand, I helped her up onto her feet, and she flopped back against the wet wall. I generously drizzled the bodywash over her, then got to work teasing and washing her.

Starting at her neck, I massaged the spot below her ears until her lashes quivered. I teased under her breasts, around her nipples, never touching them directly. Not even when she squirmed and silently pleaded me with big, hazy eyes.

I gave the same treatment to her hot, swollen pussy. I braced her feet one at a time on my legs and kneaded high up on her inner thighs. Her breaths quickly grew shallow and broken. When I got to her back, she was shaking so much I couldn't help a triumphant smirk against her hair. But I continued to torment her even as we washed off and dried up back inside the bedroom.

"Are you mad at me?" she stuttered as I *accidentally* brushed the white towel across her nipples for the dozenth time, while gently rubbing her hair dry. "Because—because I told you to be patient."

"No. Never."

"Then why are you touching me like you're punishing me?"

I held the towel still. "I'm not punishing you, Babble. I just want you to feel as frenzied as I do." Her lips parted, her lashes dropped, and my dick preened under her attention. With the towel still in my hand, I cupped her chin and forced her to look up at me. "Do you feel it?"

"Yes," she breathed.

"Really?" I said, arching a brow. "Do you feel so frenzied that you're desperate for me in a fanatical sort of way? Because that is how I feel, Esmeralda. And I don't think I have it in me to be remotely nice tonight. So, I need you to tell me if that isn't what you want."

I felt the gentle roll of her jaw as she swallowed and, "Yes. That frenzied. So don't be nice."

It was the answer I'd craved, but dark fumes spewed inside me. I ground my teeth together as they plagued me. "Are you sure, Babble?" I growled. "I might not let you come all night long."

Her eyes glowed. "Then I won't come."

"What if I change my mind? What if I make you come again and again, so much it hurts?"

Her breath shuddered against my lips. "I'll beg for more."

Fuck. "Will you let me do anything I want to you?"

"Anything you want. I'm yours, Kai."

Just like that, the fumes turned red and hot instead of dark and murky. "No, Babble," I rasped. "*I'm yours.* You control me entirely. You know I will only ever give you what you want. And if that is anything I want to do to you, then that is exactly what I will give you."

Her whimpering moan of agreement was so fucking unabashed and sexy. I plastered my lips over hers, needing to lap it up and coat my mouth in the raw honesty of it. But the moment my lips untangled from hers, I threw the towel caught amongst my fingers aside and hauled Esmeralda up from the floor, my hands cupping her arse.

I slid on my knees across the burgundy silk duvet, flopped onto my backside, and seated Esmeralda high up on my lap. Her thighs cushioned either side of my waist as I pressed my damp hair back into one the pillows, but with a little adjustment I urged her higher. And higher. Until her legs bracketed my shoulders and that cunt… Fuck, my mouth watered as I breathed in her wetness.

Above me, Esmeralda grabbed onto the headboard to stabilise herself and blinked big, round eyes like she had no idea what I was doing. But knew *exactly* what I was planning.

"Come on, Babble," I purred, giving her arse cheeks a light squeeze as I angled her hips forward. "Sit your greedy little pussy on my mouth and ride my tongue."

Her cheeks ignited as she remained adorably frozen in her hovering position. Then she gave the slightest jerk of her head, neither a nod nor a shake. "I—I—Kai…I can't."

"Why not?"

"What do you mean '*why not*'?" Her voice came out breathless and shrill. "What if I suffocate you?"

That made me smile. Had she forgotten how small she was in comparison to me? "You won't. Now sit down." She shook her head rapidly, and my hands curled over her thighs as a frustrated noise rolled up my throat. "I will not repeat myself again, Esmeralda. *Sit down. Now.*"

My Babble grasped the warning in my tone and shakily lowered herself. But not like I'd told her to, not the way I wanted her to smother me. And that was disobedience worthy of a punishment.

Lifting my head, I closed my lips around the apex of her wetness and sucked. I tugged her swollen clit into the heat of my mouth and lashed at it unforgivingly with my tongue. I reprimanded her with too much all too soon, but fuck, her perfect, warm taste was a gift for me.

Like coming home. Like making her mine. My wife, my future, my everything. My *even death couldn't do us part.*

Esmeralda's cry rung through the room as her body jerked above mine. Rising and writhing and shaking, fighting and failing to break through the confine of my arms.

She sobbed my name as her legs shook and lost all strength, dropping her right where I wanted her. On my face, smearing her wetness all over my mouth and chin. Her thighs locked around my head like a vice, fingers tearing through my damp hair, and it was so fucking satisfying I chuckled.

"Fuck!" Her flushed face scrunched in on itself.

Power and arousal thundered through my already thrumming nerves, tempting me not to take any mercy on her. But my cramping mouth eased up with a reluctant sigh.

She took a gulping breath as she bent over. "Kai," she whimpered, her eyes brimming.

Ah, fuck. Every time she said my name, I felt like a livewire caught in a rainstorm. Sparks were shooting out of me, and she was the only one caught in my path of destruction.

My tongue started moving again. Dragging between her pussy lips, exchanging full, lazy licks for her whimpered noises. But lazy wasn't what I was interested in tonight. I wanted hard and nasty and demanding and merciless. And I caught her off guard as I fucking gave it to her.

"Fu—ck," Esmeralda squeaked, trying to rip my hair out. The painful sensation had me groaning into her. "It's too much!"

Good, I wanted to say, but I whipped my tongue faster in reply instead and tortured her with pulsing suction. Despite her pleading and sobbing, my lusty Babble started rocking her hips, riding the punishment my mouth offered her with a *more, more, more* kind of neediness.

"I'm gonna come," she gasped soon enough. "I want to come. Please, please Sir, say I can come. Let me come. I'm begging you. Please, please, *please*."

I didn't give her permission. I didn't say anything. I kept working my mouth until her pussy started fluttering against my lips and her begging grew louder and desperate and weeping, and—

"Don't you dare fucking come," I snarled, gripping her by the arse and lifting her off me.

"No," she shrieked, rocking her hips for the orgasm I denied her. "No, please. Let me come."

"No, Babble. You didn't listen to me. You made me repeat myself when I told you to sit on my face. So, I won't give you permission to come until you've earned it like a good fucking slut."

"Please," she whimpered.

Excitement grazed down my spine. "Turn around." She wobbled, but this time she didn't hesitate to obey, carefully moving around so her reddened arse faced me. "That's it. Now suck on my dick, Babble. Show me how well you can earn your orgasm."

"Yes, Sir," she said, locking her fist around the base of my dick and making me hiss.

My Babble did so well, eagerly easing me into her perfect, snug mouth. My hips jerked as I hit the back of her throat, and I released a feral growl, gripping her thighs with white-knuckled fingers. She fucking moaned around me, dragging her mouth up and down and faster. Gagging, sucking, and dribbling. Choking me of my consciousness to the point canaries flew circles above my head.

"Fuck, fuck, fuck." My hips hiked up to meet her swallow. "That's it, Esmeralda. Such a good fucking whore. Earning your orgasm with that perfect, pretty mouth."

She purred and the vibrations shot through me and chattered in my teeth. Then she slipped me out of her mouth with a pop, but her hand stayed there as a tight fist pumping in the same fast rhythm of her mouth. "I love your dick so much," she slurred, lapping at one side of the crown.

I chuckled breathlessly. "I know, Babble. I can tell." Sliding my hands to her arse, I gripped and spread them, exposing the secret mess trickling onto my chest. "You're fucking dripping all over me." I licked from her clit all the way up to the puckered bud between her arse cheeks, causing her to twitch and whine. *Shit, her taste.* I snarled hungrily, needing nothing more than to have her back on my mouth. "Come here. Bring that beautiful cunt back here. *Now.*"

So eager, she didn't even bother turning around. Just scrambled back and sat her clit on my ready mouth with no concern for suffocating me this time and within minutes, I had her there again.

"Can I come—may I come? May I please come?" she chanted through her teeth as she rocked jaggedly on my tongue. But I rolled around her clit and stole it away back into my mouth.

She screamed her frustration before I could get a word out, clawing at my thighs like an angry little kitten. I hissed a chuckle, but my ball tightened as the sound played in my ears on repeat. I honestly could have come just listening to her cry.

"So impatient," I teased, tracing my hands up her sides. "Screaming before I have even said anything." She whimpered, wiggling her arse back wantonly, and a lustful sound tore from my mouth. "Oh, you greedy fucking brat, Esmeralda." She shivered. "Fine. Come for me."

As my fingers found her hard nipples to pinch and roll, I set my mouth back on her clit and worked her, wound her, wrapped her up in pleasure. And when she ripped free and screamed, her whole body shaking above me, I held her down on my mouth and lapped up every drop of it.

I unlatched my lips as she sagged forward. Not to let her rest, but to manoeuvre her legs so I could flip her onto her back. She landed as a breathless sprawl of liquid limbs, and I swiftly scrambled over her. Moving her further up towards the foot of the bed, I lowered myself.

"Kai," she gasped, belatedly reacting to what I was doing.

But I had already caught both of her wrists and pinned them to the silk duvet on either side of her hips, her thighs forced open by the width of my shoulders. She couldn't stop me from dragging my tongue, heavy and slow, over her pussy. Taunting and poking and terrorizing the ghost of her climax.

"Kai," she shrieked, her spine shooting up from the bed so roughly, I nearly lost grip of her. So, I clenched her wrists tighter, pressed my mouth down heavier, and devoured her as I rubbed my aching dick into the duvet for some pre-fucking relief.

"Kai. Kai. Sir, please!" She was thrashing so much, I didn't even have to move my tongue to torture her. "It's too much—I can't. I can't."

"It's too much, Babble?" I echoed between a lick, watching her lift her scrunched up face to look down at me. "Is it sensitive?" *Suck.* "Does it hurt?" She nodded furiously. *Lick.* "Does it *only* hurt?" She didn't seem to know if she wanted to nod or shake her head. She did a bit of both, and a smirk spread across my lips. "You like it, don't you?"

Before she could respond, I captured her clit and sucked until my cheeks hollowed. She silently screamed up at the ceiling, one heel of her foot digging between my shoulder blades. As I chuckled, I kissed over her, then swapped kiss for lick, lick for suck, and suck. And suck. And lick. And suck.

"Kai," she choked out with a jolt as I blew against her sopping cunt.

"Do you like having your sensitive clit tortured, Babble?" I panted. "Do you like that I'm holding you down so you can't escape it? Do you like that I'm doing what I want to you? Like you wanted?"

She hesitated, then whimpered defeatedly. "Yes. I like it. I love it, Sir."

"Good. I want you to love it," I said, rising on my hands and knees over her to situate myself behind her, my chest to her back. "The pain that goes perfectly with pleasure." I tucked my arm under her neck and hooked her knee back over my thigh, spreading her wet heat wide apart. "That's the only kind of pain I ever want to give you."

Wrapping my hand around her throat, I turned her face to mine and kissed her deeply. She greedily licked up the taste of herself from my mouth as I lowered my other hand to my cock. Gripping it and guiding it to her entrance. I slipped right into her with one steady nudge.

Her groan stifled my moan, the sounds tangling in our gaping mouths. I didn't have the ability to kiss her when her pillow soft pussy was wrapping ribbons of bliss around me. But neither did she as my fingers found the swollen bud of her clit again, rubbing as I pitched my hips back. She scrambled against me, feeding me choked noise after choked noise. But I held her close, my hand closing tighter around her throat, and snapped my pelvis against her arse. Pumping into her, dragging back. Again and again and again. Pistoning my hips a little too fast and a little too hard.

The twisted face Esmeralda made was everything. The helplessness. The drugged delight. The streaking pleasure flashing in her eyes. The bratty spark. The eagerness to take it. *So fucking beautiful.* I was going to get off on the memory of it every single night she wasn't in my bed.

"Kai," she whined, filling her fists with my hair and the wet duvet. "You liar."

A single huff of laughter shot through my gritted teeth. I pressed the arrogant curl on my mouth into her cheek, weighing her down into the mattress. I slowed my thrusts, pinching and rubbing her clit between my slippery fingers. "What did I lie about, Babble?"

"You said—" I licked across her skin under her ear, and she gasped over her words. "You said—Kai!" I sucked on her neck, plunged into her, and pinched her clit all at once. She shook against me, crying muffled words into the silk. "You're punishing me!"

"I'm not," I said into her ear. *But I could if I made her give me a reason to...*

"Liar," she whined just as I moved my hand from her throat and clamped it over her mouth.

"What was that?" I taunted, slipping my hand out from between the bed and her pussy. Gripping under her knee, I pressed her leg into the duvet and then rolled her half onto her stomach, pinning her under my weight.

Startled, her hands flew out above her, and I used the opportunity to let go of her leg and swipe up her wrists, locking them down in one fist on the silk sheets. She could just above move her head, but her wide eyes flicked to my heavy-lidded ones. Pleading and swimming but wanting too.

The last wire in my system labelled "gentleman" was ripped out. All that was left was the exhilaration of knowing I had completely overpowered her. That I had her trapped underneath me. To take what I gave her. To use as I pleased. And she loved it just as much as I did, if not more.

I held her stare as I leveraged myself slightly on my knees. Slowly, very slowly. Feeling the fist of pleasure turn inside my stomach at how perfectly snug she felt in this position. Going on the way she sunk her head back against my shoulder on a sigh, my Babble felt it too. The sweet, sweet—

I snapped my hips down, heavy and forceful, and she shrieked into my palm.

Each plunge jerked the entire bed as I drilled into her, grinding her into the silk sheets. I bit her neck, her brows contorted. She started struggling under me, and I bore down, hammering into her harder.

She shattered in my arms for a second time, and I was rewarded with a scream into my palm. But the way her pussy locked up and wrung my dick was the most perfect blend of pleasure and torture. It was her sweet fucking revenge, and I was stripped back to the bone, on me knees, ruined by her.

"Fuck," I roared. My mind, my lungs, my vision glitched from an overload of sensation. Instinct took over, and I bucked my hips like a young stallion breeding a mare for the first time. I only cared about filling her up, not how harsh and erratic my thrusts were.

Baby. Put a baby inside her. Get her pregnant. I want her pregnant.

The strength of my climax took me by surprise, but I came and came and came. I was left gasping Esmeralda's name into her tangled, wet hair as I crushed my pelvis against hers for forever and a day. Then a blanket of heady warmth settled over my lower body, and I nestled against her.

But the buzz wasn't gone. No fucking way.

I removed my hand from her mouth as I eased out of her, and her laboured breaths filtered through. It was so sweet the way she dropped her cheek against my palm, presuming she could have a moment to rest. I tipped her face to mine so she could see how wrong her assumption was.

"Brat," I growled.

A stillness settled over her unsteady gaze. "Brat?" she echoed. "Why?"

Shit, she was so adorable. "You didn't ask for permission to come."

Her eyes went wide, mouth agape, as I sat up on my haunches. I grabbed one of her ankles and jerked her legs apart. She stuttered a breathy noise as I forced her flat on her back.

"You should have asked, Babble. But you didn't," I tutted mockingly. "That's not how good girls are supposed to behave, is it? Only greedy sluts come without asking." I shoved her knees up to her heaving chest, displaying her swollen pussy. "So, now I'm going to punish you like one."

"But—but—" she spluttered, her fingers curling into my pecs. "You covered my mouth!"

"I covered your mouth. I didn't stop you from speaking."

She gawked, her mouth opening and closing. "Kai…"

"Sir," I corrected and dropped my head to press a kiss by her red-tipped ear. "Now hold your legs spread, and don't make me repeat myself this time, Esmeralda. Or I won't stick to spanking and fingering your cunt until I'm hard again. I will spank and finger your arse too."

She sucked in a sharp breath. I felt it in my dick.

"And there is no point begging. You will only come when I say you can."

CHAPTER 39
Esmeralda

Scientists all around Neves needed to conduct an experiment to verify whether it was possible to die from having too many orgasms.

Because I nearly died last night.

I was railed endlessly by an animal who just happened to look and sound like my boyfriend. Thrown into every position my body could contort in until the early hours of the morning. And he didn't *give* me mind-blowing orgasm after leg-shaking orgasm. *Nope.*

Kai controlled my climaxes in every sense of the word.

He didn't let me have them until I cried and begged and submitted to his every filthy command. Then he demanded them like they were in his rights to have until I sobbed and pleaded that I didn't have any more to give him. But he found them; stole them like a thief on a most wanted list. He fucking sucked every single one from me like a vampire sucked blood and left me lifeless.

Though I couldn't complain. I had enjoyed every helpless moment he had me pinned down, strumming my pleasure to whatever rhythm he wanted.

The next morning, I stirred awake under a feather-light caress of fingers shaping my eyebrow. Not to an eyeful of sexy man-chest again—Kai hated the cold too much to be the kind of guy who slept naked or even shirtless. He hadn't even let me sleep naked. But I did get an eyeful of sexy muscle-bod in a tight white thermal undershirt with an arm folded under his head.

A shy curl pulled at my lips. "Hi," I croaked, angling my face against the pillow up to his.

"Hi," he replied, his gravelly voice vibrating in my middle, as he traced his thumb down my jaw.

"How long have you been watching me sleep?"

"Ten, fifteen minutes."

I scrunched my nose. "Creep."

I could just see his dimple peeking out against his bicep even though his brows furrowed. "I'm not a creep." His thumb tugged at my bottom lip. "I like seeing you asleep next to me. It feels like you trust me. Like you feel safe with me, and that makes me…happy."

Dammit. He wasn't supposed to give a pure answer that made my heart do cartwheels like a child on a sugar rush.

I could have teased him and said I slept so soundly because he fucked all the energy out of me, but I didn't want to ruin what he'd said. Plus, maybe there was no scientific evidence that proved it, but seeing as I had lost my ability to sleep when I'd lost my sense of security, I didn't think he was wrong to say that I had found it again with him. Kai gave me every ounce of security I had ever wanted.

I smiled and wriggled closer to him, hooking a leg over his thighs and an arm over his waist. He chuckled lightly and squeezed his arms around me, tucking my head under his chin.

"No gym today?" I mumbled into his chest. He smelt so good, so warm and masculine with a sweet hint of his cologne from his undershirt.

"No." He rubbed a hand up and down my back. "I wanted to make sure you were okay."

My face knew exactly what he was talking about and heated to a hundred degrees. "My thighs are a bit sore," I said quietly. "I think the hickeys you left on my back are too."

His hand immediately lifted from my back. "I'm sorry. There is some balm in the bathroom. It should relieve the pain within a few

minutes. I'll go get it and—"

"Wait, I was kidding. It was a joke," I said with a chuckle and latched onto his arm to stop him from rolling over to the edge of the bed. "Nothing hurts. I'm fine. Just achy—maybe."

"That wasn't funny."

I tipped my chin up audaciously. "Think of it as revenge for making me beg so much last night."

His lips twitched, but his frown remained stubborn as he rolled back towards me. And closer. *And closer.* I quickly found myself shrinking into the pillow as he climbed over me, settling his weight between my legs. *Oh shit.*

"I'm going to remember your *revenge*, Babble," he rasped, eyes glinting, "and next time, you will only have yourself to thank when I keep you begging for longer."

I couldn't breathe, couldn't reply, but then he dropped his head and licked straight across my lips, morning breath be damned. I squeaked in surprise, my hands jerking up to cup his face as he chuckled. But he was already dipping his mouth to lick and kiss all over my neck.

"Kai," I squealed through a ticklish bout of giggles. "Wait." His teeth grazed my skin. "Kai!"

"I should bite you for making me worry," he growled.

Clapping my palm against his forehead, I tried to push his face back, but I just about got him to look at me through his wolfish stare. "You will get us both killed by Rose if she has to cover up another bite mark on my neck, Mr Perfect Prince."

As soon as the nickname left my lips, I regretted saying it, recalling the way *she* had spat it at him like it was an insult. The last thing I wanted was to use the same name and remind him of all his bad memories of Meg. It made me feel guilty that I might have been all this time without knowing.

Kai kissed my chin after my smile slipped away. "Say it again. I like it when you call me that." But the conflicted feeling wouldn't let me. "Say it for me. Please, Babble."

I wet my lips. "Mr Perfect Prince…"

His dimple settled in his right cheek, but he arched a brow. "Just

Mr Perfect Prince?"

I squished his cheeks in my palms. "*My* Mr Perfect Prince." I turned his face to press a quick succession of pecks to his stubbled cheek. "I love you."

"I love you too." He settled a chaste kiss to my lips.

"We should get up."

"No."

"We have to." I tried the impossible task of rolling out from under him. Basically, all I did was turn my head. And gasp when I saw the red numbers on the digital clock sitting on the bedside cabinet. "It's nearly ten-forty?"

"Hmm. So, there's no need to get up yet. We've already missed breakfast."

"But—" I stuttered as panic knocked like a ping-pong ball between my ribs.

Technically, I knew my relationship with my brother wasn't what it was, but that didn't mean I could automatically assume Kareem would be fine with me staying in bed with Kai so late on the day of the final ball. My first instinct was still to worry about his reaction.

Kai pressed a heavy kiss to my cheek. "It's okay, Esmeralda," he said softly. "When I first awoke at eight, I left the kitchen, my parents, and your brother a message to let them know we wouldn't be down for breakfast. So, he already knows. He said to let you sleep for as long as possible."

Just over a week ago I would never have believed Kareem could or would say such a thing, but it was slightly easier to imagine now. Still surreal, but just about plausible. But more importantly…

"Kareem gave you his personal number?"

"Hmm. A few days ago. So, you're not going anywhere. You're staying with me until Rose comes to help you get ready for the ball."

His adorable, clingy demand made it impossible not to smile. "Your instructions are not clear, Mr Perfect Prince," I teased. "Do you mean I have to stay away from you until the ball?"

"*Try*. If you can get out from under me."

I didn't try. *Stay away from him?* No. I had no will, no desire, no anything to. But it hit me harder than it had done at any point in these past two weeks that I didn't entirely have a choice in that.

"I don't want to leave tomorrow," I whispered sombrely.

There was a desperate intensity to Kai's expression. "Then stay."

If only it was that easy.

I was Jahandar's Crown Princess. I had a job and a duty, and for the first time, I didn't want to fulfil my role as repentance to Kareem and my parents. I wanted to support Kareem in government, to stand for my state and for our people. Without any fear or guilt or self-pity and hatred.

I wanted to make myself proud for once.

"I can't."

"I know…"

Kai had a job and a duty he couldn't abandon either. And I had no doubt he felt the same way I did.

"You haven't yet gone but it already hurts," he said, nuzzling into my right palm. "Knowing we'll both be busy. Not knowing when I will be able to kiss you and hold you next. It's already killing me." An ache ripped through my chest. "I will do everything in my power to make time to come see you in Jahandar, but what am I going to do when I can't, Esmeralda? How do I sleep without you next to me? How am I supposed to not miss you every minute of every day?"

A sting scratched across the back of my nose and eyes. "I don't know." My voice cracked. "But we can videocall every day. And I'll make time to come see you too. Whenever I can. And we can go to the same international events. All of them." I swallowed down the rock in my throat. "I know it will be hard, but we can make this work. I promise you, Kai, we will."

"I know we will," he choked out and smashed his lips over mine.

We kissed and kissed and kissed. Long and slow. Deep and feverish, taking our time to wipe away the fear and doubt and pain. Left behind was only longing that turned the space between my spread thighs damp and hot and needy. And with Kai's hard-on pressing right *there*…

"I need you. I need you now, Kai."

He shook his head rapidly, a dazed flush painted across his face. "Last night was a lot, Esmeralda. I don't want you to be sore later."

"I want to be sore," I said without missing a beat. "I want to feel you between my legs when I walk." I rolled my pelvis against his erection. "I want that ache, Kai. Give it to me. Please. I'm begging you."

Dropping his forehead against mine, he groaned, restraint and pleasure battling across his scrunched face. It was obvious pleasure was winning. "You and your filthy mouth, Babble," he growled and lifted his head. "I shouldn't make you ache. Tell me I shouldn't."

"You should." I grazed my nails down his tense back and dug my fingers into his full arse cheeks through his pyjama bottoms. He hissed above me. "You really, really should."

With our eyes locked and hands entwined above my head, he did.

CHAPTER 40
Esmeralda

"**W**ould you stop doing that?" I said sternly to Shehryar, pulling his hand away from his tie. *Again.*

He battled to fend off a scowl as he curled his hands to fists by his sides. "It's uncomfortable," he grumbled. But the restlessness flaring from his body suggested it wasn't just the tie.

He was uncomfortable, full stop.

There were two things Shehryar didn't do. One, he never wore ties of any kind with his suits. And two, he didn't attend royal events unless he was standing guard along the perimeter of the room.

But Prince Arsh had asked Shehryar and Mama Katiya to attend the closing ball of the Peace Celebrations as his guests, and the dress code as always was *as formal as formal could get.*

In other words, Shehryar sat opposite me during a five-course dinner, looking as if he wanted to sprint from Westcombe Palace's dining hall while the Dowager Queen of Khaas made conversation with him. And since the event had moved to the Grand Hall, he had stayed glued to the wall.

Now, the ball was in full swing with a live orchestra playing in one corner by the entrance staircase, and beautiful white and pale blue flower displays dotted among the hundreds of invited guests, royals, and ministers in attendance.

It took me twenty minutes to get from where I left Kai with Candy, Pierre, and Trevor in the middle of the packed gothic hall to where Shehryar was hiding in the corner after being stopped by nearly everyone I passed. I had about five minutes to drag him to his mother before the royal families took to one end so King Rami and Queen Leila could start the closing speeches.

"I know it's uncomfortable, Sher," I said sympathetically, "but you can't hide here the whole night. You should be with Prince Arsh and Mama Katiya so he can introduce you to everyone."

"I shouldn't even be here," he said, glancing around over my head as he adjusted his tie again.

I knew he was eyeing the expensive suits and designer dresses among royal tunics and dresses in national state colours, all worn by people he never usually interacted with. They made him feel out of place. A counterfeit product on a shelf of real ones.

That wasn't true. But Shehryar was a stubborn mule who rarely budged once he'd made up his mind. The stupid man didn't even realise with his tall, muscular build, he pulled off his red tie and black, fitted, three-piece suit better than nearly all the men in the room.

"You should be here, Sher," I said, tugging him forward away from the wall with a hand around his elbow. He came like a moody teenager. As his fingers went up to his tie, I swatted them away. His brows dipped but he swiftly wiped the glare off and instead gritted his teeth. I grinned fearlessly.

He couldn't tell me off. This was my turf. *Protected princess turf.*

"Touch that tie again and I will use it to strangle you later," I warned through my smile.

He blinked, having not expected that, then shifted. "You sound like Mariyah."

"Oh, you would be much livelier if your nemesis was here, wouldn't you?"

He grunted like that was an impossibility, but I didn't miss the way he rolled his jaw and glanced away for a second. *Idiot.* When was he going to admit that he didn't find my best friend as irritating as he wanted everyone to think he did?

"Then come on." I took him into the throngs of people.

"Es—Princess. I don't—"

"Crown Princess Esmeralda," a young, blonde woman called out as we passed her. I immediately recognised the blue eyes of the Touman actress in some of my favourite movies.

"Yami," I chirped.

She bowed her head. "I missed my chance to come say hi before the dinner, but I'm so glad I finally found you, Your Highness," she said, her grin outshining the stars. "It's so good to see you again."

I gave her fingers a friendly squeeze with my free hand. "It's so good to see you too. I'm so glad you stopped me. It's been so long since I last saw you."

"It has been. But look at you!" She waved her other hand down my body. "You look absolutely stunning, Your Highness. I mean, you always do, but this dress. Wow."

Coming from her, I considered it an epic compliment. My face flushed as I ran my hand down my hip over the chiffon against my skin.

I felt *wow* tonight.

My stylist, Rose, had done a great job with the gold, shimmer make-up on my face and my hair, accentuating my natural curls in a tamed, beach-curl way, pinning it half up.

As for the dark red dress and heels, I had my favourite designer in Jahandar to thank for them. The lined chiffon created a cascading skirt that skimmed the floor, with gold embroidery scattered all over, and waterfall sleeves that swished above my elbows. The V-neck was modest, but I spent ten minutes admiring my boobs in the mirror while getting ready because of the way the wrap-style overlap complimented my figure.

"Thank you so much. You look stunning too. Pink is really your colour."

"Thank you," she said and threw a quick glance to Shehryar. "I know the speeches are about to start, so maybe if you have a moment afterwards, we could catch up for a few minutes."

"Of course, I would love to," I said and then gestured to Shehryar belatedly. "By the way, this is my friend, Shehryar Timur."

Yami shook his hand. "I am Her Highness's private secretary and bodyguard," he corrected.

"I think she still considers you a friend though." I nodded in agreement. Then Yami tilted her head at him curiously. "Are you perhaps related to the beautiful woman Prince Arsh is introducing to everyone?"

I felt Shehryar stiffen next to me, but he gave a tight nod. "Yes. She's my mother."

"No wonder. You look just like her. Sorry if you find this weird but I completely understand why His Highness is showing her off to everyone. I would too if I was him. She's beautiful, and they look so happy together. Everyone is talking about how they make the perfect couple."

I could have kissed Yami for unknowingly proving my point to Shehryar. Hearing it from someone else worked though. His posture loosened. Just a touch but it was something.

"They are?" he asked.

"Yes! I don't think there's a person here who doesn't want to know when they're getting married."

Shehryar's expression was between surprise and consideration as he glanced in the general direction of where I'd last seen his mother and Prince Arsh.

"I think we're all hoping for the same thing," I said in his silence. "But we must head to the crests now, so I will come find you again, Yami."

"Of course. See you, Your Highness. It was nice meeting you, Shehryar."

Shehryar remained quiet as we left Yami and continued towards the other end of the Grand Hall.

We broke through the front of the crowd where the seven royal households were gathering themselves—minus the royal children under the age of twelve—in front of long platforms draped in red velvet carpet. Three state crests were hung on the left wall: Jahandar, Shah, and Raven. Three on the right: Prio, Dale, and Khaas. In the middle of the wall between was Touma's crest along with their state flag. Royal photographers were dotted around taking what candid pictures they could.

I followed Shehryar's gaze to where Mama Katiya—wearing a figure-hugging midnight blue dress—was trying to twist her hand out of Prince Arsh's, grinning and scolding him all the same as he kept her close. He looked at her like she was his entire world, and a happy tightness tugged in my chest.

"Love is enough when someone loves you as much as he loves her," I heard myself whisper.

I wasn't sure Shehryar heard me over the music until he hoarsely whispered, "I hope so."

When Prince Arsh finally let go of her hand, Shehryar left my side to go to his mother, and I made my way to Kareem. He was adjusting the line of five gold buttons on the fitted sleeve of his cream tunic. Down his right side draped a cape, lined in dark red on the inside, that was attached to the standing collar of his top, and his trousers had a stripe of the same red down the outer sides.

"Hello," I said quietly. It was the first time I'd been alone with him that evening.

"Hi." He cleared his throat. "How are you?"

"I'm well." I smiled, genuinely. "I finally managed to get Shehryar away from the wall."

He smiled back. It was small, but it reached his eyes. "I saw."

I felt like the new kid at school who had been complimented by someone in my class. Wary and pleased all at once. "How are you feeling?"

He rubbed a hand over his cleanly-shaven jaw. "Nervous, actually."

I was surprised by his honesty. "Why?"

"I...wrote my speech for you. But I'm not convinced it's good enough anymore."

The cogs got caught in my brain, stuttering in the same spot after he'd jammed a stick between them. I wasn't given the chance to pull it loose as someone spoke through a microphone.

"Ladies and gentlemen, Dames and Dukes," a woman said as the music died away. "May we please have your attention as the seven royal households take to their crests."

Everyone went quiet, and simultaneously, all the royals turned to face the stairs of the platform leading directly up to their crest. I automatically held my chin high and followed Kareem up the three steps before Jahandar's circular crest. My ears buzzed from the afterquakes of his bombshell, but I stood to his left and did my best to resist searching his unrevealing expression.

With all seven families in place, facing the audience, King Rami and Queen Leila stepped forward with microphones in their hands. The rest of Touma's royals lingered a step behind—the Dowager Queen on King Rami's side, Prince Arsh next to her and Adam standing at the end. That left Kai and Fay to stand on Queen Leila's left.

If the significance of Kai's position next to his mother wasn't obvious, then the change in his royal tunic was. It was still black, but rather than a red sash across his waist, it was a light blue matching the flower decorations. And the buttons and plaited ropes decorating his tunic were silver.

In other words, he was dressed in the uniform of a Touman crown prince. And he looked gorgeous.

"…and we thank everyone who has participated in these past two weeks," Queen Leila closed her speech with a smile as bright as the silver sparkle of her dress, "for making the 875th Anniversary of The Peace such a special and memorable celebration."

A roar of claps and cheers erupted through the hall. While clapping along, my gaze clashed with Kai's darker one, and a smile pulled at my lips. His eyes glittered knowingly, though his relaxed expression remained as the version of him I had once called *Orange*. It was crazy how long ago that felt and how far we had come since.

"Now, as for Touma's pledge this year," King Rami said as the cheers settled, "we are happy to announce that His Highness, Prince Arsh—with the support of all six other royal households—will initiate and see through a Change of Law proposal for the Legitimacy and Marriage Act of 22 PR. For a law that no longer represents what family, marriage, and legitimacy now mean in our society has no place in any royal household either. It is long overdue an update."

A murmur of curiosity filtered through the applauds. But so did several nods of agreement.

"And now," the Queen said, "we would like to invite His Majesty, King Kareem of Jahandar, to step forward and seal another leaf over this year's celebrations."

There was nothing about Kareem's speech that indicated he had written it for me. He thanked those who had made the celebrations possible, he made the typical jokes here and there, he talked about the progression we were making collectively to a better world. Not once did he refer to me.

Until the end.

"Before I announce Jahandar's pledge, I would like to take a moment to gloat," he said with a light grin and chuckles bubbled through the air. "This year, for our annual royal game, Crown Princess Esmeralda and I were paired together in a team. And my sister and I won."

I heard the split-second noise of cheering, but my ears went numb as the pounding behind my ribcage grew silent. It didn't restart.

He called me "his sister." *In public. Not his heir.*

Kareem grinned around the room. "It was a reminder of the days we used to play in the corridors of the palace, and a reminder that I ought to use the gym more often." More laughter travelled the Grand Hall. "But more than that, it was a moment for us to bond again as family."

His voice took on a softer, sincere tone. "In the rush and intensity of politics and running government, it has become far too easy to forget that we are siblings. Work becomes central and we don't stop to reminisce our childhood nor create new memories. But at the end of the day, we are there for each other even though it may not always be obvious that the unconditional support is there. That is what being family means, no matter what form it comes in."

My head was ringing again, but the hall was pin-drop silent.

"However, there are many children in Jahandar and in all of

Neves, who like my sister and I, have lost their parents in one shape or another, and do not have the supportive family system they need to thrive. It was something the late Queen—our mother—cared about immensely, and it is something Crown Princess Esmeralda has dedicated so much of her time to as well.

"Therefore." Kareem lifted his chin. "Jahandar pledges seven billion Raal to set up the Amara-Ayla Foundation, which will provide grants and loans to shelters, schools, and universities to support and guide orphans and abandoned children with their education and life choices, while also giving them the chance to have normal childhoods with fully funded trips with their found families."

Amara-Ayla…as in…for mother and me?

It was turmoil inside me. A mix of good feelings and sad ones roaring as loud as the echo through the room as Kareem lowered the mic. Years of practise from holding back my emotions was the only reason the liquid in my eyes didn't start gushing down my cheeks in waterfalls, but my hands shook by my sides. I couldn't make out Kareem's expression through the blurry veil.

Once he moved back, his attention went straight to Shah's monarchs as they received the mics, but his arm pressed heavily against mine, shoulder to elbow. Strong and steady and unmoving.

A simple guarantee.

I had my brother back. No matter what happened in the future.

It took the rest of the speeches and pledges for me to regain my composure entirely. From full-on tears to trying not to grin like a fool who was floating around weightlessly. It was even more difficult to school my features when a mic was placed on a stand on Touma's platform.

"Now, before we make some room for a dance or two," King Rami said, his smile of pure fatherly excitement, "Her Majesty and I would like to make an announcement that we know many people have been expecting and speculating on for some time." He paused. "*Touma's next crown prince.*"

Electricity zipped around the hall until the clack and creak of the wooden doors being opened on the right side of the hall silenced everyone. The crowd of guests parted in two as six guards dressed in red breeches, tailcoats and black boots walked in. Three on either side of Pierre in the middle, holding a gold velvet cushion in front of him. He looked dapper in a black, three-piece suit, with his silvery brown hair neatly gelled back and his ruby red eyes steadfast.

Everyone ogled at the antique silver crown sitting atop the cushion, stained beautifully with age but still impeccably shiny. Each arch and peak looked sharp even from a distance as if the crown had been crafted yesterday, not five-hundred years ago.

About a metre from where Touma's platform was, the two guards at the front stopped and the rest, including Pierre followed suit. I held my breath when Queen Leila turned to her left.

"Prince Kai."

One lone person somewhere in the hall gasped, but the atmosphere was too intense to laugh. I was starting to feel nervous, and all I was doing was watching my boyfriend step forward to face his parents as the rest of his family took a step back. The only noise was coming from the royal photographers' cameras going off and a staff member moving the mic stand.

"Take one knee," King Rami instructed Kai.

Kai got down on one knee, lowered his head, and placed his right palm over his heart.

"Before this hall of witnesses and the six other ruling families," Queen Leila said, "do you, first-born prince, Kai Touma, vow to take upon the role of crown prince with honour and pride?"

"Yes, I vow," Kai replied, his voice deep and certain, booming through the mic placed next to him.

"And do you solemnly swear to show your loyalty to the people of Touma by serving and protecting all, from those in the furthest regions of the north and south, to the coasts of the east and west?" King Rami asked.

"Yes, I swear."

"And finally, do you promise to rule by the treaty of our foremothers and forefathers when the privilege of the crown is placed in your lap?" said his mother.

"Yes, I promise."

A single hushed heartbeat pulsed through the silence. "Raise your head."

Kai lifted his head, looking straight ahead at his father's torso. Pierre walked up the three steps of the platform and behind Kai to the Queen. She picked up the silver crown in both hands.

"Then," King Rami announced loudly. "Queen Leila Rani Touma and I, King Rami Landon Ayaan Touma elect you, Kai Touma, to be the next rightful ruler and Head of Government."

A proud, happy block landed in my throat as Queen Leila placed the crown on Kai's head, adjusting it with a little twist. "You may rise, Crown Prince Kai."

Kai just about got to his feet when the howl of cheers and hooting and clapping threatened to rip the ceiling off the Grand Hall. It only grew louder as he tipped his chin up, catching the yellow light on the silver, and smiled so fucking gorgeously.

I wanted to be the loudest of everyone. I wanted to jump up and down and cheer and yell out, "That's my boyfriend!" Unfortunately, that *undignified* behaviour was not a possibility as Princess Esmeralda. I had to wait for a moment when I was Girlfriend Esmeralda—his Babble—to do that.

So, I grinned as far as my mouth could stretch and clapped so hard my palms stung. Pierre took the first bow before Kai—*I meant my sexy, handsome Crown Prince Kai*—followed by each royal family. I was bouncing on my feet when it was mine and Kareem's turn.

Side by side, Kareem bowed his head and I sunk into a deep curtsy, then Kai returned the gesture of high respect with a low nod.

"Congratulations, Your Highness," Kareem said. "You truly deserve this."

"Thank you, Your Majesty," Kai replied, his bright gaze slipping to me.

"Congratulations," I said coyly.

His lips twitched as he tugged at his left earlobe. "Thank you."

Damn it. What I wouldn't have given to throw myself into his arms and kiss him all over his perfect face. But it was his moment to shine, and I didn't want to take away from it by giving people a reason to talk about us and not him and only him.

I walked away when I had to, even though I wanted to glue myself to his side, and he looked like he was promising to buy me said glue and paint it on me himself.

He climbed down from the platform and the crowd of invited guests swallowed him up. But over the heads of so many people his glowing eyes latched onto mine. I winked at him and turned away, walking the edges of the hall to find Yami while everyone else praised and congratulated my man.

There wasn't a breeze outside, but the midnight air was cold and crisp against the sheen on my skin as I stared up at the clear, twinkling sky, the moon hanging huge and bright.

I'd snuck out ten minutes ago while Kai had still been surrounded, nearly two hours after the announcement. I was the only one there in the small, gated garden around from the Grand Hall, though I could hear some distant laughter over the melody of the orchestra. My arms rested against a low mossy wall as the bushes whispered to each other around me.

I was so lost in the beauty of the night sky I missed the crunch of steps on the gravel behind me. So, the large hands that slowly snuck around my waist and dragged me back against a broad, hard chest scared a gasp out of me.

My favourite scent and warmth filled my senses as a heavy weight settled against the side of head.

"You left me in there alone," Kai grumbled into my hair and a smile spread across my lips.

Without glancing up, I settled back into him, wrapping my arms over his forearms. "I didn't think you would notice if I disappeared for a minute."

"Of course, I noticed." He swayed me gently from side to side. "Candy was so fed up with me asking where you had gone that he went to ask Shehryar himself."

I giggled quietly. "How did you sneak away?"

"I excused myself to the bathroom."

"You lied? That was naughty."

He squeezed me tighter, weighing me into the crook of his arm. "I needed to see you, but you weren't there. I had to find you."

Ah, shit, my heart. "You're now the guest of honour, Crown Prince Kai. Everyone wants to speak to you and congratulate you. I didn't want to ruin that by lingering."

"You weren't ruining anything. You were the only reason I hadn't bolted from the hall sooner." He pressed his lips to my hair and took a deep breath. "There were too many people around me."

My chest did a little twist at how tired he sounded. "I know. But you did such a good job talking to all of them. Everyone loved you, and I felt so proud watching you."

I felt his heart pick up pace, knocking incessantly against my back. Assuming he liked the praise, I offered another, more playful one. "And you looked absolutely gorgeous too." He grunted, and I grinned. "What? You did—oh, wait. I haven't even looked at you properly with your crown on. Let me turn around."

"You don't need to look." Just from hearing his tone, I knew he was blushing.

"Kai!"

It took a bit of wriggling, but he eventually let me turn around and step away to get a good look at him. I nearly doubled over from the impact.

The little lock of hair falling against the side of his forehead from under the silver crown was absolute perfection paired with his half embarrassed, half grumpy frown.

"How did I ever get so lucky?" I sighed. "You're so beautiful." He rolled his jaw as he glanced away and tugged at his left earlobe. "Are you blushing?"

"No," he grumbled.

I chuckled and flopped forward against him, encircling my arms around his waist. His dimple appeared in his right cheek as he hugged me back before planting a long kiss to my forehead.

"Should we go back inside?" I asked moments later as we swayed gently.

"Probably."

Neither of us attempted to move and the frolicking melody coming from the hall changed into something softer and slower.

"I should have a gift to give you right now," Kai said quietly, a frustrated line forming between his brows. "A birthday present that was from me, and not my family, and something more, something else, because you deserve all the gifts in the world, Esmeralda." His hand skated up my back. "I wish I'd had more time. I should have made time, because now all I have—"

He abruptly cut himself off and clenched his jaw. "Never mind."

"What?" I protested. "No. You can't do that to me. You can't tell me you have something for me and then say, '*never mind*'."

"It isn't anything close to a gift. It's stupid really."

"That doesn't matter. Show me."

After a moment of confliction, he reached into the left pocket of his black slacks and pulled out a crinkled, folded piece of paper. I took it from him and opened it up. I probably wouldn't have realised what it was if I hadn't spotted the name swirled across the top. Even then, it took me a moment to place it, but when I did, I felt a breathless giddiness whizz through me.

"Is this…the receipt from the ice-cream parlour we went to?"

His brows were pinched. "I told you it was stupid."

Stupid? He didn't understand the kind of romantic gesture he had just pulled?

"You kept it?" I croaked. He glanced away. "Why did you keep it?"

He tugged at his ear. "I don't know. But I didn't want to throw it away." His black irises swallowed me up. "I had fun with you that day and I didn't want to forget it. I wanted something to remember it by—"

Hand on his nape, I pushed up on my heels and crushed my lips against his, bruising his mouth with everything I felt for him rather than actually kissing him. But with a slight adjustment, our lips were moulding and moving in sync. Slow and sensual and passionate.

"Do you realise," I said through a pant, "I'm going to frame this in my room back in Jahandar and stare at it for hours every night?"

"It isn't much..."

"It's everything, Kai. It's romantic and sweet, and I love it. I love that you kept a memento from that day." I lifted it up between us. "Where's the other half?"

"I have it."

A grin blossomed across my mouth. "I had no idea you were such a romantic, Mr Perfect Prince."

"I still wish I had more to give you," he said, tucking a strand of hair behind my ear.

"In that case..." I snaked my arms around his neck. "I would like two jumpers and two t-shirts you have worn but haven't washed yet, and two pairs of boxers that I can use as pyjamas."

His lips crept up. "That's nearly all my clothes, Babble."

"Considering you have nearly all my underwear from this trip in your drawers, I would say my request is fair."

His gaze grew hooded and hot. "I want something else too."

"And what might that be?"

"Your white silk skirt."

A stab of heat struck right down my middle. "The one stained with your handprints?" I asked, my eyes on his mouth. It was the only white skirt Rose had packed, but I wanted to hear it from him.

"Hmm, that one," he rasped.

"Done." He caught my lips, kissing me like he could have kissed me for ever.

"You know, we've never danced together before," I said when the symphony of the orchestra changed again.

Kai considered it, then frowned. "That is my fault. I don't dance very often."

I nodded with mock earnest. "The fact that I was too nervous to be anywhere near you when it was time to dance had nothing to do with it, did it?"

My sarcasm made him smile. "And now? Do you still feel nervous?"

I raised my brows. "Are you asking me to dance, Mr Perfect Prince?"

"I am."

"I would love to."

For a man who didn't like being the centre of attention, Kai didn't hesitate to take me by the hand into the middle of the ballroom floor.

It didn't matter that everyone was watching us.

His eyes never left mine and mine never left his as he led me through a dance.

Our first dance of many, many, *many* more to come.

MARIYAH

DUUUUDDDDDEEEE!!!!!

MARIYAH

I woke up to pictures of u and TRG EVERYWHEREEE

MARIYAH

a dance and him driving u to the airport ahughdjdkhfdg

MARIYAH

Y didnt u tell me??!?!

MARIYAH

U guys have fucking broken the internet

MARIYAH

AND PRINCE ARSH AND SHEHRYAR'S MUM?!!!!!!!!

MARIYAH

GIRL FUCKING EXPLAIN BEFORE I EXPLODE

EPILOGUE

Esmeralda

9 MONTHS LATER

Long-distance relationships were *hard*.

Kai and I discovered that the first week we spent apart.

With me taking lead on the setting up of the Amara-Ayla Foundation and Kai attending more events and an official ceremony for his appointment as Crown Prince, we just about made time to talk between endless hours of work. Figuring out when either of us could visit had been impossible.

Within the first month, tears were shed multiple times. On phone calls and videocalls, and alone on those sleepless nights when I missed his warmth and smell and tight hugs. It was only towards the beginning of May—just over two months after the Peace Celebrations—when things calmed down a bit for both of us, allowing Kai to come visit me for four days in Jahandar.

It didn't exactly get any easier after that. It was painful actually, only having a few days together and then being torn apart again. But having no other choice, Kai and I learnt to adjust to the workings of a long-distance relationship. Constantly being in contact, figuring out phone sex, and looking forward to the days we could be together made being apart slightly more bearable.

We learnt to appreciate the time we had with each other too. Even if it was only two visits and one international animal welfare event in the six months after his first visit to Jahandar.

It helped that my relationship with Kareem improved significantly. We started movie nights once a week. Awkward as fuck at first, but at some point, we began sharing a sofa and a bowl of popcorn.

We had dinner together every night too, where we talked about things other than work, and laughter became a common sound in the dining hall. He asked me regularly about Kai, though I never once told him I knew he dropped Kai the occasional message.

Otherwise, the only other person the entire Jahmal Palace was missing was Mama Katiya.

It took four months for all of us, including Shehryar, to convince my long-distance-relationship mentor to go live with Prince Arsh in Touma. Mama Katiya had been reluctant to leave Shehryar, me, and her work behind. But when we found a brilliant new hire, Mona, Mama Katiya packed her bags and left to be with her man. Although I suggested he go with her, Shehryar outright refused to resign from his role as my private secretary and I didn't dare bring it up again.

I had to admit, as much as I'd been happy for Mama Katiya, it sucked big time that I couldn't just pack my bags and go live with Kai or vice versa the way she had.

That being said, nine months passed by quicker than I expected, and November came around bringing with it cooler weather. And Kai's thirtieth birthday.

Except, guilt was eating me alive.

"Are you sure it wasn't wrong of me to tell him I wasn't going to make his birthday?" I asked Mariyah as she turned the page of her book, reclining in the seat opposite me.

"It wouldn't be a surprise if he knew you were coming, would it?" she said without lifting a lash.

I flicked nervously at my nail. "But he was really upset on the phone…"

Kai and I had been planning my trip to Touma for his birthday since he visited me in Jahandar in May. He extended the invite to Mariyah so I could spend some time with her there too. But two weeks ago, Prince Arsh had called and asked me to tell Kai I could no longer come until after his birthday, so they could surprise him on the morning of his birthday with my arrival.

I hadn't slept properly since, because all I could hear was his upset "You can't come?" in my head day and night and it was killing me. Even though it was a lie, and Mariyah, Shehryar and I were on a private state plane, just over an hour away from landing in Touma.

Mariyah closed her book with a set of fingers marking her page and shuffled in the cream leather seat. Her blue eyes were soft, and her blonde hair was plaited into two boxer braids.

"When he sees you there, he'll be so happy that he'll completely forget why he was upset in the first place," she said, then smirked. "Plus, I'm sure there are *other ways* you could convince him not to be upset with you too. Ya get what I'm saying, Princess?"

My cheeks smarted. She knew about the toys and handcuffs I had packed in my suitcase.

"I didn't need to hear that."

I grimaced at the discomfort in Shehryar's voice. I'd momentarily forgotten he was scrolling through his laptop in the seat on the other side of the aisle.

Mariyah scoffed and rolled her eyes. "Then go somewhere else."

Shehryar's jaw tightened. "We're on a plane. There isn't anywhere else for me to go."

I let out a heavy sigh, but neither of them seemed to notice. *Why would they though?* They were so enamoured with each other that when they argued the entire world disappeared around them.

"You could jump out of the plane," my best friend snarked in a sickeningly sweet voice.

"Ladies first."

"Then please, by all means, step up first. Because the peanut-sized knob between your legs doesn't count as a dick."

"O—kay!" I quickly interrupted as Shehryar's expression turned thunderous. "That's enough. *Please.*" Mariyah lost her defensive posture. "The moment we got on this plane, you two have been at each other's throats. Did something happen? You two are never normally this bad."

They looked away like scolded teenagers, refusing to answer. Clearly, something *had* happened.

I shook my head tiredly. "Whatever it was, can you forget about it for the next twelve days, please? I want to spend time with Kai and have fun with all of us there. That isn't going to happen if you two won't stop bickering." I searched their turned away expressions. "Please. For me."

"Okay. Fine," Mariyah grumbled, her eyes lifting to me apologetically.

"Thank you." I smiled at her and looked to Shehryar. "Sher?"

"Hmm, okay." He flicked a glare at Mariyah then picked his laptop up and made his way to the door on the left opposite us, disappearing through it.

I caught Mariyah staring at the closed door with something that wasn't hatred, but she played it off as if her pale cheeks weren't brushed with a guilty pink tinge.

"What?" she harrumphed. "He started it."

I clenched my teeth.

One of them had better end it. *Before I ended them.*

Prince Arsh was at the airport to pick us up when we landed in Touma just after nine-forty in the morning. I ended up in one car with him while Mariyah and Shehryar rode the other, but I was less worried about them killing each other than I was about getting to Kai as quickly as possible.

An hour later, Shehryar, Mariyah and I were being smuggled into Chaukham Palace through the staff doors on the side where Mama Katiya, Pierre, Fay, and Adam were waiting for us.

On a mission of speed, stealth, and silence, Prince Arsh led us quickly through the palace down to the kitchen. Familiar faces popped up everywhere, beaming as they saw us and followed behind.

"Why does it seem like everyone was expecting us—I mean, Esmeralda?" Mariyah whispered.

"Because they were," Prince Arsh replied, throwing a smirk over his shoulder from beside Mama Katiya and Shehryar walking with their arms linked. "Everyone except Kai had to know so preparations could be made."

"And no one let it slip? Even by accident?"

"Nah, none of us would. We're good at keeping secrets," Pierre said from behind me and Mariyah.

"Everyone except Michael," Adam added. He seemed even taller than the last time I saw him two months back.

"Well, yeah. Everyone except Michael. But we only told him this morning."

"His Highness didn't pick up on anything either?" Mariyah asked in disbelief.

Fay grunted, walking between Adam and Pierre. "Kai is absolutely oblivious to these things. And with him moping around, I doubt he would have noticed if the world exploded around him."

I was beginning to feel nervous, but as we turned into the corridor, the number of staff gathered outside the kitchen shocked my nerves into non-existence but trebled them all the same.

Michael, Kai's equerry. Raj, the nightguard. Jorge, the stablemaster. Nearly everyone was there.

"Woah," Mariyah mumbled next to me.

As they spotted us, half the staff chirped, "They're here," "They're here," like a flock of seagulls, before the other half went, "Shh," "He'll hear us," "Shh." They all quickly bowed their heads and moved aside to make a path for us.

"Are you sure Prince Kai has no idea?" Mariyah questioned as Prince Arsh turned around.

He chuckled, his hazel eyes crinkling. "I'm sure." He settled his gaze on me. "Are you ready?"

Emotion stirred and solidified in my throat. I gulped around it.

"Yes."

Feeling the pressure with everyone's eyes on me, I headed for the silver double doors of the kitchen. My heart slammed against my ribcage when I saw the back of Kai through the circular windows on each door, and my eyes began to prickle.

One month, four weeks and four days. That was how long it had been since I last saw him. I'd missed him every second of every day. Now, he was right there. On the other side of the doors.

Michael beamed at me as he slowly and silently pulled one long doorhandle. "We'll be right behind you, Your Highness."

"You mean…the light fittings?" Kai's deep voice was the first thing I heard as I stepped through the slither of space between the doors into the kitchen.

"Yes, the light fittings," King Rami said cheerfully, staring up at the tube lights on the ceiling. "Now that you're the Crown Prince, your mother and I would like to delegate palace maintenance work to you, and the first task at hand is the kitchen light fittings. We've been wanting to change them for years, haven't we, honey?"

"Yes, we have," Queen Leila played along with an earnest expression. "We can't delay changing them any further, and Nur was very much on board with having your input, sweetie."

"Oh, yes," Nur, the head chef, gleamed, his silver moustache curling up with his grin. "I think your thirtieth birthday is a brilliant occasion to make your first design choice."

I pressed my palm over my mouth to hold in a laugh as Kai shuffled from foot to foot, his fitted, dark blue suit moving fluidly with his awkward steps. He was so adorably confused.

"I'm…" He cleared his throat. "I'm not sure I'm the correct person to ask about…light fittings." From an angle, I watched him scratch his stubbled jaw; it didn't look like he'd shaved recently. "Fay might have something more to offer…or the palace maintenance team."

"What about Princess Esmeralda?" Nur said and my stomach hiccupped. "Her Highness might be able to help."

King Rami clapped a hand on Kai's back. "That's a brilliant idea. We should ask Esmeralda."

I assumed that was my cue, but I couldn't seem to get my swollen tongue to cooperate. Except I heard myself croak, "I think spotlights would look nice."

Kai spun around so swiftly all I saw was a blur of dark blue. Then his round ink black eyes sucked me in and locked me down in my favourite place to be.

My mouth blossomed into an aching smile. "Happy birth—"

A thousand Newtons of force hit me as I was engulfed in a bear hug. And by bear hug, I meant *bear hug*. Arms trapped by my sides and hauled straight off the floor with his face buried in my neck.

I giggled, nose stinging, and wriggled my arms free to wrap them around him. He let out a huge shuddering noise. "I thought you couldn't come," he croaked, his muffled words tickling my skin. "You said you couldn't come."

My heart shattered and fit itself back together again in the space of a second.

"I was never going to miss your birthday, Kai," I whispered, cradling the back of his head in my hand.

It might have been minutes or moments later, but sudden rattles of movement filtered through in all directions before a roared, "Surprise," echoed around the kitchen seemingly endlessly.

Kai lifted his head, and I watched his awe-filled expression before following his gaze. All the kitchen staff had gathered behind Nur, everyone who had been in the corridor had come in, and Kai's family were huddled together with the addition of Gigi and Mariyah standing next to Shehryar and Pierre.

There wasn't a single face that didn't have a grin going from ear to ear.

"Did you..." Kai uttered, and his attention flew back to me. "*You planned this?*"

Everyone burst out laughing and I giggled. So, he was *a little* oblivious, but it was adorable. Especially as he blushed at his own cluelessness.

"Your family planned it," I said, glancing over my shoulder. "I just played my role in their plan."

"It was my idea," Gigi said, tipping up her chin haughtily.

"It was not," King Rami and Prince Arsh said at exactly the same time.

Laughs filtered through again, but as Kai set me down on my feet, they turned to *oh's* and *ah's*.

Two chefs carried a big square wooden board with a three-tiered iced cake, decorated with blue macarons and silver spheres of different sizes. On top were big silver *three* and *zero* candles.

"Whoever put the candles on, I very much appreciate you reminding Kai that he's now middle-aged," Fay taunted as the two chefs set the cake on the metal serving island in front of us.

Kai scowled at his younger brother, his cheeks pink as he tugged at his left earlobe. "Thirty isn't middle-aged," he grumbled, scattering chuckles through the kitchen.

"He's going to start complaining about back pains soon," Pierre added with a massive smirk.

I giggled into Kai's arm as he growled over my head, "You're older than me."

Pierre sniffed. "By five months."

"Might we stop insulting everyone over the age of thirty and cut the cake?" King Rami huffed, giving a jokingly dirty side-glance to Pierre and Fay.

Nur chuckled and stepped forward, a knife and box of matches in his hands. "Would you like to do the honour, Your Highness?" he asked me.

I untangled my arm from around Kai's waist and took the small box, stepping up to the big cake. On the counter, it was level with my height, the candles just sitting above my head.

"I don't think she's gonna be able to reach," I heard Mariyah tease.

I glared at her, cheeks aflame as everyone laughed. Mariyah wiggled her eyebrows at me cheekily. *I fucking knew she was going to make a height joke.*

"I *can* reach," I said, a reluctant smile taking over my mouth.

I had to stand on my tiptoes, but with a flick of my wrist, I lit a match and little orange flames latched onto the wicks of each candle. I put the box down and turned to Kai. He gave me a beautiful lop-sided smile as he shuffled forward. Everyone else followed suit, phones out for pictures and videos.

"Are we ready?" Prince Arsh called out then waved his hands like a conductor. "One, two, three…"

The chorus of "Happy Birthday" shook through the entire kitchen, belted out a little off tune but full of happiness and love. And Kai's blushing grin was the most beautiful thing in the entire universe.

As the closing note turned into whooping and hollering, I cupped my hands around my mouth and cheered the loudest. Kai blew out the candles, tugging at his ear as he stood straight. Then he sunk the knife into the bottom tier of the cake, carving the first slice.

"Feed Princess Esmeralda some," a woman shouted out and an agreeing roar followed.

I didn't think he was going to do it, but he cut off the edge of the cake slice, picked it up in his fingers and brought it to my lips. I couldn't stop grinning giddily as I swiped the piece into my mouth, holding his glittering gaze the whole time. He looked so happy and proud as he brushed his thumb across my bottom lip. I wanted to pounce on him and bite him for being so cute. Instead, I broke a piece off the cake and fed it to him, indulging the crowd.

And indulged they were feeling, because another woman yelled out, "Now kiss," and soon everyone was chanting, "Kiss, kiss, kiss, kiss."

I looked up at Kai. He looked down at me. I bit my bottom lip as I raised my brows in question. His eyes tracked the movement before he lifted his lashes. Something glinted in his ink black irises.

Before I knew it, he caught me and swooped me around, dipping me as if we were dancing. The wild squeals all around drowned out my gasp as I clung onto him. The only thing keeping me from toppling backwards was his strong hand at the back of my head and his arm banded around me.

His tongue snuck out and licked across his smirking lips before his expression softened. "I missed you so much, Babble," he whispered for my ears only.

My chest clenched. "I missed you too, Mr Perfect Prince."

And then he settled his mouth over mine and kissed me.

It wasn't a light kiss for the satisfaction of the watching eyes. It was so much more than that. Nights apart. Promises of days together. It was sweet, it was deep, it was beautiful. *And it was for us.*

But I was glad someone caught it on camera. Because tucked against Kai's naked body that night, I got to watch him set the picture as his screensaver on his phone.

He looked so pleased when I promised to give him thousands of more moments just as good as that one, if not better. Before he rolled me under him and loved me so long and slow, making up for all the hours we spent loving each other from a distance.

The End

ACKNOWLEDGMENTS

Wow. I mean, hi.

If you're reading this that means I actually published my first book.

Me from five years ago would have had a fit. "You showed people what we wrote? Why the fuck would you do that? Are you insane? We can't do that!"

Five years ago, she was probably right—I have buried those manuscripts never to be found or seen or read. But I've come a long way since that girl first decided to start writing the stories she pictured in her head, further than I could have ever imagined.

Last September, when I started writing this book, I still wasn't sure I had what it took to become a published author. And now here I am, writing my first acknowledgments and thanking the people who got me there.

First of all, of course, I would like to thank my editor, Amy Briggs. I'm so glad you emailed me back that day and took a chance on my manuscript. Your guidance and prompts of improvement were everything, and when I got it right, you cheered me on and wiped away the imposter syndrome. You were patient and kind and I promise, I will be careful with my capital letters from now on.

To Book and Moods who helped create my book cover and made my book look pretty on the inside too, thank you, thank you, a thousand times thank you! You worked with all my tweaks and never told me it wasn't possible, and just look at what you created!

To Sonia, the AMAZING artist, who took my awful stickman drawing and turned it into my stunning book cover art, you brought my characters to life perfectly, and I hope you know that you're stuck with me for ever now.

To Elizianna, you too took my awful sketch and drew me a map that is perfect! You understood all my random squiggles and you made all the changes I asked for without a complaint. You gave me gorgeous artwork too and I can't thank you enough for it! You're stuck with me too!

To the bookish friends I made on Bookstagram, you were there to hype me up even before I started planning a publishing schedule for Tall, Royal and Grumpy. Emily and Antonia, I owe you so much for picking me up in my moments of doubt and just always being there for a good chat. And thank you Emily for BETA reading too!

To the girl I met in Piccadilly Waterstones. Laura, you beautiful girl, I need a whole book to thank you for your friendship, your support, and for all your overdramatic, hilarious comments as you BETA read. You made me giggle and blush and roll my eyes at how many book husbands you collected as you read. I threw random spicy scenes at you before I'd even fully finished writing TRG and you drank them up like such a good little whore for me. You have hyped me up more than I could have ever asked for and you've always believed in me whole-heartedly. I love you, dude.

I haven't forgotten my dearest friend, Dabira. First of all, you need to come back from Japan so I can see you! Secondly, I apologise for how many years you waited for this book and how much the plot has changed. Don't kill me, please.

To Kai and Esmeralda.

This isn't the story I wrote for you two five years ago. Kai, you were mean, and Esmeralda, you still had a crush, but that plot didn't work, so I set you aside while I worked on another project. Thank you for being patient with me while I figured out your story. Thank you for cooperating with me while I rewrote you. I apologise to the old versions of yourselves I asked you to leave behind, but I think you'll agree with me that Mr Perfect Prince and Babble are the versions you were meant to be.

And finally, to those of you who picked up my debut book, whether that was as an ARC, as a Bookstagrammer/Booktoker or just as an avid reader, thank you so much for taking a chance on me.

I hope you enjoyed my writing, my plot, my characters, my spice, and the world that I created.

I hope you stick around in the world of Neves, because there is definitely so much more to come!

Nylah xx

ABOUT THE AUTHOR

Nylah Monroe is a born and bred city girl from London, UK, who is still unconvinced she can call herself an author yet. She writes contemporary romance books with New Adult drama and emotional damage, and a sprinkle of romantic comedy fairy dust. She believes in the motto "equal parts pain and happiness" when it comes to her writing.

A lover of winter, coffee, and cats, she claims she doesn't believe in love in real life but give her a romance book and a solid book boyfriend, and she's a goner. Regency, dark, New Adult, rom-com, monster romance, she isn't fussed, but her favourite tropes are age gap and enemies-to-lovers.

When she isn't writing or dreaming up more characters and plots than she has time to write, she has her head stuck in a book, is out book shopping, or is trying to convince her family there is enough space in the house to build more shelves.

Instagram – @nylahmwrites
Tiktok – @nylahmwrites
Facebook – Author Nylah Monroe
Pinterest – Nylah Monroe
Goodreads – Nylah Monroe
Nylah's Facebook Reader's Group – Good Little ***** of Neves